AMERICA'S
WIFE

BOOKS BY CELESTE DE BLASIS

WILD SWAN TRILOGY
A Wild Hope
A Wild Heart
A Wild Legacy

AMERICA'S DAUGHTER TRILOGY
America's Daughter

AMERICA'S WIFE

CELESTE DE BLASIS

Bookouture

Published by Bookouture in 2021

An imprint of Storyfire Ltd.
Carmelite House
50 Victoria Embankment
London EC4Y 0DZ

www.bookouture.com

ISBN: 978-1-80019-328-4
eBook ISBN: 978-1-80019-327-7

BOOK II

THE MID-ATLANTIC STATES

Chapter 1

New York, Summer 1776

Her wedding was over, and life for Addie Bradwell now seemed to revolve entirely around General Washington and the Continental Army in New York. So much had changed since she had witnessed the Boston Tea Party and now she and her brothers, Justin, Ad and Quentin Valencourt, and her new husband Silas, were firmly caught up in the American fight for independence. After the decision was made to sell the Valencourt possessions, Addie's brothers and Silas stayed in Boston only long enough to collect money from the first sales, and then, pockets plump, they left the city. Purchasing horses on the way, they hastened to join General Washington.

Addie worked feverishly to close their affairs in Boston. Her heart had gone with Silas and her brothers, and that made it easier to prepare the house for strangers. Aside from items she'd sold and those left in the hands of agents to be disposed of when the asking price was met, many furnishings would remain in place for the renters. She and Tullia packed away personal belongings left by Marcus and Mary, as well as mementos of Lily. Tullia insisted that pieces of the childhoods of Lily's children be preserved, too, in favorite playthings, drawings, and games.

"Someday you will want to remember what it was like before the war came and you grew up," she said.

Addie continued to be amazed at Tullia's complicity in her scheme, but she also worried that it was going to be far more difficult for Tullia to leave Boston than for her. Tullia would be forty-one years old that year, and though she appeared to be as strong and spry as ever, to Addie, forty-one seemed to be an age when one ought to be settled.

"I know you have friends here, a life here," she said. "If you wish to stay, I'll make sure you are comfortably situated before I go."

"Are you saying you don't want me to go with you?" Tullia's voice was sharp, but her eyes were so sad, Addie couldn't bear it.

"No! I don't mean that at all! It would be very, very hard to leave without you, but I want you to know that you have a choice. We're grown up now."

"The last time I had such a choice was before I came north with your mama," Tullia said. "She worried like you, said she wouldn't make me go so far away from Castleton if I didn't want to. Up to then, a few other plantations and Williamsburg were the only other places I'd seen. I was afraid of leaving, but I'd missed your mama when she was gone to England without me, and I couldn't let her go without me again."

Tullia's eyes sparkled with sudden mischief. "I know you think I'm too old to go with you, but I heard that General Washington is three years older than I am. If he can lead the army I can follow it."

Addie threw up her hands in laughing surrender and ceased to feel guilty that she was relieved Tullia would be with her.

She was more grateful by the day for it. Left to her own devices, she would have set out on horseback to travel to Silas as swiftly as possible. But she could not do that with Tullia, and Tullia made her see that they had to go with more equipment than a change of clothes and an extra blanket. They needed a wagon, and they needed to furnish it with everything from bedding, to staples and cooking utensils, to clothing (including winter garments in case they were gone that long), to a brace of pistols, a musket, and ammunition for protection. They were going to follow an army and, as Tullia pointed out, they could not depend on finding decent lodgings every night along the way.

With people coming back into the city, Addie was able to purchase a sturdy wagon and team, and out in the countryside she found a passable riding horse. On the same expedition, she arranged to store some Valencourt possessions at Mary's farm. The tenants had accepted Mary's transfer of ownership to Addie, but she could tell how relieved they were that she wasn't requisitioning any of the farm's livestock for her journey.

As she and Tullia inventoried everything remaining in the house on Summer Street in the South End, Addie was struck anew by how much her father had left behind: the prized Turkey carpets possessed by few; the wealth of linens for various uses, all neatly embroidered with the date they were made and, if they were for the bedchambers, with symbols indicating specific beds; the finely wrought chairs, tables, cabinets, and chests, some made in the colonies, more imported over the years from England; the porcelain and glassware also from over the sea; the mirrors and the mirrored wall sconces that reflected light; even the andirons in the fireplaces were of the best manufacture. Every item that had been sold and every one that still graced the house was evidence of how successful Marcus had been in America and of the elegant comfort he had provided for his family. It filled Addie with sorrow to think of her father and Mary in exile.

"If they go to England, they won't be alone," Tullia reminded her. "Callista is there, and your father still has a sister and a brother living. They might not seem so real to you, but they're part of where he came from, and maybe the Loyalists will just go to New York, after all, and Darius is there."

Addie was comforted by Tullia's words, but they both knew it was doubtful, with the Continental Army heading there, that New York would provide refuge for the Loyalists. It was also doubtful that Marcus, wherever he went, would ever again be so much the master of his world as he had been in Boston.

On the day they left the city, Addie looked back once as they crossed the Neck, but then she turned her attention to the horses. Everyone who mattered to her was ahead.

Tullia had dissuaded her from cutting her hair, but Addie had won the argument over clothes and was once again dressed as a boy. Whatever slight curves she had been developing had disappeared with the weight she had lost during the siege, so that binding her breasts presented no difficulty. Her hair was pinned up under her hat except for a little false queue, and Tullia had to admit, albeit reluctantly, that Addie could easily pass for a lad. Nor could Tullia dispute that the disguise was safer for the trip than Addie's normal mode of dress. Addie did regret the necessity of removing her wedding band, but in spite of that she felt freer than she had in a long time.

They traveled south without incident, keeping to themselves. They were far from the only travelers; men of all ages were on their way to join the Continental Army, some with their families. It wasn't difficult to understand that if the British could take and control New York, they might thereby drive a wedge that would divide New England from the rest and break the unity of the colonies.

The army had taken twelve days to march to New York and had arrived in the early weeks of April. Even with all the arrangements Addie and Tullia had had to make in Boston before leaving, they were there by mid-May. Addie changed back into feminine attire a day out of the city so that she would not scandalize her brothers or her husband. It amused her to imagine the travelers who had seen her before wondering at the change if they saw her now.

It was apparent that the Continentals had been busy since their arrival, for, in anticipation of a British attack by sea, there were fortifications being dug and built everywhere, on both sides of the North or Hudson River, on Long Island, and all around Manhattan. The city of New York itself was only twelve blocks long by five blocks wide, occupying the southern tip of Manhattan Island, but it was home to some twenty thousand souls and had in the recent past begun to eclipse Boston and other port cities as a major trading center. For many of the country-bred soldiers in the Continental Army, it had to beckon as a place of great temptation and worldliness.

Because Ad and Justin were on Washington's staff, they were easy to locate, though Addie and Tullia were questioned repeatedly about their business the closer they drew to headquarters. Washington was using two sites, one a country estate north of the city, the other an office at the bottom of Broadway, close to the main fort at the Battery on the Hudson River. He and his staff were at the city office at present, and the guards responsible for the general's safety took their duties seriously; no one was going to harm him if they could prevent it.

It was the first time Addie had considered what a gain it would be for the British if they could assassinate the commander in chief, and she realized how naive she was not to have thought of the possibility before. She shivered, thinking of how lost they would all be if General Washington were not there to lead them.

She rubbed her wedding band, back on her finger now that she was dressed as a woman again, and her longing for Silas was suddenly so sharp, she barely kept herself from cursing at the next sentry who challenged them.

"My three brothers and my husband are with General Washington, and the weapons I have are in plain sight." She gestured to the musket and displayed the pistols. "Now, may we pass?"

The soldier put up his hands in mock surrender. "Better than that, I'll take you to 'em! You look enough like two of the general's aides to convince me."

Ad saw the wagon first, and forgetting all decorum, he raced to swing his twin down from the seat. "Thank God you've arrived safely!" All the fears he'd had about the journey were clear in his exclamation, and he hugged her tightly.

"Ad, you shouldn't have worried. Tullia and I are very competent," she chided him, but she was touched by his concern.

"If you think I worried, you should have witnessed your husband's behavior these past weeks. It was all we could do to keep him from turning right around and heading north again." He chuckled when he saw his sister's fond expression at the words "your husband."

"And where is my husband?" she asked.

"He's out somewhere with his beloved guns—my pardon, I am sure you are first in his affections, but the cannon are a close second. I'll send someone to find him, but in the meantime I'll take you to your lodgings. Silas has found rooms in a private house."

There were questions she could not wait to ask, though she was already sure of the answer to the first one. "The refugees from Boston, they did not put in here, did they?"

"No. It was a wild guess that General Howe would bring them here. It seems they went the other way, north to Canada, probably Halifax in Nova Scotia."

Addie shuddered at the thought because all she had ever heard of that town was that it was a bleak, noisome place. "Papa will hate it!"

"He won't stay there long," Ad said. "I'm certain he will take Mary and the children to England as soon as he can." He studied her face. "Did you really think you would see Papa here?"

Her voice was as soft as his. "Not really. Despite the rumors, it wouldn't have made sense. But some small part of me held a foolish hope." She straightened her shoulders and asked, "Darius. Have you seen him?"

"Justin and I checked as soon as we got here. Darius's house and the shops are closed. We expect he and his wife fled out to the country when they heard our army was on the way."

This time, Addie was relieved by her brother's negative answer. She had been very uneasy with the prospect of coming face to face with Darius under the present circumstances. And though she disagreed with his politics, she did not want him to come to harm at the hands of the Patriots.

The rooms Silas had rented for them were clean and well appointed. Mistress Chaffey, the landlady, was a widow who had more need of company than of money. Although she had no children of her own, she was a motherly sort and very concerned about a nephew who had joined the army. She thought it romantic that Addie had followed her husband to war, and the room she had let for Tullia's use was no less agreeable than Addie and Silas's. Addie knew Silas must have taken special care to make sure Tullia would not be condemned by prejudice to discomfort.

The house did not have its own stable, but Mistress Chaffey knew of a good livery nearby, and Ad arranged for the wagon and horses to be kept there.

By the time Silas arrived at the house, Ad had gone back to his duties, and Addie and Tullia were settled in. Addie had fussed over her until Tullia had agreed to lie down for a rest, and when Addie had checked on her a bit later, she had found her fast asleep.

Addie meant to read while she waited for Silas, but the bed in their room looked very inviting. She took off her shoes and lay down, intending to close her eyes only briefly, but within minutes, she was as deeply asleep as Tullia.

Silas found her so, with the last light of afternoon fading from the chamber. She looked so beautiful, his pulse quickened. But with her usual vitality quenched by sleep, she also looked fragile.

He stood beside the bed and said her name softly and then again, and she awakened, joy lighting her face at the sight of him. She held out her arms. He gathered her close and just held her for a long moment before his mouth found hers and they kissed as if they'd been separated for years instead of weeks. She stroked his face and his neck and ran her hands down his back, thwarted by his clothing, frantic, as she became more alert, to know that no hurt had come to him while they were apart.

Silas knew Tullia was close by and that Justin and Ad would be at the house soon. It didn't make any difference. He disentangled himself long enough to lock the door, and then he forgot about everyone and everything else except for making love to Addie.

They couldn't tell whose hands were shaking the harder as they worked to get rid of their clothing, and they gave up before the task was complete, coming together in a nest of garments half on and half off. Despite their haste, Addie's body was more than ready for his, and Silas heard her throaty purr of pleasure as he thrust home. He wanted to go on and on, but his body would not wait. When it was over, he barely had the strength to shift them so that his weight would not crush her. He felt her shaking against him and heard small sounds, and he was lost, sure she was weeping, sure he had hurt her. Then he realized she was laughing. The sound welled up and broke free.

"Oh, Silas! Just look at us! What a shameful pair we are! And how wonderful, how marvelous we are!"

He laughed with her, but as he gazed about the room, his happiness faded. He could not fault the cleanliness of it, but it was so plainly furnished compared to the Valencourt house in Boston.

"I am sorry. The city is in a great state of confusion, and this was the best I could find. But it isn't nearly good enough."

He sounded so disconsolate, Addie could hardly speak for the lump in her throat. She propped herself on his chest so that she could see his face. "My love, for such a steady, sensible man, you can be very foolish.

This is a fine room! It is clean, warm, and kind, as is Mistress Chaffey. She welcomed me so graciously and is so fond of you already, it was almost like coming home. She means us to be happy here, and so do I."

She held his chin so he could not look away. "Husband, I have left my father's house. Even though he left before I did, you know I could have stayed there had I wished it. But what I want, the only thing I want, is to be with you. Tullia and I with our wagon of goods were prepared to sleep on the ground if need be, and we did for a few nights on our way here. She wants to be close to her children and I to be close to you. Consider what luxury this is compared to the bare earth!"

He could feel her trembling with urgency to convince him.

He doubted himself, his ability to provide adequately for her—he was ever mindful that all he possessed had come from the Valencourts—but he could not doubt her. Tears stung his eyes, and he pulled her down against him, burying his head against her neck, drawing comfort from her.

Addie wished they could stay like this forever, but she reminded Silas that her brothers were due soon. As it happened, they were still making themselves presentable when Justin knocked on their door, calling their names.

"We will be with you directly," Silas said, striving to make his voice calm, but Addie spoiled his effort by giggling because he looked so embarrassed.

"We'll wait for you downstairs," Justin called through the door, and he sounded as amused as Addie.

"If you meant to keep it a secret that we love each other, it's much too late," Addie told her husband, and despite her teasing tone, Silas took it as another gift from her, for she was so intent on letting him and everyone else know how proud she was to be his wife.

When the couple joined them, Addie's brothers did not have to ask how the reunion had gone, and for an instant, Justin had to look away from the contentment he saw in their faces because it reminded him so much of his days and nights with his wife Sarah, now dead from smallpox. But when he greeted his sister, none of the pain showed.

Ad and Justin looked the same to Addie, but Quentin seemed to have grown noticeably in the weeks since he'd left Boston. His voice was low and steady, with no squeaks left, and his cheeks were beard-shadowed.

"You look so much like Papa!" Addie told him, and he ducked his head, flattered by the comparison.

Mistress Chaffey had prepared a delectable supper for them, and to Addie's mind, the only thing lacking was Tullia's company. But Tullia refused to act the part of friend and thus push the limits of Mistress Chaffey's tolerance. "I will be well treated as a lady's maid; anything more might cause a battle, and there is war enough now without that."

Addie had to accept her words because she could not push Tullia where Tullia would not go. And she knew that if any of the servants in the Chaffey house thought to push Tullia too far, they would find themselves confronted by her implacable dignity.

Addie wanted to know everything about her husband's and brothers' duties, though she was dismayed to learn that Quentin was due to be sent to serve on Long Island, which meant his visits to the city would be limited.

"None of us knows from one day to the next where we'll be," Justin admitted. "There are more of us by the day, but still, it would take a vast army to guard every shore of this watery place."

Addie understood only too well what he meant, for though Boston was vulnerable by reason of being connected so tenuously to the mainland, here it was worse. Deep bays and rivers defined Manhattan Island, Staten Island, Long Island, and the Jersey shore, and deep navigable waters meant access for Britain's navy, which could transport huge numbers of troops.

Addie studied each face in turn, and then she asked, "You do not believe our army can hold New York against the enemy, do you?"

"We can and we will!" Quentin protested, the fire of his youth and his belief making his dark eyes very bright.

"We will try," Ad corrected gently. He regretted having to gainsay his younger brother, but he didn't want Quentin's enthusiasm to blind him to the dangers they all faced. "The reason we don't know what is to happen next or where is because we don't know where Britain's General Howe is, or General Clinton either. Howe sailed north with the refugees from Boston." He swallowed hard, thinking of Marcus. "And Clinton has, if the rumors are true, been causing trouble in the Carolinas. But General Washington expects the British to come after us here, and I believe he's right."

Addie could see that the British had few choices. They could ignore the rebellion, hoping it would lose strength while they punished the colonies by continued restraints on trade, or they could seek out Washington and his army. And the first course was really no choice at all for a nation that prided itself on its military might and thought badly of the colonists' performance under arms.

Addie felt very proud as she studied the men's faces. Quentin was the only one who did not doubt a Patriot victory, but the others were no less willing than he to risk all to achieve it. This was the essence the redcoats seemed unable to understand, but there was no way to measure how far this dedication and determination would carry the Continental Army.

The talk of what was to come did not end when her brothers had departed for their quarters, and she and Silas were settling down for the night.

Silas held her in his arms, but now it was more in comfort than in passion.

"I want a promise from you," he said, "and no arguments." He felt her stiffen against him, ready to protest because she knew it was something she would not like. "Please, Addie, we cannot fight about this. I want you to check on your horses and the wagon often, and when the redcoats threaten the city, I want you to go north, off the island. I will try to send word when you should go, but I need to trust you to use your good sense and go even if I haven't been able to get a message to you. Promise?"

She heard the words he did not say, that it would make his duties that much harder and more dangerous if he were worrying about her getting out of the city.

"I promise, and you can be sure that Tullia will not let me delay too long."

They lay together in the darkness, and she waited until she was sure her voice would hold steady before she asked, "When we lose this city, what then?" Deliberately she used "when" as he had, not "if."

"Why then we fight them somewhere else, and somewhere else after that until they learn they cannot win. Losing this city need not mean we lose the whole colony. In Europe, capture a major city or two, and you have caught the country. That isn't true here, and the redcoats will learn it to their sorrow."

Listening to him, Addie realized that in his own way, he was no less optimistic than Quentin. A host of logical arguments—among them the wealth of England's manufactories for arms and every other kind of finished goods, and the presence of large numbers of colonists who were either indifferent or opposed to the Patriots' aims—occurred to her, but she did not voice them. His survival might well rest on the strength of his belief.

Her father had taught her the value of logical thought and rational planning that life might assume a measured, prosperous pattern. But she was learning to live by the moment and to regard each one with Silas as precious.

She willed herself to patience in the days that followed, accepting the fact that Silas spent as much time with her as he could, but his duty with the army was pressing, despite there being no sign of the enemy. Quentin didn't have much time to spare either, and Justin and Ad left the city with General Washington, accompanying him on a hurried trip to Philadelphia where he had been invited to consult with Congress, so Addie lacked their company, too.

Colonel Knox's wife Lucy was in New York with her husband, and Addie called on her because the colonel, in charge of the Continental artillery, was not only Silas's friend, but also his commanding officer. This made the visit more formal than it would otherwise have been, and Addie was somewhat nervous.

She had only a passing acquaintance with Lucy Knox, who was four or five years older than she, and she found her a bit intimidating. With bright black eyes, a plump figure, and the pride of having recently produced a healthy daughter, Lucy was an imposing matron with a firm idea of her own consequence. On the other hand, she was well read and good humored, and the two women felt a special bond for having Loyalist families who had left Boston with the British.

Lucy's father, Thomas Flucker, had been Royal Secretary of the Province of Massachusetts Bay. Her family had held a high social position and had been heartily opposed to her marrying Henry Knox, the bookseller. At the time, Henry had been discreet about his support for the Patriot cause, but he had refused to proclaim himself a Loyalist. Lucy had married him in 1774 in defiance of her family, and she had become as fervid a Patriot as Henry.

"I long to hear from my family, to know that they are well," Lucy confessed.

"I, too. I am sure my father will not stay in Halifax but will take the children and my stepmother on to England," Addie said. "But I wonder what life will be like for him there, for all that he considers himself an Englishman."

They were silent for a moment, both considering the changed circumstances of their parents and how difficult communication had become so that something as basic as the exchange of a letter was complicated enough to be nigh impossible.

They did not discuss the strain of waiting for the British to strike, but they found easy ground in praising each other's husbands.

"We appreciated that your husband honored us by witnessing our marriage in spite of how busy he was. Silas thinks Colonel Knox is the finest artillery command the Continental Army could have," Addie said, and she meant it, for Silas had nothing but praise for Knox. He admired the man's theoretical knowledge and his willingness to handle the big guns himself. The year before Henry had married Lucy, he had lost the two smallest fingers on his left hand in a hunting accident. He never mentioned the incident, and he kept the injury hidden, bound in a silk handkerchief. The Valencourts knew others, including Richard Henry Lee in Virginia, who were missing fingers or bore other scars from mishaps with small arms, and every artilleryman knew that he had nearly as good a chance of being maimed or killed by his own cannon misfiring or exploding as of being hit by enemy fire. But though Colonel Knox had suffered a grievous injury from a firearm, he showed no fear of any of them from musket to cannon.

"My Harry places great faith in Captain Bradwell," Lucy told Addie in return. "He believes that officers like your husband are vital to the success of our army."

They talked awhile longer, and Addie had the privilege of holding baby Lucy before she took her leave. It was common knowledge that Henry and Lucy Knox adored each other, and after her visit with Lucy, Addie was glad of it—anything that served to comfort the colonel could only be good for the men he commanded. She did not envy Lucy for having a baby, for though she hoped one day to bear children, she knew that were she pregnant now, Silas would use that as an excuse to send her far from danger, far from him. Time enough to be a mother; for the present, her single passion was to be with Silas for as long as possible.

Addie was not foolhardy enough to go about New York unattended. When Silas or Quentin could not be with her, she had Tullia to act as chaperone, and they were careful about where they went. Much of the population had vacated the city, and those who remained were uneasy with the sudden influx of Patriot soldiers and with waiting for whatever would happen. The whores were doing a brisk business with the soldiers, and decent women stayed away from the district ironically known as "Holy Ground" where the prostitutes reigned. Even the better streets were not without their hazards. New York had its share of Loyalists, but it also had one of the most aggressive branches of the Sons of Liberty. They had staged their own tea party some months after the one in Boston, and they were not above doing harm to the persons and property of those who opposed them. Many of them strutted about quite openly now, as if final victory were already theirs. Many Loyalist leaders had been sent away to be detained in Connecticut.

Addie, unable to resist, went to view the Valencourt shops. She was sure the broken windows and damaged goods strewn around were the work of the Sons of Liberty, and she wondered how much inventory had been stolen or if Darius had had the time and forethought to store some of it safely.

"Shame on them, shame!" Tullia said. "Makes no sense to go breaking things in the place where you live, just makes a big mess for everyone. I know Master Darius. He's patient for a time, but he has a high temper when he's pushed. He won't forgive this."

Though Addie was related to Darius by blood, she did not know him nearly as well as Tullia and she did not doubt Tullia's judgment of him. She shivered, suddenly sure that Darius, no matter where he was now, would not quit the field as their father had.

Justin and Ad had made discreet inquiries, and it did not seem that Darius was among those Loyalists who were being held in Connecticut. Since Justin and Ad were on Washington's staff, there was some embarrassment over the fact that Darius's house, like the residences of some other Tories, was being used for officers' quarters, but the brothers had made it clear that they understood the circumstances and would not, could not protest. Addie prayed that they would never face their half-brother in the battlefield.

She avoided going near the shops again, but wherever she and Tullia wandered, they were reminded that this was not Boston. Both towns were seaports, but that was where the similarity ended. New York had been in English hands for more than a century, but its Dutch origins were still evident, in the architecture of some old buildings, in the names of various establishments and areas, such as the Bowery from "bouwerij" meaning a green leafy place, though the once rural lane was now a busy thoroughfare. But the most profound differences between the two cities lay not in these superficialities, but in the spirit, for New York had been established as a trading center, not as a refuge for one religious sect, and its population was a broad mixture of people and beliefs. From its earliest days as New Amsterdam, the state of one's finances rather than one's soul had been the measure of acceptance, and this had not changed under British rule.

New York was about a mile in length and half of that in breadth, and had been a town of large, pleasant houses on well-shaded streets, with handsome public buildings, churches, and schools, and with businesses so conveniently located, cartage was rarely more than half a mile. But now defenses were being built everywhere, the big trees being chopped down to clear the view, the wood used in the fortifications. Public buildings were being turned to military use, open spaces to parade grounds. The shutting down of the city's trade showed in the deserted docks and warehouses. New York was being transformed from a flourishing port to a garrison, and even the country estates outside of the city were being adversely affected.

Much the same thing had happened to Boston under British rule, but Addie did not believe New York would be so soon abandoned as a military post. It was located between New England and the Southern colonies, and it was, with its deep harbor and rivers, an ideal spot for an army supported by a powerful navy. Unfortunately, that was an apt description of the British Army. The Americans lacked a navy other than privateers, and the cohesion of their army was questionable. Many of the troops who had joined Washington over the past weeks were militia, and there was no way to judge accurately how well each group was trained or how well they would face the enemy.

The wide variety of uniforms of both Continental troops and militia underscored the lack of unity. Here there were light gray surtouts, there green short coats, here blue coats, there butternut—on and on in a seemingly unlimited array of apparel. Most disquieting of all to Addie were the differences between the peoples of the diverse regions of the country from north to south, for General Washington was charged with forming these disparate souls into one army—a task more fitting for a worker of miracles than for a soldier.

General Washington, and Ad and Justin with him, were back in New York early in June, while Martha Washington remained behind in Philadelphia to recover from the effects of a smallpox inoculation. Carried by the soldiers who had been returning from what had proven a disastrous campaign in Canada, the disease was as much of a problem here as it had been in Boston, and despite her reservations about inoculation, Martha had finally seen the necessity of it. Addie's brothers reported that Mistress Washington had weathered the treatment well and would be rejoining her husband ere long.

Ad escorted his twin for a brief visit with General Washington at the Richmond Hill headquarters. The estate belonged to a Loyalist who was now the Paymaster-General of the British Army, and its pastoral setting in Lispenard's Meadow, with a garden overlooking the Hudson to the Jersey shore, belied its military usage. Indeed, because Richmond Hill was two miles from the Battery—a likely scene of action, but not a comfortable place to lodge—the situation of comfort versus necessity kept the general and his staff moving from one location to the other.

General Washington could not forebear reminding Addie that following the army was hazardous business.

Addie used the same weapon she had used against her brothers and Silas, saying, "I have heard that your wife has taken the risk quite willingly, sir," and the general smiled at the just hit. It was common knowledge how greatly Martha added to the general's comfort; he was much more approachable when she was near.

"Thank you for giving Silas Bradwell permission to wed me," Addie said, and for an instant, the general became once more the gallant with no more pressing business than turning the proper compliment.

"The young men of Virginia must weep to have lost you to a New Englander." Then the war intruded again as he added, "But it is not all loss. Knox tells me your husband is a skillful artilleryman, and that makes him most vital to our enterprise."

He gave her a courtly bow, and she curtseyed in turn, but before she had left the room, he was once again poring over maps and documents. He wore his sword and spurs even when at his writing desk, a measure of the immediacy of the war.

"What work he must do! So much for one man," Addie said.

"Yes, but there is as much honor as burden in it," Ad said, "though the burden would be lighter did he not have to deal with Congress's appointments." Ad was referring to the brigadier generals chosen by the Congress. They had been selected more for political reasons than for military skills, though some were cast in a favorable light in both, and General Washington had little choice except to employ them as well as he could. "I have to believe that Congress must be impressed by the general each time he appears before them. Otherwise, our journey to Philadelphia was a waste of effort."

Addie shared her twin's tension; everyone was showing signs of wear from the waiting. And Addie knew the general must feel the unease more keenly than anyone else.

Martha rejoined her husband on June 16, and two days later the Provincial Congress of New York entertained and honored General Washington and his staff. But following closely on these events were arrests of men suspected of plotting the abduction or assassination of the general. One of them, Thomas Hickey, was already in jail for counterfeiting, but he had been one of Washington's guards and thus had had access to the general. A fifer and a drummer were among the others who were said to have been bribed with money supplied by Governor Tryon. The Tory governor was safely aboard a British warship but still directing his agents in the city in actions against the Patriots.

Hickey was tried by court martial, and on June 28, he was hanged by the neck in a field near Bowery Lane. The officers and men of the brigades in Manhattan were there under arms, and thousands of civilians turned out to watch. Addie was among them. Because her husband and brother were there by command, she felt as if she also had to obey.

Hickey was brought on to the field to the funereal beat of drums and the wail of fifes. The buttons had been slashed from his uniform coat, the red cloth epaulet of a sergeant's rank ripped from his right shoulder. His composure faltered only once, when the chaplain shook his hand at the foot of the gallows. But then Hickey wiped the tears from his face and mounted the platform.

Addie saw the body drop, jerk briefly, and die. It reminded her of some cleverly constructed marionette. She was standing far enough away so that it was almost possible to pretend it was not a man. But the worst part for her was that she did not have to pretend. She discovered a vein of savagery in herself that approved this ultimate punishment, despite the humanity Hickey had shown in his tears. She had considered how lost they would be without the general, and now it seemed that they had come close to that pass.

Silas was not so convinced. He winced when she admitted she had witnessed the hanging. "You and all the rest of us, even little children," he grumbled. "The wages of sin, fair enough, I suppose, if the sin were committed."

"You think Hickey was innocent?"

"I don't know. I wasn't part of the court that found him guilty. But there are rumors on top of rumors, and many names have been mentioned, yet only Hickey is hanged. It seems too convenient, though I don't doubt that Governor Tryon, along with every other Tory of means, has been doing his best to corrupt our army." He rubbed his face wearily.

"There's something else, isn't there?" Addie asked, not liking the way his eyes had avoided hers when he had spoken of the rumors.

Silas didn't have the energy to try to keep the truth from her. "It is being whispered that General Washington has a mistress, that she has read secret documents while he slept and has passed information on to the enemy."

"You believe this?" Addie's eyes were wide with shock.

"No! I don't. Oh, hell! I don't want to believe it, but what if it is true?"

"It isn't," Addie said with utter conviction. "It is not that I think men are incapable of such behavior—though do not think you can stray without horrible consequences—but pray tell me, how could the general accomplish this? His wife was only absent from his side for a brief period; Justin, Ad, and others are with him constantly; the work is never done; and can you imagine a man of the general's great size and distinctive mien sneaking about unnoticed and carrying bundles of documents besides? It sounds to me that some have decided he would be less threatening did he serve Venus instead of Mars."

Her words were balm to his spirit, particularly sweet because she knew the general personally. Silas had such admiration for him, it frightened him sometimes. He had enough awareness of his own heart to know that in losing Marcus, he had transferred much of his hero worship, as had Ad and Justin, to Washington, and he understood the danger in that, the blindness to faults that could come from it, and the pain that would come if the trust were betrayed.

"I'll wager that if you ask Ad or Justin about this, they will answer the same and with more authority, for they are constant witnesses to the general's life. They are on duty, within his call both day and night."

But Silas didn't have to ask because Ad brought it up, shaking his head in exasperated amusement. "The poor man, where would he find the time or the energy, even if he did have the inclination?"

"Or the invisible cloak?" Justin asked. "Not to mention the invisible horse, for he would need both to travel unremarked."

"His wife is a patient woman, and I hope she remains so, for before this war is over, there will probably be scores, nay, hundreds of woman who will claim intimate knowledge of her husband."

"What a dreadful prediction!" Addie said, but she was grateful to her brothers who, though they had disguised it with humor, were as sensitive as she to Silas's need for reassurance.

However, underneath the fellowship and love of the little group, they shared the knowledge that this might be the last supper they would share at the Chaffey house. Already there was a change because Quentin was on Long Island and could not get away to be with them. But the biggest change of all was the presence of the frigate *Greyhound* in New York waters.

Despite some losses to Patriot privateers, British ships, with the British Navy in command of the seas, sailed where they pleased, and the waters off Manhattan Island continued to be cut by the hulls of British ships of one kind or another even while the Continental Army was settling in on the land.

The *Greyhound* was different because on board was General Howe. The ship was constructed and named for speed, and the report was that Howe had sailed from Halifax, Nova Scotia, only a couple of weeks before. No one believed he had sailed alone; troop ships would take longer to arrive. Already other sails had been sighted, but no one knew how many ships or how many troops were coming.

"Perhaps General Howe is here to offer more reasonable terms for reconciliation." Addie's voice sounded quavery to her ears, like a child's whisper against the dark.

"More reasonable than being hanged for our crimes against the Crown?" Justin asked. "Reasonable meaning that we will lay down our arms and let everything go back to the way it was, with England dictating how life will be here forever?"

"Howe's intentions will be made clear enough when we see how many soldiers are set to join him." Silas had had enough of wild rumors and wanted no part of starting new ones.

It was difficult to avoid them with so much at stake and with so many conflicting reports. But some of them were well substantiated. There was no longer any doubt that Canada was a lost cause and would not come in on the American side. The troops who had gone north last year had, after some initial success, failed. The well-liked Major General Richard Montgomery had died before the gates of Quebec. Colonel Benedict Arnold's force had been severely mauled, and the survivors had had to escape southward through wild forests. Colonel Arnold himself had been wounded. Now the best hope was that British soldiers in Canada could be prevented from gaining ground in New England and northern New York.

"I never understood why it was thought that Canada would join us," Justin confessed. "There are a good many Roman Catholics there and Anglicans. They have little in common with and little liking for New England's Congregationalists, and what they do have in common—fishing grounds and land boundaries—are perpetually in dispute. And they see this as New England's war."

"If they had better intelligence, they would not regard it so any longer," Ad said. "Moore's Creek Bridge in North Carolina is a fair distance from New England."

News from there had been positive, for in February, a force of Loyalist Highlanders had been defeated by militia, and the area was firmly in Patriot control. It was significant because of the Scots' reputation for fighting, and it was reassuring to know they could be beaten. Some of the captured soldiers had been part of the newly recruited "Traverne's Highlanders."

"Do you think your Scotsman was taken with the others?" Ad asked his sister.

"He is not my Scotsman!" she snapped, but it was startling how clearly his image appeared in her mind at the mention of his name. "But I doubt he was captured, for we have not heard that their commander is among the prisoners, and that would seem an important detail." That he could be less than their leader did not occur to her.

"Perhaps he is safely in Scotland," Justin suggested. "Some commanding officers never take the field at all, even when it is their names their troops bear."

"Some, but not John Traverne," Addie said flatly. "His brother did it before him, but his brother is duty-bound at home now, I believe, for the lot of his people is a hard one. If men bearing the Traverne standard are to be here, then John Traverne will be with them."

Silas made no comment then, but she could feel his tension, and when they were alone, he said, "I know I am an idiot to be jealous, but I am, jealous of the Scotsman. He made a deep impression on you, for all that you did not see him often."

Addie decided on part of the truth. "He is an impressive man. I wish he were on our side. He commands the respect of other men with little effort. I watched him do it with the redcoats, though he himself was not in uniform. That alone will make him a formidable enemy."

Her words made Silas relax because she was describing a soldier, a foe, not a romantic figure.

Addie felt no guilt for neglecting to mention the human, vulnerable side she had seen of Traverne when he had told her of the deaths of his wife and child, but she could see his face exactly as it had looked then, so bleak and sad.

Silas loved her fiercely that night, and they held each other until the dawn, both aware that with General Howe so near, the semblance of a normal life that they had created in New York was surely coming to an end.

Chapter 2

The Bradwells and Valencourts did not have long to wait. Within a couple of days, General Howe's fleet of more than a hundred ships arrived, and on July 3, British troops were landed on Staten Island. Still, General Howe took no action.

Addie saw less of Silas and her brothers as they remained close to their posts, but when Silas reminded her of her promise to leave, she replied that she would when there was danger of the city being overrun.

"The redcoats have made no attack on Manhattan yet, and I vow there will be a good deal of warning before they march up to Mistress Chaffey's door," she told him, but she was faithful about seeing that the horses and wagon were kept in readiness.

On July 9, a new document, released by the Continental Congress in Philadelphia five days previously, was read to the troops in New York. Many civilians came to the reading, among them Addie, Tullia, and Mistress Chaffey. As they listened to the words they knew that a great step had been taken.

> *When in the course of human events, it becomes necessary for one people to dissolve the political bands which have connected them with another, and to assume among the powers of the earth, the separate and equal station to which the laws of Nature and of Nature's God entitle them, a decent respect to the opinions of mankind requires that they should declare the causes which impel them to the separation.*
>
> *We hold these truths to be self-evident, that all men are created equal, that they are endowed by their Creator with certain unalienable rights, that among these are life, liberty, and the pursuit of happiness. That to secure these rights, governments are instituted among men, deriving their just powers from the*

consent of the governed. That whenever any form of government
becomes destructive of these ends, it is the right of the people to
alter or to abolish it, and to institute new government, laying
its foundation on such principles and organizing its powers
in such form, as to them shall seem most likely to effect their
safety and happiness...

The document then proceeded to list in detail the offenses committed by the "present Ring of Great Britain" against these "states," and the people of Britain were also admonished for failing to heed the warnings and appeal of their brethren.

The years of supplication were over. As much as a "Declaration of Independence," as it was titled, it was a declaration of revolution, of self-generated change so profound, it was impossible to find its match in history. Addie and her companions, like the rest of the listening crowd, drew breath as the last words were read, and then their voices joined the cheers of the multitude.

"The United States of America," Mistress Chaffey said. "I like the sound of that. All my life, I've been an Englishwoman. But I was born here, not across the sea. If it is good enough for those fine men in Philadelphia to be Americans, it is good enough for me."

"And for me," said Addie and Tullia in chorus.

Her companions remained with Addie until the troops were dismissed and Silas found them where they had arranged to meet. But as soon as he appeared, the two older women left, clearly wanting the couple to have this time to themselves.

Watching them go, Addie smiled. "It's kind of them, but their presence could hardly make a difference in this sea of people."

But, strangely, as Addie looked up at Silas, it was as if they were alone.

"What do you think of it?" he asked.

The words tumbled out. "I think that every discussion of politics we have had since we were young was leading to this. I think we've just stepped off a cliff, thousands of us together, and somehow we must learn to fly before we hit bottom. I think it's very, very dangerous, and

wonderful. I want to weep and to laugh. I wish Papa could hear the
words and understand. I wish Sarah had lived to witness this. This is
truly the New World now."

As the crowd swirled around them, they gazed at each other with
perfect understanding, not ignoring the menace of British troops so
close by, but allowing themselves an instant to imagine the culmina-
tion of their dreams.

Silas took her hands, and they wandered with the jubilant throng,
watching as the huge gold statue of George III was pulled down. The
gold was only gilt over the thousands of pounds of lead beneath, lead
that could be melted and molded into musket balls for the Continental
Army. The idea swept the crowd as the statue crashed to earth.

Addie didn't protest when Silas suggested it was time they return
to Mistress Chaffey's. The crowd, a mix of soldiers and civilians, was
growing more boisterous. Many were consuming more than the spirit
of independence as they stopped often to quench their thirst at the
taverns.

The Bradwells walked along, both of them thinking that only a year
ago, even the most avid Patriots still thought of the King as their father
and as separate from the machinations of his ministers and Parliament.

Addie shivered suddenly, though the night was hot and sultry with
intermittent flashes of lightning. "I enjoyed watching that statue come
down," she admitted, "but it is frightening to see how quickly the
mob—we—can turn on someone we once professed to love."

Silas could not dispute her observation, and it was as if Marcus
were walking with them, Marcus who so feared the disruption of order.

When they reached the house, they found Ad waiting for them.

"We've had word from Uncle Hartley," he said, digging a crumpled
letter out of his pocket and handing it to his sister. "For all the caution
that has guided his steps before, he was ready for this. He is very
proud of the work the Congress did and particularly that of his fellow
Virginian, Mr. Jefferson, who did the writing, with a little editorial
help from others."

The identity of the author did not surprise the twins, for Tom
Jefferson was familiar to them from their Williamsburg days as a

well-educated lawyer and member of the House of Burgesses, and he was as well known for his eloquence on paper as for his shyness in public speaking. It was fitting that he should have been the one to compose the Declaration.

"Mr. Jefferson would have accused the King of foisting the evil of slavery upon us, among his other sins, but he was persuaded to omit that clause for fear of offending too many slave owners. I think Uncle Hartley would rather have left the words in, for all that he owns slaves himself." Ad shook his head in wonder. "Strange that he should grow so radical while Papa moved so far in the other direction."

"Papa didn't move. He just stayed where he has always been, and we all journeyed away from him in our minds," Addie corrected him sadly.

Ad wished he had another chance, just one more, to change their father's view, though he knew in his heart that the attempt would be futile.

Ad could not stay the night, not with so much to be done at headquarters, but even after he had departed and the rest of the household had settled down, Addie and Silas remained awake for hours, too excited to sleep.

Silas was as moved by the Declaration as anyone could be, but he was also obsessed with ordnance—their own and that of the British.

"All those ships and more to come, all of them armed. We're doing our best with what we've got, deploying our cannon in the forts and batteries on both sides of the Hudson and around Manhattan and Long Island, but there is too much shoreline to defend."

"But more men are joining General Washington every day," Addie pointed out. "That must count for something."

"It does. But men with muskets cannot stand forever against cannon."

"The wagon and the horses are ready," she told him calmly, before he could ask. "Remember what you told me, 'we will fight them somewhere else, and somewhere else after that.'"

"The general could use you on his staff," Silas said. He pulled her close, and so they remained through the night, in spite of the summer heat, drawing comfort from each other in a world that had suddenly grown impossibly vast. They were Americans now. They were no longer attached to the mother country. They would no longer suffer the tyranny, but neither would they have the protection nor the pride of the tradition that had shaped their lives and the lives of so many before them. No longer unless their cause was lost and they were hanged as enemies of the civilization that had formed them.

The next morning, Silas kissed her hard and was gone. And the day after that, Admiral Lord Howe's fleet appeared off Sandy Hook. When the ships hove into view, they were saluted by General Howe's vessels already in the harbor, and the sailors on board and the soldiers on Staten Island cheered wildly.

Addie, Tullia, and Mistress Chaffey would no more miss this than they would have forgone the reading of the Declaration. And if the noise of the enemy was deafening, the sight of all the ships coming in was a spectacle of terrifying beauty.

Admiral Lord Howe had with him one hundred and fifty transports loaded with troops. Addie stared at the rows and rows of figures on the decks until her eyes ached. The sun glinted off buttons, badges, gorgets, and sword hilts, and picked up bright slashes of color from uniforms. The cheering and the salute of guns battered at her ears, and she fully understood Silas's apprehensions.

"So the Howe brothers are together in this, together against us. They have ties here and have been well regarded in the past. I wonder how this sits with them?"

"Not ill enough to keep them away. The King bids them come against us, and so they do." The contempt in Mistress Chaffey's voice did not hide her fear for her nephew's safety, and Addie could feel the same fear rippling through many of the spectators. It was bitter to know that there were those who stood among them silently applauding the show of Britain's power.

Nor was the power for show only. The *Phoenix*, a man-of-war of forty guns, and a smaller ship, the *Rose*, sailed through the Narrows between Long Island and Staten Island. The American batteries along the shore opened fire, and the British returned the compliment with heavy broadsides.

Suddenly Addie and her companions were being shoved this way and that by screaming adults and shrieking children, and Addie was more afraid of being trampled by the crazed crowd than of being hit by British shot. The three of them sought shelter by a huge stack of barrels and huddled there until the press of people had eased.

The most horrifying thing of all was that the *Phoenix* and the *Rose* proceeded on their way, seemingly impervious to fire from the shore.

"God help us, Silas was right!" Addie cried, and she mourned that all the hard work the army had poured into building defenses against British ships seemed to matter naught.

That night, she and Tullia packed their things, ready to leave on the instant if need be, but when morning came, no battle had yet been joined. The two ships were said to be continuing unharmed up the Hudson River, passing easily through the barrier that had been laid across the river to impede British vessels. It was clear that some Loyalist had supplied the enemy with information about the supposedly secret channel meant to allow only American traffic through. More British troops were being disembarked on Staten Island, but an attack did not appear imminent.

It was several days before Silas could come to Addie, and he was furious that she had not fled at the first sound of the guns. Mistress Washington, Lucy Knox, and most of the other officers' wives had been sent away when the British ships had been sighted, but that had only stiffened Addie's resolve.

Martha Washington had departed in her green coach, her coachman and postillion in the scarlet-and-white Washington livery, her enslaved Black maid Oney with her. Martha's hair had been powdered and topped with a fresh lace cap, and her traveling gown fit her small, round figure with simple elegance. She had bowed and waved from the window to well-wishers as the coach, accompanied by a mounted escort, left the city.

Addie had had a brief meeting with her after she had arrived back in New York from Philadelphia. Martha had greeted her warmly, pleased as she always was to see anyone known as a friend back in Virginia. They had reminisced about their last visit two years ago in Williamsburg, before the war began, and they had chatted about domestic affairs, including Martha's concern that Jacky's wife Nelly be safely delivered of her first child, due this summer. But inevitably the conversation had turned to the war.

"He will never allow me to stay once the enemy appears," Mistress Washington had said softly. "I understand, but it is so difficult to leave him!" At that moment, her face had been openly adoring of her husband.

"Everyone knows he is content only when you are near, ma'am," Addie had offered, and Martha had blushed as prettily as a young girl.

As if reading Addie's thoughts, Silas said now, "You should have left when the general's wife and the others did." But he had to concede, albeit reluctantly, that she was right when she claimed that despite the exchange of fire, few could really have believed a full attack was being launched.

"The British line up for battle, like peacocks displaying their tails," she said. "They would never do anything so clumsy as to tumble off their ships in a mad scramble after us."

He surprised her with a sudden smile. "I think they may be learning that we are not so clumsy as they thought, either." He laughed outright. "Oh, Addie! I wish you could have seen it! I went as an aide with Colonel Knox and Colonel Reed to meet with an emissary from Admiral Howe. The British were approaching by boat under flag of truce so we met them by barge. The redcoat captain stood, all starched and proper, and announced, 'I have a letter, sir, from Lord Howe to Mr. Washington.'

"'Sir, we have no person in our army with that address,' Colonel Reed told him.

"Then the redcoat directed him to look at the address on a letter. It read: 'George Washington, Esquire, New York.' But Reed insisted, 'No, sir, I cannot receive that letter.'

"It went on a bit longer, but Reed would not be swayed, claiming he had to obey orders, and there was nothing the redcoat could say to that. And the story is widespread that it happened again at headquarters with Colonel Paterson, Howe's adjutant general, trying to persuade General Washington to receive a letter addressed to 'George

Washington, Esq., etcetera, etcetera.' Colonel Paterson tangled his tongue trying to induce General Washington to overlook the insult, calling him 'Your Excellency' too many times to count and claiming that the et ceteras indicated all formal titles."

Ad and Justin had witnessed this exchange firsthand, and when Addie saw her twin, he added details. He was as amused as Silas, but he was also deeply moved. "Colonel Paterson was there to tell General Washington that Lord Howe had been granted great powers to make peace, if it were possible.

"The general said, 'Yes, power to pardon. But he came to the wrong place with his pardons; the Americans have not offended, therefore they need no pardon.' And then he sent his compliments to Lord and General Howe, as one commander to others.

"Addie, I tell you, Paterson looked stunned, as if someone had hit him between the eyes. I am sure he did not expect to find a man of our general's presence and dignity leading the Rebel army." He pronounced "rebel" exuberantly, turning insult to praise. "We were all so proud of His Excellency, we would have marched straight into hell for him had he asked it." Some of his animation faded. "That may be where we're going anyway," he admitted wryly. "And if we are, I'd just as soon we set out. The waiting is wearing at everyone."

But the waiting went on. The *Phoenix* and the *Rose* sailed back down the Hudson, returning within six days, undeterred by American batteries. The British forces on Staten Island continued to organize their bivouacs, while Loyalists flocked to them from the countryside. On the huge fleet of ships, sailors went about their duties, and Loyalists were entertained as they anticipated the restoration of the world as they knew it. And adding to the general tension, the weather was hot, sultry, with periodic heavy rains.

"Maybe those redcoats will boil away in their uniforms," Tullia suggested one stifling afternoon. "Not so wise to send them here in the middle of summer dressed for winter."

"The British think even the weather should obey them," Addie said, but she remembered how the heat had affected the redcoats on their retreat from Lexington and Concord, and she hoped it would do worse to them here. With every day that passed, they were becoming less individual, less human to her, not at all like they had been in Boston when she had had daily contact with them in her father's house. In spite of her kind memories of Captain Byrne, redcoats were becoming, in her mind, demons sent to kill her husband and brothers.

The American attempts to fortify their position on Manhattan went on at a furious rate, and no able-bodied man was exempt. Not only did soldiers and officers work side by side, but civilians were called out, too, to wield spades and pickaxes, though Black and white were to work on alternate days.

Life in the city degenerated. The humid heat, bad water, sewage, refuse, and too many soldiers living in inadequate, overcrowded conditions caused all manner of diseases from rashes and boils to ague, camp fever, the flux, and smallpox to spread like fire. Some men made crude attempts to inoculate themselves against the smallpox, causing more cases until orders were issued that any man who did so would be considered an enemy to his country.

The stench of the city was foul and crept in everywhere, but Addie did her best to ignore it. She was ever conscious of how lavish her simple quarters were in comparison to the wretched conditions being endured by the soldiers. And at least there was no shortage of fresh fruit and produce, as well as fodder for the animals, coming in from the surrounding countryside. The only overt manifestation of war occurred when British foraging parties came too close to Continental troops, and shots were exchanged.

Silas, Justin, and Ad managed to spend time at Mistress Chaffey's every few days as the summer wore on, but Quentin appeared only once. He brought with him a set of miniatures he had painted of himself, his siblings, Silas, and Tullia.

Though she had long known how talented Quentin was, Addie was amazed nonetheless at how well he'd captured all of them in vivid colors. Looking at the one of herself was like peering into a mirror, albeit a flattering one in her eyes.

"You ought to be in the atelier of a great master, not camped on Long Island," she said. "This is such fine work, more people than just your family ought to see your genius."

Quentin grinned at her. "They do. I've got a brisk business going because so many soldiers want likenesses of themselves for their wives or sweethearts or mothers. Or they want portraits of General Washington. I have so many orders, I cannot fill them all in the time I have away from duty. My worry is that I will not be able to keep myself supplied with all I need to paint. My case is nearly empty, I have used almost everything I brought from home."

After Quentin had greeted Tullia and allowed her to make a fuss over him, he and Addie went shopping for artists' supplies, using the excursion to pretend that nothing was out of the ordinary.

Only when it was time for him to return to camp did his cheerful manner falter. "I don't want to make you sad, but I need to beg a favor. Please keep these safe for me, and when we know where they should go, I want to send them to Papa, to remind him that we are still part of his family." He handed the little portraits to her.

"Together we will send them off someday soon," she said, willing herself not to cry.

Quentin bid goodbye to Tullia, gave Addie a final hug, and was gone.

"It isn't right that so much beauty goes to war," Tullia said. Weeping, she buried her face in her apron, and Addie's own tears overflowed.

And still the enemy ships kept coming. New York's harbor was so crowded with British ships, it was a wonder they did not run afoul of each other. There were dozens of warships, hundreds of transports and supply vessels, and thousands of men. Sometimes when Addie stared at the scene, it lost its reality, becoming a senseless tangle of shapes—hulls, bowsprits, and masts—etched against the sea and sky. And now there were Highlanders among the troops, too. Addie thought of John Traverne and the men he would lead, and she wished they all had stayed in Scotland.

By mid-August, the British with their mercenaries were estimated to number more than thirty thousand, while Washington commanded considerably fewer than that, with sickness continuing to take its toll from both armies in the summer heat. But the biggest difference between them was not in the numbers, but in the fact that the British forces were, for the most part, professional soldiers, and no one could foretell how the Continental Army, with its citizen soldiers, would fare against them in formal battle, a drill that would be quite unlike the shoot-from-behind-the-wall action of Lexington and Concord or the surprise occupations of Breed's Hill and Dorchester Heights.

It did not help that sectional rivalry continued to cause such dissension. In particular, the Virginians, who were generally well disciplined and deferential toward their officers, were appalled by the rough democracy of the New Englanders, who did not take kindly to being ordered about by anyone. And the New Englanders and New Yorkers, longtime business rivals, despised each other no less now than they had before the war, their prejudices unchanged by the appearance of a massive enemy force.

The problem was so acute, Washington addressed it in general orders on August 1, entreating the officers and soldiers to work together because everything depended on that harmony, but also declaring that punishment and dismissal would fall on those who failed to act accordingly.

"If the plea fails, perhaps the threat will succeed," Ad said, flexing fingers cramped from copying these orders and other official papers.

"Perhaps, but these are old rivalries, as comfortable as a feather bed. I think new friendships will be easier formed at the point of the enemy's guns than by the scratch of our quills." Justin regretted the words as soon as he spoke them. His cynicism was of no use to his brother, and he tried to make up for it. "At least we have General Greene on Long Island."

Washington's forces were divided among three major positions, with part in New York City itself, part farther north, and part on Long Island, under the command of Nathanael Greene. It was reassuring to the Valencourts and Bradwells that one of the army's most able generals was in charge of the area where Quentin was serving.

But in mid-August, Greene took to his bed with fever, and his duties were given to General John Sullivan, who was not of Greene's caliber. The best hope was that Greene would recover quickly but time ran out before Greene was back on his feet. On August 22, General Howe began to debark troops on Long Island. By noon, fifteen thousand fully equipped soldiers had been landed. A storm had raged the night before, but now the weather, bright and clear, favored the British. The display of military precision sent a message as clear as the weather: if the Rebels would not agree to the government's overtures of peace through pardons, then the problem of the intransigent colonies would be solved with an iron fist.

In the city, the American warning guns on Long Island could be heard and smoke was seen drifting up into the sky. There were confused reports about what the smoke might mean, but the most likely story was that the Americans were pulling in their outposts, burning hayricks so that the British would be unable to get fodder for their livestock.

The Americans' forward defenses were now on a ridge of hills, the Heights of Guian, through which there were four passes. And behind and to the west was the main American position at Brooklyn Heights. From where the British had landed and from the way they were massing, it seemed that they would assault the western passes, and these were heavily guarded by the Americans. But Howe would begin the battle when he was ready and not before. Three days after he had landed the first troops, he brought in German troops with the same show of flawless maneuvers.

Things were not going so smoothly for the Continental Army. Addie listened as avidly as anyone to the rumors and speculations about what was happening. For her, the irony of the situation was that Silas, Justin, and Ad were, for the moment, close at hand, her brothers waiting on their general and Silas ready to be sent to Long Island with artillery reinforcements if need be, but she saw little of any of them. And their brief contacts were wholly unsatisfactory.

Silas wanted her to leave immediately, but she refused. "The enemy isn't coming to the city yet, and I will not go until I know that Quentin is safe."

It was impossible for him to push too hard because he shared her apprehension. It filled them all with dread that Quentin was to be the first of them to face a full-blown enemy assault.

On August 27, Howe put an end to the guessing game. While part of his force made a noisy feint against the western passes, another detachment, which had proceeded in darkness, marched through the easternmost pass, Jamaica Pass, in the morning and arrived behind the left center of the American defensive line. With careful elegance, aided by the Americans' neglect of Jamaica Pass, Howe had set and sprung a trap.

Quentin was one of the thousands of Americans who found themselves ensnared. Though he would not have admitted it to anyone, he had hoped that his brothers or Silas would be near when he went into battle, to steady him in case he panicked, but he did not need them, after all. He felt as calm as if he were in the still eye of a great storm. The smoke of the guns rolled over everything, and he knew the voice of his fife must be so strong and true it would pierce the haze and direct the men. He played each note as if it were a word, telling, cajoling, pleading for the men to move this way and that. While he played, the battle roiled around him, but in his mind and in his soul, the music was all.

The musket ball slammed into his heart, killing him before the last notes from his fife ceased to dance on the air.

At headquarters with Washington, Ad and Justin gleaned news from one courier after another. Some units were being attacked from front, flank, and rear. Many were fighting ferociously despite their disadvantage, but they were heavily outnumbered, and many, unable to get back to the main American position at Brooklyn Heights, were being captured by the British. Most horrifying of all, there were reports that German troops were slaughtering those who were trapped and trying to surrender.

"Oh, God! I pray Addie doesn't hear of this!" Ad met his brother's eyes. Neither of them said Quentin's name aloud, but he filled their minds.

General Washington was sending reinforcements across the East River to Brooklyn—Ad and Justin wrote orders moving troops and delivered messages to various officers as fast as they could—but with the troops on Long Island in such disarray and the enemy there in such force, there was great uncertainty about risking more men. The one thing in the Americans' favor in an otherwise disastrous day was that the wind was from the north, preventing British ships from sailing into the East River and thus blocking the enemy from that route to the American rear.

Ad wrote the orders that sent Silas's unit across to Long Island. With effort, he kept his hand steady, but he could not help feeling guilty for remaining in the relative safety of headquarters while his younger brother and his brother-in-law faced the enemy. And he knew Justin felt the same; he was so tense, the cords of his neck were hard ridges.

It was a relief to cross over to Long Island with Washington when he took direct command, though it increased the chances of harm befalling the general. But even his appearance on the scene could not change the course of the day, though it put renewed heart in his discouraged troops to see him. The drenching rain of the afternoon was the best weapon they had against Howe, but by then, the battle was over anyway. Two generals were prisoners of the British, and estimates had up to a thousand other Americans captured. There were hundreds of American dead, with enemy losses much less.

Additional troops continued to be ferried over from the city to reinforce the American position on Brooklyn Heights, seemingly a sure indication that Washington meant to mount a stiff defense. However, it was a precarious perch with Howe in front of them and the East River behind them.

Justin and Ad rode back and forth, taking messages from various commanders and bringing back replies. They took whatever mounts were available, and if they had brief minutes out of the saddle, they spent them with quills in hand. Wherever they went, they searched for glimpses of Quentin and Silas, though it would be hard to pick out their faces among the thousands and the confusion. And so many had been killed, taken prisoner, or separated from their units, accurate information was impossible to obtain.

The next day was little better. After his stunning action, it seemed certain that Howe would attack again immediately, but the heavy rain driven by wind from the northeast that increased the Americans' misery also seemed to keep Howe from bestirring himself.

All day long, Washington checked pickets and every other detail of the deployment while his aides reeled in their saddles or squinted at their writing with eyesight blurred by exhaustion.

Ad felt relief well within him when Silas hailed him during one of his rides. He dared pull up only briefly, but his grin was wide. "Well met. Justin and I have been looking for you. Any sign of Quentin?"

Silas shook his head. "No, but I'll keep asking." His face was suddenly grim. "I do know that his unit was hard hit; a lot of them were taken prisoner." Silas could not bring himself to say that many had been killed, too, but he was sure Ad must be aware of it.

Ad rode on. "Not Quentin, not Quentin," sounded in his brain to the beat of his horse's hooves, and he knew Justin was thinking the same thing after he told him about seeing Silas.

During the night, they could hear the ring of pickaxes and other sounds of the enemy digging entrenchments, sounds more ominous than their own scant chorus of muskets firing.

Boats had been taking the most severely wounded across the East River since the end of the battle, but those who were still able to shoulder weapons had remained with their regiments. Ad pitied the men he saw with bloody, rain-soaked bandages wrapped around their heads or limbs. A few were dull-eyed with pain and shock, but most of them looked grimly resolute, determined to face Howe's next assault, whenever it came. Despite the rain, the air reeked of gunpowder and wood smoke, of sweat, of thousands of men.

The storm continued through the night, as Washington and his staff kept on making rounds of the encampment. Justin, Ad, and the rest of the aides were so fatigued, they could scarcely stay awake, but if the general could keep going, then so would they.

On the next day, the weather showed signs of clearing, the rain reduced to occasional bursts. The British were pushing their works closer and began a preliminary bombardment, and Washington gave every sign of being determined to hold the line.

"We can't allow them to kill him or take him prisoner if they overrun us," Ad said to his brother, not caring that his desperation showed.

"What exactly do you propose we do to prevent either case—kidnap him?" Justin asked. "I can't believe he means to let it end here, but it will if they take him."

In the evening, Washington called a council of war that his generals might approve his plan for immediate withdrawal. By then, the Valencourts already knew that withdrawal was imminent, for in spite of staging the show of asking his generals, Washington had already acted to implement his plan, sending orders for every kind of craft with oars or sails to be collected and in the East River by dark.

Ad rode hard, jerking his horse's head up when the beast nearly went down in the slippery soil. The general's plan was a daring one and required that each man do his part, for he planned to get every one of his soldiers off Long Island before the sun rose again.

One by one officers were ordered to march their men down to the shore as quietly as possible, leaving their cooking fires smoldering behind them so the British would think the troops were still in place. The men had kept their firewood as dry as possible, and here and there, they added what was left before they moved out. Fog diffused the light, making the fires glow, phantom camps in the night.

No unit was told the overall plan; each thought it was the only one being moved, and each followed orders. If the enemy had launched the attack with admirable precision, at least the Continental Army was matching them in discipline this night.

Justin heard a familiar voice in the darkness of early morning.

"We don't go until every damn gun is secured!" Silas swore as he checked the lines, working to make sure the cannon could be safely transported to Manhattan.

Justin went to him, and Silas smiled at him briefly before asking, "Any sign of Quentin?"

"No," Justin admitted, "but we'll keep looking… and hoping."

They clasped hands for an instant and went back to their separate duties, conscious that dawn was not far away.

Colonel John Glover and his Marblehead regiment, which included a good number of Salem seamen as well as Marbleheaders, acted as sailors all night long, performing a near miracle as they carried more than eight thousand men to safety. At first the wind was too strong to allow for sails or full boats, so the men rowed with muffled oars in the churning water. At midnight, the tide turned, the wind lessened, and in the calmer water, the boats were able to carry sails and more passengers.

Hour after hour, the men labored on, crossing back and forth from two sites. They used every kind of vessel that would float and they transported not only men, but horses, ammunition, field guns, muskets, and other equipment.

Ad felt a deep pride of place, Marblehead and Salem being little coastal towns close to Boston and noted for their fine fishermen and sailors. Their tart voices in the darkness comforted him.

But the most important passenger remained on the Long Island shore. Muffled in his cloak, Washington had overseen every step of the evacuation, his presence and his commands calming the men when they had grown anxious to get into the boats. But as quiet and orderly as the maneuver had been overall, with every minute that passed there was more chance of discovery. His aides, Justin and Ad included, had given up trying to persuade him to leave before all the rest had gone, but when the last boat was readied, Washington got in with them.

"Did you fear I would breakfast with General Howe?" he asked Ad, and Ad answered his commander's brief smile with one of his own. "The thought occurred to me, Your Excellency."

Ad knew the general must be sore of heart for their losses on Long Island, but his steadiness had not faltered. And as Ad thought of all that had happened, he realized that in some ways, they had won by not losing more. Despite being outnumbered and outfoxed, many units had stood fast and fought well in a conventional battle rather than by frontier rules. And now, General Washington had gotten his soldiers away in a bold move that must surely make the enemy imagine their prey had simply vanished into the fog. Ad considered how difficult it was going to be for the British to understand an enemy that could count gain in anything short of complete disaster.

Such musings ended abruptly when they landed, and he saw Silas waiting for them, Silas with his face looking like a death's head in the misty light and with a brass-bound case clutched against his chest. Justin saw him, too, and Ad heard him breathe, "God, no! Please, God, no!"

Ad and Justin recognized the box, the fine case made to hold artists' supplies for painting in the field, the box given to Quentin by Marcus years ago so that his talented son could take it with him to Virginia. Quentin had never traveled without it; it had been with him when he had run away to the army in Cambridge, and it had been with him on Long Island.

"By your leave, Your Excellency, there seems to be some news of our brother Quentin." Ad could barely form the words.

General Washington nodded. "Go. I trust no ill has befallen him."

Ad and Justin went to Silas, who seemed unable to take another step toward them.

"A sergeant had this, he was looking for you. He knew Quentin's brothers were on General Washington's staff, but he didn't want to give this to you over there"—he jerked his head in the direction they had come—"for fear you would do something rash and displease the general. I heard him asking after you, and I told him who I am. He wept when he gave it to me. He said Quentin was a good lad, a good soldier. He said they would miss his music and his clever paintings. He…" Silas's monotone trailed off.

"Captured? Wounded?" Ad couldn't make himself say the next word.

Silas bowed his head, and his hands clutched the box harder. "The sergeant said that Quentin died in the battle. He said it was very fast, a shot to the heart. He is sure Quentin lies with the others. The regiment was being pushed back, they could not bring off their… dead." He did not say that the sergeant was certain the shooting of Quentin had been very specific; Ad and Justin would have suspected that anyway because during a battle the fifers and drummers were vital for the signals they gave and were thus better shot down as soon as possible. And Quentin had been very, very skilled at creating the piercing musical language of war. He had practiced and practiced that he might never endanger the troops by making the music misspeak.

Silas saw the blotches appearing on the case and was distantly surprised to realize they were marks of his tears. "How will I tell her?" he whispered.

Ad wanted to say that Addie didn't have to know yet because they didn't know for sure, not absolutely, but even as he considered it, he accepted the veracity of the sergeant's report. Nor was there any way to conceal from his twin that Quentin had not come back with them.

"We'll go together," Justin said.

Silas looked away from them and back again, struggling for control. "We can't all be away from our posts. For all we know, Howe will be on our heels as soon as he discovers we're gone. And it is my place to tell her." He turned away from them, and they let him go.

"I hope the British do attack today, damn their souls!" Justin swore. His body was surging with rage and sorrow so intermixed, he trembled.

Ad shared his need for action, but more, the part of him that had always been so attuned to his twin could scarcely bear being separated from her now. He knew how deep her grief would run. And he knew that Silas was sparing him from witnessing the initial onslaught of it.

They made their way through the press of men, and no one impeded their progress.

When Silas saw Addie, he did not have to say the words. At first her eyes lighted at the sight of him safe before her, and then she saw the darkness in him, and she saw Quentin's paintbox.

She froze, staring at the case, and then she reached out and stroked the wood, leather, and brass with gentle fingers. "He's dead. The youngest of us. So much beauty gone." She spoke softly, as if trying to remember the words to an old ballad. The sudden harsh sound of weeping came from Tullia, not from Addie.

Very carefully, Silas put his burden down, and then he put his arms around Addie. "Ad and Justin are unharmed. I just took my leave of them." He felt her nod against him in acknowledgment. He spoke past the rigid constriction of his throat. "The sergeant who saw Quentin die said it was very fast."

"'Cross my heart and hope to die.'" The words went through Addie's mind, but she didn't know that she had said them aloud—words soldiers said because a quick death was a blessing compared to the lingering agony so many wounded suffered before they expired. She thought of Captain Byrne and her sister-in-law, Sarah, and she thought she should have been with Quentin when he died. Because no matter how hard those other deaths had been, this was worse, and part of her could not believe it had happened at all and was sure he would turn up in the next day or so, proving that it had all been a mistake.

She stared at his case with its sturdy leather straps for carrying. It was not logical proof that he was dead, but somehow, it was proof enough.

Grief, rage, and guilt filled her in equal measure, but she could express nothing. She felt a huge knot inside as if her ribs were being squeezed too tightly for breath. She wanted to scream and cry and pound the earth until it gave up all of its dead or engulfed her entirely. But she did none of these things.

She reached out and touched Silas's cheek. "I know you must go. When General Howe pursues, every gun will be needed. If not tomorrow, then the next day or the next, he will come. Tullia and I will leave. If we cross the Hudson, we will have plenty of room to run. We won't be trapped on this island, and you won't have to worry about us any longer."

It was what Silas had wanted—to have her out of harm's way—but he hated the flat, calm tone of her voice, the shocked white pallor of her skin, as if all the life had drained away from her.

"Addie, I…"

She put her fingers over his mouth and warned him, "Don't try to make this easier. I know you want to, but you can't. All you can do is to keep safe. We can't lose anymore. We cannot." Even these words did not break the dull cadence of her voice.

He pulled her into his arms, and she neither resisted nor relaxed. For the first time, he fully understood those soldiers who could scarcely keep their minds on their duties for the worries they had about their families. Addie was usually so strong, but she needed him more now than she ever had, and he was helpless to offer comfort or even to stay.

"I love you," he said, and he let her go. "I'll get word to Justin and Ad. They are better able than I to arrange passage for you."

She heard him clearly then, heard his old fear of being unworthy, and it pierced her heart, sharp and clean through the fog of misery. She closed her eyes for a moment, and when she opened them again, the gold had eclipsed the brown so that they glowed fierce and feline.

"I love you more than anyone else in all the world. More than my brothers, living or dead. More than my father. More than myself. I will wait for you across the river. I will wait for you to come to me."

This time it was she who put her arms around him. She kissed him, trying to say more with her touch than she could with words. And she watched him out of sight, lifting her hand in farewell when he turned back to look at her. She had never so craved the release of weeping, but the tears would not come.

It was as if Tullia were weeping for both of them. All her normal competence and composure had deserted her with the news of Quentin's death. Even her sturdy body seemed to have grown smaller and weaker, and Addie found herself taking care of Tullia instead of the other way around. But it was fitting; Addie needed to see the grief even if she couldn't express it herself, and having to make the final arrangements for their departure gave her small tasks on which to focus, though she and Tullia had practiced this so often, everything was in good order. And within a few hours, a message came that her brothers had arranged for them to go north, across the Harlem River to the mainland of New York and on until they could be ferried across the Hudson. Thence, they would go south again, to Fort Lee on the Jersey side, unless Howe was attacking by then or the river was filled with British ships.

Word also came to Mistress Chaffey, assuring her that her nephew was unhurt, and she had been joyful, but when she learned of Quentin's death, she began to behave oddly. She offered her condolences, but her eyes avoided Addie and Tullia's, and she kept finding excuses to be as far from them as possible. Everything was so hazy for Addie it took her a while to understand, and she went in search of their landlady.

"You mustn't feel guilty," she said. "I am so glad your nephew has survived, so very glad. It would not have helped my brother had your nephew died, too."

Mistress Chaffey sighed with relief and dabbed at her eyes. "I am so very sorry. It seemed indecent to be happy about anything, but war jumbles everything." She paused before she added, "I am going to miss you and Tullia, but it is right that you are leaving."

"You may come with us if you wish," Addie said, uneasy at the idea of this kind woman being in the city when the British took it.

"I thank you, but it's different for me. I could go stay with my brother out in the country, but his wife is a terrible shrew. I'd rather face the enemy." Mistress Chaffey grimaced. "This is my home. I won't abandon it. And I can't imagine that the redcoats will bother with an old widow. I've thought about it, and I will not be foolish. I might even rent rooms to them. But I will pray for the day when they are gone forever."

Mistress Chaffey knew as well as anyone that there was little chance Washington could hold the city.

Addie didn't sleep at all that night, and when dawn came with no sign of movement from British troops, she and Tullia left the city, heading north with two outriders sent as escorts by General Washington, though he could ill afford the gesture.

Ad and Justin saw them briefly before the journey began, but they were all beyond anything except the tritest words, able to exchange nothing more than cautions to take care and promises that they would be reunited soon.

But just for an instant, as Ad looked at her, Addie felt their old connection, and she was comforted.

"We will see you across the river," Ad called to her as the wagon began to move.

All of them except Quentin.

His artist's case was in the wagon, a casket of dreams, filled with the ghosts of beauty and talent that would have grown to full flower had the boy been given time to become the man.

Chapter 3

It was nearly three weeks before Howe attacked again, but when he did, either by luck or good intelligence, he directed his forces against the soldiers least able to withstand an assault.

During the night of September 14, five British frigates made their way up the East River and anchored off Kip's Bay. In the morning, the ships' guns bombarded the shore. It was militia that held the shore, not Continental troops, and perhaps they could have withstood a battle of muskets, but the roaring cannon tearing up the earth terrified them. Without firing a shot, they began to run from the enemy, and their panic infected the support troops in position behind them.

When Justin, Ad, and other aides rode onto the scene with General Washington, they beheld chaos, with smoke and dust clouding everything.

Ad saw rage sweep over the general's face, and then Washington was striking out at the fleeing men with the flat of his sword and bellowing curses, "Good God, have I got such troops as those! Damn you! Stand and fight! Damn you!" and more furious words Ad had never imagined him saying.

Ad was paralyzed in the middle of bedlam, so shocked by the general's display that he couldn't think. But he heard Justin yelling, "Please, Your Excellency, you must quit the field! The enemy is too close!" And Ad began shouting, too, and before he considered his action, he grabbed at the headstall of Washington's plunging horse.

Ad saw the general's sword raised above his head, and for an instant he thought he was going to be dashed from his saddle. "We lose you, we lose all!" he screamed.

He heard General Greene adding his own pleas, and the sword was lowered. The general's big body slumped momentarily in defeat as the rage died away, leaving such despair in its wake, Ad looked away. But then Washington straightened and allowed his aides to lead him out of the enemy's range, for not only was the space open, offering little cover, but also the frigates were so close to the shore, their swivel guns were being used to rain grapeshot down on the Americans.

Ad managed to mumble his thanks to General Greene, thinking that Greene's recovery from fever might well have saved his own life. But he was so taken aback by his actions and by their leader's loss of control, he felt physically ill and had to fight not to puke as he had after the first time he killed a redcoat, after the battles of Lexington and Concord.

"He will understand," Justin said, riding up beside him. "We had to get him off the field. He is too big and too obvious a target. I'm proud of you."

Justin's words reassured Ad, but his spirit eased much more when General Washington looked directly at him, nodded, and said, "Breakfast with General Howe seems to have been postponed yet again."

After so many days of inactivity, now events were happening too fast. General Washington sent orders for those troops left in New York City to pull out. General Putnam went south to collect the units coming north, but it was a near thing. The British moved so quickly to cut off the retreat, they would have succeeded had not Putnam's aide, Aaron Burr, a young New Yorker who knew the land well, led the way to the west and around the British advance.

Colonel Knox and Silas were among the last ones into camp, but far from being concerned about his safety, Silas was distraught that some much-needed cannon had been left behind.

"Better the guns than you," Ad snapped, betraying how worried he had been about his brother-in-law.

The Americans gathered along Harlem Heights in the northernest corner of Manhattan Island, digging in.

"It's one thing we do very well," Justin said to Ad. "Give us shovels, and we'll turn the world into ditches and embankments. But ask us to fight—now that's another matter entirely."

"That's not fair," Ad protested. He was as shaken as his brother, but he feared despair as much as he feared what the enemy could do. "We ran today, but we'll stand tomorrow or…"

Justin continued for him, "The next day or the next, I know." But he did not sound convinced.

They were both thinking of Quentin, as they did constantly, and because of his sacrifice, defeat became ever more unthinkable.

It depressed everyone's spirit further when cold rain fell in the night. Many of the men who had come in to the position hadn't eaten for a day or two and had difficulty getting a meal now. Many had abandoned their packs in their haste to reach Harlem Heights and thus were without blankets and cooking utensils. And there was a severe shortage of tents.

At their newly established headquarters in another mansion vacated by a Tory, Washington's aides had never seen the general's spirits at such a low point, and that was hardest of all to bear. Yet, he continued to pore over dispatches and maps, trying to ascertain the possibilities for the morrow. New York City was lost, and there was little chance of holding any part of Manhattan Island, but he had to try. He had written an appeal to Congress, explaining why the city could not be held and pointing out that "on our side the war should be defensive; it has been called a War of Posts; we should on all occasions avoid a general action, and never be drawn into a necessity to put anything at risk." He had gone on to say that the enemy meant to winter in New York and that there was no doubt they could drive out the Americans. But Congress was thinking in political, not military, terms and did not want to face the political consequences of deserting the city.

In the morning, Washington sent Lieutenant Colonel Thomas Knowlton and one hundred and fifty Connecticut rangers to reconnoiter the enemy's position. As dawn broke, the sound of firing reached the camp. Washington rode to his forward posts, and from there he dispatched Colonel Joseph Reed to find out what was happening to Knowlton. He nodded at Justin, sending him with Reed.

Justin felt no fear, just wild exhilaration. Staying behind the lines was galling his soul until any excuse for action was welcome. And when Knowlton's force came into view, Justin wanted to crow in triumph. Knowlton's troops were firing volley after volley, holding off two light infantry battalions, a part of the Forty-second Scottish Highlanders, nicknamed the "Black Watch," and a body of Traverne's Highlanders.

Reed and Justin wheeled around and raced back to Washington. Reed advised sending reinforcements, volunteering to lead them. Washington gave the order, and Justin again went with Reed. When they were in sight of Knowlton's position again, they found that the Black Watch and Traverne's Highlanders were threatening the flanks of the small American force, but the Americans were pulling back in good order, not fleeing in terror.

The enemy's advance guard was in open view and their bugle horns began to sound the "a fox gone to earth" of the hunt. It was a calculated insult, and enough of the Americans understood it that when Reed tried to direct a measured counterattack with the reinforcements, the men were too eager and rushed the British in a fury. Colonel Reed and Justin tried to control them, but it was impossible.

"At least they're going the right way today," Justin said, and he and Reed went with the tide. When their soldiers roared a halloo in mocking foxhunt counterpoint, Justin yelled as loudly as any.

The Americans kept moving, firing, reloading, seeking cover, firing again, picking out targets carefully despite the speed of the action, driving the British before them as if they would chase them off the earth.

The foot soldiers had their muskets, but Justin was well armed with pistols and his sword. He still felt no fear, nor did he feel pity. He wanted to kill every enemy soldier before him. Quite clearly he saw a man's jawbone shatter from one of his shots, but he was unaware that he was saying Quentin's name over and over as he fought.

Near noon, some of the enemy made a stand. The steady fire from the cannon checked the American advance enough to keep the enemy's light infantry from being totally annihilated, and when they withdrew again, they had more and more reinforcements joining them on the field.

Justin knew the American advance was over even before the official command came from Washington to quit the field. They were in peril of going so far from their lines that the British, with their growing numbers, could turn and engulf them.

Ad was one of the aides carrying the orders to withdraw. Justin hailed him, saying, "I take it back—digging is not the only thing we do well."

Even as Ad rode on, he saw his brother's face, mud-splattered with damp earth, lips pulled back in as much of a snarl as a smile, life and death in equal measure blazing in his golden eyes.

And Ad knew Silas was part of the reason American artillery had kept up such a steady punishing fire on the enemy and that his dark eyes would hold the same ferocity as Justin's.

The furious activity of the afternoon did not keep Ad from feeling lonely. It was only a matter of time before Justin would leave Washington's staff to seek a more active combat role, as had other aides. Ad knew the inevitability of it as well as if Justin had already announced his intentions. He had seen how the endless piles of paperwork at headquarters, the meticulous clerical work needed to report to Congress and to keep the army working, had begun to chafe at his brother.

Ad thought of the mad riding and the sword practice he had done on his last visit to Virginia, and he knew the only time he would be riding into action would be beside General Washington or to carry his orders; that most of his time would, indeed, be spent with quill and ink, not a sword; that he would stay beside the general until he was no longer needed.

The moment he made the decision, he felt a great calm settle on him.

That night, despite the rigors of the day, there were dispatches and orders to write, and Ad settled to the task with ease while Justin fidgeted, splattering ink with too much pressure on his quill, cursing under his breath.

Justin studied his brother for a moment, and then, voice low so that others could not overhear, he asked, "How do you stand it? I feel as if I am going to jump out of my skin!"

"We're different, you and I. This is a good job for me, and right now, His Excellency needs both of us. But if you will just have patience, the time will surely come when you will have a command more to your liking."

Justin stared at him, feeling as if his brother had become the elder of them, but Ad's understanding and certainty soothed his troubled spirit, and he went back to work with a steady hand.

Though the Americans had gained no ground today, neither had they lost any, and they had forced some of the most elite troops in the British Army to turn tail. They had fought like a real army, with officers doing a splendid job of encouraging their men. They had suffered losses, including gallant Lieutenant Colonel Knowlton, who had died in Joseph Reed's arms still concerned only for his men, not for himself. And yet, it had been a glorious day. Justin grinned as he recalled the way their soldiers had turned the fox-hunting jibe back on the British.

However, he was not so light-hearted in the following days when he had to write out reprimands to officers who had acted without direct orders or who had gone beyond the bounds of such orders.

Ad, engaged in the same task, agreed with his discontent but defended their commander. "The army is no place for independent action."

They were working in a small space crowded with writing tables, and another aide, Tench Tilghman, was with them, but he made no attempt to join their conversation, giving them the illusion of privacy until Ad addressed him directly, asking his opinion.

"Well, it seems to me that an army is like a good horse. You want it to have spirit and speed, but if it doesn't do what you want it to do and if it won't go where you bid it, then it really isn't much use, no matter how prettily it moves." His mouth twisted with self-deprecating humor. "Of course, I probably find the simile apt because of losing my mount on the day of the battle."

Tilghman had ridden as hard as any of them that day, carrying Washington's messages, and his horse had collapsed and died, probably from bot fly, though the animal had seemed sound. The Marylander was an expert horseman and careful of his animals, so he had some guilt over not having seen that the beast was ailing.

But as Ad watched Justin relax while he and Tench discussed the superiority of Southern horses to Northern stock, Ad was convinced that the Marylander had broached the subject with careful purpose to put the Valencourts at ease.

Tench had joined the staff as a volunteer aide the month before, and though there was nothing forward about him, he had already established himself as a valuable member of Washington's official family. He was related to most of the major citizens of Maryland, and of the city of Philadelphia, too. In his early thirties, he was slender, a couple of inches under six feet tall, and comely, with auburn hair and gray eyes. He was well educated and had been a successful merchant before joining the war effort. With all of these attributes, and with his extensive social connections, he could easily have been an arrogant man. But he was unassuming, steady, with a honed wit and a keen sense of humor. He wrote a particularly fine hand, and his prose was so clear, General Washington was entrusting him with more correspondence by the day. And heaven knew, his services were needed because Washington's staff was so short of secretaries, piles of correspondence remained unanswered.

Although he was older than they, both Ad and Justin were drawn to him. He reminded them of the family and friends they had in Virginia. And they shared intellectual interests, having studied many of the same classic and contemporary works and also being fluent in French, a somewhat unusual accomplishment in a country that had fought hard to oust the French from their midst in the last war. Until Tench joined the staff, the Valencourts had been the only aides who spoke the language. It was a talent of limited use for the present, but it might prove valuable in the future. It was a badly kept secret that American envoys were even now seeking aid at the French Court.

But beyond these graces, Ad and Justin shared a deeper bond with Tilghman, for his father, like theirs, was a Loyalist, as were three of his five brothers. One of the three was now in England while another had run away to join the British Navy. His father was in Philadelphia, and though Tench had not as yet spoken of him to them, the Valencourts knew how worried he must be about his parent. And while this was the situation in many families, there was no doubt that having such close Loyalist connections meant that some would never fully trust them and would cavil behind their backs about their proximity to the commander in chief.

Tench had been reticent about his family problems, but he had been direct in extending his sympathies to Ad and Justin for the loss of Quentin.

"I do not like to contemplate how I would feel were I to lose one of my brothers or my sisters," he said. "And from what I have heard of him, it was not your loss alone, for your brother was reputed to be a talented artist and musician. I am sorry that all of us have been deprived of such a creative soul."

His courtly tribute was balm to their bruised hearts, for not only were they haunted by Quentin's death, but they were also horrified by the raw manner of his burial—a soldier's grave dug by strangers whose main concern had been to get the bodies covered as quickly as possible lest the elements and wild animals disperse the corpses and cause disease. Justin and Ad knew that dead was dead and nothing else should matter, but it did.

Addie was never far from their thoughts either, and though she had been gone only a short time, Silas missed her so much it was better not to mention her when he was near. But all of them were glad that she was not on Manhattan Island anymore.

General Howe made no move against them in the days immediately following the Battle of Harlem Heights—the ferocity of the American response having been a shock to him—but there was little doubt that he would move against them again.

Then on the night of September 20, only four days after the battle, fires started in New York City, burning through the night and into the next morning, destroying both great and small buildings until a quarter of the city was gone. A brisk wind from the south had fanned the flames, and Howe, fearing a ruse to cover an attack, had not committed all of his forces to fighting the fire.

From their position on Harlem Heights, the Americans could see the lurid glow some eight or nine miles away. In the morning the sky was stained with a thick curtain of smoke. Rumors flew like embers in their camp because there had been discussions about burning the city as they evacuated it in order to deny it to the enemy as a base of operations. But Congress, with a strong representation from New York, had decided against it. Nonetheless, there was speculation that the fires had been set by American agents or by New Englanders on their own account because of their jealousy over New York's growing prominence as a port.

"You must be most relieved that your sister has already left the city," Tench said. He had yet to meet Ariadne Bradwell, but her brothers spoke of her so often and with such affection, he felt as if he knew her.

"Truly we are. God knows Justin and I would be crazed, but Silas would be tearing the city apart looking for her," Ad said. He thought of Mistress Chaffey and hoped she was unharmed, and he thought of Darius and the Valencourt properties. He glanced away and then looked squarely at Tench and at Justin. "Do you think we caused the fire?"

Neither of the men mistook his meaning.

"I wrote no orders for it," Justin replied.

"Nor did I. I am rather new to this, but you are both in His Excellency's confidence. If the fire were an official act, you would know. To my mind, the most important factor is that Congress forbade the burning of the city, and His Excellency would not disobey. He is ever conscious that he serves at their pleasure, no matter how difficult that is." Tench's faith in Washington's integrity was absolute.

They had to trust their instinct for, though the general was often quite open with those closest to him, being in his confidence did not mean knowing all of his thoughts. His response to the fires was perfectly measured between distress for the citizens and acknowledgment that the damage would make the city much less hospitable to the enemy, but he did not betray any strong personal emotion about either circumstance.

General Howe pursued the Americans at his leisure. It was the second week in October before he started a landing at Throg's Point where a regiment of Pennsylvanian riflemen killed enough redcoats so that the rest backed off. Six days later Howe struck to the northeast, at Pell's Point, but here Massachusetts regiments under John Glover held firm.

The riflemen gained those six days for the Continental Army, and the action by Glover's command gave them a couple more, but Washington knew he had to keep his troops from being forced into a big battle on British terms. By the time Howe's forces arrived at New Rochelle, the Americans were digging in at White Plains, and it took Howe six days to catch up with them. But when he did, he put on an ominous show in front of the American lines, deploying his whole army in preparation for an attack.

Justin looked at the bright uniforms and battle standards and watched the precision of the troops wheeling into position. "I hate to admit it, but it's an awesome sight."

"A parade of power meant to show us for rabble. At least I've got a good horse for our next journey." Tench's normally calm voice had a sharp edge despite his attempt at humor. He had acquired a pretty black mare and, on an optimistic day, he had speculated that she would be a good brood mare could he get her home to Maryland.

Looking at the display before them, Ad wondered if any of them would leave this place, let alone go home, though he wasn't sure where that was anymore. When he thought of the house in Boston, he felt no longing for that empty place. His uncle's plantation, Castleton, was a more comforting thought, but it was far away and not his by any right except the kindness of his mother's family. He rubbed his neck wearily. They were all exhausted. No matter how hard they worked, they could not get ahead of the piles of paperwork that had to be done to keep the war in motion. They started work early in the morning, continued into the night, and were often summoned from sleep.

This night, there was little rest as every aspect of the battle that would surely come with the new day was considered. They had already abandoned Manhattan and the territory south of their present position, but they were making the enemy pay for their gains, and their hope was to extract penalties again at White Plains.

When they went into battle, Washington himself led the center, his aides with him, but the key American position was on Chatterton's

Hill, on the right flank. At first things went badly there, with British cannonading sending some of the militia fleeing, though Continentals held the line. The battle grew more confusing on both sides, but finally American artillery was in place on the hill.

Silas shouted orders until he was hoarse, and his eyes burned from the smoke of gunpowder and from straining to see how accurate their fire was. And for a while, it looked as if they were forcing the enemy back. Silas wanted it so much, it was like a physical blow to his heart when he saw that the redcoats, along with thousands of their German mercenaries, were turning the American right flank.

The hill had to be vacated, but Silas and other officers were determined they would do it in good order, and to that end, Silas encouraged the gun crews. "That's right, secure the ropes, we'll need this one again," on and on until the men and their ordnance were safely away.

At the end of the day, it was clear that both sides had made mistakes, for while some of the militia had panicked, some British units had pressed too hard and lost more men than they should have. On the whole, the Americans had fought well, inflicting more casualties than they suffered.

But now the enemy held the high ground and had brought up artillery to place it on Chatterton's Hill. They fired on the American positions during the night, forcing the soldiers to seek shelter in hastily dug entrenchments that were shoe-deep in cold water that seeped up from the ground.

With permission, Ad left headquarters long enough to seek out Silas, and he was greatly relieved to find him unhurt, not knowing until that instant how much he had feared he would have to carry bad news to Addie.

"Well met," he said.

Silas managed a tired grin in response, but then his face settled into a grim mask. "We tried so hard." His ears were still ringing from the boom of the guns, so he wasn't sure whether he was shouting or whispering, and he didn't flinch as another round came in from the British.

Ad squatted beside him. "You were outnumbered. I'd far rather you got off the damn hill in one piece than that you stayed there to be blown to bits or hacked to death by Hessians."

Although the Germans came from various principalities, many were from Hesse, and "Hessians" had become the general term for them, spoken with contempt as if it were the hissing of geese. They had no personal stake in the outcome of the war beyond keeping themselves alive, and they believed that plundering and raping were rewards they should enjoy. The rumor was that their British allies didn't like them much better than did the Americans. But like them or not, the redcoats were certainly making use of them; there were thousands of them out there, waiting to help finish off Washington's army when morning came.

Silas made a conscious effort to keep his voice low. "We're in a bad way. We need to get our guns to higher ground, but I don't see how it can be done."

Ad had nothing to say to that, and he knew he had to get back to headquarters. He ached all over from the hard, tense riding he had done at Washington's side during the battle and from the same despair he felt in Silas. He clamped his hand on Silas's shoulder. "Take care of yourself. I don't want Addie's heart to be broken again."

"And you," Silas said.

Just for a moment, Ad saw a Silas other than the exhausted soldier, saw the man who loved Addie so much that the mere mention of her name had made his dark eyes shine, his face soften until he looked years younger.

Ad didn't feel guilty for the short time he had been away from his duties, for decisions had already been made about how to shift their defensive positions to take less punishment from enemy guns on the hill, and beyond that, there was little to do except wait for the dawn. He fell asleep to the sound of Justin, Tench, and others breathing nearby, all of them within call should the general need them.

Justin awakened him, shaking him and saying, "Behold! Providence has smiled on us by weeping!"

During the battle of the day before, the sun had glinted on bayonets, swords, and every other bright piece of metal, but there was no sun this

morning. Rain poured down, shutting out visibility, making renewed
battle impossible for the time being. Washington didn't hesitate. In
short order, they were moving out, withdrawing to a more advantageous
position five miles away at Castle Hill.

When the weather cleared, they waited for Howe to pursue
them, but scouts soon brought the news that he had turned back to
Manhattan.

"I'm not sure whether we ought to feel pleased or insulted by this,"
Ad confessed to Justin.

"I don't think General Howe quit the field out of fear, though this
would be a hard place to assault," Justin said. "More likely he's longing
for the comfort of regular quarters and is weary of harrying us with
no great gain. He doesn't seem inclined to tax himself unduly, and
for that we should be grateful. But he surely knows that many of our
enlistments are over at the end of the year. Perhaps he is just waiting
for us to disappear with no help from him."

"I mislike the division in our army," Ad confided, conscious that he
would not say such a thing to anyone else, for fear of sounding disloyal.

But Justin shared his disquiet. There were still nearly three thousand
men in and around Fort Washington, on the Manhattan side of the
Hudson River, and men on the opposite shore at Fort Lee, together
the last hope of denying control of the river to the British. In addition,
Washington was leaving seven thousand men at North Castle Heights
to block northward movement by Howe should he face about again.

The Valencourts were glad Silas was with Washington's troops as
they went north to Peekskill to cross the Hudson. But the dividing
of their forces continued, with nearly four thousand men left on the
east side of the river to guard the Hudson Highlands.

Crossing the river was complicated and tedious, and Washington
supervised it personally, keeping his aides frantically busy with orders.
However, not even the rush of duties could keep Ad and Justin from
feeling as if their noble venture were heading step by step toward
disaster. And though Silas was too honorable to question them about
what they knew of their commander's plans, the tight planes of his
face and his shadowed eyes revealed much to them. The only light any

of them could see in the darkness was that they would soon see Addie and Tullia again, but since they didn't know what Howe would do next, they had to face the fact that the reunion might prove precarious. The last news they had had of the women was that they were staying in a farmhouse not far from Fort Lee.

By the second week of November, Washington had moved into New Jersey and had established his headquarters at Hackensack about nine miles from Fort Lee.

With each passing day, the Valencourts had seen evidence that Tench Tilghman's loyalty to Washington matched theirs, and so they knew how much it cost him when, within moments of their arrival at Hackensack, he expressed his doubt for Addie's sake.

"When your brother-in-law goes to visit your sister, I suggest he bring her back here, to make sure she is behind our lines. Fort Washington is across the river, I know, but if it does not hold..." his voice trailed off.

Silas was in complete agreement and half mad to get to Addie, leaving as soon as he had permission. He had scarcely dismounted at the farmhouse before she was running to him, the tears she could not shed for Quentin streaming down her face in relief at seeing her husband before her.

He opened his arms, and she burrowed against him as if she wanted to get under his skin.

"I love you, Addie, I love you!" Silas whispered urgently, his throat suddenly too tight for normal speech.

Addie pulled away and began touching him, his face, his hands, and through the layers of cloth, his shoulders and chest, until Silas managed a smile. "If you explore much further, we will scandalize the countryside. I really am all right, and so are your brothers."

She leaned her head against him again, beginning to shiver. "I have been so afraid for you, my love." He felt lean and hard, every spare ounce of flesh stripped away, as if the war were fining him down, and his face was thin and lined.

He didn't want to compound her distress, but there was no help for it. "I want you and Tullia to come back with me now."

Instinctively, Addie glanced toward the east, toward the river forts, but she did not question him. "Tullia and I have been ready to go for days, ever since we heard Washington had crossed the Hudson and was heading for New Jersey."

Addie was more determined than ever that Silas have no complaints about her suitability as a soldier's wife. She had learned much in her stay here, for there were quite a few soldiers' wives and children camped near Fort Lee, most of them living in very poor conditions because they had little choice with no one to provide for them at home, but they were doing the best they could in bad circumstances. It made her feel guilty that she could afford adequate lodgings for herself and Tullia while others were in want. But she was a lady and an officer's wife, and whether she approved or not, that set her apart from the wives of common soldiers. There were strict rules in the army against familiarity between officers and their men, and Addie had learned that the women seemed to prefer the same divisions. It was not really a change, for few of the women were those she would have known personally in civilian life, but it was frustrating to want to help and have so little chance to do so. She and Tullia had managed to offer aid in a few cases of illness among the children, but that was all.

As she was getting ready to retreat inland, she worried, asking Silas, "What about the families around Fort Lee? I'm sure there are some near Fort Washington, too. What about them, will someone tell them to move?"

"You know better than that," he chided without heat. "It is the British who admit the need for domestic comfort. They set quotas for women accompanying regiments and allow rations for women and children. We, on the other hand, do not want such encumbrances and so deny the reality entirely."

The situation frustrated him as it did Addie, for he had gunners whose wives and children were with them, and he knew how the men worried about them, as he worried about Addie. "At least the redcoats do not normally attack our families anymore than we do theirs. Not even the Hessians have shown any inclination for that."

"No, they only rape women of property while they plunder their houses," Addie said in disgust. Addie knew of the enemy regiments encamped near Fort Washington, and the Hudson River no longer seemed to be much of a barrier.

Addie and Tullia had no objections to leaving their present quarters. The couple who had rented a room to them were neither friendly nor hostile, simply pleased to be paid for the space. There was no wrench in leaving them. It was just as well; it was hard enough to wonder how Mistress Chaffey had fared in the fire.

Tullia greeted Silas with a smile, but he could see that she had not recovered from Quentin's death. She looked smaller somehow, and older, and Addie was obviously the one in charge. He felt a jolt of anger and self-blame that Addie had had no one to care for her in these past weeks, but then he thought that perhaps her grief might have been assuaged or at least contained by having Tullia depend on her.

He thought of something else, too, as he helped the women ready the horses and load the last of their belongings. He thought he would give just about anything to have Addie alone. The force of his lust astonished him. He was bone-deep tired and had anticipated nothing beyond seeing her again and assuring himself that she was safe. But now the soft floral scent of her, the tawny glow in her eyes, and the way the sunlight caught in her hair, the way her slim height had fit against him, the deft movements of her hands as she made sure the wagon was neatly packed, the way she caught her lower lip in her teeth as she studied the arrangement of goods—everything about her made his blood run hot and pool in his groin. He nearly protested when she donned her wide-brimmed hat, hiding her hair and shadowing her face.

He had been doing the heavy work, but his hands stilled as he stared at her, and she turned her head to look at him, as if he had spoken to her.

"Silas?" But beyond his name, she had no other question to ask. His face wore the same expression as when they made love, his dark eyes narrowed and intense, the planes of his face sculpted by passion—and in that tiny instant of recognizing his need, she acknowledged her own, her body singing in answer to his.

"I hope your brothers have found some private place for us to sleep tonight," he muttered.

She laughed, surprising herself with the sound of it. She had not thought to feel this way again. She hadn't felt anything but fear since Quentin's death, fear that she would lose another brother or her husband.

While Tullia drove the wagon, Silas and Addie rode their horses, talking and flirting with each other as if the war had vanished. And even when they arrived at headquarters, having passed the inspection of sentries as darkness was falling, and Addie greeted her brothers, the couple's attention was still so fixed on each other. Ad hid his amusement by turning a laugh into a cough. Justin was less subtle.

"Addie can pay her respects to His Excellency tomorrow. We'll see to the horses and make sure of Tullia's comfort. You and Addie go along now," he told Silas, and he gave him directions to the house where he'd rented a room for them. "There's little available here since we've filled the town, but the house is clean enough, and I don't think you'll notice much about it anyway."

"Thank you," Silas said. He felt deep affection for his brother-in-law, who, despite having lost his wife, did not begrudge others their happiness. Then all thought fled except the fact that he and Addie had at least this night to themselves.

As Justin had predicted, neither of them noticed much about the room. Their senses were filled with the rediscovery of the familiar territory of each other. Their bodies remembered every curve and hollow, every rough and smooth texture, every scent and sound of the other, remembered how to fit together, how to give, how to take.

At the peak of her pleasure, when her body was burning with the fire Silas had conjured in her, when she was so filled with him that every movement of her body was echoed in his, Addie was startled by the deep contentment that swelled beneath the passion, and even when her body had reached completion, the contentment grew.

"I never thought it would be like this," she said when they were both on the edge of sleep. Curled against him, head resting on his chest, she could hear the steady beat of his heart. "I knew I loved you and that I wanted to be with you always. But I didn't know that you could make me feel as if the most peaceful, happy times in my life were happening again, all at once. Riding for hours and hours at Castleton, spending time with Papa, new books, adventures with Ad, laughing with you and my brothers—all those sweet, sweet times are now found in you."

"Oh, Addie," were the only words he could manage. He understood, for she had been his special source of joy for a long time, but beneath his wonder that she felt the same about him, there was terror as the reality of the war flooded back into his mind. He wanted to warn her that their situation was too uncertain for her to invest so much of herself in him.

"I know what you are thinking," she said, her voice calm in the darkness, her body tuned to the sudden tension in his. "But no one, save he who takes his own life, knows when death will come. Perhaps the war has made us more alive because it has given death more rein. Perhaps without it I would be a complacent wife forever fiddling the household accounts to hide extra gowns, and perhaps you would be a husband who spends so many hours at his work and in the coffee houses, he has but little time for his wife."

She got the response she wanted when he laughed at her fancies.

"Never, war or no, never, ever would we be like that!" Still laughing, he rolled atop her and began planting little nipping kisses wherever he could reach. "I never could find a book or printing press or coffee house as delectable as you, and you are too precise to fiddle accounts, though there are other things you fiddle quite well."

"I come from a very musical family," she said, her voice prim, her hands wanton, and even the flashing memory of Quentin making music did not dim the play.

They spent the night in love and nonsense and cherishing, sleeping only when they had to, and it was not until dawn had broken that Silas allowed reality to intrude on them again.

"No one knows what is going to happen next, but it's a fair guess that the redcoats will come after us now that our army is so spread out. Above all else, they must want to defeat General Washington. But if it is to be done this year, it must be soon. Winter is coming, and I cannot imagine the enemy forgoing the comfort of winter quarters to chase us through the snow. So, if we are overrun, you and Tullia will be on your own again. I will trust you to go back to Boston or south to Virginia."

"You may trust me to use my best judgment," she said, and that was as much as she could give him. The thought of being too far from Silas and her brothers to help them was even more intolerable now than before Quentin had been killed.

Chapter 4

New Jersey, Winter 1776

Though they sent Tullia to Addie in the morning, Justin and Ad did not have time to see their sister. Instead, they and Tench rode with General Washington and some of his generals to Fort Lee.

The situation across the river at Fort Washington was deteriorating rapidly, with the Hessians in place and British troops converging on the position. Boats continued to go back and forth across the Hudson River, and Washington wanted to check for himself about whether or not Fort Washington could be held.

At the fort they were greeted by Colonel Magaw, the officer in command there. As the officers conferred, the sound of gunfire from the outer defenses crackled through the air, but, undaunted, General Greene and Colonel Magaw maintained that the fort could be held at least until December.

The Valencourts were accustomed to their commander's insistence on considering his officers' recommendations, but they were shocked when Washington agreed that the fort should continue to stand against an enemy so confident of victory that terms of surrender had already been offered.

Ad wondered if the general was just too exhausted to make a good decision. He glanced at Tench and saw his own doubts reflected there, but none of the aides had the right to gainsay their superiors. At the moment, what they wanted the most was to get Washington away from this threatened place. At least that was accomplished as the firing increased and Colonel Magaw bid them to get back across the river, though he was still sure the fort would not fall. They left him there and made their hasty way back down the cliff and into their boat.

They were halfway across the river when the colors of the fort fluttered down out of sight, and the firing stopped.

"Dear God!" Justin breathed, and then there was silence in the boat as the full significance of the capitulation hit them.

Ad blinked back sudden tears, and others, including General Washington, were having the same struggle. The terrible swiftness of the change in their fortunes was nearly impossible to credit.

None of the fort's troops had been evacuated, and because the fort had been captured there were sure to be casualties, particularly with the murderous Hessians on the scene. Nearly three thousand men were thus lost, killed, or taken prisoner, so many from an army that needed every soldier.

Washington had already begun to pull troops back from Fort Lee, but now the task took on a hellish urgency with Greene in charge while Washington returned to Hackensack to lead his troops out of harm's way, if that was possible. Pursuit was so immediate, cooking pots were still heating on the fires, and much more vital equipment was left behind when thousands of the enemy came across the river and took the fort. However, all of the troops had been gotten out except for a handful of men too drunk to move.

Rather than leading the expedition himself, Howe had sent General Cornwallis, and Cornwallis did not share Howe's desultory nature. He chased the Americans with the intention of finishing them, and it seemed he would have a good chance of doing that, as Washington's forces numbered only some fifty-four hundred men with half of those enlisted only to the end of the year and many too sick to be of any use in a fight.

They fled west and then angled to the south with Cornwallis hunting them. Addie quickly discovered that running for one's life made the need for normal comforts, such as palatable food and a cozy bed, unimportant. She and Tullia were with the baggage train much of the time unless she rode her saddle horse, though she didn't like to get too far from Tullia. There were other women, and children too, and she and Tullia tried to help transport the weariest.

The baggage train and the food supplies were meager. The enemy had seized several thousand head of cattle as well as two thousand barrels of corn, and Washington's soldiers were hungry. With winter coming on, they were also ill-clothed, many having only pieces of summer-weight garments, some lacking even stockings and shoes. Bits of broken equipment marked their passage, but it was the broken men who tore at Addie's heart. Some dropped back, too worn down to go on, resigned to waiting for the enemy so that they could surrender to them. Others left for home.

One woman, Mistress Willis, whom Addie had helped when her baby had been colicky, confronted Addie directly with the news. "We be goin' home," she said, her expression defiant but also pleading, as if she feared Addie's condemnation. "We got to. Don't seem much reason for stayin' now, an' it ain't no good for the babies."

Besides the infant in Mistress Willis's arms, a small boy peeked from behind her skirts, smiling shyly at Addie, who had held him on her lap several times as the wagon trundled along. Mistress Willis wasn't yet twenty, but she looked much older.

Addie wanted to plead that Washington needed every soldier he had, including Private Willis, but she couldn't. Instead, she said, "I understand. Safe journey."

Mistress Willis turned away, but then she turned back again. "Thank you for helpin' us." She looked over to where her husband waited for her. "I know my man. If there still be a war come next year, he be back. An' if I can, I be with him."

Addie nodded. "His Excellency will still have need of soldiers for our army." She did not allow any quaver of doubt in her voice, but she thought it would be a miracle if the Continental Army still existed for anyone to rejoin by the end of the year, let alone beyond that time.

Mistress Willis squared her shoulders, hoisted her baby higher on her hip, bid the toddler to keep close to her, and walked away toward her husband, who stood with his head bowed, as if too ashamed to meet anyone's eyes.

Watching them go, Addie wondered how many more would leave. There was little hope of the army gathering more men on its way. Most of the people who watched them pass the towns and farmsteads regarded them with barely veiled suspicion, dreading that the soldiers would steal from them, or worse, cause trouble for them with the pursuing enemy.

But no matter the hardships and the fear of what was to come, Addie would not have been anywhere else. At night Silas slept beside her, usually under the wagon or in the little tent he had acquired for them, unless they found shelter in a tavern or farmhouse. Tullia was always close by, and Addie knew her brothers were not far away. She could not have borne to be apart from any of them, fretting over what was happening to them, and her unwavering determination to stay with the army was wearing the men down so that they hardly bothered to argue the point anymore.

In fact, with Washington's permission, she was adding her fine script to the paperwork that went on despite the retreat. Though she was given only the most routine work, with no security risk involved, she took great pleasure in the task. The steady scratch of a quill was soothing, giving order to the chaos.

But one evening as she worked beside her brothers and Tench, Tench drew breath so sharply, everyone looked at him.

Since meeting him, Addie had come to share her brothers' respect for the Marylander, and his manner toward her was at once courtly and warm, as if there were nothing out of the ordinary about her traveling with the army. And in spite of the burden of these days, she had never seen him shaken from his habitual calm, so it was disconcerting to see his distress, visible on his face even in the dim, flickering candlelight.

Feeling their eyes upon him, Tench licked his suddenly dry lips. "I… that is… I'm sorry." He shrugged helplessly and handed the document he had been reading to Justin.

Justin stared at the report for a long time before he looked at the twins. "This is an account of the units Cornwallis has with him. One of them is 'Valencourt's Rangers,' a company of Tories outfitted in green coats."

After a long silence, Ad said, "I expect their coats fit very well and are warm."

Addie said, "I wish our name were Smith or Brown, even Jenkins would do. At least I am a Bradwell now, but even marriage could not change your lot."

Justin cast his eyes heavenward. "I know you have brothers and sisters," he said to Tench, "but you haven't had to put up with twins. It is a trial no singly birthed sibling deserves."

Justin waited long enough to see the tension ease in their friend's face before he went on. "We appreciate your delicacy in telling us first about our brother's activities. And I ask that you inform His Excellency of this difficulty. We will do what he thinks best. We do not want to be an embarrassment to him. But I trust you to tell him that we will follow wherever he leads even to the gates of hell."

Tench doubted they knew how powerful was the effect of three pairs of golden Valencourt eyes trained on one person. He cleared his throat. "I will speak to His Excellency, but I remind you, if everyone who has Tory relatives had to leave the Continental Army, there would scarce be any troops remaining, and we're few enough as it is. You know I would be one of the many who would be gone."

"Thank you for your optimism, but you don't have a brother leading a pack of Tories close on our heels," Ad muttered, thinking of the great pressure Washington was under and that he'd learned firsthand how the general's temper could flare, though he was usually sorry enough afterwards to make some kind of amends. He also thought of how uneasy it made him feel to picture Darius pursuing them.

"It will be best for all if this were settled now," Tench said, and, plucking the offending document from Justin's hand, he left the room.

They were sheltered for the night in a tavern, the secretaries working in one small room while Washington met with General Greene and other officers in the next, from which they could easily summon an aide if notes were to be taken.

"It's chilling to think of Darius riding with the enemy," Addie said quietly, "though it should not be such a shock. He stands to lose all if the British are defeated."

Hearing his twin say what he'd been thinking was a comforting reminder to Ad of their bond, and he carried her musing further. "How easy it has become for us to speak of the British as the enemy, as being totally separate from us, as if we were never the same people. But for Darius, like Papa, the separation was never made."

Silence stretched among the three as they thought of the wreckage of their family, and then Tench returned. His attempt to present Washington's reply in formal military style was spoiled by his grin. "His Excellency sends his regrets. He already knew of Valencourt's Rangers, having been informed of their existence by General Greene. He intended to mention the matter to you, lest you be unpleasantly surprised by the news, just as you were. He is sorry that he forgot about it." Tench emphasized his last words with relish, and the Valencourts breathed a collective sigh of relief. The general had sent them a very deliberate message, designed to assure them that their Tory connections concerned him no more than they had before.

Ad did not speak of their remaining worry until he and Justin were alone. "I hope to God we do not face him on the field."

"If we do, it will be because Cornwallis has caught up with us, and I expect Darius would be the least of our worries then."

"Only war could so skew things that the worst possibility might provide some benefit," Ad conceded ruefully. "Likewise, we have so little, we move swiftly while the enemy is so well supplied, it slows them down. And no matter what kind of soldier Darius has become, I cannot imagine him enduring any discomfort if he could avoid it."

Having managed to burn the bridge across the Passaic River, despite an exchange of shots with Cornwallis's advance guard, Washington's force gained a little time. Cornwallis had no boats in his baggage train and would have to improvise to cross the river.

The army paused at Newark, New Jersey, and the respite was both welcome and trying, increasing as it did the risk that Cornwallis would catch up with them. But Washington was desperate that General Charles Lee, for whom Fort Lee had been named and who had been left in charge of the seven thousand men at North Castle Heights, bring his men to join them. Washington's aides had been sending their general's polite missives, and Washington hoped Lee would appear at Newark. But he showed little inclination to comply.

His aides understood Washington's admiration for Lee, an Irishman in his mid-forties who had served as a regular officer in the British and the Polish Armies, but they were growing increasingly uneasy about the man, despite his knowledge of military matters. They could overlook the fact that Lee was an eccentric character, big-nosed, bandy-legged, so physically unkempt that his clothes always bore food stains, and dog hairs from the pack of hounds that accompanied him, but it was harder to forgive the contempt he was showing toward Washington.

Lee had fought in America with the British Army during the French and Indian War, but his current sojourn in the country had begun only three years ago when he had returned and settled in Virginia. Because of his military experience, and due to his ability to convince Congress of its value, he had been made second in command of the Continental Army.

"I suspect he means to have our commander's job," Justin said bluntly, and no one contradicted him.

"His military experience is of little use if he will not take to the field when he is ordered to do so," Ad offered.

"Ah, but there's the rub. His Excellency has only requested that Lee come to us; he has not ordered it. He is no dictator. He serves at the pleasure of Congress, as does General Lee." Tench ground out the words in frustration. "I wish His Excellency would allow us to frame the next letter to General Lee."

They all knew the impossibility of that. No matter how much trust Washington placed in them, and no matter how much paperwork emanated from his headquarters, he retained control of it. If he did not like the tone in a letter or order he had directed his aides to compose, he struck out the offending parts and had it redone.

Lee did not appear, but the rear guard posted outside of Newark came in to report that the enemy was rapidly approaching the town. The Americans had to scramble to get out of reach, and the rear guard was just leaving the town as Cornwallis's advance guard entered it.

Ad and Justin were glad to be so far forward that they could not see which enemy units came in first, though later they saw the reports that noted German jaegers had been given the honor.

"Perhaps Tory units aren't so well thought of, like some of our militia," Ad noted, taking some satisfaction in the knowledge that if that were the case, it would surely irk proud Darius.

Ad imagined the two armies were engaged in a bizarre dance—one moved and thus the other; one rested and so did the other, lest too much of the dance make them too weary to fight. But should the two partners finally meet, the dance would end in death. That was incentive enough to keep the steps lively.

Cornwallis almost caught them again as they tried to destroy the bridge over the Raritan River after they had crossed on it. They could hear the fifes and drums of the British, and this time enemy fire drove them off before the bridge was completely destroyed. But Cornwallis's troops were exhausted, having suffered a forced march made worse by rain and bad roads. He had to rest his men while Washington pushed on.

Washington left a small detachment behind in Princeton to delay their pursuers and went on to Trenton, planning to go from there across the Delaware River into Pennsylvania. They reached Trenton on December 3, and the general ordered that every boat be collected from Philadelphia and seventy miles along the river above the city. Many citizens of Philadelphia were already heading out into the country, convinced the British were on their way to take the city, and Washington and his staff foresaw the same thing and no way to stop it. But the general was determined that the enemy not take both the city and the army.

Ad and the other aides helped implement the plan, issuing promises of payment when they could find the owners of the boats and confiscating vessels that were unattended.

Ad felt a stir of guilt as he gave an elderly man a promissory note for payment in Continental currency at a future date. The currency itself was so devalued, it was worth less by the day, but the army didn't even have that to offer.

"Want my boat," the old man muttered. "Need my boat not this worthless scrap." He dropped the paper onto the muddy earth, ground it under his battered shoe, and glared defiantly at Ad.

"Sir, I'm sorry, but better to deal with us than with the Hessians. They'd pay you by slitting your throat." As soon as the words were out of his mouth, he was disgusted with himself for acting as if he were a mother speaking to a child: "Take this foul medicine or the Hessians will get you." But at least General Washington was making every effort to prevent his army from acting like an occupying force entitled to plunder without repercussions.

Once the baggage and supplies were safely across the river, Washington turned back, intending to join the troops he had left in Princeton. He hoped that General Lee would meet him there, for he had at last sent a letter that, while still calmly worded, left no doubt that he expected Lee to come to him.

Addie and Tullia were across the river, their wagon and horses having been transported over with the army baggage, and Addie had made no protest over this separation, being grateful to have had help in getting across the Delaware.

By December 8, they were all on the Pennsylvania side. Washington had never made it to Princeton. Instead, the detachment he had left there had met him on the way, having been driven out by Cornwallis. The only question was why Cornwallis had delayed so long in Princeton that all of the Americans had had time to get across the river. And once they were across, there was a nearly audible collective groan of exhaustion as they collapsed in their camps, spread out for fifty miles along the river in positions they could not possibly hold if the enemy came against them.

When Cornwallis appeared at the river, General Howe was with him, and they had troops vastly outnumbering the Americans. But with all the boats in American hands, the British had no means to cross the formidable water, and having driven the Americans out of New Jersey, there was little cause to make the effort that would be needed to continue the campaign with winter coming on and Washington's ranks so diminished. Daily it became more evident that pursuit was over for the time being and that the enemy was going into winter quarters in New York City, leaving some British and Hessian units in encampments in New Jersey.

Daily, too, was the decline in Washington's strength as more men fell ill and more went home. Word was again sent to General Lee, whose defiance was growing more and more inexcusable, to come in with his troops, and Washington was also requesting reinforcements from part of the Northern Army posted at Fort Ticonderoga.

Three regiments from Fort Ti did arrive, led by General Horatio Gates and Colonel Benedict Arnold. Gates was a British-born Virginian, and Washington had served with him in the French and Indian War. He was nicknamed "Granny" Gates for the care he took of his troops, but he also took very good care of himself, always seeking to promote his self-interest. Arnold shared this trait, but after his exploits in the unsuccessful Canadian campaign, the slight, dark man could not be faulted for lack of courage.

For Washington's aides, it was difficult to deal with the currents that ran beneath the surface cordiality of the hierarchy of the Continental Army. No one would dare voice complaints against Washington to his aides, but they knew what was happening from a phrase here and there in the correspondence, a whisper here, a conversation broken off there.

Long Island, the city of New York, the whole island of Manhattan, and the state of New Jersey had been lost to the enemy. Newport, Rhode Island, had been taken with little effort to serve as a convenient naval base from which to harass American shipping. Congress had fled to Baltimore for fear that Philadelphia might also be captured.

Some of the losses had been caused by serious bungling, men continued to leave the army in droves, and there was a severe shortage of food and equipment for those who remained. As commander in chief, Washington had to shoulder the blame for many of the disasters, and he did not shirk from that part of his duty. But knowing he might have made some decisions differently or listened less to other officers was not the same as claiming another man could have better served and led. Yet the Valencourts and Tench knew that too many thought exactly that. It made the aides even more fanatically loyal to their commander than they had been before, and it made them suspicious of many.

"I count Knox, Glover, Greene, Mercer, and Stark among his best support," Justin said. Though Greene had made the wrong decision at Fort Washington, Justin did not doubt his basic worthiness.

"And I would add General Schuyler. He is a powerful man in the state of New York, and it is he who sent the regiments from Fort Ti,'

Tench pointed out. "There are others, too. There may not be enough of them, but the best men in the army know that General Washington is worthy of his command."

"I don't care what General Lee's military experience has been, I don't count him among the best," Ad grumbled. "The last word we have is that he has established his headquarters at Peekskill and is lavishing more care on his dogs than on his men. He is surely guilty of insubordination, if not worse."

He thought of his attempt to explain to Addie why General Lee could get away with his behavior. Addie had heard him out and had then said, "If the commander in chief of our army can be so defied, then we are in grave peril with little effort from the enemy." Ad agreed with her.

The next word they had of Lee was stunning. He had started to move his troops, albeit slowly, but at Basking Ridge, New Jersey, he had been captured by a patrol of the Queen's Light Dragoons, being neatly plucked out of White's Tavern by a little troop of seven men. He was three miles outside of his lines and gossip had it that he had been dallying with a woman. It was a good indication of his slovenly habits that at ten in the morning, he had just sat down to a delayed breakfast with his staff and that he was wearing his dressing gown when the enemy got him. His staff officers had been killed or wounded, but Lee was taken unharmed.

In contrast to his aides' fury at Lee, Washington reacted with profound restraint. "It was by his own folly and imprudence, and without a view to effect any good that he was taken," he said.

His aides had to take their tone from his, though Justin confided to his brother, "I wonder why he was really at White's. What woman would suffer him? Perhaps he arranged to be taken. I hope they keep the bastard! It would be a favor to us."

There was immediate benefit from Lee's capture. General Sullivan, who succeeded him, marched his men to Phillipsburg, crossed the Delaware, and came down to join Washington. And Knox was back, too, with more artillery. Unfortunately, many of the enlistments of these additional troops were running out, so the fact that they had arrived in the Delaware River encampments didn't mean they would stay through the end of the year. And many were being enticed away by higher pay and bounties offered by the state militias.

Congress had managed to accomplish one useful thing before it fled; it had resolved "that until Congress shall otherwise order, General Washington be possessed of full power to order and direct all things relative to the department and to the operations of the war." Others might covet his position, but for now, he had as much power as anyone in the country. However, in the fashion typical of him, Washington had immediately assured the Congress, "Instead of thinking of myself freed from all civil obligations, I shall constantly bear in mind that, as the sword was the last resort for the preservation of our liberty, so it ought to be the first thing laid aside when those liberties are finally established."

Nonetheless, his humility in the face of the power bestowed on him did not prevent him from sending requests for additional soldiers and money to every provincial assembly in range. Sometimes his aides wrote steadily for so many hours, they could scarcely straighten their fingers. And again Addie helped when she was allowed to do so, glad to be useful.

Despite these efforts to increase the army the men kept drifting away with too few new recruits coming in. Ad and Justin saw Washington's depression, and their spirits were as heavy as his. And then, after their numbers had been somewhat increased by an influx of Pennsylvania and New Jersey militia, the general chose a course of such risk, the Valencourts would have given much to talk him out of it. But it was his decision and too delicate a matter for their interference.

"He was a gambling man in Virginia," Justin reminded his brother.

"But never for such stakes as these," Ad said, and yet, for the first time since they had begun the retreat across New Jersey, he felt as if they were marching toward something better than a catastrophe.

While Howe surely had a better spy network than the Americans, Washington had received what seemed to be reliable reports from agents in New Jersey that the British and Hessian garrisons in that state were small. The reports were quite detailed, giving troop returns

and placements. Washington decided the country needed bold action
in order to hold it together; his soldiers needed the same; and he knew
how to accomplish it.

He held his crucial staff meeting on Christmas Eve at Samuel
Merrick's house located a few miles above Trenton on the Pennsylvania
side of the Delaware River. They shared a beggarly supper, and then
the officers were reminded of the events that had brought them to
their present situation, though it was doubtful that any of them had
forgotten that in twelve weeks, they had lost five battles and about
forty-five hundred men, most of them taken prisoner.

Washington, his voice heavy with the cold most of them had
contracted, proposed his plan to them: the army would cross the
Delaware on Christmas night, slip down its east bank, and creep up
on the Hessians at Trenton when the Germans' Yuletide revelry would
have taken its toll.

Ad wondered if he were going a bit mad as he worked with the
other aides on the plans. He wasn't afraid; he was euphoric, as if drunk
on potent New England rum.

Justin eyed him and grinned knowingly. "It is so impossible, it
must surely work."

"Only His Excellency would have thought of this, and only he
could accomplish it," Tench said.

Ad wished he could share their excitement with Addie and Silas,
but they would know soon enough. Silas had been grumbling that
the horses used to haul the guns were slipping for lack of proper ice
shoes, and Ad could well imagine what a task it would be to get those
horses and those guns across the Delaware again now that the river
was filled with ice but not frozen solid.

There was little marking of Christmas in the American camp.
They were too short of supplies for feasting and, in any case, only the
Anglicans and the few Roman Catholics there were would have made
truly merry had they the means.

The river, though a good barrier against Tory spies and deserters carrying word to the enemy, was closely watched. The soldiers
were issued three days' cooked cold rations, such as they were, and

these, their muskets and blankets would be all they would carry. On Christmas Day, Washington proclaimed the password would be, "Victory or death."

On the same day, the commander received news that a company of Virginians had made an attack on the guards at the north end of Trenton and had then withdrawn. In fury, Washington turned on the officer who had ordered the attack, for now, if they had any sense at all, the garrison at Trenton, the target of Washington's planned raid, would be alerted. It was as good a reason as could be to cancel the operation, but it was as if desperation and the hope of success, slim as it was, had merged into one compulsion with its own momentum. Washington would go as planned.

As a diversion, one group was to cross downstream of Trenton and to engage General Carl van Donop's Hessian garrison at Bordertown. Others were to come to the Americans' support from Philadelphia. Another detachment was to cross directly opposite Trenton in order to hold the bridge over the Assunpink River so that the Hessians couldn't escape. The main force of twenty-four hundred men would be led by Washington himself from McKonkey's Ferry to land about nine miles from Trenton, advancing on the town from the north. The general had chosen this location because it gave him access to three ferries that were fairly close to each other.

Nearly every able-bodied man was committed to the raid and the general was overseeing the operation himself. Someone had brought an empty skep to serve as a makeshift chair, and from this perch he gave his orders to Henry Knox, who relayed them to the soldiers. This was an amusingly efficient system because Knox had a voice as big as the rest of him and could easily make himself heard over the elements and everything else.

The soldiers had to wait for hours to embark as the boats were brought down to them. Most of them were ill-clad, the snow was cold under their feet, and they huddled in their blankets, trying to find protection from the wind that bit ever deeper as the temperature dropped.

John Glover and his seamen-soldiers were again in charge of getting the troops across. They were using Durham boats, cargo craft normally employed in hauling grain or iron, vessels unfamiliar to most of the men. They had a fleet of more than forty of the boats, some forty feet long, some sixty feet, pointed at both ends with a shallow draft, designed to be rowed downstream by oars and poled upstream. Familiar or not, boats were boats to the sailors, and they worked with steady strength to move the men back and forth across the river. On the flat ferries, which were transporting the horses, artillery wagons, and guns, the horses snorted and whinnied in protest and terror as they slipped and lurched on the icy decks.

The river was giving them no help. At McKonkey's Ferry, it was about three hundred yards wide, and it was full of huge, floating chunks of ice. Even over the hiss of the wind, the eerie shrieking and moaning of the ice assaulted the ears.

"Ghosts ride tonight," Silas heard one man mutter, and he couldn't blame him for the fear he heard in his voice.

Rain had turned to snow that was freezing into sleet, and with every hour that passed, it was more doubtful that the men could keep the firing pans or the powder for their muskets dry. That meant that the artillery would be vital to the enterprise, for it was far easier to make a cannon rather than a musket fire in such weather. Colonel Knox and his officers were determined that the artillery be gotten across.

Silas did not think about the impossibility of such a task or that the bitter cold was making handling the guns more difficult. He didn't think that as an officer, he could let the soldiers do all the heavy work. He was infected with the same mad hope as his brothers-in-law, and he was willing to do anything he could to get the guns across the river.

He did think of Addie because she was never far from his mind, but it was with amazement, not worry. In these past weeks, she had changed. He had assumed that as conditions grew rougher, she would decide, with no advice from him, that the sensible course would be to establish herself and Tullia in comfortable quarters at some remove from the army. Instead, she had adapted without complaint, becoming, in her own way, a soldier. She would always be tender and welcoming for him—he did not doubt that—but whatever other softness there had been was gone.

When she had learned of this night's mission, she had told him, "Go, drive them away or kill them. They do not belong here. This is our country, not theirs! They killed Quentin. It is enough. I trust you and my brothers to come back to me. The enemy is complacent; they misjudge our will."

Silas carried the image of how she had looked as she spoke, so fine and fierce, as caught up as the rest of them in the belief that this bold stroke would succeed. And he felt a moment of gratitude that General Washington was acquainted with her because otherwise she might have donned her boy's clothing and marched with them.

Silas knew they were running behind schedule. General Washington had wanted everyone across by midnight so that they could be in Trenton by dawn. But it was 3 a.m. before Knox's operation was complete. Still, the guns had been safely ferried across.

The Valencourts were even more aware of time slipping away than Silas was because they were with Washington, witnessing his tight-lipped control as he calculated the diminishing odds for their success. He was near despair at the idea of losing the chance to surprise the garrison at Trenton, and yet they had come too far to turn back, for with daylight close, the enemy would certainly discover them in retreat, and they would be easy targets, trying to get back across the icy river. And to add to his burden, news came that both the diversionary force and the support ordered from Philadelphia had turned back.

It was 4 a.m. by the time the soldiers were formed up and ready to march. Officers were to be identified by white paper tucked in their hats, not a particularly good choice with snow in the air. In about two hours, dawn would break.

They hadn't gone far before one of his generals sent word to Washington that, despite the best efforts of the men to keep them dry, the firing pans of their muskets were too wet to fire.

Washington told the messenger, "Tell your general to use the bayonet and penetrate into the town. The town must be taken. I am resolved to take it."

Justin hoped it wouldn't come to that because their army wasn't proficient with the bayonet; unlike the enemy, who used that weapon with deadly skill.

They stopped briefly near the hamlet of Birmingham to eat of their cold rations, and Justin and Ad, like most of the officers, didn't bother to dismount. Some soldiers fell asleep where they stood, only to be shaken awake by their companions.

As the force led by Washington himself headed cross-country from Birmingham, Ad began to understand the whispers he heard from the soldiers as they made out the big figure of their leader on his tall bay horse.

"He's here," "He's with us," "There he is," they said, as if his mere presence blessed them and made whatever he asked of them possible. The loyalty of these men touched Ad deeply, and he ignored the cold seeping into his body. After all, he was riding while these men were on foot.

The general's voice came to him as Washington encouraged the troops, "Stick close to your officers, boys—press on—press on."

Bone-weary and cold, half-blinded by the snow and sleet, stumbling over the bad ground, some with bloody feet, moving as quietly as possible, the men pressed on as he asked. Torches on the artillery pieces leading them had been allowed until Birmingham, but after that, the lights were extinguished, so they marched in darkness until the first feeble light of dawn broke.

More than once, Ad saw men help comrades back into line when they had fallen.

Not long after the sun had risen, its glow pale in the heavy weather, Washington ordered the column halted. He rode down the long line of men, and over and over again his voice, solemn and deep despite its hoarseness, rolled over them. "Soldiers, keep by your officers. For God's sake, keep by your officers!"

By the time they neared Trenton, the soldiers had already accomplished much, having covered nine miles in four hours. Washington had detached columns under generals Sullivan and Greene before they reached Trenton, so that by the time the Hessian pickets sighted Washington's force and began to scream their warnings, "Der Feind! Heraus! Heraus!", the Americans were closing in from various directions and had most escape routes closed off.

While the Hessians had surely celebrated Christmas well on the previous day, they turned out in force to rebuff the invaders only to find the storm was in their faces, obscuring their vision with a sting-ing mixture of rain, sleet, and snow. The Hessians were accustomed to formal battle lines, not to having the enemy appear suddenly and hit from every direction, but they made an effort to rally and impose their order. But Ad could see they were having the same trouble with wet muskets as the Americans and were trying to get within bayonet distance. And the American artillery so laboriously brought across the river and divided among the attacking columns was causing great damage and confusion.

Silas saw the Hessians trying to wheel their artillery into position with horses, and he directed his six-pounders toward them. Three horses fell over on one gun, two on another. For a moment, Silas's stomach twisted at the sight of the beasts spewing blood and entrails over the guns and the snow, but the dead and dying horses did as much to stop the Hessian guns as did wounding and killing much of the gun crew. He averted his eyes when he recognized an odd object as a man's arm.

The battle was being won by American artillery, but the soldiers with muskets that were dry enough and with bayonets and spontoons that could slash flesh in any weather picked off Hessians wherever they closed on them.

Wooden buildings blew apart from the artillery assault, and to add to the cacophony and confusion, citizens of the town screamed and ran in terror.

Colonel Rall was commander at Trenton, and his regiment had sought shelter in an orchard to regroup. Knox had set his men on some abandoned Hessian guns, training them on the orchard, and as soon as Rall and his men emerged, they were hit with grape and cannister from their own guns. Rall himself was thrown from his saddle by the shot that hit him. With their leader down, the men fled, only to find themselves surrounded when they broke onto open ground.

Silas watched their colors coming down as they surrendered on the spot.

Washington was ordering cannon to be brought to bear on some Hessians who had gathered beyond the town when Justin rode up to him to announce, "Your Excellency, they have struck."

"Struck?"

"Yes, sir. Their colors are down!"

Washington stared through a glass at the figures, their bright uniforms made even more colorful by the contrast with the white field. "So they are," he said.

Justin saw his own joy and relief reflected on his brother's and Tench's faces. And as they rode through the town with their commander, a messenger approached to tell him that Knyphausen's Hessians, who were also part of the Trenton brigade, had also surrendered.

With that, Washington's delight showed. "This is a glorious day for our country!"

As they realized what they had done, the American soldiers threw their hats in the air, cheering themselves and laughing. The Hessians, babbling in German for the mercy they themselves seldom granted, now looked more ridiculous than fearsome with their greased pigtails and big, waxed mustaches.

Helpless against the tide, Washington joined the laughter, startling his aides until he calmed himself and sent them to calm the men.

The attack had lasted only about an hour, but the numbers were astonishing. They had a few wounded but no deaths except for two poor souls who had frozen on the march. The Hessians had twenty-two dead and eighty-four wounded. The number of prisoners captured came to over nine hundred.

It was briefly tempting to push on and take the Hessians at other Jersey outposts, but Washington's staff pointed out to him that the weather, already so grueling, might get worse and make the river impassable. There was also the matter of the men having found ample supplies of liquor. Washington ordered the hogsheads of rum stove in, but many had already been broached by his soldiers, and guzzling the rum on their nearly empty stomachs was bound to cause powerful effects. Not all of them had the sense to partake of the Hessians' copious stores of food.

The wisest course was to cross back to Pennsylvania. So once again, John Glover's men put their backs to the oars to carry not only their army but also the prisoners across the Delaware. There was captured artillery to take, too, in addition to their own, and horses to load on the ferries, horses with ice adorning their manes and tails, and the decks as slick under their hooves as during the first crossing.

Ice formed so quickly on the boats, impeding progress, that the prisoners were asked to stomp up and down to break it loose. They did it vigorously, their faces revealing their terror of being lost in the frigid waters.

Glover's men got them all safely across.

Addie was waiting for her husband and her brothers when they rode back into camp in the early hours of December 27. Silas swept her into his arms, his cloak swirling around both of them.

"We did it, Addie! We won! We won because the men were willing to keep on; hungry, cold, and so weary, they were willing to go on and on because General Washington asked them to do it for our country. We won at Trenton, and we will win the war because of them, because of him."

Beyond his words, Addie could feel the excitement coursing through his body as if lightning had replaced the blood in his veins, and she shared the triumph of the victory, made sweeter because of all the losses of the past months.

But the success at Trenton did not change the reality of most enlistments expiring at the end of the year, so little time that it could be counted in hours. To have struck the enemy so boldly, and then to have to have his soldiers fade away, back to the farms and hamlets from which they had come, was intolerable to Washington. He was determined to risk not only his pride, but also his personal fortune, for he was going to offer a bounty of ten dollars to those who would stay on, and if Congress could or would not provide the money, Washington himself would stand good for it.

When the men were on parade, Washington spoke to them. He begged they not go home, assuring them their services were still sorely needed.

The drums beat for volunteers, but not one man turned out.

It was not enough that his aides and the most loyal officers would stay. There was no army without the common soldiers.

Ad kept his eyes straight ahead, his face devoid of expression, but he wanted to bow his head and weep.

The general wheeled his horse around, rode in front of the men, and spoke to them again. "My brave fellows, you have done all I asked you to do, and more than could be reasonably expected; but your country is at stake, your wives, your houses, and all you hold dear. You have worn yourselves out with fatigued hardships, but we know not how to spare you. If you will consent to stay only one month longer, you will render that service to the cause of liberty, and to your country, which you probably never can do under any other circumstances. The present is emphatically the crisis which is to decide our destiny."

Justin was as frozen as Ad, imagining news of failure with this regiment traveling swiftly up and down the line, but then he felt a stir, heard quiet murmurings, one man to another.

"I will remain if you will."

"We cannot go home when he bids us stay."

"We leave now and lose all, our wee sons must carry our muskets for us ere long."

A few men stepped forward, and then, quite suddenly, nearly every man who was fit for duty joined them until there were about two hundred of them.

An officer inquired of General Washington if the men should be enrolled, but Washington shook his head. "No! Men who will volunteer in such case as this need no enrollment to keep them to their duty."

For an instant, such joy blazed on his commander's face, Ad's own control faltered, and he felt tears warm against his cold cheeks. He didn't care. He felt like throwing his hat in the air and whooping in triumph. Two hundred men would not change the course of the war, but the appeal would be repeated down the line, and the example of these men would be followed by others. Washington had asked from his heart that they follow him despite their grim situation, and from their hearts, they had answered him. It was the one factor the enemy would never be able to anticipate—a weapon forged not of metal, but of spirit.

Chapter 5

Winter 1777

With his officers adding their pleas to his, instead of being utterly abandoned, Washington retained a force of a few thousand men. And having convinced them to stay, he led them back across the Delaware to harry the enemy again.

The Hessian prisoners had been sent to Philadelphia, tangible proof of the success at Trenton. The raid had heartened Americans, but shaken the British. General Cornwallis had been on the point of departing for leave in England, but General Howe quickly recalled him and sent him into New Jersey with eight thousand men.

A battle with Cornwallis would be suicidal, and Washington avoided it by leaving four hundred men near Trenton to tend campfires and make the noise of a greater force while the rest slipped away in the night toward Princeton, where Cornwallis had stationed part of his force. The decoys left their positions just before dawn to rejoin Washington. However, this time surprise did not work as well as it had at Trenton, for most of the enemy left at Princeton was out and marching to reinforce Cornwallis.

Washington had dispatched a brigade to secure the Post Road to Trenton, and as the Americans emerged from the woods, the advancing British spied them and attacked. The two sides fired at each other, but when the British advanced with bayonets, the Americans fled. Some Pennsylvania militia coming up to support them did no better. Continentals arriving on the scene tried to turn the action, but it was Washington himself who rallied his army.

Riding with him, there was nothing his aides could do except pray no British bullet found the large target he made as he led the attack, calling to those who were fleeing, "Parade with us, my brave fellows. There is but a handful of the enemy, and we will have them directly!"

Ad saw the men turn and follow their general, and he gave a whoop of joy.

The British, realizing they were facing the whole of Washington's force, used their bayonets again to break through to the south, toward Trenton. The Americans pursued them gleefully, taking prisoners, until Washington called them back so that they could go after the remainder of the British force in Princeton.

As it was, most of them had escaped from the town except for about two hundred who had barricaded themselves in the College of New Jersey's Nassau Hall. But two rounds of artillery fired into the building and the threat of the Americans storming the position convinced those inside to capitulate. Though the damage to the building was minimal, it gave Ad an odd turn to see violence inflicted on this place that had sheltered him during his student days at the college.

The new year of 1777 was only three days old and dealing another blow to the enemy had been a heady way to begin it. It was again tempting to keep on, but reality intruded on the plan. American casualties were disproportionately among the officer corps, who had emulated their commander in chief and paid a heavy price. One sad case was that of General Mercer, who was in British hands and so severely wounded, death was sure.

Nor was it possible to deny the toll that cold and the long months of marching and fighting had taken on the men. Most of them were so exhausted, they lacked the stamina to go into battle again so soon. What they needed most of all was the time and a place to rest.

Given the British Army's aversion to fighting in winter conditions, Washington and his staff trusted that Cornwallis would not come after them unless directly challenged. They left the enemy to return to winter quarters while they sought theirs, reaching Morristown, New Jersey, on January 7.

Washington chose Freeman's Tavern on the Common as his headquarters because there was room for his staff there. The troops were billeted in barns or public buildings, but they set to work to construct huts of logs chinked with clay and moss, and most would move into the huts as soon as they were habitable.

Addie and Tullia had traveled with other families and the baggage train, avoiding contact with the enemy as they left Pennsylvania to rejoin Washington's army on its march to Morristown. Silas and Addie found lodgings for themselves and Tullia in a house nearby. The couple who owned the modest dwelling, the Dolbys, welcomed the extra income provided by their boarders, and they were glad of the presence of the American Army. They were aware of the British's, and more particularly, the Hessians', reputation for dealing harshly with civilians. Not every soldier in the Continental Army behaved impeccably, but Washington's policy was against harm to any but the enemy, and when transgressors were caught, they were sternly punished.

The Dolbys had three grown children, all daughters, all married and living in their own homes. The Dolbys were proud that one son-in-law was in the Continental Army and another in the militia. They were noticeably reticent about the third son-in-law, leaving Silas and Addie to assume he was probably a Loyalist.

"Do you think the divisions caused in families by this war will ever heal?" Addie asked Silas as they lay snuggled together, waiting for sleep. The room was cold, but they were warm in the nest of their bed.

Silas stroked Addie's back gently, knowing they were both thinking of Marcus without saying his name. "I hope so, but it is hard to judge. It must surely depend on how long the war goes on, on how it ends, and on how much damage is done before the finish. No one can foretell any of that now. But I know Marcus will send word to us before long." He hoped that was true. He knew how constantly Addie and her brothers thought of their father, and Marcus was scarcely ever absent from his mind. And they would have to inform him of Quentin's death. He quailed inwardly at the knowledge of the pain that would cause the man.

He didn't feel much better about what he had to ask Addie, but he was running out of time.

"General Washington has asked General Knox to go to New England to oversee the casting of cannon and to establish laborato-

ries for the manufacture of powder. He is also to tell the provincial
legislatures how desperate we are for men. The militia with us have
increased our numbers, but we have scarcely a thousand Continentals
in camp now."

"And General Knox wants you to accompany him," Addie finished
for him, her voice faint. She wanted to shriek at him, forbid him to
go. After the hard months of campaigning, to be settled in one spot
with no dangerous battles looming in the near future was bliss. The
few days she and Silas had already spent at Morristown had been
some of the best since the war began, and she had wanted them to
continue as long as possible. She had little doubt that if she turned
either supplicant or shrew, she could prevent Silas from leaving, for
Knox and Washington were not only friends, they were also gentlemen
who were loath to distress a lady. But she heard the pride in Silas's
voice when he called Knox by his new rank, Congress having made
him a brigadier general. And she had her own pride in how much
Knox valued the loyalty and talent of her husband.

"It will be to our good for you to go," she conceded. "We have
trusted agents seeing to our affairs in Boston and at the farm, but it
would be well to remind them we still exist. Soon it will be a year
since we were there."

She stated it as a fact, with no wistfulness for the place that had
been home. It underscored the truth that for Addie home was wherever
Silas and her brothers were. Knowing that, he loved her more for
letting him go without protest, for not asking that she go with him
because she knew she would be of no use on this military assignment
undertaken in winter weather.

"We stored things, Tullia and I, including clothing. I hope you can
manage to bring some back with you. We have all grown threadbare
in this enterprise."

Silas was so relieved that his mission with Knox would cause no
complaint from her, it was easy to promise that he would check on
their interests. "And I will bring back as much clothing as I can.
Indeed, we have become scarecrows." He brushed his lips across her
temple. "My practical Addie; General Washington should appoint

you quartermaster. I warrant you could do a fine job of supplying the army with its wants."

"I fear Tullia and I did not pack away so much as that." The levity went out of her voice as she added, "I wish we had been able to. It is so hard to see how many of the men suffer from the cold. And it is worse for their families. It is no wonder so many have gone home. I hope General Knox will be able to persuade all of New England to be generous."

She nuzzled her face against his neck, breathing the scent of him, trying not to think about how much she was going to miss him. "It is well that we have known this campaign only by the day; seeing too far ahead would have been daunting for the stoutest heart."

Silas agreed with her to a point, but he wished he could see the end of the war, could see the victory that would make all of their sacrifices, even Quentin's death, worthwhile. And then he pondered what he would do if he saw that it was all in vain, that Britain triumphed. It was better, after all, not to know. He was grateful he did not have to make the decision of what he would do if he knew their cause would be lost.

He shifted until their bodies were even more closely aligned than before. They drew comfort from the familiar fit, needing nothing beyond the contentment that wrapped around them and narrowed the boundaries of the universe to this small space.

When Silas left Morristown with General Knox, Addie saw him off with a determined smile. It helped that she was flanked by her brothers. They had consulted with Silas about their Boston properties, and Silas was leaving charged with a considerable list of family duties to perform. They did not worry that Silas would not have the time, for in addition to his official business, Henry Knox was going home for a reunion with his Lucy and his children, an infant son being a new addition. It was certain that Knox would not spend all of his hours on government concerns.

"We'll help keep you busy, and Silas will be back before long," Ad told his twin, feeling her sorrow under the bright front she had presented to her husband.

He was as good as his word, for though a couple more aides-de-camp had joined Washington's staff in the past months, the piles of correspondence to be answered continued to grow, and general and special orders had to be written to guide the daily life of the encampment. Addie was pleased to pass the time doing something useful at headquarters.

There were also families of soldiers to see to. There wasn't much she and Tullia could do, but they offered their help with sick children and with women who, themselves being unwell, were thankful to have someone watch their offspring for a while.

Most of the families were living in wretched conditions, their shelters having been constructed only when the official huts were finished. Squalor and lack of adequate supplies of food, bedding, and so basic a commodity as soap made the situation unhealthier. Some didn't have the habits of cleanliness even if they could obtain soap, and that made a delicate situation, for as much as Addie and Tullia wanted to improve the lot of the children, they understood that accusing the parents of slovenly habits was not the way to do it. After all, the problem had been so serious since the beginning that General Washington had issued orders about bathing. But those rules had little power in the winter cold, and the best Addie and Tullia could do was to clean as they went, doing it without preaching.

Addie had once considered the aroma of vinegar sharp but pleasant, but now she wished never to smell it again. The whole encampment reeked of it due to its liberal use as a weapon against contagions. Perhaps there was some merit in the stuff since it was so strong and so widely used, but combined in such quantities with the odors of unwashed bodies, sodden clothing, dirty cooking pots, damp wood, and smoke from the fireplaces, it formed a lethal perfume.

The differences in how the officers and common soldiers lived were apparent. While the officers laughed at each other for their tattered appearance, they did not go hungry. And on some nights they managed to create the semblance of a social life with dancing, the gatherings attended by the officers, those of their wives who had come to Morristown, and by ladies and gentlemen, prominent citizens loyal to the American cause, from the surrounding countryside.

These assemblies made Addie long for Silas, but at the same time, she needed the additions to her depleted wardrobe that his journey would allow him to retrieve. She had never cared much about such things, but after months of traveling with the army, she made a poor showing compared to the other ladies.

In spite of Silas's absence, Addie did not lack for dancing partners, for the women were definitely in the minority. Washington loved to dance, and when he was moving gracefully to the music, it seemed as if the awful burden he carried was cast aside, and he was transformed into the charming Virginia gentleman he had been before the war began. When he danced with Addie, she felt as if she were in Williamsburg or at Castleton again, and she was touched when he used his wife's nickname, saying, "I suspect you miss your husband as much as I miss my Patsy. Never fear, Knox will have him back before long."

"And your wife? Will she join us soon?"

"I fear subjecting her to the rigors of winter travel and tearing her away once again from all that is familiar to her. Yet, every day I am tempted to ask that she risk the journey."

"Your Excellency, if I may be so bold. I do not know your wife well, but I do know that there is no place she would rather be than with you. You are her comfort as much as she is yours. When you send her word, she will come."

The general looked so gratified by this assurance, Addie did not regret her temerity.

But the process worked in reverse, and it was Addie herself who received a letter from Virginia, from Aunt Camille. With her usual perception, Camille had included all sorts of small details about life at Castleton, knowing that the Valencourts would welcome such news in the midst of war. But the war intruded even on Camille's country life, for she noted that the Valencourts would undoubtedly see their cousins Hart and Reeves soon:

> *Now that the depredations of treacherous Lord Dunmore have ceased, they will be released from their military duties here and will surely travel north to join General Washington. Their*

mother and I would like to keep them here, but they are men,
not boys, and the truth is, Catherine and I can run Castleton
without them for as long as needs be. We worry about your
uncle, for his work with the Continental Congress continues to
wear on his health, but he, too, has a duty to our new nation.

I find no gentle way to tell you this, but I have news of
your father. He, his wife, and children are safely in England.
They are staying with your half-sister Callista but will probably
remove to their own establishment before long. They are well.
Marcus has not sent word to any of us directly, but I trust the
accuracy of this report from a friend in England. And when
you are ready to inform Marcus of the loss of dear Quentin, you
may send to England through diplomatic channels.

As carefully as Camille had tried to state it, the cruel fact was that Marcus could have sent word himself, had he so desired, for he knew his children were with Washington and knew where the Castletons resided. It was Marcus, not they, who had been lost to communication. There was additional hurt for Addie and her brothers, for they had no doubt that Marcus had kept their half-brother Darius informed of his movements. Though it was possible for them to contact Darius, as letters did go back and forth across the lines, they did not feel it would be suitable to write to him since he was actively engaged in the war on the British side.

Even Tench, who kept in touch with his Loyalist relatives, particularly his father, conceded that their position was a difficult one. "I doubt not that His Excellency would understand, but to other eyes, direct correspondence with so active an enemy officer might appear in the worst light."

Tench's father was not in uniform and, as far as the Valencourts knew, Tench had little contact with his brother Philemon, who had run away to the British Navy. In any case, Philemon would be only seventeen this year, a youth hardly to be compared with Darius Valencourt, a man who had raised and equipped his own company of soldiers.

"'Tis a damnable coil when families are so divided and a sad reflection of the division between us and England." The dark tone in Tench's voice was a reminder of why he had proved so valuable a friend to the Valencourts; they never had to defend or explain their own Loyalist connections.

Though they felt cowardly, Ad and Justin were relieved when Addie volunteered to write to their father. "I have Quentin's miniatures to send to him, though I would rather keep them by me. But I promised." She wondered if it would always hurt so much to say Quentin's name, to think of him. She hoped the day would come when she could recall the beauty of him without being crushed immediately by the remembrance of his death.

Despite the lack of blood ties between Quentin and Tullia, Addie knew that Tullia's grief was as deep as her own and could not have been more had Tullia borne Quentin of her own flesh. While she never shirked from the work at hand, her spirit had been quenched for all the months since Quentin had been killed.

But now, with Silas away, and with more time to spend with Tullia, Addie noticed that the deep pall of sorrow seemed to be lifting. Tullia even spoke Quentin's name aloud, saying, "You tell your father that Quentin was brave and that the other soldiers thought well of him and mourned his passing. Lily gave your papa fine children, and he has no business turning his back on you because of that royal master in England. Has no business turning away from Silas either; that boy loves and honors him as much as any son could." Her expression turned sly as she regarded Addie. "You write to him, and Lily will speak with you—you are so like her. He never could resist her, and when he gets your letter, he will hear her voice, too."

Addie wished she could be as optimistic as Tullia, but as the long months had passed, she had become convinced that this separation from Marcus was not a break of the moment, but a chasm that would never be crossed. She wished she did not know her father's heart so well. He had been the most kind and indulgent of parents, but he was also a man of unyielding principle. And in his ordered world, Lily's children and Silas had become agents of chaos. Addie thought they would have had some chance for reunion had Marcus been able to remain in America as Tench's father had. But Marcus was across the sea in England, undoubtedly surrounded by those who shared his loyalty to the mother country and his disgust for the Rebels. To them, the Declaration of Independence and, with it, the colonies' determination to become a sovereign nation, would be the gravest insult and threat.

There was nothing Addie could do about her father beyond writing to him, but she eyed Tullia with keen interest. Here was the woman she had known of old, full of spirit and hope, determined that things would go well for her family. With her attention focused, Addie noticed other things, too, and wondered when the transformation had begun and how she could have been so blind until this instant.

Tullia was ever a clean, well-kept woman, but in the past months, her high standards had faltered, not only from the hardship of traveling with the army, but also from her sorrow. Now that was all changed, and she somehow managed to appear as crisp and tidy as if she were presiding over her old domain in Boston. She had even managed to give her cracked shoes a soft shine. There was a brightness in her eyes, a soft glow, and Addie realized she had never seen Tullia look quite like this.

The truth hit her so abruptly, she asked without preamble or tact, "Who is he?"

Tullia opened her mouth to deny there was anyone, but instead, a smile brightened her face. "His name is Prince Freedom. He's a blacksmith and a teamster, but he's fought with a musket, too. He's been with the army since right after the Battle of Lexington, but we just noticed each other lately.

"Like me, he was born a slave, but he was freed on the death of his master. That was more than twenty years ago. He took the last name 'Freedom' instead of his master's name. I think Prince Freedom is a grand name. Don't you?"

Tullia giggled, and Addie's eyes widened at the girlish sound. She had never heard such from her friend.

"I think it is a splendid name," she said, but her mind was spinning. When they had set out together on their journey into war, she had worried that Tullia was too old. Now she was seeing a woman completely different from the one she had always known. Tullia had ever been the matron, the woman who had become mother to Lily's children after Lily died. This Tullia who spoke Prince Freedom's name with such delight was someone entirely out of Addie's experience, and Addie struggled to collect her scattered wits. She had never thought of Tullia in relationship to a man, and she felt some shame for judging her so sexless. She also felt a flare of panic at the thought that this Prince Freedom might not be suitable, and that thought immediately made her feel as if she were the mother, concerned about her daughter's suitor.

All in all, she was dizzy with the turn Tullia's life had taken, and the best she could manage was to ask, "When may I meet Mr. Freedom?"

"You worried that this old woman has chosen badly?" Tullia asked, but there was no sting in the words.

"I think only a fool would call you an old woman," Addie said, giving her a quick hug. "But I would like to meet the man. If I were not married to Silas, if I had fallen in love with a soldier in this camp, wouldn't you insist that he be introduced to you?"

Tullia nodded, and then her expression grew soft and dreamy. "He is a fine man. I will be proud to have you meet him." She hesitated and then went on. "I never thought this would happen to me. There was a young man I fancied at Castleton long ago, and your mama's family would have let me stay with him, but I would have been with Lily no longer, and I couldn't do that."

"I'm sorry," Addie said.

But Tullia shook her head. "Don't be. I loved your mother more than I loved that boy, else I would have stayed with him. My life in Boston with Lily, with your father, with you children—all of it was better than it would have been for me at Castleton."

Tullia did not have to elaborate for Addie to know the stark truth. Had Tullia stayed at Castleton, she might have had children of her own, but she would have remained a slave, and her children, too. She would never have become the free, self-possessed woman she was now, the woman who carried herself with visible pride.

Addie thought of how oddly mixed the Black presence was in the Continental Army. Some were slaves accompanying their masters—as

Washington's own slaves were with him, from his steward Billy Lee to those who did his laundry and saw to various other domestic chores. Some were slaves who served in the army at the pleasure of their masters; some, by giving their enlistment bounty to their owners, were declared freedmen, served as such in the army, and if they survived the war would remain free. And some were like Prince Freedom, free Negroes who were choosing to fight against Britain's tyranny.

She was acutely nervous when Tullia took her to meet Prince, not knowing what she would do if she didn't like the man. But in the event, she need not have worried. He was enormous, over six feet tall and so broadly built, Addie thought he must cast the shadow of two average-sized men. His years of smithing had given him muscles that bulged beneath the rough homespun he wore. His tightly curled hair was flecked with gray, but there were few other signs of age. His dark skin was smooth over his broad nose and cheekbones, and his mouth was full.

Addie stopped her inventory at his eyes. They were nearly as golden as hers, brown glowing with light, and they were likewise filled with apprehension because he was as anxious that she approve of him as she was that Tullia not be duped by a dishonorable man. And in his eyes Addie saw intelligence and a kindness that made it easy for her to understand why Tullia had fallen under his spell.

Addie smiled at him. "I am pleased to meet you."

His smile was wide in return. "Likewise, Mistress Bradwell. Tullia has told me much about you and your brothers."

"Oh, my! I'm sure much of it were better left untold. Tullia has put up with a great deal of mischief from us over the years."

Prince's eyes sparkled with good humor. "In her words, you were all little angels come down from heaven."

"Not exactly angels," Tullia protested demurely, and in shared laughter, it was as if the three of them were old friends.

Prince Freedom was proud of his children, explaining to Addie that he had one son and two daughters, all married. Prince's wife had died after the birth of their younger daughter, and he was sure the children had missed the presence of their mother, but he'd done his best with them. The greatest tragedy they'd suffered, aside from the loss of their mother, was when the boy, Isaac, had been run over by a heavily loaded wagon.

"We thought we'd lose him. His foot was crushed real bad, and he was in a fever for weeks. But he lived to grow to a man near as big as I am. He's lame, but his arms are strong enough to do any job a blacksmith needs to do."

Prince described the business he had built, a business being run in his absence by his son and one of his sons-in-law. Located in Dedham, southwest of Boston, it was a manufacturing smithy, both forge and nail factory, and in addition it produced edge tools and anchors. The workmanship was widely known for being of superior quality.

Listening to him, Addie understood that this man, while somewhat embarrassed at speaking so candidly about his accomplishments, was doing so as a necessary step in his courtship of Tullia. He intended that Addie know Tullia would be well looked after by him. Addie doubted it would make any difference to him if he knew that Tullia had a portion of her own from Marcus. Prince Freedom was the sort of man who would expect to provide for his wife.

That he wanted to marry Tullia was as clear to Addie as if he had proposed within her hearing. She felt hollow inside at the thought of Tullia leaving their lives, and then she acknowledged to herself how selfish that was. No one deserved a life and family of her own more than Tullia. And as long as the couple remained with the army, things need not change so much.

When they took their leave of Prince, Addie met his eyes and a long look passed between them, and when Tullia moved just out of earshot, Addie whispered, "I know you will take good care of her."

"I will. Bless you, Mistress Bradwell," he said, and his eyes were shining with so much love for Tullia, Addie had to blink back tears.

Tullia and Addie walked along, and Addie knew Tullia was waiting for her to speak, but she had to swallow several times before she found her voice. "You and Mr. Freedom are very fortunate to have found each other. He is so kind, I am sure his children will be kind, too, and will welcome you as his wife and their stepmother."

Tullia stopped walking so abruptly, Addie took several steps beyond her.

"How can you think I would marry that man and leave all of you?" Tullia hissed.

Only then did Addie understand that her fear of losing Tullia was less than Tullia's fear of leaving.

"What do you plan to do? Do you intend only to dally with him while he offers you his heart and his home? Because that is what he wants to give you, whether he has said it or not."

Tullia's tears overflowed, and she wiped at them angrily. "It would be so easy for you to see me go then?" she mumbled.

"You know better than that," Addie protested. "It is nigh impossible to imagine not having you with us. You have cared for us all of our days. You will always have a home with Silas and me, and I know Ad and Justin feel the same, though none of us have much in the way of homes to offer at the moment." She paused before asking softly, "Have I mistaken the matter? I do not doubt Prince Freedom's love for you, but perhaps, though you have some feeling for him, you do not return his love in measure full enough to marry him. You would not be the first woman to feel so, but the decision must be made for your own sake, not for ours. We are all grown now. Only you can choose what is best for yourself."

Tullia struggled to regain control of herself and gave up the fight as more tears flowed. "I do love him, more than I ever thought I could love a man. But I stopped thinking of being a wife a long, long time ago and now I am afraid. It would be such a change, such a big change."

"It seems to me that the war has been the biggest change anyone could experience, yet we are managing," Addie offered carefully, mindful of the memories of Quentin that lay between them. "It isn't just your happiness that is at stake; it is also Prince's.

"Of course, you don't have to answer the question until it's asked, and we'll all be together as long as we continue with the army. And it appears that the army will be needed for a good while to come." It was peculiar to find something good in their perilous situation, but she saw the tension ease in Tullia's face as she realized she really didn't have to make any decision right now. It continued to amaze Addie that Tullia could be as confounded as anyone by love.

Since Addie knew the secret, Tullia was resigned to having others know as well, so Ad and Justin were duly introduced to Prince Freedom, and they came away as impressed with the man as Addie was, but even more astonished than their sister that Tullia was in love.

Having learned the truth before they did, Addie could afford to be amused by their attitude.

Ad actually blushed, stammering to his twin, "I just never thought she would... I mean..."

Addie laughed at him but admitted, "Poor Tullia, all these years we've regarded her as the perfect mother for us, but not as a woman."

"I am infinitely relieved that Tullia has chosen such a worthy man and that we do not have to fight for her honor," Justin said. "Prince Freedom is one of the largest human beings I have ever seen. I have no doubt that he could dispatch me, you,"—he nodded at Ad—"and Silas all at once without strain. But I inquired after his reputation and discovered it is without blemish. He is known as a fine craftsman with a special talent for calming the beasts when he shoes or drives them, be it horses or mules or oxen. There aren't many smiths who can serve as teamsters, too." He gazed into the distance for a moment. "I think he will suit Tullia very well, but all in all, it is passing strange to think of her having a secret suitor."

Ad snorted at that. "Prince Freedom is too big to have been kept a secret for long."

Tullia tried not to neglect Addie, but it was natural that she wanted to spend any free time she had with Prince. Addie was cheered by the proximity of her brothers, but they weren't always in camp, for General Washington sent his aides out in the countryside with foraging and scouting parties that were further charged with harassing the enemy when they could. It was heartening to know that though the British had controlled most of New Jersey a short time ago, now they held little of it, the battles of Trenton and Princeton having driven them back, and the current forays against their remaining outposts kept them unsettled.

Addie knew her brothers and the other officers had no intention of engaging in a real battle with the enemy, but that didn't keep her from worrying about them when they were out of Morristown. And even when they were close by, their duties kept them occupied. Her best chance of their company was when she helped with the correspondence or when they all attended an evening gathering. The fact was, she missed Silas, and no one else's company, not even that of her twin, could make up for her husband's absence.

When Silas and General Knox rode into camp, Addie flew to Silas with no thought of dignity, throwing herself into his arms as he dismounted. She heard General Knox chuckle, not a small sound from so large a man, and then she was aware of nothing except Silas's arms coming around her and lifting her off her feet.

"Oh, I missed you so much!" Addie breathed in the scent of him, a heady combination of leather and horse and this particular man, and her body was suddenly flooded with warmth despite the cold day.

But it was Silas who said, "You smell like flowers."

"You don't." Addie's words were a purr of approval, and Silas laughed.

"You are dismissed from duty for today, Major Bradwell," General Knox said, his amusement still evident.

"Thank you, sir!" All Silas wanted to do was to whisk Addie away to their room, but first he had to see to the precious cargo he had brought with him. "You and Tullia did a good job of storage. I've got clothing for all of us as well as blankets and such. Your brothers and I will be the only men in the army with breeches that aren't in tatters."

"I give credit to Tullia. She's the one who organized the packing. Had it been up to me, we would have frozen ere this, for we would have come away with little, and no winter clothing at all. All I wanted to do was to follow you. And now Tullia has found someone to follow." She described Prince Freedom, and Silas reacted with the same surprise she and her brothers had. "I've only been gone a short time, and yet Tullia has found a new life. Did anything else happen while I was away?"

"Just some evenings of dancing when I wished you were here to partner me."

Silas groaned—such assemblies were not his favorite diversion, but it was some compensation to be able to watch Addie's graceful movements.

Their chance to slip away to their room was lost when Ad and Justin, who were at headquarters this day, came out to greet Silas and to question him about his trip.

"We'll be alone later," Addie murmured, though she was no less frustrated than he, and she knew if her siblings weren't so anxious for news, they would be more sensitive to the moment. But she was as interested as they when Silas began to talk.

"The Boston house is still rented and all is in order on the farm. The last harvest was good. Your business interests"—he corrected himself at Justin's grunt of impatience—"*our* interests are all well tended, but with the lack of hard money growing worse every day, we must expect to receive payments in Continental paper before too long. And that means our income will be much diminished in value."

"We still have silver in reserve, don't we?" Addie asked.

"Yes, and I brought some coin back. But we have no way of knowing how long the war will go on, so we must be careful." He smiled ruefully and put his hands up, pretending to fend off Addie before she could protest. "I know, we are not prone to expensive vices as it is. We don't gamble or drink to excess, and I keep no greedy mistress, nor do your brothers, as far as I know."

Justin gave him a sharp jab on the arm. "That might change if you've truly brought me decent breeches."

"I do not understand why your breeches must be in good repair if your intention is to take them off," Addie observed.

Justin and Ad were shocked for an instant, and Addie and Silas exchanged a look of amusement.

"Marriage has made my wife bawdy," Silas said with obvious pleasure, but then he sobered. "There is more news for us from Boston. It's awkward. Now that Darius is so notorious a Tory, his right to the properties Marcus deeded to him is in question. I'm sure everything would have been confiscated by local authorities were it not for us. But since we are with the Continental Army, there is a chance the properties will come our way. Nothing is clear now. No one knows what the final disposition of Loyalist properties will be, any more than anyone knows how the war will end. But, at least, I think we will be consulted before anything is decided."

They all considered this in silence, sharing a feeling of unease rather than triumph. Marcus had been precise in his arrangements. And he had been generous to his and Lily's children, despite the fact that he considered their actions treasonous. Likewise, he had rewarded Darius, as he wished to do, for his loyalty. To them, though Darius was actively their enemy and though they had feared just this circumstance, what Marcus had decreed about his property should stand, no matter the shifting currents of war. For it to be otherwise made it seem as if they were picking Marcus's bones, as if he were dead.

Justin stirred restlessly and shifted the subject to the public mission that had taken Silas to New England with General Knox.

"General Knox did his best, and I hope some good will come of it. He proposes that Springfield, Massachusetts, is the most favorable place in New England for a cannon factory and a powder laboratory. And he asked all four New England states to provide more men for the army, but there are problems with that. For instance, Massachusetts has already provided a good many men. And with both our army and the enemy's in winter quarters, it is difficult for most to see the purpose of early recruitment. It is as if they think the army should spring forth fully organized at the first sign of renewed campaigning. Finally, and perhaps most importantly, some of the states are giving such generous bounties for men to join their militias, they make the bounty offered by the Continental Congress seem paltry. Massachusetts is offering eighty-six and two-thirds dollars per man, and that is more than four times what Congress will give a man for signing up."

Addie and her brothers considered how much more difficult a late enlistment of soldiers would make the task of forging an army for the next campaign and, worse, that sufficient men might not come.

Silas rubbed his face wearily. The travails of winter travel were catching up with him, and he cast a longing look at Addie.

Ad intercepted the look and said to Justin, "We ought to be getting back to our duties. Silas may be free for what is left of the day, but we are not."

With an abstracted air, Justin agreed, still thinking of recruitment problems.

"I do have time to see to the disposition of the baggage," Ad said. "We will see you on the morrow."

Silas breathed his heartfelt thanks.

Mistress Dolby welcomed Silas home warmly, and she didn't blink an eye when he told her that he and Addie were retiring to their room and asked that she explain to Tullia they would see her in the morning.

Addie lagged behind long enough to beg hot water from the kitchen fireplace. She knew Silas would want to wash away the grime of travel and that he would be perfectly willing to do so with the icy water that would be waiting in the pitcher in their chamber. But Addie had it in mind to pamper her husband.

Silas had already stripped down to his breeches when she arrived with the hot water. "That will feel good," he said, eying the steaming bucket.

"Better than you know," Addie purred. "Let me care for you."

Silas was spellbound by the glow in her eyes. He allowed her to lead him to the bed, and he sat down and watched as she added wood to the embers in the fireplace and coaxed the flames higher. She put a square of linen down on the hearth and filled the washing basin with hot and cold water, blending them until she was satisfied with the temperature. Then she returned to him, pulled him to his feet, and led him to stand on the cloth where the fire was dispelling the winter chill. She held her hands together to warm them before she ran them lightly down his chest and began to unfasten his breeches.

Silas shivered at her touch, though not from cold. She was touching him gently, but his body was so sensitive to her, it was as if streaks of fire radiated from every contact, and he wasn't sure he could control his response enough to allow the seduction to continue.

He sighed as she stripped the last of his clothes from him, teasing with her hands as she knelt and pulled his breeches and stockings down. She stroked his feet as she lifted first one and then the other so that he could step out of the clothes.

Then her hands traveled back up the inside of his legs, slowly, slowly, until her fingers encircled him.

"You are beautiful, husband, every inch of you." There was laughter as well as passion in her voice.

"Every inch of me will be swiftly diminished if you continue so," Silas muttered, but her laughter eased the sharp edge of his need. A sweet languor flooded through him, as if they had all the time in the world, and suddenly he understood that that was exactly what she intended.

No matter that they had known and loved each other before the war began; all their married life had been colored and dictated by the war, by the battle just fought or the one to come. But Addie was intent on stealing time from it.

Looking down at her, Silas wondered when he had last seen her so clearly, or if he ever had. She was kneeling before him, gazing up at him, and yet, he felt as if he were the supplicant. Her face was at once young and ancient, her expression an enticing blend of love, desire, and mischief. Her gown was in sorry shape, but it was no more than a worn shell around the beauty of her. There was nothing voluptuous about her form. If such had ever been possible, the constraints of war had eclipsed it. But all the attenuated lines—the graceful arch of her neck, her delicate shoulders, the slight but insistent curves of her body, and her clever hands caressing him with easy familiarity—all of this was Addie and all he would ever need or want from a woman.

She bathed him with complete absorption, stopping now and again to lick at the moisture on his skin. She savored the various textures of him—the taut skin of his neck, the smoothness of his back, the silk beneath his arms and the crisp hair on his chest, the firm sculpture of his buttocks. She followed the furred line that bisected his muscled belly and then widened to frame his rigid sex. She felt the heat of his desire flowing from his body, felt her own heat rising to meet his until, when she touched him, it was as if his hands and mouth were tracing her own flesh. And soon they were when Silas could no longer govern his need.

He stripped her clothes from her and pulled her down on the bed with him, changing the slow rhythm she had led to the swift pace of his passion. This was one dance he knew well. Unable to wait any longer, he plunged into her, thrusting hard and deep again and again, her body taking him in, welcoming him without restraint until he shuddered with the force of his release and felt her tremors echoing his.

When he had caught his breath and regained enough strength to focus on Addie again, any fear that he had been too rough was dispelled by her expression. She looked so content, so pleased with herself and with him, he was startled into laughter.

"Perhaps I should go away more often. I will ask General Knox to allow me to accompany him on his next mission."

"Then Knox will think you are disaffected with me and wish to be apart from your shrewish wife." Her lazy smile belied her words, and both of them could hear General Knox's amusement when she had flown into Silas's arms.

"No one will ever think that, not as long as I draw breath." His humor was eclipsed by amazement that his hunger for her was so swiftly renewed.

Addie knew she would have to give Silas the news of her father, knew it would bring him the same mixture of relief that Marcus, Mary, and the children were safe, and hurt that he had not seen fit to send them word. But she did not have to tell him now. She did not have to do anything except steal this time to love her husband.

She let everything go—the cold, the winterscape of the army's encampment, the precariousness of their lives—everything except Silas. He filled her body, her soul, her mind, and her heart until he was the universe, and the beat of his heart was the pulse of the stars.

Chapter 6

To Addie's joy, Silas was not required to accompany Knox when he went off to inspect forts along the Hudson River. Instead, she and Silas settled in and worked at the pretense of being a normal married couple, not members of an army that would surely be annihilated before long if many more men did not flock to its banners.

Addie wrote the letter to Marcus, but her brothers and Silas added their signatures with hers. In the letter, she told her father of Quentin's death, of why the miniatures were being sent, and she expressed gratitude that their family had reached England safely. She allowed not one word of recrimination for Marcus's refusal to send them word, but neither did she shy away from the truth.

> *We are strong and well. We do not falter nor will we fail in our cause. But we will mourn forever what we have lost, not only our dear Quentin, but also your presence and kind counsel. Though you are far from us in body, you are never distant from our hearts.*

They agreed that there was nothing to be gained by arguing anew the principles of the American cause. The time when Marcus would listen to their political views was long past, had been past before the first shots had been fired. But they hoped that the collection of portraits, each little oval so lovingly and skillfully painted by Quentin, would remind Marcus that they were still part of his family.

However much they missed Marcus, the reality of their lives was in Morristown, passing the days until the next campaign would begin. And because Addie was so happy to be with Silas, she was pleased when Ad told her that General Washington had sent for Martha.

"He does not demand that she come, only suggests it, so perhaps she will not. It is a hard journey in winter, and she has family obligations aplenty at Mount Vernon," he said.

"How little you know of women," Addie teased. "She will come because there is no place she would rather be than with her husband."

Then suddenly they all knew terror that was worse than any they had known since the war had begun. General Washington fell ill with a putrid sore throat, the infection worsening so quickly the big man lost all his strength within a matter of hours. His fever soared, and his throat closed until he could scarcely draw breath.

They had seen him sit his saddle with steady grace and little respite for days at a time and still have the energy to complete reports to Congress, while aides far younger than he staggered from exhaustion. They had seen him dance for hours after more than a full day of work. And they had come to depend on his enormous endurance and vigor. They had never seen him like this, helpless and beyond speech. His slave Billy tried to assure them that the general would get well as quickly as he fell ill, but the dread in his eyes stole all conviction from his words.

Washington's staff kept the news as secret from the encampment as they could, but among themselves, they had to face the fact that within a matter of hours, they could be without the one man who had the power to bind them together and lead them on against impossible odds. Without him, their cause could be lost so swiftly, they would be hanged for treason before spring had thawed the snow.

But to a man, fear for their own necks was overwhelmed by grief. Ad's throat ached so badly from unshed tears, it was as if he were suffering from the same malady that was killing the general. In the candlelight, he could see the sheen of tears in his brother's eyes and in the eyes of their fellow officers. The night was deepening, and they were all aware of how often death came to steal life in those dark hours just before the sun rose.

Finally a voice, so distorted by emotion that Ad couldn't recognize the speaker, asked from the shadows, "Who will lead us if you cannot?"

Washington's throat was too filled with pus and phlegm for speech, but his glazed eyes searched one face after another until his gaze settled with grave certainty and affection on Nathanael Greene.

Ad and Justin exchanged a look of understanding. General Greene, the fighting Quaker from Rhode Island, was a sound choice on all accounts, notwithstanding his mistake in judgment regarding Fort Washington. He was utterly loyal to Washington and the American cause, and he was from a state that was neither too far to the north nor too far to the south.

But Greene, obviously not sharing the others' high opinion of him and overcome by the honor done him, made a sound that was somewhere between a hysterical laugh and a despairing sob. He tried to say something to ease the terrible tension in the room, but his voice shook so much, the words were unintelligible. But his grip was firm as he took Washington's hot, dry hand in his own, and the men watching knew that he would risk everything to his last breath to shoulder Washington's burden, if it came to that.

They kept vigil as the slow minutes ticked by until the first glow of dawn, and then they drew a collective sigh of relief. Washington's breathing had eased, his fever was going down, and he was sleeping peacefully.

As soon as he could get away, Ad hastened to take the good news to his sister. She and Silas looked as exhausted as Ad felt, for they had been unable to sleep and had kept vigil together.

"He's going to recover," Ad announced, and with that Addie burst into tears, her body shaking with the force of the release as Silas held her. Both of the men felt helpless in the face of this uncharacteristic outburst from her.

"The smallpox has been so bad in the camp, but most have been inoculated now, and, anyway, I didn't worry about General Washington because he is protected for having had the disease long ago." Addie's voice was so unsteady and muffled against Silas, the men had to strain to understand her. "But this, he has nearly perished from a sore throat! Anything might take him from us. Anything! Some other ailment that runs out of control or a shot from an enemy gun—the general

is so large and easy a target! He could die as swiftly as Quentin did!"
She jerked away from Silas and clapped her hands over her mouth, as
stunned as the men by her outburst.

Silas drew her back against him, gently stroking the tears from
her face. "All will be well, sweetheart. The general is a strong man.
When we go into battle again, he will be there." He did not allow
a trace of doubt in his voice. He understood that for her, as for her
brothers and himself, devotion to Washington went beyond political
or military loyalty.

For the umpteenth time, Silas wished he had more to offer his
wife, specifically a loving family of his own so that he could send her
to them to be indulged for a while, away from army life, but the best
he could do was to suggest that she go to Castleton.

Just in time, he stopped himself from saying it, knowing what
her reaction would be. She was usually so strong for all of them, it
had shaken him and Ad to see her so distraught, to hear her mention
Quentin's death. But she had the right to let down her guard now
and then without being threatened with exile, which was exactly how
she would view it. She had proven already that she would endure any
hardship to remain with him and her brothers.

"My apologies," Addie said. "Such a foolish reaction when the
news is good."

"It is the truth when I tell you that there was not a dry eye at
headquarters these past hours," Ad told her. "I hope never to pass so
terrifying a night again."

"The general needs his lady beside him. I hope she arrives soon,"
Addie said, making Silas doubly glad he had not proposed Virginia to her.

Once his fever had broken, the general began to recover rapidly, but
no one could deny the benefit that Martha's timely arrival provided.
She had scarcely removed her traveling cloak before she was in the
kitchen, concocting a fragrant brew of molasses and onions that had
previously been efficacious when her husband had ailed with a throat
or chest complaint.

Everyone on the staff was relieved. It was easy to see how much
comfort Martha's mere presence brought to their leader, and in her

quiet way she was firmly in charge of the general within minutes of her arrival. It was a responsibility the staff was only too happy to relinquish.

When Martha arrived in mid-March, the grip of winter was just beginning to wane. Weeks later, in May when spring was on the land, more Virginians appeared in camp. Among Colonel Bland's cavalry of well-dressed riders on magnificent horses were Harry Lee and Hart and Reeves Castleton.

"Heaven save us! There's another one," Tench exclaimed to Ad and Justin when he first saw Reeves, who looked so much like the tawny Valencourts he knew. "If you count your sister, and I certainly would, you are on your way to having a regiment of your own."

For Addie and her brothers, the arrival of their cousins was a wonderful reunion though somewhat embarrassing in its generosity. For besides news from Castleton, delicacies from Castleton's larder, and two new gowns of homespun for Addie, Hart and Reeves had brought far more lavish gifts—sleek, powerful thoroughbreds from Castleton's notable stable. With both sides of the conflict desperate for good mounts, the horses were even more valuable here than in their native Virginia.

These horses from Castleton, with bloodlines that traced back to English champions, would have been judged prizes in peacetime; in war they became invaluable. There were two chestnut geldings and two mares, one bay, one black.

"Papa wants you to have the black mare—her name's Nightingale—and your brothers and Silas can decide for themselves about the others," Hart told Addie. "Where is your husband, by the way? Is he in camp? Sissy wants a detailed description from our unbiased eyes."

"Silas is about. He's with General Knox, but I'm sure the stir you have caused will bring him here before long." Addie had to make an effort to keep her voice steady, she was so touched that Silas had been included in Castleton's largesse. But then it occurred to her that Silas's pride was apt to make trouble.

She hadn't long to wait to see the proof of that. Ad chose the bay mare, Ember, for himself, and he and Justin decided Blaze, the taller of the two geldings, would be best for Silas.

"For all that he comes from Massachusetts stock, Silas is as long-legged as any Virginian," Justin told his cousins, "and he's getting to be just as fine a rider, too."

Hart and Reeves exchanged a glance, pleased that the Valencourts were still in such sympathy with Silas. They were very fond of Addie and wanted to be able to report home that she had married a good man. But some of their enthusiasm faded when Silas appeared and they were introduced to him, Silas being told by Ad in the same moment which horse was his. This tall, dark man was so stern-faced, despite his surface politeness at the introductions, the Castletons could scarcely imagine him with Addie.

Addie wanted to kick him in the shins and hug him at the same time. She could see his insecurities as plainly as if they were medals pinned to his coat.

"I thank you for the gesture, but I can't accept——" was as far as Silas got before the Castletons took matters in hand.

"I'm so sorry that things haven't been made clear to you," Hart said with elaborate courtesy.

Reeves fell in with him, saying, "It is difficult, we know, learning all the twists and turns of our family."

"But the fact is," Hart continued, "when you married Addie, she became a Bradwell, but you became not only a Valencourt but also a Castleton. In Virginia, *kin* is a short word that covers a lot of ground."

"Covers cousins to more degrees than all the tribes in the Bible," Reeves offered helpfully.

"So, you being kin to us, and Addie being very close kin, the giving of this wedding gift to you is just in the normal way of things." Hart paused, scratching his chin. "Of course, if these were normal times, we might have given you something that didn't walk here on its own four feet, a set of silver, or perhaps——"

"An armoire. A sturdy, highly polished one from England would have been just the thing before the war," Reeves suggested. "Or a carriage, though then you would have had to provide the horses."

Silas could not resist them, not with Reeves looking so much like Addie and her brothers, not with the two Castletons being so ridiculously charming, and not, particularly, because he could feel under their light-hearted banter their earnest desire that he accept the gift, and their offer of a place in their family as well.

"I surrender," he said, laughing. "That is as heavy a rain of well-directed shot as I've experienced since the war began. I thank you for the princely steed and for being my kinsmen."

The Castletons' reservations about Addie's choice of a husband faded. They saw the potent charm of the man, but, more, they saw the tenderness of the look he and Addie exchanged. They were immensely relieved that they would be able to write home that all was well with Addie's marriage.

Silas also met Harry Lee and tried not to flinch at the warmth he saw in Lee's greeting to Addie. Though Addie might judge her ties to the Lee family too distant to claim a relationship with that powerful family, Silas was sure Harry saw her and her brothers as no less deserving of his special favor than the Castletons, whose mother was of Lee blood. All in all, despite his acceptance of the Castletons' goodwill, Silas found this contingent of Virginians intimidating. It was not just the physical beauty they shared—a beauty he could see only too clearly when he imagined looking at them through Addie's eyes—it was their absolute self-assurance, as if it had never occurred to them to doubt their ascendancy in every area of social and political life.

"I am sure there are many things you would change in me, had you the chance," Addie began when they were at last alone and in bed that night, and it took all of Silas's will to remain supine and listen. "But there is so little I would change in you. I would not change this or this or this." Light as butterfly wings her fingers traced his face, his torso, and lower still, and then her hands settled on his chest and his forehead. "Most of all, I would not change anything in your heart and only one thing in your mind."

Her voice grew very soft. "I remember when you came to us. I remember that ragged little boy who appeared on my father's doorstep. I remember him, but he is gone. In his place, there is a fully grown man, a man of intelligence and passion and grace. I can see him clearly;

everyone can except for the man himself. That is the one thing I would change. I would that you could see yourself as the rest of us do."

He thought again of the proud, well-connected Virginians who had ridden into camp to join others of their kind, and he knew he would never be as sure of his position in the world as they were. But Addie was forcing him to see that he did not have to be exactly like them. Addie had met these men, had known others like them from the time she had first gone to Castleton as a child, and yet she had chosen to marry him.

He whispered her name and drew her close, his heart too full for further words, but he was more resolved than ever that she would never regret marrying him, no matter how uncertain the war had made their lives.

Silas was not the only one who had been discomposed by the new arrivals. Mistress Washington's coming had been taken as a signal by other officers' wives that they, too, should join their husbands. With their appearance plus the advent of Colonel Eland's cavalry and the advance of spring, life in the encampment took on a festive air, despite continued privations.

But the gaiety did not reach Justin. He felt so restless in his duties, each day was a struggle, and he took every opportunity to ride out with the foraging parties and liked nothing better than when the exercise involved a brush with the enemy.

He knew that by most measures of success, he and Ad had done well. They were both respected members of Washington's staff, each with the rank of lieutenant colonel. And Silas had been promoted to major and, as before, he would go in with the artillery the next time there was a battle. Justin envied him. He wanted to be attached to an active fighting unit, specifically to the cavalry with his cousins and Harry Lee, but he did not know how to leave the general's family.

Washington depended on his staff for the official duties they performed and for something less tangible, for the moral support and human companionship they gave to him. And the general had been hurt more than once by the defection of those on whom he relied. Because of that, he put great trust in those who had been with him the longest—the Valencourts, Tench Tilghman, Robert Harrison (an affable Virginian nicknamed the "Old Colonel" because he was older than most of the aides), and a couple of others. Justin felt guilty and small-souled to know this and still to want to quit his post. But the want gnawed at him constantly.

At least there had been recent additions to the staff, men Justin hoped would prove useful. One was Richard Kidder Meade of Virginia, who could ride like the very devil, even by Virginia's high standards, and the other was Alexander Hamilton, late of New York, but originally from the West Indies. His birth was rumored to be illegitimate, and his background was obscure, plainly not like that of the other aides, who were all from eminent families and mostly known to the general before the war. However, though just twenty-two years old, Hamilton, called "Hammy" by his friends, had already earned a reputation for being a fine artillery officer, having most recently distinguished himself at the Battle of Trenton. Silas had the highest praise for his skill.

Physically, Hamilton was one of the prettiest men Addie had ever seen. He was of slender build with delicate features and nearly violet eyes. She had first seen him in New York City, and his beauty had struck her then. But there was nothing feminine in his manner, and he was openly appreciative of women. Even when Addie was dressed in drab homespun, he made her feel as if she were clad in silk. But she was not overly charmed by the man, and she asked her twin his opinion.

Ad thought about it and shrugged. "He is intelligent and a man of action. And he has spoken French since childhood. Tench continues to insist that France will become more and more involved with us, beyond the Frenchmen who are joining the army individually, so another French speaker is all to the good."

"But?" Addie pressed when Ad hesitated.

"I doubt my view of him. Perhaps I have some jealousy of the fellow, for I swear he has done nothing untoward. Quite the contrary, he has made every effort to find his place among us. He is congenial and does not shirk duty. He believes in our cause. But I do not think he holds the commander in chief in the same regard as do the rest of us, and I think he will always have more of an eye to his own advancement

than to the good of others." He shrugged again, his discomfort with
his reservations vexing him. "Who am I to judge him when I am one
of those who have been handsomely served by family connections?"

Addie could not deny the justice of Ad's observation, and thinking
that, for all Silas's insecurities, he did not have to contend with bastardy,
she was resolved to suspend her unease about Hamilton.

"What about Justin?" she asked abruptly. "Even with her preoccupation with Mr. Freedom, Tullia has noticed something is amiss.
Our brother is behaving like a nervous colt."

Knowing denial was futile, Ad told her the truth. "He wants to
leave the general's family. He wants to join our cousins and Harry
Lee in the cavalry."

"Of course," she said, recognizing it as the obvious cause of Justin's
unrest. "And you would like to do the same." It was not a question.

Again Ad spoke honestly. "Very much. It is hard not to imagine
what it would be like to spend the days in the saddle instead of
hunched over endless piles of paper. But I would never leave the
general unless he asked me to go—never! I love the man like a father
and would serve where he has most need of me." He twisted his hands
together, rubbing at the calluses, the one from holding a quill now
more prominent than those from handling the reins of the horse. "Our
brother loves Washington no less than I, but he is different. He has
more restlessness inside of him, and it is making him miserable. But
he dreads requesting a change of assignment."

They fell silent, both aware of how little they could do to help
Justin with so thorny a matter.

Finally pressed by the knowledge that the summer campaign could start
at any moment, Justin asked for a private interview with the general.

His courage faltered as he took note of how harassed the general
looked. With the season advancing, the pace was quickening at headquarters so that the riding aides were in and out all day long, swords
and spurs a constant jangle, while the secretary aides scribbled away,
all of them working as hard as they could to get the army ready to

fight. Vegetables for the men and forage for the horses were becoming more plentiful by the day, but the numbers of men and beasts had to be increased, by avid recruitment of the former, by almost any means in the case of the latter. All else was in short supply, too, so that there was a constant push for everything from beef to uniforms to blankets to ammunition to hospital supplies and countless other necessities. Though Congress had returned from Baltimore to Philadelphia, placing the government closer at hand, it continued to be slow to respond to the army's needs.

"Your sister is proving to be of great value in helping to organize the camp women for hospital duties," the general said, putting down a sheet of paper.

Justin recognized Addie's handwriting, and his courage slipped a little more. In most matters, the general was straightforward, but Justin knew him well enough by now to know that he was not above manipulation when it suited his purpose, and his mention of Addie's efforts was hardly subtle. General Washington was telling him that other members of the Valencourt family were carrying out their duties.

Justin took a deep breath before he spoke. "Yes, Your Excellency, my sister is no less a soldier than my brother and I. She will not fail you or our cause. Nor will I or my Castleton cousins fail you, not as long as we live. But I ask your leave that I may join them in the cavalry."

Justin watched the expression of disappointment followed swiftly by rage in the general's face, and he braced himself for the white-hot blast that was sure to hit him. But instead, the rage vanished as swiftly as it had appeared.

"You remind me of myself years ago. When I marched out with General Braddock, I would have been in torment had I been confined to the duties of a secretary. Your request is granted. And may the God of armies protect you. Patsy and I would not wish to hear of injury to you, nor would we want to impart such news to your brother or your sister."

In those brief words, the general gave him such blessing, Justin felt his will caving in to the point that he wanted to take it all back and school himself to headquarters' duty for the duration.

But Washington forestalled him. "You must never give up the high ground when you hold it so firmly. Even the cavalry knows that."

"Your Excellency." Justin bowed and left.

He told his brother first, dreading his reaction, but Ad said, "Congratulations. I know how much you want this, and the cavalry will be fortunate to get you. Remember I told you months ago that you'd have a chance like this."

"So you did," Justin agreed, recalling his words. And the memory went a long way toward easing his conscience, for hurting Ad was the last thing he wanted to do.

But Ad was regarding him with clear eyes, and he answered before Justin could ask the question, "No, I won't ask for a new assignment. I am content to remain with the general."

And that was exactly what Ad told Washington when his commander asked him outright if he too wished to ride with Bland.

"Your Excellency, as long as you are satisfied with my work, I am satisfied to do it. I would not like to leave your family, not even to ride with my own."

"Well said. So be it." There was a wealth of relief in Washington's brief words.

While Ad felt more peaceful and resolute with every move he made to curtail his freedom to leave the general's staff, Justin felt increasingly unsure that he was making the right choice. He felt particularly strange when he gave the broad green riband to his brother. Worn across the breast over his waistcoat and under his coat, the riband had identified him to all as one of Washington's family. Giving up its slight weight was physically wrenching.

"Why don't you just fold it away?" Ad suggested.

With a rueful smile, Justin shook his hand. "Everything is so scarce, even something as small as this should not be wasted. Better you or one of the others get some use of it."

The other aides were cordial in their good wishes, and Justin could discern no envy at the choice he had made. At the general's direction, it was Tench who penned Justin's new orders, orders that would be confirmed by Congress and which included a complicated compromise on rank. Justin would become an acting captain but would retain the seniority of his lieutenant colonelcy. In this way, he could be part of Harry Lee's troop under Colonel Bland and yet would not lose the benefits, such as they were, of the rank he had earned while in Washington's service.

Tench saw the doubt in Justin and scolded him gently, "You are not going over to the enemy. You will still be serving the general and our cause... and on a fine new horse, too." Then his smile faded. "Your brother and I, we will be more useful here, but you belong with the cavalry. Godspeed."

The two men shared a hard, quick embrace, both of them knowing that in addition to Justin no longer being a part of the intimate group at headquarters, there was a good chance that he would often be absent from camp altogether since a pattern was already established of detaching troops of cavalry to where they could do the most good, though the danger to them increased the further they were from the support of the main army. Harry Lee and the others were presently some twelve miles away in a forward position with General Lincoln at Middlebrook.

Addie was as calm about Justin's decision as Ad had been, a circumstance that did not surprise Justin since the twins so often thought alike. But Addie spoke more to the heart of the situation. "I expect you feel a bit shaken, but I am sure you're doing what is best for you and for the army, too. Good cavalry officers are as rare as those who can write a legible hand. After all, many of the men from this region and New England have never ridden anything better than plow horses."

"Spoken like a true Virginian," Justin teased, the tension inside of him lessening.

"Or a Marylander like Tench," Addie allowed, and she giggled. "Oh, Justin! You won't be giving up your rank, you'll just be sitting on it."

Only then did Justin realize the amusing irony that his new horse was called Colonel, his sire having been General Wolfe, a stallion named for the tragic hero of the French and Indian War. He and Addie laughed until tears came into their eyes, and the mirth served as a release for Justin, easing his doubt.

Colonel Bland welcomed him, and the Castleton cousins and Harry Lee were delighted by Justin's choice.

"Not all Virginians are born in the state," Hart declared.

Reeves said, "We hoped a good horse from home would nudge at least one of you in the right direction."

"The twins are good riders, too. I doubt your sister's husband or our colonel would allow her to join us, but what about Ad?" There was a speculative gleam in Harry Lee's eyes.

"There is no chance of that." Justin was firm. "Ad insists he is content to remain on the general's staff, and I thank God for it! There is always so much work to do at headquarters, it is bad enough that I've left." He could trust only that the cavalry would prove useful to Washington here, unlike in New England where there had been little use for it.

In addition to Justin's joining them, the Castletons soon had something else to celebrate when they received news from home via one of the express riders' pouches of official and unofficial messages. Sissy's husband had not come north in order that he could wait with her for the birth of their first child, and now Sissy had been safely delivered of a son, Randolph James Fitzjohn.

Proud and relieved, Sissy's brothers managed to collect enough food and liquor to have a credible celebration in honor of their new nephew, delaying the event until they could visit Morristown and share with Ad and Silas.

When Silas returned to her late at night, Addie was hard put not to laugh at him. Silas was ever a controlled and sober man; she could not remember ever seeing him so tipsy. His efforts to be quiet and avoid waking her failed as he lurched through the door and stumbled against the bed, muttering, "Musn' wake Addie, musn'..."

"Addie is already awake," she told him.

"Oh, then I doan hav' t'be qui... qui-et." He sat and then sprawled backward on the bed. "Virninians drink as well as they ri... ride." He sighed gustily.

Smiling at his pronunciation, Addie drew his head into her lap, untying his queue ribbon and stroking his disheveled hair away from his face. She hoped one of the muffled sounds she'd heard had been his hat dropping to the floor and that he hadn't lost it on the way back. But it didn't really matter. She was glad he had been accepted by her cousins and had in turn accepted them enough to relax his guard in their presence.

"I use a want a baby, too," he confided.

Suddenly Addie was wary rather than amused, but she kept stroking his hair. "You did? But you changed your mind?"

She could feel the effort he was making to order his thoughts.

"No, still want 'em, mebbe lots, but differ'nt reason. Before thought I could send you away from this." One arm flailed in the darkness as if to encompass the whole encampment, and Addie caught it and pressed it firmly down across his chest before he could accidentally smack her with it. "If there were a baby, keep you safe. But you good soldier, good wife, an' I doan want you go away, not ever."

"Then if a baby comes, we'll both stay with you," Addie said, but her voice trembled, and she was swept by a great swell of love for him.

She had been delighted by Sissy's news from the time she had read of her cousin's pregnancy in a letter months before, but at the same time, she had felt some guilt because she herself had not conceived and because she was relieved that she hadn't. She wanted to stay with Silas and her brothers, and despite what she'd just said, a baby would make that very difficult. Though a considerable number of the common soldiers' wives stayed with their husbands for as long as they could, their children with them, women of her own station were seldom with the army once the winter encampment had broken up. This was particularly true for those with children; they either had to bring them with them to winter quarters or make provisions for their offspring to stay with relatives or friends, an arrangement that left most mothers ever anxious to return to their little ones.

Addie was well aware that her privileged position of remaining with the army was because General Washington allowed her to be there. She doubted he would be so indulgent were an infant involved.

In spite of being pulled this way and that about whether she would want to be carrying Silas's child now, she had begun to be more concerned that she had not conceived. But when she had broached the possibility that she might be barren, Tullia had dismissed her fears.

"You are just twenty years old, you've only been married a year, and this year hasn't been a normal one by any account. Don't be in such a hurry. Once babies start coming, women haven't time to think of much else." She had hesitated, reticence overtaking her usual bluntness. "And if it never happens, well, just you remember it isn't always the woman. Lady Washington had babies by her first husband, but she hasn't had any by the general, and I don't expect it's for lack of trying. It's not so unusual that way, either. I've known other times where a widow brought children with her to a new marriage but didn't have any more."

Addie had been a little shocked by Tullia's observations about the Washingtons because she wasn't in the habit of considering them as lovers, but then she had rebuked herself for being foolish; she had seen the Washingtons together enough to know that their bond was more than simple friendship. And Tullia's explanation had done what she intended; it eased Addie's fear of being barren.

She smiled in the darkness as Silas sighed again and fell asleep; it was certain they were not going to explore the possibility of conceiving a child during what was left of this night, and she suspected Silas would have some sharp curses for his "Virninians" when he awakened in the morning with a bad head.

Chapter 7

Spring 1777

Washington moved his headquarters south to Middlebrook at the end of May. There was a long forested ridge running east and west to provide a good defensive position, for Washington expected General Howe to come after them in the Jerseys once again.

Most of the army would be going into tents now, and Jacky Custis came to escort his mother, Lady Washington, home to Mount Vernon. Martha's departure was the signal to most of the other officers' wives to pack up and leave. The road to Mount Vernon led through Philadelphia, and it was important to the general that his wife be beyond that city before the British could block the way. The best guess at headquarters was that the redcoats would try to take Philadelphia in the new campaign. British transports at New York were seen being loaded, and that indicated the enemy planned to move by water as well as by land, though where the fleet was going was unknown.

Equally ominous was the intelligence that General Burgoyne, returned from England to Quebec, was to lead a large force southward toward Albany, New York, where he would expect to be joined by some of Howe's force coming up from Manhattan. If this were accomplished, New England would be cut off and the blow to the young nation's unity in war could be fatal.

Ad and the other aides knew how disturbed Washington continued to be about the jealousies over the commands of various divisions of the Continental Army, most of the trouble stemming from regional distrust. And the political reality was that many members of Congress seemed to take a fiendish delight in making major military decisions without consulting the commander in chief. To be sure, having suffered at the hands of an occupying army, there was a strong American bias against allowing even their own military establishment to have too much power, but in the view of Washington's aides, Congress seemed intent on making foolish, dangerous mistakes that at the very least further snarled Washington's already complicated job. The Castleton cousins told Ad that their father was near despair sometimes when he could not persuade his fellow representatives that they must trust Washington's judgment more.

To further add to the general's woes, Congress kept accepting the flood of European adventurers who appeared before them with letters of introduction from American agents abroad. Most of these Europeans had some military experience in their histories, but nearly all of them, for deigning to join the Americans, expected to be amply rewarded with hard money and a command. And most expected to be given rank that would elevate them above American officers. They did not heed that Congress had neither the money nor the regiments to give them and too often played sleight of hand with rank to the end that no one was sure of who superseded whom.

With the exception of a few good men, mostly French, who were serving with the engineers, most of the foreigners had made themselves thoroughly unwelcome, and Ad and the other aides would gladly have sent them back where they came from.

"I don't know why the general doesn't resign," Ad said to Tench one day as they labored over an especially demanding piece of correspondence destined for Congress.

"Ah, but you do know, if you think about it," Tench replied. "And Congress does, too. They know the man they've got. They know he is proud of his strengths, of his ability to finish the task, no matter how difficult it is."

"Are you accusing him of vanity?"

"Some, but only what a man needs in his position. It is more an affair of honor. Still, such strength can be played for a weakness by the unscrupulous, at least for a time. In the end, though, I believe it will come around again, and he will prevail."

"The philosopher secretary," Ad remarked, but he was comforted by his friend's attitude. Tench had no need for their commander to be perfect; he expected only that Washington would hold steady because he was a strong, competent man who knew his worth.

It was bound to raise the general's spirits that recruits were coming in to the Continental Army. It seemed there would never be enough and, as always, desertion continued to be a serious problem, but the growing numbers were certainly an improvement over the thin ranks of winter. Many officers who had chosen to spend their winter in more luxurious quarters than those of the Morristown encampment also returned to their posts. Whatever the general thought privately about these officers who had not shared the trials of winter with him, he was unfailingly warm in welcoming them back. He knew goodwill as well as good fortune would be needed to knit all of these pieces together into an effective fighting force to meet the British if they did make an attempt on Philadelphia.

Addie felt the same urgency in a different quarter. The more time she spent with the families of the soldiers, the more she respected their courage and pitied their straitened circumstances. There were trulls who plied their trade and too often spread disease, but most of the women in the camp were honest, poor, and hardworking, and they made do with very little. They served as laundresses, cooks, seamstresses, and nurses. Without them, the army would have been in trouble even more serious than usual, though official policy continued to vary from ignoring the women's presence altogether to issuing orders designed to get them out of the way or to at least limit their numbers.

Addie and Tullia kept on as they had been doing, helping with the children when they could, organizing groups of women to make bandages in anticipation of battles to come, trying as discreetly as possible to suggest healthy additions to the bland camp diet, but even if the people were willing to eat vegetables and greens, these foods remained in limited supply, although the growing season was advancing. Even basics such as salt, vinegar, and soap were still hard to come by.

Disease was a constant problem, too, though the cold weather had passed. Many of the country dwellers were fairly isolated until they joined the army, and they had little resistance to the contagions that came with large concentrations of people—thus dysentery, fevers, measles, and such were enemies as formidable as the British. And because mass inoculation was practical only in the winter when troops were mostly inactive and could be isolated, the threat of smallpox returned with the warmer weather and the new recruits.

Tullia was very proud of Addie. Because of Addie's social rank, because of having lost one brother to the cause and because of having two other brothers, a husband, and two close cousins serving with the Continental Army—no matter that there were also Tory connections—she would be granted respect with no effort on her part. But she was earning affection. She was greeted with smiles and nods of recognition everywhere she went in camp. There were even kindly meant jokes so that men could be heard to whisper overly loud when she was near, "Best be ready to run, that Mistress Bradwell will set you to washin' everything in sight does she catch you. Then she'll make you graze in the meadows with the horses," and other variations on her determination that they take care of themselves.

Tullia saw how Addie managed just the right degree of friendliness, avoiding being too familiar, which would have made the other women uneasy, and yet not being aloof either, and always showing enthusiasm for any recipe or skill or scrap of knowledge for surviving that the women shared with her.

Addie did her best to remember as many names as she could, though it grew increasingly difficult as she came in contact with more and more people. And one day, she was at first baffled when a wiry little man approached her, and blurted out, "Th' wife bid me tell you I came back. She made me promise. She' would'a come, her an' th' little ones, only she's too close to her time with th' new baby."

The hazy image sharpened in her mind, and she saw him standing off to the side, looking furtive and ashamed, as his wife tried to make her understand why they had to go. She remembered young Mistress Willis quite clearly with the infant in her arms and the child peeping from behind her skirt. And now she was going to have another baby.

"Oh, yes, you are Private Willis."

"*Willets*, ma'am," he corrected her nervously.

After a slight hesitation, she gave a small nod of complicity. Officers might manage to go home for the winter without repercussions, but for common soldiers like this one who left before their enlistments were up, the official punishment for desertion was hanging. However, if every American soldier who went home to tend to domestic affairs were hanged for it, there would be more executed than marching. And the easiest way around the problem was to enlist again under a different name or in a different region, which carried the added benefit of providing the soldier with a new enlistment bounty.

Addie didn't begrudge the man nor his family this second small windfall; she was amazed that he had returned at all. "Private... ah, Willets, conditions were very bad when you left. They are scarcely better now. And you have a growing family. I do not wish to offend, but will you tell me why you have returned? Was it the tax on tea, the restrain on shipping and trade, or some other specific?"

Willis regarded her steadily for a moment before he replied, "Never drunk no tea; it were ever too dear even when th' King tried to dump it cheap on us. An' I never had nothin' to do with ships or what's in 'em. But I'm a sensible man, an' there ain't no sense at all in havin' th' King who lives all those miles away across th' sea tellin' me what to do an' sendin' his redcoats an' his Hessians to make me do it. Mebbe it were fittin' all that time ago when we were just beginnin', but not anymore. We are a country now, all on our own." His thin shoulders straightened.

Addie thought of all the philosophical arguments that had raged in her family as to why or why not loyalty was owed to England, and she was humbled by how direct this man was in his reasoning. She envied him. He would never have to justify his actions by elaborate circumlocutions of the mind; for him, the King had become a bully, and Private Willis was prepared to risk his life rather than bow to a bully, even one who was supported by thousands of troops.

"All General Washington needs is that men of your resolve continue to enlist, under whatever names. With such purpose, we cannot fail."

Addie could see that he was at once pleased and embarrassed by her praise, but then he flushed darker red as his hands fumbled through his pack, and she had no idea what he was about until he handed her a packet carefully wrapped in worn paper.

"Th' wife made this for when your firstborn comes, to keep th' little one warm."

When Addie unwrapped the package, she found an exquisitely made infant's quilt. The colors of the squares were muted because the Willises had nothing but homespun, home-dyed fabrics, and the texture was as soft as velvet from many washings before the original garments had been consigned to the scrap basket.

It didn't matter that she and Silas might never have children; what was important was that despite the endless chores that measured her days, Mistress Willis had found the time and cared enough to make this lovely gift.

Addie brushed the edge of the quilt against her cheek. "I have never received anything so fine before," she said, meaning it. "Please tell your wife for me when you see her again."

Both of them were aware that he might not return safely to his wife, or indeed, that his wife might not survive the birth of the expected child. But neither of them spoke of these possibilities. Instead, he said, "I'll tell her. It'll please her that you favor her work."

Addie hoped not only that Willis would keep safe, but also that he and others like him would stay with the army long enough to be of use. She could well imagine that many men would leave out of sheer frustration.

The roads, such as they were, had long since hardened from the muddy thaw of winter and the ruins of spring and could now support men, horses, gun carriages, and wagons. As predicted, General Howe moved troops in large numbers into the Jerseys, and in late June, General Lord Cornwallis was set out to encircle and drive the Continentals out of Middlebrook, but he never got into an advantageous enough position to make the plan work.

Howe's movements were baffling, leaving Washington and his staff to speculate that Howe was waiting for the Americans either to try to march north to assist in repelling Burgoyne's forces or to instigate a full attack on the British in the Jerseys. However, neither idea made much sense since Howe had far more soldiers than Washington, despite the fact that winter in and around the city of New York had not been kind to the occupying forces, inflicting outbreaks of smallpox and other contagions on them.

Instead of a major campaign on either side, the summer's action was a series of alarms and excursions, of marching hither and yon and back again, raiding back and forth in the Jerseys and along the Hudson, but never meeting in main force.

The truth was that Washington hadn't the resources to attack New York or Howe's deployed army and must wait for the British to make a major move, then do his best to counter it. Even to march north to assist in the defense against Burgoyne was not an option for the commander in chief, for such action would leave the way open to Philadelphia.

Whether or not Washington had the military means to keep the enemy from taking Philadelphia was beside the point. Philadelphia was serving as the capital of the young nation, and after the loss of New York in the previous year, it was politically untenable that Philadelphia should also be lost. It was yet another case of politics and military reality being far apart. At headquarters they worked feverishly over various plans, but they were all aware of the odds against them, odds made particularly bad because the British controlled the waters with their navy and could thus move troops with far more ease than could the Americans.

Ad didn't want to admit it, even to himself, but he envied his brother because at least Justin was spending his days in the thick of things, riding hard in cavalry raids, which, if they accomplished nothing decisive, at least pricked and stung the British and garnered much-needed supplies.

For his part, Justin was more sure by the day that he had made the right decision. His new assignment pleased him in every way. He fed on the swift, hazardous action. The jingle of spurs and bits, the creak of leather and thunder of hooves were music to him. The hot scent of sweating horses and the dry rise of dust stirred by their passing were perfume. Even when he had been in the saddle for hours, he did not feel weary; rather, he felt as if he were as close to flying as a human could get, somehow at once weightless and powerful.

His euphoria was brutally checked one afternoon when he burst through the trees with the others, riding down on the enemy. The report had been of British regulars, but instead, they were faced with regulars and Valencourt's Rangers, and as if his eyes had suddenly developed magnified vision, Justin saw his half-brother Darius riding at the head of the troops, mouth open to shout orders as he caught sight of the Continentals.

Valencourt's Rangers were earning a reputation for savage fighting, being as they were prominent Loyalists fueled by personal hatred and apt to lose all if the Rebels triumphed. All of this flashed through Justin's mind, but the only thought he could hold in his head was that Darius looked so much like Marcus, it was as if their father were in the battle.

Suddenly Reeves was beside him, a sharp nod of his head telling Justin he knew whom they faced, and it was as if Justin could hear his cousin saying, "Steady on. It's just another battle like any other."

Justin saw the shock on Darius's face as he recognized them, though he probably thought it was Justin and Ad who were coming at him.

Carbines were discharged on both sides, and then the riders closed on each other, and sabers shattered the light until they were too coated with blood to reflect the sun.

Colonel was a bold mount, unafraid of contact with other horses, willing to work in close and even ram against an enemy's beast when Justin asked him. Using his knees and his heels, hardly having to use the reins at all, Justin was able to concentrate his energy into his sword arm. Parry, thrust, slash, vary the stroke and the rhythm in counterpoint to the opponent's actions, watch the back, ignore the ache that ran up the arm clear to the neck and jaw after long sword play. A blade skittered over the leather of his boot, and he struck with his own weapon while the man's arm was still down. Blood soaked instantly into the green coat, and the man pitched out of the saddle.

Justin felt a streak of fire along his ribcage, but he didn't look down to see how badly he'd been cut. It was on his left side and did not interfere with his sword arm nor with his handling of the reins with his left hand. The pain faded as swiftly as it had come.

He was face to face with his brother, his blade coming up to parry Darius's. He saw the battle lust in the dark eyes and knew one of them was going to die. Their eyes locked as tightly as their blades, and suddenly Darius yelled, "No!" and jerked his saber back, leaving himself open to Justin's attack. Justin nearly followed through, pulling back at the last second.

For an instant they stared at each other as if the battle were not raging around them, as if time had slowed and they were the last two men on earth. Then Darius backed his horse, raised his sword in angry salute, and wheeled away.

It all happened in the blink of an eye, and the next thing that penetrated Justin's consciousness was that they were being ordered to retreat. They had been more than holding their own, but Justin didn't stop to question the order as they raced for the shelter of nearby trees. He turned his head for a brief backward look and saw more British dragoons coming in support of the enemy.

"Come on, Colonel!" he urged, and the chestnut leaped forward with an added burst of speed. Justin bent low in the saddle to avoid the slap of branches.

The headlong dash ended as they realized there was no pursuit, the enemy obviously leery of being lured into an ambush in the thick brush.

"They know us well. We always have hundreds of men in reserve," Harry Lee commented wryly, and the men around him laughed, the stress of battle evident in the volume. "That's a damned fine horse you..." Harry's voice trailed off as he came up beside Justin, and then he swore, "Christ's blood! Or rather, yours. How badly are you hurt?"

Hart and Reeves were suddenly there, too, staring at Justin in consternation. He looked around, seeing that there were other wounded and one man who was slung over his saddle, his horse being led. As the excitement of the battle wore off, the pain in his side returned, burning down his ribs, and he felt the wetness of the blood that was soaking his shirt and jacket and running down to his breeches. But he was more dazed by the encounter with Darius than by his wound.

"Did you see that? He pulled back?" Justin said. He was not aware he was swaying in the saddle.

"Actually, we are the ones who pulled back," Harry said, eying him with increasing alarm.

"No, I mean Darius," Justin corrected him fretfully, biting back a groan as Colonel sidled, jolting him.

Hart and Reeves exchanged a look, and Harry said, "If there was a pursuit, we'd know by now. Justin, it's safe to stop here." When Justin did not respond, Harry reached out and brought Colonel to a stop. "Justin, we need to stop to see to your wound."

Justin blinked at them, trying to understand, but things were growing hazier by the second. His cousins hauled him unceremoniously from the saddle and laid him on the ground, stripping off his jacket and pulling up his shirt to expose a gaping slash so deep that two of his ribs were visible, gleaming gray-white through the gore.

Hart blanched at the gruesome sight, but Reeves was all practicality as he surveyed the damage. "You're lucky. Nothing vital has been hit. We just need to stop the bleeding."

Harry was already tearing strips from Justin's ruined shirt, and he and Reeves exchanged a look, silently acknowledging that Justin could just as soon die of blood loss as of organ damage. They bound the wound as tightly as they could, causing Justin enough pain in the process to rouse him somewhat from his stupor, but his mind remained fuzzy. He saw how worried his cousins and Harry Lee were, but why seemed to be just beyond his grasp. Then he thought he had it.

"Don't tell Addie. She'll worry."

"No, of course we won't tell Addie," Hart lied.

"Let's see how good this horse of yours really is," Harry said. He was the lightest of them, so he got on Colonel, and Hart and Reeves lifted Justin up to sit in front of him.

Justin wanted to say he could ride by himself but found that he didn't even have the strength to form the words. It took all of his concentration to sit in the saddle. Even the pain was being washed away by the dark wave that swirled around the edges of his vision and then closed down the last spots of light.

It seemed only moments later when he opened his eyes again, and he thought he must have dropped his reins until he remembered that Harry Lee was guiding Colonel. He tried to straighten in the saddle and gasped at the pain.

"Just lie still or you'll pull at your stitches." Addie's voice trembled, but her hands were steady as she lifted his head enough to give him water and then wiped his face with a cool cloth.

He frowned up at her. "Weren't supposed to tell you."

She wrung out the cloth and dipped it in the water again, bathing his shoulders and the part of his chest that wasn't covered with bandages, using the rhythm of her hands to calm herself. "You were rather a large package to keep secret. The wound is clean, but you lost a lot of blood. It will take some time for you to regain your strength."

And don't you frighten me like that ever again, she wanted to scream at him. When he had been brought in, his clothes had seemed more blood than cloth, and he hadn't stirred even when they had cleaned and sutured his wound.

Hearing other voices speaking to him, Justin turned his head slightly and saw that Tullia, Ad, and Silas were there, and that all of them looked very tired, though they were smiling. Vaguely he realized he was in the farmhouse room that was serving as Addie and Silas's newest temporary home.

The first words he had spoken to Addie had taken so much energy, he had to fight to ask, "How long?"

He stayed awake just long enough to hear, "Two days."

He slept for most of the next twenty-four hours, rousing only to drink the water and broth Addie or Tullia held to his mouth. He had some fever, but it was not dangerously high, and the pain of the wound was bearable unless he moved unwisely.

He was touched and flattered to awaken once to see General Washington looking down at him.

"I trust you will heal quickly," the general said, a smile underlying the gruff tone of command, and it was typical of him that he refrained from pointing out that had Justin stayed on the staff, he might be in better health.

As soon as Justin could think clearly, he was impatient to be in the saddle again, but he knew how fortunate he was. Most of all he wanted to tell his siblings about Darius.

The twins knew that Justin had been in a battle with Valencourt's Rangers. And because Justin had mumbled Darius's name a few times before he regained consciousness, they dreaded learning that it was their half-brother who had wounded Justin. Their cousins and Harry Lee had done nothing to alleviate this fear because they suspected the same thing, particularly because Justin had mentioned Darius right after he'd been wounded. Thus, when Justin told the twins what had really happened between him and Darius, it took them a moment to accept it.

"He didn't do that?" Addie gestured at Justin's bandaged side.

And Ad asked, "He stopped the action?"

Justin frowned at them. "Isn't that what I just told you?"

"Yes, but we thought…"

Justin interrupted his sister. "You thought he was a savage Tory who would let nothing stay his hand. I did, too." He took a deep breath, wincing as his ribcage expanded. "It was he, not I, who stopped. I had no thought of that. I would have gone on fighting him. As it was, I had all I could do to halt my own blade in time. He risked all, leaving himself open to my attack." He closed his eyes, seeing Darius's face again. "He looks so much like Papa! You saw him on your way back from Virginia, before war began, but it has been a long while for me, and surely he must be looking more like Papa with every passing year, for I don't remember the likeness being so close before."

The twins thought back to the last time they had seen Darius and realized in the same instant that Darius had always favored their father, as had Quentin, but before the war, it had had no special significance.

"Thank God for it!" Addie exclaimed. "Did he not look so like Papa, you might have struck when he would not."

Justin shook his head wearily. "Oh, Addie, I'm relieved, too, that neither of us killed the other. But war cannot be waged like that. I have sworn my loyalty and pledged my honor to our cause, as Darius has to his. To refuse to fight is a violation of loyalty and honor."

Addie wanted to protest that any cause that demanded fratricide deserved no loyalty, but she had to accept that that was too simple an ideal for this civil war. Her heart had hardened and she had become soldier enough so that she wanted no words from her to haunt Justin or to stay his sword when it needed to strike, even if their half-brother was the target.

"In order to keep you or Ad or Silas safe, I would kill Darius myself," she said, and she saw his gratitude for her support.

July 4 marked the first anniversary of Congress's public release of the Declaration of Independence, and there was as much trepidation as celebration. With that document, they had ended all hope of reconciliation with England, yet it was more than two years since the opening shots had been fired at Lexington, and their chances of prevailing in their fight for independence seemed to lessen by the day.

Still, there was some satisfaction in observing that whatever Howe had marched into the Jerseys to gain had eluded him. He had earned the particular enmity of the populace, as well as the Continental Army, because he had allowed his army to plunder the countryside. Everywhere the British Army marched, officers and common soldiers were picked off by hidden gunmen, stragglers were cut off and captured, and life was made generally miserable for this far superior force.

After nearly a month of futile maneuvering, Howe quit the Jerseys. Beginning on July 5, great numbers of British and Hessian troops, and even a regiment of light horse, were observed being loaded aboard transports, though they did not sail for more than two weeks. The Americans kept a close watch on the operation, and among the regiments, they noted Traverne's Highlanders.

"I'll wager your Scotsman wishes he were home in the cool mist," Ad teased his twin.

Addie snapped her standard response, "He's not my Scotsman!" but she did think of him and his men with reluctant pity. She thought they should not be here fighting against the Americans, but she could remember John Traverne's strong presence only too clearly, and she did not like the idea of his being weakened and perhaps killed by the fevers that would undoubtedly flourish on the ships. The weather was stiflingly hot, and conditions would be hellish for men and horses alike.

When the ships finally sailed on July 23, there was still the question of where they were going. The best that Washington could do was to keep watch, wait, and hope that more men continued to come in to his army than to desert from it.

Meanwhile, Burgoyne's force had continued its inexorable march southward, taking Forts Ticonderoga and Edward on the way as the Americans abandoned them. The loss of Fort Ti was particularly dismaying because in the public mind it was a major fortress, despite the reality of a garrison too small and too badly supplied to stand against the enemy. Burgoyne's mission seemed to be to terrify all American sympathizers while overrunning American outposts on the way. Terrifying the countryside was not a difficult mission since Burgoyne, in addition to British regulars and Tories, had with him a large number of Native American allies—Algonquin, Abnaki, Ottawa, and Iroquois, the latter being a league of six tribes. Despite the fact that Native Americans had been pushed back everywhere that white settlers had landed on the American continent, the mere mention of unrest among them was enough to send whole frontier communities fleeing for shelter.

Then the weapon of terror turned back against the British when a Tory with Burgoyne's army, David Jones, sent some Native Americans to escort his fiancée, Jane McCrae, safely to camp, but instead they returned carrying her scalp. No one except the Native Americans themselves knew exactly what had happened, and they offered no excuse. The best guess was that the original party had met with a few others; they had argued over who should escort the girl and what reward there should be; and they had solved the problem by killing and scalping her.

It didn't matter that Jane McCrae had been set to marry a Tory. It didn't matter that such atrocities had occurred before and undoubtedly would again. But somehow her story caught fire in people's minds, outraging Loyalists and Patriots alike. And men who had thought to tend their shops or their fields and ignore the war bid farewell to their families and came in to the Northern Army and to Washington's force.

Tullia reported that Prince was behaving as if Native Americans were on the way to kill every woman in sight, and Addie saw the effect of the story on her menfolk and tried to be patient. With no subtlety at all, Ad suggested his sister not wander too far when she was exercising Nightingale; Justin fabricated excuses to keep Addie close by; and Silas found so many reasons to check on her, Addie finally said, "Burgoyne's Indians are not going to find me here! They are far to the north, and I have all General Washington's army around me. I am perfectly safe from everything except you and my brothers' fussing."

In answer, Silas wrapped his arms around her and laid his cheek against her hair, but before his head came down against hers, she glimpsed the stark horror in his eyes, and she could no longer avoid imagining what it had been like for Jane McCrae. She must have been nervous in the company of the Native Americans even when she had thought she was being taken safely to her fiancé, and then had come the moment when it had all gone wrong. The reports had said that Jane's body had been terribly mutilated in addition to the scalping, but Addie hoped that a blow to the head had freed Jane from the scene, that she hadn't known the unspeakable things that were being done to her.

Addie shuddered in Silas's arms, trying to force the images away. Day by day, the savagery of war was eating away all that had once been peaceful, secure, and familiar until Addie felt stripped of everything except the frantic need to keep Silas and her brothers safe. She was as anxious for them as they were for her. It was hard to let any of them out of her sight even though she could not follow them about as they performed their military duties.

When General Howe and the British fleet weighed anchor and put out to sea, heading south, Washington quickly began to march his force south, too. Justin was growing stronger every day, but he was not yet fully fit, and Addie recognized it was her duty to stay behind with him at the farmhouse, though it was agonizing to watch Silas and Ad leaving without them. Tullia insisted on remaining with them, and

Addie was grateful for her company, though she wondered if Prince Freedom would always be so patient with Tullia's divided loyalties.

As it happened, those who remained behind missed nothing but frustration, for when Washington reached the Delaware on July 29, expecting to find that the enemy had gotten there before him, there was no news of the British at all, no sighting of them off the Delaware Capes, nothing. That raised the possibility that they were doubling back to sail up the Hudson River after all, which left the Americans no choice but to head back into New Jersey. When, at the end of the month, a message came that the British had been sighted at last off the Capes, the army went south again. But the British put out to sea, disappearing so completely that it seemed certain they were heading for Charles Town in the Carolinas.

By the time Justin, Addie, and Tullia rejoined the army, they found Silas and Ad ready to chew nails.

"We've been wearing out men, shoe leather, horses, and everything else without accomplishing a damn thing!" Ad swore.

Silas said, "I hope the men remember how to fight when the time comes."

"It's not as though the general has much choice unless the enemy sends him a copy of their plans," Addie pointed out mildly. She did not want to confess that her cowardly heart was quite satisfied by the lack of battles, but she could not deny the tension it was causing in Silas. Normally so patient, he grew more short-tempered by the day. He drilled his artillery unit mercilessly despite the heat, and he did not relax even when he and Addie were alone. Sometimes they sought shelter in a farmhouse, but more often they slept in their tent like most of the army, and Addie could scarcely imagine what it would be like to have a settled domestic life in a home of their own.

Their tent bore little resemblance to the large double marquee General Washington used, the confines of theirs so close, it was difficult to be anything but intimate. And yet, even when they retired for the night, Silas continued to review battle plans in his head. He didn't have to say anything to Addie about it; she could feel him doing it, could feel it in the restlessness of his sleep when he finally closed his eyes, could feel it most of all in the emotional distance that was growing between them, no matter how small the physical space they shared. The more Addie needed the comfort of his touch, the more Silas curled in on himself They made love rarely now, and when they did it was as if they had lost the music to the dance their bodies had performed so effortlessly from the earliest days of their marriage.

Finally one night, Addie's temper snapped after Silas had found his pleasure and rolled away while her body was still seeking.

"I am not a mare squealing to be serviced by any stallion!"

"Aren't you?" Silas asked, voice like silk, and then silence fell between them, thicker than the muggy heat of the night.

Addie blushed in the darkness as his words found their mark; she had been the one who had initiated the lovemaking, and she hadn't been subtle about it, wiggling against him, touching him—everything short of squealing aloud for service.

For his part, Silas loved Addie's wholehearted partnership in their joining, and to strike out at her for his own inadequacy was so alien to his nature, he felt as if some wicked other had asked the question.

"I'm sorry," they said in chorus, and then their words collided. "I was too quick…" "… too slow." "I didn't mean…" "I shouldn't have…"

And their thoughts raced parallel. Addie suddenly understood that it could be much easier for Silas were she somewhere else like most of the officers' wives, and Silas pictured what it would be like to be without her for all but the months of the winter encampment.

"They try so hard, but they are so untrained compared to the enemy," Silas began, and then the words poured out. "I feel responsible for every man under my command and for their wives and children, too, whether they're here or left at home. And the men are as apt to be killed by our own guns exploding as by enemy fire. It's the waiting, the hellish waiting! One day I think they cannot fail, and the next I think they cannot do anything else. And I cannot think of anything but them."

Addie wished she could tell him that her need for physical lovemaking was only an expression of her terror that the new battles would come and the ones after that and that in one or another of them she would lose him or one of her remaining brothers or one of her cousins, but telling him that would only add to his misery. For the first time, she saw clearly how separate their burdens were—hers only to be a good soldier's wife and soldiers' sister, no matter what else she accomplished while they were with the army; his to be responsible for the lives of all the men he commanded. Her brothers and cousins had lighter loads to carry, for they served, they did not command. It was such a stark difference everything else paled before it.

"Your men are fortunate to have you and so am I," she said. "It is sufficient to be close to you. Time enough for loving and even for bickering if needs be when we go into winter quarters."

She stroked his face gently and then began to knead the knotted muscles of his shoulders, relieved when he did not push her away. He should have been with her brothers and cousins this evening, for Sissy's husband had finally come north to join the cavalry, and the Virginians were hosting another celebration, with complete disregard for whether or not the enemy might show up on the morrow. But Silas had gone only out of courtesy, had stayed a short time, and had come to her entirely sober. She smiled sadly, remembering how relaxed and funny he had been when he had spent that riotous evening with the "Virninians." She thought she must be the only woman in Christendom who wished her husband had gotten drunk this night.

At last, she could feel him beginning to relax, and then he murmured, "For a while maybe, but not until winter quarters. I don't think I can wait that long." He fell asleep to the sound of Addie's soft laughter.

Addie stayed awake for a long time, comforted by his nearness, but gradually a chill settled on her, despite the heat. Like trying to picture them having a home of their own, her mind went curiously blank when she tried to see their marriage outside of the war. It seemed an evil omen that she could not conjure the image of days shaped by peace.

Chapter 8

Pennsylvania, Summer 1777

Sissy's husband, James Fitzjohn, was not the only new addition to the army. Among the influx of new recruits and volunteers, yet another European officer arrived, having appeared before Congress with recommendations from American agents abroad and having then been given the lofty rank of major general and sent along to Washington.

But this situation was even more ticklish than was usual with the European adventurers. This Frenchman, for all that he was still some days away from his twentieth birthday, was from a wealthy, respected family himself, and was allied with the powerful Noailles family through marriage to the daughter of the Duc d'Ayen, all of which made it unadvisable to anger him while the country was so in need of aid from France.

"I hope he is more a soldier and less a peacock than most of them," Silas commented sourly.

"Maybe he will choke on his name." Ad wrinkled his brow and then recited, "Joseph Paul Yves Roch Gilbert du Motier, Marquis de Lafayette—a name that long should be enough to do it." He couldn't mention the secret communication that had come from Congress telling the general how crucial it was to treat Lafayette well. It would have been easier had the fellow been a Pole or some other nationality besides French. Many American veterans of the French and Indian War were offended by the idea of French participation in this one even while they knew they needed assistance from whatever government would offer it, and even though there were already Frenchmen fighting with them. Ad sympathized with his brother-in-law, knowing that Silas shared the feelings of those older men because his father had died as a result of that conflict. But it didn't matter what Silas or anyone else thought about it, the Marquis de Lafayette was to be welcomed heartily, and somehow the fact that his rank was more honorary than real and brought no troops to command with it must be glossed over.

First appearances were not reassuring, for while Lafayette was not overly impressive on a horse due to his rather clumsy seat, his obviously new and ostentatious uniform was galling to officers whose own apparel was threadbare at best. Fairly tall for a Frenchman, Lafayette was of wiry build with reddish hair, a rather sharp nose, and a wide forehead that slanted back at an oddly acute angle. In spite of his aristocratic lineage, there was something a trifle awkward about the young man, as if a country bumpkin existed beneath the title.

He had studied English diligently on his voyage to the United States and continued to add to his vocabulary, but his accent was so thick, it took some inner translation on the part of the listener to be sure of what he said.

All in all, despite his illustrious background, Lafayette could have become a figure of fun as well as being resented, but quite the opposite happened, and it was due to the man himself.

His eyes were alive with intelligence and passion, and, he seemed to be embracing all things American with genuine enthusiasm. There was no arrogance in his manner, quite the contrary. When Washington, knowing how shabby the Continental Army must look to the marquis, said, "We must be embarrassed to show ourselves to an officer who has just left the French Army," Lafayette responded, "I 'ave come to learn, not to teach."

When Ad tried to tell his twin about that first meeting between Lafayette and Washington, he found it difficult to put into words. "I'm not sure exactly what happened, but something extraordinary did occur. The marquis is a man who knows the King and Queen of France, and yet he looked at the general as if he had never been in the presence of such greatness. Either he is a great actor, or he is as ingenuous as he seems and in our leader he sees a man who meets all of his requirements for a hero."

"And His Excellency, how did he react?" Addie asked, wishing she could have witnessed the event.

"He seemed relieved that Lafayette is not an overbearing popinjay, but it went beyond that. I think he was genuinely touched by the marquis's humility in his presence, but more, I think he was as unable as the rest of us to resist the Frenchman's charm. I tell you, Addie, it is lethal. God knows things are not going well for us, and yet, Lafayette makes me want to smile, forget the war, and take him to visit Boston and Virginia, too, to show him a little of America. I vow, the man will charm even Silas when they meet."

That meeting was not long in coming, for Lafayette was quickly accepted as an honorary member of the staff. When he met the Bradwells, he swept Addie a formal bow as if they were being introduced at court, causing Silas to shift uneasily at her side until the marquis said to him, "Monsieur, you are so fortunate to 'ave your wife beside you at this time. My own wife, she is 'ome in France with our little daughter."

His words did exactly what he intended, putting Silas at ease and establishing common ground by referring to his married state.

Addie thought perhaps Lafayette, despite his boyish energy, was quite sophisticated after all. And Silas thought that if he weren't careful, he was going to be unpardonably rude and laugh aloud at Lafayette's English. Then he realized he had not felt so light-hearted for a very long time.

"I was utterly engaged," he confessed to Addie later. "General Washington should send Lafayette against the British; surely he could make them laugh and go home where they belong."

"He has the same quality Washington has," Addie said, "something beyond charm, something that draws other people like a magnet. And I think that, notwithstanding the political problems that have come with him, the marquis will be good company for the general. He smiled more tonight than he has in a long while."

"So did I." Silas nuzzled her neck. "Perhaps winter is coming early this year."

Addie turned into his embrace willingly, giddy with the thought that she would be in the Frenchman's debt, though never able to tell him so.

They took their time with each other, learning that they could wander away from each other emotionally and physically and still find the way back.

When it was over, body satiated, Addie lay listening to the camp. The night was still, and sounds, small and large, near and far, carried as if equal—the hiss and whirr of insects, the restless stir of livestock, the occasional footsteps and the challenges of sentries, muffled voices, and the fretful cry of a child. Even after the official day was over, the fifes and drums silent, there was no way such a sprawl of humanity and animals could be quiet. Washington's force of Continental regular and Pennsylvania militia now numbered more than ten thousand and that number did not include the many families or the sutlers, peddlers, prostitutes, scavengers, and the myriad others who traveled in the wake of an army as inevitably as the dust of summer roads. This night music had become so familiar, soothing rather than discordant, Addie wondered if she would ever be able to sleep in silence.

Then the increasingly familiar sorrow welled up in spite of her effort to stem it. She swallowed hard and opened her eyes wide in the darkness to stop the tears from overflowing. "Can you imagine us old, settled, and together?"

Silas's even breathing went on, and Addie, regretting the question as soon as she had voiced it, was glad he had not heard.

But Silas heard every whispered word as he kept up the pretense of sleep. Only inside did he allow the answer: No, but I will love you, Ariadne Valencourt Bradwell, until the day I die and can love no more. He would never admit to her that no matter how hard he tried to see even so simple a thing as himself selling books and working a printing press again, the images would not come.

But it did come to him then that he was no longer responsible for peering into the future. Before the war, that had surely been the charge on every married man of good faith and average ambition, for one could not, in conscience, take on the responsibility of a wife, not even one as independent as Addie, without a plan of how he was going to support her and the children that might bless the union. But he and Addie no longer existed on a plane where anything was predictable.

Acts of nature were always a risk, but nothing was more threatening than war when even those acts of nature went awry so that men died of a snake's bite, or disease, or too much heat or too much cold, or a fatal fall or other accidents in places where those men would never have been were it not for the conflict.

Everything Marcus had taught him had been about a reasoned, measured life, and all of it had been blown apart just as effectively as the cannon in Silas's regiment could demolish their targets. Accepting that and understanding that the best he could do was to perform his military duties day by day until there was no more need brought him a sense of peace, the only peace possible in the midst of war.

His muscles relaxed, and he let sleep take him. His last thought was that his impatience was foolish. Sooner or later, General Howe would reappear, and the fighting would start again.

And indeed, within days word came that the British were sailing up Chesapeake Bay. And on August 24, a Sunday, Washington marched his army through Philadelphia in a brave display as they went south to meet the enemy.

Good news from the Northern Army heightened their spirits, for not only had a body of Hessians been defeated at Rennington, in the New Hampshire Grants, but an enemy force, which included hundreds of hostile Native Americans who had been menacing settlers and forts in western New York, had been turned back and dispersed. This western flank of Burgoyne's invasion had been scheduled to join with Burgoyne's army and now it would be that much less.

In Philadelphia, Addie stood with her Uncle Hartley to watch their army pass, and she was glad of his protection. The city was beautiful and it was serving as the capital of the United States, but it was no secret that a large part of its population was Tory. Addie was certain that a great number of those who were watching and even cheering today would suffer no disquiet in welcoming the British should they take the city.

As if to prove her thoughts, behind her Addie heard a woman's muffled laughter and then her whispered voice saying, "Oh, what an army of ragamuffins they look!" The titter of mirth came again, and Addie wanted to swing around and slap the woman's face. Uncle Hartley's hand on her arm restrained her, and she looked up into his lined face. The war was making him into an old man, but it had not diminished his humanity, and his patriotism still burned with a steady flame. The night before, he had entertained them all—his sons and son-in-law, Addie, her husband, and her brothers—with a supper at a popular city tavern, and for a little while, Addie had been able to pretend that they were a family with nothing better to do than share a meal together. Uncle Hartley had given them all the news from Castleton, assuring them that everyone was well, particularly little Randolph James. Addie had had to hide her smile, for every time there was any mention of his wife or their baby, James Fitzjohn was sure to get an endearingly dreamy expression on his face.

But inevitably, the talk had turned to war, and looking around to make sure they could not be overheard, Uncle Hartley had said, "I know you will all comport yourselves with courage, but I pray you take no unnecessary risks. I am not the only member of the Congress who doubts that Philadelphia can be held if the enemy is determined to take it."

"But, Papa, we have already lost New York; it is unthinkable that we should lose Philadelphia, too!" Hart protested.

Hartley corrected his son gently. "It will be embarrassing, not unthinkable. Philadelphia is not an ancient capital like London or Paris. We are so new, our government exists wherever its representatives meet."

"Well, then, make sure the enemy does not capture you with the city," Reeves cautioned his father, the serious look in his eyes belying his light tone.

"You needn't worry about that, my boy. We may be slow to enact legislation, but we've proven ourselves amazingly quick to get out of harm's way."

Hartley's smile had been wry the night before, but now as he watched the army marching past, watched his sons and nephews and the thousands of others who were willing to hazard their lives, his expression was such a poignant mixture of pride and tenderness,

Addie's eyes burned with tears. She picked out each of their men—Ad near the front with the other aides accompanying Washington and Lafayette; Justin, her cousins, and James Fitzjohn with the cavalry; and Silas with the artillery.

The goal of having every soldier in proper uniform was still far from accomplished, and many wore garments that were visibly patched, but at the general's bidding, they had washed their clothing as well as they could, and they'd decorated their hats with sprigs of greenery to symbolize hope. Their shoes were worn and cracked, but as Washington had commanded, they did their best to keep in step to the music of the fifes and drums. Some had nosegays attached to the ends of their muskets, and the little knots of flowers bobbed in cadence.

Addie understood why the general had ordered that the camp women not come through the town with the army, and she knew how infuriated many of the women were. Washington judged that they, most of them even more shabbily dressed than the soldiers, would detract from the dignified spectacle he was trying to create. But toward the end of the parade, when Addie heard a commotion from some of the side streets, she guessed the source before she caught sight of women, children with them, streaming after their men in defiance of Washington's order.

"Oh, mercy! Would you look at those slatterns!" the woman behind her hissed to her companion, and Uncle Hartley, in spite of his patriotism, looked discomfited by the camp women's actions.

Addie resisted the impulse to cheer the women on. Instead, she said, "Uncle, it must be difficult for anyone who has not seen those women work day after day to credit how important they are to the army. It is they who do the laundry, the mending, much of the cooking, the nursing, so many tasks. And many of the women also have children to care for. Most of them have very little, and yet, they persevere in the harshest of conditions and endure everything to stay by their men."

Addie had made sure her voice was loud enough for the woman behind to hear her, and with a wink, Uncle Hartley answered at the same volume. "Then they should have their own place in today's procession, just as they claimed it."

Addie had the satisfaction of hearing the woman behind snort in outrage when the man with her observed quite affably, "I cannot imagine you lasting very long in such conditions."

Addie and her uncle exchanged broad smiles, like naughty children, but both of them sobered when Addie bid goodbye at the livery where Nightingale was stabled. Her uncle had arranged an escort to see her safely to Silas, but it was he who gave her a leg up into the saddle.

"Take care, child," he said.

She leaned down to kiss him on the cheek. "You take care, too. You are father to us all now."

Hartley watched her ride away, thinking all the while that Marcus Valencourt was a stubborn fool who had lost a great deal more than his life in Boston by remaining loyal to the King.

Washington's army kept watch on the British as they unloaded their ships at Head of Elk in Maryland. It was no surprise that being so long aboard ships in the heat had debilitated both men and horses. The horses that hadn't died and been tossed overboard were emaciated, and their condition worsened when they were allowed to gorge themselves in a cornfield, and the colic that resulted killed many of them.

General Howe offered pardons and protection to any Maryland-ers who would submit to the authority of His Majesty's forces, but most of the populace in the area fled, taking what they could of their possessions and livestock.

Still, it was too much to hope that these setbacks would put an end to the enemy's intentions.

Washington sent out detachments to harass the British at every opportunity and to move out of their reach supplies that had been collected along the Elk River. The American raiding parties were adept at capturing small groups of enemy soldiers who were drawn away from their camps by the prospect of food for themselves, forage for their animals, and, in some cases, plunder.

With the shortage of light horse in the Continental Army, those units of cavalry that existed were much needed. Justin and his comrades spent most days in the saddle dawn to dusk, and some of the skirmishes they engaged in were sharp. They admitted to each other that it was exhilarating to hunt the enemy down, but they said little about the darker side of what they were doing. They did not always show mercy, for the plight of the inhabitants of the region fueled them with rage. It was a pathetic sight to see men, women, and children dragging what they could with them, trying to get away, while the enemy, particularly the Hessians, stripped the countryside of everything they could carry or, with livestock, drive away.

One day they caught three Hessians with their packs full of stolen goods. They hanged them on the spot, leaving the spoils in their packs to show the reason for the sentence. Justin felt no regret, not even when the Hessians squealed in terror, and he saw the same hard resolve on other faces. But Sissy's husband looked away from the scene and, for an instant, Justin wondered if he himself would be softer had Sarah lived and more, if he carried an image of her with a child.

Justin did not see fellow human beings when he looked at the Hessians; he saw predaceous beasts ravaging the countryside, raping the women, stealing all. In their packs, among the other spoils, had been a woman's necklace made of rose-petal paste beads that still carried the scent, a pewter candlestick, even a child's carved wooden horse—homely treasures that made Justin think the family must have been there when the Hessians came upon them. Perhaps the men of the homestead were with the Continental Army, leaving the women and children unprotected. He shuddered inside imagining what might have been done to them.

But he found he was not as devoid of pity as he thought when he heard that two enemy soldiers had been caught in the woods and had their throats slit. He was glad he and the men he rode with had had nothing to do with it, for even the most boastful versions of the story did not claim the dead men had been after anything but food. And in spite of the general insanity of war, there were limits he still recognized. Hanging was a standard punishment for many offenses in both armies, many of them crimes less vile than what the Hessians were doing, but throat-slitting was murder by any measure.

Some of Washington's officers had wanted to attack the enemy immediately. Some of his staff wanted the same—Hamilton for one—and Ad was inclined to agree with him on the basis that the sooner the enemy was engaged, the less time they would have to recover from the effects of more than seven weeks at sea. It was, however, the commander in chief's responsibility and choice, and with General Greene's advice, Washington chose to shift slightly north, to Pennsylvania again, and to make a stand along Brandywine Creek where the hilly, thickly wooded terrain and the water, which could be crossed only at specific fords, would make assaulting their position difficult.

On September 11, the enemy came against them. The morning dawned in fog and heat, so there was confusion from the beginning, confusion made worse by the Americans' lack of reliable intelligence and shortage of light horse to scout for it—they did not know even so basic a fact as how large the British force was.

The action began opposite Greene's position at Chadd's Ford, but aside from lobbing some artillery shells across the creek, the enemy did not seem intent on a full attack. And though there were British regulars with them, the majority of the estimated four or five thousand were Hessians. The assumption was that there were additional troops coming up behind the Hessians, and that once they arrived, the attack would begin in earnest.

As the minutes ticked by, Ad grew more uneasy and frustrated, and he could see the same emotions reflected on the faces of the other aides as they rode from position to position, sometimes with the commander in chief, sometimes to carry messages for him. Even with the fog lifting, the densely wooded landscape severely limited visibility. Ad rubbed his eyes, knowing it was foolish, but feeling that if they could all see just a bit farther, secrets they needed to know would be revealed.

Riding with Colonel Bland's light horse, Justin was more mobile than Ad but no less frustrated. As they scouted through the woods on the west side of the creek, their visibility was very limited, too, except when they broke into clearings here and there, and they were mindful of the need to gather information without getting trapped by a superior force.

And then they caught sight of them—redcoats crossing the west branch of Brandywine Creek at unguarded Trimble's Ford. Colonel Bland sent word back immediately to General Sullivan. Justin's blood pounded in his ears, and he wanted to ride on, ride the redcoats down, but like everyone else, he had to curb his instincts. He reminded himself that surely additional troops would cross the creek so they could engage the enemy, especially since a more detailed report followed the first and included the information that General Howe was believed to be with this force.

When word came to General Washington he didn't hesitate. He sent orders back that Sullivan was to cross and attack with his three divisions, and he also ordered Greene, with the main army, to attack the Hessians. But before these maneuvers could be accomplished, another report came in from General Sullivan, this one stating that he had fresh, firsthand intelligence that there hadn't been any movement of the enemy, after all, and he was "confident that they are not in that quarter..."

Acting on this assurance, Washington countermanded the attack orders.

Ad felt a twist in his gut when he understood what had happened. He knew the original warning had come from Colonel Bland. He thought of Justin and his cousins. He could hear the desperation in his voice when he waylaid Tench. "I know my brother, my cousins, Harry Lee, the others in the cavalry. I swear, they would not imagine thousands of redcoats where there were none!"

Tench's face was rigid with strain. "I agree, these are not men to see phantoms. If Sullivan's man did not find the enemy, 'tis only because they've moved on." He reached out and gripped Ad's arm. "But we are not the generals. We follow General Washington; we follow his orders." His hand dropped away, and then he added, "And we keep our eyes open for thousands of missing redcoats."

Justin was as baffled as he was angry. It was a relief to be sent out again to scout further, proof that General Washington had not totally discounted their report. But even being sure of what they'd seen the first time did not prevent their shock at the second sighting. Justin heard the soft oaths from more than one man as he saw two brigades of the enemy moving rapidly and a great cloud of dust on the horizon marking the passage of a much greater force.

"Damnation!" Justin joined his oath to others. "It's Long Island all over again!" There was grudging admiration as well as horror at the realization that General Howe had managed to outflank the Continental Army once more, this time coming around by unguarded fords as he had, only a year before, used an unguarded pass to get behind the Americans to inflict the disastrous defeat that had taken Quentin's life along with so many others. The enemy was heading for the rear of Sullivan's right flank and taking the high ground as they did so.

It was two o'clock in the afternoon by the time Washington had the news that a large enemy force had circled around behind his army. Frantic orders were sent to wheel various divisions about so that they would be facing their foes, but the main body under Greene still faced the Hessians across the creek. The Hessians had provided the diversion Howe needed to slip away, but they were no less a threat for that role.

When Ad wasn't scribbling dispatches, he was racing off with them, but still, it was as if a giant clock were ticking in his head, counting the minutes until the British would open fire. All initiative had been stolen from the Americans, and by three o'clock, it appeared that the enemy was in position. For another hour the Americans kept up their hectic pace, trying to shift their troops, guns, and battle plans enough to make up for having lost the advantage of terrain.

When Howe's forces opened fire, the Hessians started action against Greene, so that all the activity that had gone before seemed like silence. The fire of cannon and muskets exploded the air, and smoke obscured everything. Bugles and trumpets directed the cavalry while for the infantry, fifes and drums and the eerie skirl of bagpipes added to the cacophony so that voice commands, "Incline to the right!" "Incline to the left!" "Charge!" "Halt!" on and on, had to be shouted and relayed.

Beyond the noise, Justin was finding another hazard. He was suddenly aware that he had never before been under such heavy fire in an area so densely wooded where not only was the earth churned up by small musket and big cannon balls, but the air above became an arboreal battlefield with leaves raining down in the early autumn of grapeshot, and trees dropping branches severed by artillery.

As Justin was blessing Colonel for his surefooted charge through the falling debris, he heard a wrenching scream of tortured wood even as the horse sprang forward with a grunt of effort, just escaping the huge branch that thudded down behind him, smaller branches lashing the horse's hindquarters and making him kick out in outrage as he continued on. One glance back at the branch was enough for Justin to see that it was big enough to have killed him easily and his horse, too. The tender tissue across his ribs ached from the jarring ride.

"What a good fellow, Colonel, what a fine one." Justin wasn't surprised at the unsteadiness of his voice. He thought the falling forest might well kill them before the enemy had a chance.

Even as he thought it, he caught a flurry of movement to his left and saw James Fitzjohn going down in a tangle of horse and timber. He reined Colonel to the side, vaulting out of the saddle before the horse had come to a full stop.

"Christ, oh, sweet Christ!" he muttered over and over, half curse, half prayer, not aware that he spoke at all until he started calling, "James! James, can you hear me?" though he was sure the man had to be dead as was the bay he'd been riding. Under the fallen branches, the animal lay motionless, the beautiful head twisted at an odd angle on the broken neck.

At first he thought James must be under the horse, but then he heard a moan and saw that he had been thrown clear.

James sat up gingerly, gripping his head. His dragoon's helmet— leather reinforced with metal and designed to shield the head and neck from saber blows—was nowhere in sight. "Can you ride with me?" Justin asked, eyes searching the surrounding countryside as he went to him. They had only seconds. He couldn't see any of the rest of their troops, and he was sure the thrashing he heard in the nearby thickets was from foe, not friend.

James glanced at his horse and regret flashed across his face. "Go on. Two of us are too heavy a load."

"Not for Colonel; he's already performed one miracle." As he spoke, he helped James to stand. "Besides, it would be worth my life did I have to tell Sissy that I left you in the woods."

James wasted no more time arguing, mounting Colonel behind Justin. Colonel took off with a will, given extra power by his frenzy to be away from the dead horse and the terrible falling forest. Shot whistled around them as they fled.

Privy to all the information that was coming in to the commander in chief, Ad had a wider view of the battle than did his brother, and it wasn't reassuring. Too many divisions were giving way, which in turn threatened those who were standing fast and fighting well. When word came that the heaviest fighting was centered around the Birmingham Meetinghouse, and Washington wanted to go there, Ad and the rest of the aides had to confess they did not know the way.

Ad looked away from the expression on the general's face at this news, but no explosion of temper came. Ad almost wished it had, for he suspected Washington was so close to despair at the unraveling of the day, even rage was beyond him.

Then they found an old man who admitted he knew the way, but he refused to lead them. While Washington might be beyond temper, his aides weren't. The old man was given the choice of dying by the sword or leading them. When he chose the latter, he was boosted up on a good horse, and he took off, proving himself a good rider if not a good Patriot as he rode at a full gallop, keeping his seat when his mount soared over fences on the way.

Despite their situation, or maybe because of it, Ad had to restrain his laughter as he and the other aides and Lafayette rode behind Washington, who, close on the heels of the reluctant guide, kept shouting, "Push along, old man—push along, old man!"

They arrived at their destination to discover that the enemy was pressing so hard and close with bayonets, only the thick cover of the countryside was saving the Americans from being completely routed. Ad saw the sun glinting off the metal, saw their men falling back from the stabbing blades as fast as they could, despite all efforts to rally them.

Washington had sent orders shifting various divisions as quickly as possible, and Greene's men marched four miles in only forty-five minutes, abandoning their now untenable position at Chadd's Ford in order to support the American right flank, but all hope of decisive action against the British was long gone. The best Washington could do was to save his army once again from destruction. In this, he had good practice, and he used the strongest troops to keep a corridor of escape open as the rest retreated to the east. He was aided by the sheer exhaustion of Howe's troops, for their long march to outflank the Americans, the heat of the day, and the grueling fighting had rendered them incapable of pursuit.

Not until most of the army had straggled into the town of Chester later that night was Ad able to take stock of his relatives. Silas was all right, though distraught that the artillery had been hard hit and had had to abandon some of their precious guns. Justin, Reeves, and Hart were unhurt, and James Fitzjohn insisted he was fine, too, though a huge ugly bruise was swelling on his forehead from where the branch had hit him and thrown him off his horse.

Justin drew Ad aside to tell him what had happened to James. "He insists he is suffering no ill effects, but damn, he took a terrific blow to his head! We found a horse for him, and he rode in on his own, but he's said little for the past few hours, and not all of what he has said has made sense."

Ad knew he had to get back to the general momentarily, for there were still dispatches to write. He wished Addie and Tullia were here to consult regarding James, but they were with the main baggage train and the other camp women, and they hadn't caught up to the army yet.

There were injuries among the staff, too. The new aide, John Laurens, with them for less than a week, had been hit by a musket ball in the ankle. Like James, he was insisting he was fine, that the bone wasn't broken, but the contusion was so severe, he hadn't been able to get off his horse or to walk without help. The South Carolinian was the son of a prominent member of Congress, Henry Laurens, which made his continued good health a matter of some interest.

Worse, the Marquis de Lafayette had taken a musket ball through the leg. Washington and his staff had intended that Lafayette be kept out of danger as much as possible, but the marquis had had other ideas and had been shot while trying to rally troops. He had ignored his wound until someone had pointed out that his boot was full of blood. Still protesting his good health, he had fainted when he reached Chester, and Washington was having him transported by water to Philadelphia where the best care was available.

Ad studied James where he sat against a tree, flanked by his brothers-in-law. It was hard to see him clearly in the flickering torchlight, but Ad could tell that he was very pale except for the darkening bruise. "Perhaps a cool cloth to lessen the swelling. His head must hurt terribly. I know you will all keep close watch on him. But I don't know what else can be done; even in the best of times, there is little remedy for head injuries."

"And this time surely does not qualify as the best." Justin's mouth twisted as if he tasted the bitterness of his thoughts. "To be fooled again! In the same way as last year! It is intolerable! We saw them, we saw the damn redcoats slipping around us, and we reported it. How could General Sullivan have believed we were mistaken? How could General Washington?"

Ad shook his head, suddenly so weary, he could barely stand. "I don't know. The mischief was done with that second report from Sullivan, the one saying there was no trace of the enemy in that quarter." His eyes slid away from his brother's, away from the unspoken words between them, words of disloyalty about their commander in chief, words about Quentin dying because of the same deadly error in judgment. "It all seemed to go bad very fast and yet, at the same time, slowly, like a nightmare. But I am not sure it would have been much different even had we known what General Howe was doing. His Excellency had some eleven thousand men in the field, more than a quarter of them undependable militia. It's hard to be accurate, but I believe the enemy outnumbered us by several thousand."

He turned away, but Justin's voice followed him. "Little brother, do you think to comfort me with the knowledge that we could not have prevailed under any circumstances this day, that so many died in vain?"

"No, I offer no comfort," Ad said, and he kept walking away, feeling as divided from his brother as he ever had. Justin had made the transformation completely; he was now a fighting man who wanted—needed—to win every battle. Ad regretted the mistakes the army command, including Washington, had made today, but he was a staff officer who saw all the twists and turns the battle had taken and understood that the general's duty above any transient hope of victory or gain, above *all things*, was to preserve the army so that the struggle could continue.

By the next day, there was a rough casualty count of captured, wounded, and dead, the total close to a thousand. Among the dead was James Fitzjohn. He had assured his companions that all he needed was a good night's sleep and had bedded down with them. But in the morning when they awakened, James lay still, blank eyes open to the dawn.

Chapter 9

Autumn 1777

One look at her twin's face and Addie knew something terrible had happened.

He caught her close as she slipped from Nightingale's back. "Silas and Justin are all right, so are our cousins. It's James."

His explanation of the death was brief and straightforward. Addie heard Tullia's gasp from behind her where Tullia had drawn up the wagon, but she herself had a difficult time comprehending Ad's words. There was a roaring in her ears that made it difficult to sort out her jumbled thoughts.

Her husband, brothers, and cousins were safe—that was the first thing she understood, and relief and joy shot through her. But then the rest of it penetrated, and she immediately thought of Sissy with their son, waiting for James to return to them. She thought of her cousin on the night of the party at Castleton when Sissy had finally gotten James to see that she had grown up. She thought of James with his quiet, steady manner, his good humor, his love for his wife and child. She thought of Sissy never seeing him again. And she thought that it was all somehow made worse by the fact that he hadn't died from enemy fire hitting him but from falling timber. It made his death seem not only wasteful but undignified. The thought was foolish—death in battle came in many guises—but she could not banish it.

When she saw Silas, she held on to him, trembling so hard she couldn't speak. His words of reassurance flowed over her until her shivering subsided. His solid strength steadied her as nothing else could. As long as he was in her world, she could bear anything. She acknowledged the selfishness of it even as she resolved that she would follow the drum to the last beat to be with him.

Her cousins, Harry Lee, and others who had known James were heartsick at the loss of him, but it was more than that with Justin. Seeing his sister broke his control.

"I knew he was badly hurt, I knew!"

Because she was so accustomed to Justin being the older brother and sure of himself, it was unnerving to witness his self-doubt, but Ad's description of what had happened told her enough.

"Had you not stopped for him, he would have died in the hands of the enemy. Is that not sufficient? Do you truly believe there is something else you could have done? Perhaps cure a head wound no one else understands?"

"Sarah, Quentin, and now James—it is too much!" He growled the words angrily, but Addie heard the enormous grief and the helplessness beneath the rage, and she had nothing to offer beyond the love she had always had for him. It seemed a paltry weapon against his despair.

They arranged for James's burial, but someday after the war was over he would surely be carried home to Virginia. Addie had an awful vision of rough wooden caskets being shipped hither and yon in some year to come, a last gruesome act. But even then Quentin would not go home, for he was buried in some common grave.

They had little time to mourn, for though it seemed impossible to prevent the British from taking Philadelphia, Washington was determined to make it as difficult as possible and to make their stay there unpleasant should they triumph.

The army marched via the city and took up a position some twenty miles west of it. Washington sent word that members of the Continental Congress ought to seek other quarters and that everything that might be of use to the enemy should be removed. His goal now was to deny the British access to the fords across the Schuylkill River, which was a far more formidable barrier to Philadelphia than Brandywine Creek. He also sent out raiding parties to remove stores that had been kept in mills along the river.

Returning from one of these raids after a close brush with the enemy, Justin and Harry Lee were filled with dread at having to tell their commander in chief that one of his aides, Hamilton, had perished in the mission. When Hammy appeared, equally distraught at having to tell Washington that Harry Lee had been killed, the two men caught sight of each other. They fell into each other's arms, laughing uproariously as they exchanged the unusual greeting of "I thought you were dead!"

"Had I seen you 'die,' I doubt I would have returned at all," Hammy told Justin. "It would take a braver man than I to face the twins with such news."

Justin didn't care that he was grinning foolishly in relief to see Hammy safe. Any small victory over death was to be celebrated.

Victories of any size were few for them. The enemy came after them a week after Brandywine, and they were in danger of being overrun on both flanks when the heavens opened up and rain poured down in such blinding sheets, ceasing the "Battle of the Clouds". The Americans retreated west and west again, needing to resupply with dry powder and other necessities.

Brigadier General Anthony Wayne was left behind near the hamlet of Paoli with some fifteen hundred men to prey upon Howe's baggage train, but instead Wayne's camp was attacked at one o'clock in the morning, the enemy descending by the thousands on the Americans who were so clearly illuminated by their campfires. Using only bayonets, the British caused utter havoc in short order. Those Americans who did get a shot off with their muskets had no time to reload before the blades were upon them, and few of them had bayonets of their own. More than fifty were killed, and a hundred wounded before the detachment fled westward away from the night terror that quickly came to be called the "Paoli Massacre," though the British had been only clever and determined.

Congress fled, too, to Lancaster and then on to York, a small, rough Pennsylvania town sure to discommode the many members of Congress accustomed to the refined atmosphere of Philadelphia. In a particular act of kindness, Henry Laurens, John's father, took the Marquis de Lafayette up in his coach to convey him to a safe place for recovery from his wound.

Addie could not stop thinking about the sorrow Uncle Hartley carried with him into exile and knew how much he must wish he were going home to comfort his daughter in the first days of her grief.

Despite this continuing tide of misfortune, Washington was still determined to do all in his power to prevent General Howe from crossing the Schuylkill River and taking the city. He brought his army into position to parallel the enemy's movements across the river. Howe seemed to be playing the game, but then, once more proving himself master of the flanking movement, he countermarched his forces one night, crossed the river, and was clear to enter Germantown on September 25 and to take possession of Philadelphia the next day.

The report that Tories had turned out in huge numbers to cheer the invaders came as no surprise to anyone. Addie thought of the woman who had laughed at the Continentals, and she indulged in the spiteful hope that the woman would find life under the occupation most unpleasant.

General Washington intended it to be just that, planning to strengthen forts along the Delaware River in order to make it difficult for the enemy to bring foodstuffs and other supplies into the city. As Boston had become prison for the British, so Washington hoped to make Philadelphia. Nor did he allow the British peace at Germantown, the little community about five miles north of Philadelphia where Howe set up his main encampment while General Cornwallis commanded the garrison in Philadelphia. It was especially insulting—and tempting—to the Americans that Howe, by his neglect of solid entrenchments and by the casual placement of his troops, showed how little he regarded the threat of further action from the Continental Army. It was enough to entice Washington to attack. He had one advantage in that men continued to come in to his army, more than were deserting, while Howe had no access to fresh troops; the Philadelphia Loyalists might cheer the British, but it was unlikely they would join the fight in large numbers.

The army left camp at dusk and marched all night, taking their positions early in the morning. At four o'clock, Washington gave the order to attack. Some of the militia seemed to have gotten lost and were nowhere to be found; others, though present, appeared to be disinclined to fight too aggressively; and heavy fog complicated everything. But it didn't matter, the Continentals were carrying the battle. They made contact with an enemy infantry battalion some five miles from the main British camp. The redcoats fought hard at first, assuming they were facing nothing more than scouting parties, but when they began to be overwhelmed by the Americans, they fell back rapidly to the support of additional troops. It was a sight, however hazy in the smoke and fog, to gladden American hearts and to quicken the pace of pursuit.

But the retreat of the enemy was not uniform; an untold number took shelter in a large stone house and fired from the windows on any Americans within range. When Washington and his aides came on the scene, the commander in chief was faced with a classic military dilemma, for part of his army was already ahead, engaging the enemy, while he had reserves with him. Yet, there was no easy way to dislodge the men in the house and press on.

Silas ground his teeth in frustration. Despite his men's best efforts, artillery shells simply bounced off the stout stone walls. When General Knox asked his opinion, he gave it.

"Sir, we could fire at those stones for the next week, and the house would probably still provide good shelter. Nor does the roof seem likely to catch fire, and we can't get close enough to set fires around the walls to smoke them out." He wanted to suggest that perhaps they should just march on, but he wasn't sure that was good advice either. According to all the treatises on military history he and Henry had studied, to leave an armed fortress intact behind one's army was deemed among the worst of miscalculations.

When Washington consulted with Knox, the two decided they could not risk leaving the enemy in the house, and Washington ordered an assault. The brigade that got the job immediately began to suffer heavy casualties as they advanced on the house again and again. And the losses were not confined to that brigade, as the British continued to pick off anyone they could.

When something thumped into Ad's left shoulder, nearly knocking him off his horse, he didn't know what it was until he looked down, saw the blood, and realized he'd been shot. There wasn't any pain yet, though he knew it would come, and when he pulled his coat and shirt aside, he was relieved to see that the bleeding wasn't excessive. But knowing his usefulness for the day was over, he did not protest when Washington ordered him to the rear. Nor did he have much choice except to submit to the rough ministrations of a surgeon's mate, who made quick work of digging out the musket ball, assuring him that he was fortunate it wasn't lodged deep and had not hit anything vital. Ad didn't feel so fortunate as the metal probe awakened the nerves in the wound and sent pain streaking down his arm and chest, but he knew the man was right. He could still move his arm and his fingers, and considering the marksman had undoubtedly been aiming for his heart, he had gotten off lightly. He discovered that the broad green riband that identified him as one of Washington's aides made an admirable sling. The riband seemed the last thing that worked as the day wore on.

Silas and Justin suffered no physical wounds, but their mental anguish was acute as the American attack wavered and dissolved in a hideous series of mishaps and malfeasance. The confusion of the Continentals was more than enough to stop the flight of the British and swing them around, and it was the Americans who retreated, chased for ten miles until the day ended with a fierce rear guard action, with exhaustion, and with memories of a broiling hot day of such fog stained with the smoke of battle, that the whole could have been played out in the landscape of Hades.

Like Ad, John Laurens had gotten a shoulder wound and was using his riband as a sling so that Tench teased, "Is this some new fashion for the staff?" to cover his concern for his friends.

Though his shoulder throbbed, Ad was feeling strangely pleased with himself that he, like Justin, had been blooded and had survived it, at least so far. But Addie was so shaken by his having been wounded, his cavalier attitude infuriated her. She fussed over him and scolded until he asked, "Would it make you feel better if I felt worse? I can moan and groan if you like."

He still looked so cocky, she threw up her hands, muttering, "Men! I think you enjoy war!" But she couldn't stay angry with him, and Tullia agreed that, barring putrefaction, his wound looked as minor as he claimed it was. And though she knew it was irrational, deep inside Addie clung to the idea that this lesser hurt would save him from greater harm, as if the grotesque flesh-hunting specter of the battlefield would pass over him the next time, as it must surely pass over Justin, too.

Not all the casualties were as lucky as Ad, and in helping to tend the wounded, Addie discovered Private Willis, now Willets. He had lost part of his right foot to an artillery shell, but he had no intention of dying.

"We had 'em, for a while there, we had 'em on th' run," he told her proudly.

"I know you did. I heard that many units fought very well."

"T'was muddlin', you know, th' plan for all them columns marchin' to meet up—no offense to General Washington—an' mebbe we got a little lost here an' there, but…"

His voice trailed off as he tired, and Addie finished for him, "But even if we didn't win, we didn't lose either." They exchanged a conspiratorial smile of veterans grown accustomed to finding victory in loss as long as the army remained more or less intact.

"Remember to thank your wife for the quilt."

Neither of them said goodbye, but they knew when he had recovered enough to leave, they would not see each other again. He would go home for good now, home to his wife and children, including the baby he had never seen. Neither he nor his wife wrote well enough to exchange letters, so he did not yet know the sex of the child or even if it and its mother had survived.

Addie swallowed the lump in her throat at the realization that this man's life would always be a war of sorts, because he would still have to fight all the battles against poverty, disease, and misfortune to provide for his family and to keep them safe. And there were so many like him in the army—tough, enduring, and eternally optimistic despite the hardships of their lives. They were the best weapons Washington had, made more powerful by the enemy's unchanging, blind contempt for them.

General Burgoyne had surely underestimated them in his confrontation with the Northern Army. His fortunes had declined in one encounter after another until late in the month, news reached Washington's headquarters that Burgoyne had surrendered his entire force of nearly six thousand British and Hessian troops to General Gates on October 17 at Saratoga, New York. It was a stunning victory made all the more impressive by comparison to the losses Washington had suffered in the past months.

Ad had never felt prouder of the general, for not by the slightest word or gesture did he betray anything but great satisfaction in Gates's success. But Ad and others of the staff ached for him even as they rejoiced in the northern triumph. Their commander in chief had been given the impossible task of holding Philadelphia against the enemy, while Burgoyne had gone a good distance to assist in his own downfall, his heavily laden troops traveling ever more slowly in dense forests while their food supplies dwindled and their Native American allies proved less and less use as scouts and warriors until they had quit the job entirely. Nor had Burgoyne received the assistance he expected from other quarters, for not only had the western arm of the expedition failed and turned back before it reached him, but General Clinton had also marched too late from New York to aid him. Even poor Jane McCrae had helped defeat Burgoyne, her murder having encouraged so many to join the Northern Army and having spurred many militia men to fight more effectively than ever before.

There were whispers that perhaps Gates would make a better commander in chief, but Washington gave no sign of hearing them. Instead, he continued to pursue every avenue to bedevil the British in Philadelphia and even to hope that he might yet force them to quit the city. He had somewhat better intelligence than previously, and Howe's troops in and around the city were estimated to be between seventeen and twenty thousand. Such a number required an enormous amount of provisioning. With the Continental Army roaming the countryside, Howe needed an open passage up the Delaware River for ships to bring supplies. Chevaux-de-frise, specially constructed barriers, were strung across the river to impede shipping, and forts along the river were heavily manned. But Washington still wanted at least one more direct action against Howe, and to that end, he sent Hamilton north to request additional men.

Although his origins were dubious, when Hammy had come to New York from the West Indies, he had come with introductions to some of the most powerful commercial and political interests, contacts he had cultivated from the day of his arrival, and his good service as a pamphleteer in the Patriot cause and as a skilled artillery officer had enhanced his standing with them. He was a good choice for the mission, but Ad had misgivings. He had grown quite fond of Hammy, finding, like most of the staff, that the energy and intelligence of the man were hard to resist. But he had also come to see that Hammy had the most excitable temperament of all of them and a deep streak of gloom that could pitch him into black despair with little warning. Hammy could not abide less than perfection in himself or others, and to fail at anything he attempted was unacceptable.

"If anyone can get those extra troops for us, it is you, but I hope you will not take it to heart if the request is denied. After all, the Northern Department is run much as a separate army; even His Excellency treats it so. He asks for reinforcements, he does not demand," Ad reminded him, but Hammy shrugged off the warning.

"It is only logical that the men be sent to His Excellency," he insisted, and knowing it was futile, Ad did not point out that logic seemed to have little to do with the way the war was being conducted. At twenty-two, Hammy was two years older than he, but Ad often felt as if he were the elder, as if he had grown beyond the fire of youth while Hammy still burned with it.

Spies brought word from Philadelphia that the blockade of the Delaware River was, as Washington had planned, causing hardship that was edging toward panic. But in November, the British attacked Fort Mifflin, and though the defenders held out for days against a continuous bombardment by artillery, in the end they had to abandon the fort in the middle of the night when two warships got close enough so that marines aboard could toss grenades and fire muskets from the foretops. The obstructions meant to keep the enemy ships out had created a new channel in the current, a channel wide and deep enough to allow the ships' passage.

Three days later, Fort Mercer, too, had to be abandoned.

Some troops did come from the Northern Army to join Washington, but not enough and not in time. General Gates claimed reluctance to deplete his forces because, while General Clinton had not helped Burgoyne, he had gone north from New York City to make mischief in the Highlands along the Hudson River. Gates did not want to tempt Clinton to further action.

When word came that Hammy had fallen ill on his mission and was too weak to return to his post immediately, Ad confided to Tench, "I doubt not that he is fevered, but I suspect his heart fell ill before his flesh because he could not bring the whole Northern Army to the general."

"His passions are wound too high for this work of patience," Tench agreed. "He craves action as much as Justin does, but I think him less likely than your brother to relinquish the honor of being close to the general. Thus he is trapped between action and ambition, an uncomfortable place to be, as we all know to one degree or another."

It was typical of Tench to understand without censoring, but Ad thought there was no less ambitious man than he. From the day Tench had joined the staff, he had had only one goal—to serve Washington as well as he was able—and he had never deviated from that. He was still here in the capacity of a volunteer, drawing no pay. Ad would never embarrass him by telling him, but his admiration for the older man was boundless.

"Hammy will come back to us when he can," Tench said, but his voice was abstracted, and he gazed off as if he could see thousands of miles across the ocean. "I hope we will have troops from another quarter before long. The defeat of Burgoyne should convince the French that we are worth the gamble of an open alliance."

Ad thought that despite their general's wish for further action, most would be relieved when this campaign season was over and they could rest in winter quarters.

He worried about both of his siblings—Justin with his battle fever a constant high flame, and Addie more finely drawn with each passing day until now she looked waiflike, her golden eyes huge in her thin face. He tried to be careful not to infringe on the bond between her and Silas, no matter his prior claim. But finally he couldn't stand it, particularly because he saw that Silas was as baffled as he, watching Addie with such love and anxiety, Ad felt nearly as much worry for his brother-in-law as he did for his sister.

He thought of various ways to approach her, but when it came to it, he took the direct route, asking, "What is wrong? And don't tell me nothing because I know better than that."

Addie hadn't meant to confide in anyone, but her guilt had grown so heavy that simply being questioned by her twin broke her control. "I know what you are thinking, you and Justin and our cousins, and probably Silas, too. You think I should go to Sissy, but I can't! I can't leave any of you. Most of all, I can't leave Silas. I want every minute with him that I can have."

There was such pain on her face, Ad had to look away, and guilt became his. "Justin and I did talk about it," he admitted. "We thought not only of what comfort you would be to Sissy, but also of how good it would be for you if the aunts could pamper you for a while. But I swear to you, we discarded the idea as we spoke. We know better than to think you would leave Silas."

"You didn't ask him?"

"No, of course not! Allow us some sense. We also know Silas, know that he would tear his heart out and hand it to any one of us if we asked. But this is between the two of you."

"You understand how I feel, and so will he." Addie's smile was wobbly, but genuine.

Ad's lack of condemnation eased her burden, so much that Silas noted the change in her immediately, and she found the courage to speak honestly to him. She was as direct with him as Ad had been with her.

"I'm sorry," she apologized. "I know I've been difficult of late." And then she explained.

Despite the lateness of the year, they were quartered in their tent, cuddled together for warmth, and the instant Addie mentioned

Virginia, she felt Silas tense, and then he made his own confession. "I am not so noble as you think. I know I should have urged you to go to your cousin, but God help me, I don't want you away from me. When you said nothing about going to Virginia, I also said nothing. I should have known how much it was distressing you."

She nestled her head against his shoulder, kissing the tight cords of his neck. "No matter how close we are, we cannot always know what the other is thinking. And I will go to Virginia. I'll go when the war is over and you are safe, and you'll go with me so you can see Castleton and meet everyone. I want to show you the gardens and the horses— everything! I want to dance with you in the moonlight near the river."

It was too cold for them to sleep without clothing, but when Silas pulled Addie over on top of him, even through the layers of cloth, she could feel his growing arousal.

"I do this better than I dance," he said, running his hands down her back, pressing her close as he stroked her buttocks.

"Then we'll do this in the moonlight by the river." Her laugh was low and husky as he eased his hold on her enough so they could push clothing out of the way. But in spite of their mutual seduction and the fantasy of a time of peace, the reality of their situation stayed with them so that even at the height of their passion, they did not cry out lest the sounds carry beyond the canvas walls of their tent.

Ad noticed the change in his sister and brother-in-law as soon as he saw them again, but he was wise enough not to remark on it. His peace of mind increased for more prosaic reasons. Though General Howe did come out once more in early December, and the two armies maneuvered back and forth, no real battle resulted, and it was evident that active campaigning was at an end for this year. Raids would go on, but major troop movements would not resume until the snows of winter and the rains of spring had passed and the roads had dried.

Ad knew how disappointed Washington was to have struck no decisive blow to Howe, but he judged that the general needed a respite as much as did the rest of the army. He qualified the thought—the rest of the army with the possible exception of Lafayette.

The Frenchman had rejoined them in fair health and high spirits and had marched with General Greene in the attempt to keep Fort

Mercer from falling to the enemy. That had failed, but Lafayette had been part of a force that had attacked a strong line of pickets belonging to Cornwallis's troops, driving them back into their camp, after which the Americans had retired with no losses. It had been a bold reminder to the British about the dangers of complacency.

Lafayette was prepared to slay any dragon for General Washington, and now he had troops of his own, having been given command of General Stephen's men. Ad had no doubt of Lafayette's fitness to lead, though he felt sorry for Adam Stephen. The man had proved himself gallant, but age and ill health had begun to wear away at him. Ad suspected he had drunk too much on the day of the Germantown battle in an effort to banish his pains long enough to fight. But Ad could not fault the commander in chief for removing the man from a position where he could cause further harm. He did not envy Washington the awesome responsibilities of his office that allowed scarcely a day to pass without some vital decision having to be made. And worse, what had once been whispers about his unfitness to command had grown in volume, with enemies becoming more identifiable.

In the army, the most disaffected seemed to be General Gates and Thomas Conway, an Irishman who had served in the French Army for thirty years and was yet another of the European adventurers. Conway had been granted the rank of brigadier general, and was a credible officer on the battlefield, but he wanted to be promoted to major general, regardless of Washington's opinion of the matter. And both Gates and Conway had powerful adherents in Congress, men made bold by Washington's losses and Gates's victory. It did not help Washington's cause that only a handful of the men who had chosen him to lead in 1775 remained in the Congress.

After Saratoga, in an unmistakable indication of how independent he regarded his command, Gates had sent his report to Congress. He had sent no account to Washington. It was an insult, but Washington had done his best to control his temper.

That was scarcely the end of it, and not even the aides were spared. John Laurens's father had recently been made President of the Continental Congress, and he sent John much news of the muttering and plotting among representatives. Henry Laurens was loyal to Washington, and there was no doubt that he meant what he wrote to his son to be passed along to the commander in chief. But it put John in the terrible position of being the tale-bearer who could only make the general feel more frustrated and disheartened.

"It's like molasses spilled over everything," Ad complained glumly. "We're all stepping in it wherever we turn."

"I would liken it to something less sweet," Tench said. "But the general will prevail, because in the end, Congress will not be able to face continuing this war without him, however his enemies bluster." His was always the voice of reason, but he was as disgusted as Ad and as anxious that their foes be routed.

There were comforting signs of this happening because Congress had expanded Washington's powers of late, in spite of the general's insistence that the only chance for the new nation was rule by a civil government, not by the military. And Washington had the open support of many of the most prominent officers in the army who believed in the man himself and in his strict adherence to the policy that promotion must come from seniority and service, not favoritism.

Still, it was galling that Congress saw fit to award Gates a gold medal and to make him President of the Board of War and to then create the post of Inspector General and to give the appointment to Conway. These officers made the men independent of Washington, answerable only to Congress. The situation was made more difficult by the fact that there was no way to determine if the whole miserable affair had been an organized plot to remove Washington as commander in chief or was just the result of the petty jealousies and ambitions of small-souled men who cared more for their own advancement than for the country.

Although Washington was beleaguered by these political matters, nothing worried him more than the condition of his soldiers. Many of them were already so ill-supplied with clothing and food, it was hard to imagine how they would survive the winter.

Chapter 10

Winter 1777–1778

It was a weary band that arrived at Valley Forge on the night of December 19. They were about eighteen miles west of Philadelphia, at the junction of the Schuylkill River and Valley Creek. Its name was misleading, for it was high ground, and the iron forge that had given it its identity had been burned down by the British in September. The heavily wooded slope ran for about two miles, and at the western end there was higher ground yet, a hill called Mount Joy. With proper fortification, the position would be nearly impossible for the enemy assault, while it was close enough to Philadelphia to allow Washington to keep track of enemy movements.

Though the general took no chances, planning elaborate defensive works, the Americans were heartened by the knowledge that it was most unlikely that Howe would come after them now. The weather was cold, with icy rain and snow, and General Sir William Howe was not a man to sacrifice the comforts of winter quarters in the city, especially when, by all accounts, his blond mistress, Elizabeth Loring, was keeping him warm and warmly pleasured. Her husband, Major Joshua Loring, was apparently content to have traded the favors of his wife for the position of Commissioner of Prisoners.

For the present, it was more probable that Washington's army would be defeated by lack of supplies than by General Howe. During the campaign of the early fall, when the weather had been terribly hot, many men had lost or discarded their blankets. And the marching and countermarching of the past months had worn so hard on their clothing, more than two thousand had arrived barefoot at Valley Forge, and there were more in rags than in complete uniforms. Exposure was a constant danger, hunger no less so, and these harsh conditions so weakened the men's constitutions that, though the most seriously ailing had been sent to Reading, Pennsylvania, before the army got to Valley Forge, more soldiers were falling ill, and the toll could only grow.

On Christmas Day, the general was unable to issue rum to the troops as was his wont on special occasions, and the best he could offer Lafayette and the other officers who were invited to dine with him was meager fare—small portions of veal, mutton, potatoes, and cabbage, with only water to drink.

Ad was honored to be included, and however sparse the meal, he knew they were eating far better than most of the troops. By custom, officers enjoyed more privileges than their men, but there was enough of the democratic New Englander in him to make him feel some guilt for the difference.

He thought of his family. Addie would be content because she had Silas to herself for this day, but Justin and their cousins were on detached duty in New Jersey, foraging and guarding against incursions by the British. He hoped they'd found the means to celebrate, and then he smiled inwardly—his cousins and Harry Lee were accustomed to lavish Christmases, and he doubted they would allow even a war to prevent them from enjoying the holiday.

The thought rose unbidden—Marcus would keep Christmas, too, in England among the Anglicans there. Food and drink would be plentiful, and a Yule log would provide long hours of warmth. Marcus would be surrounded by his English family and by Mary and the children. He would certainly think of Darius, his Loyalist son, but would he think of his Castleton children at all? Had he banished them forever from his heart?

Ad shoved the image of his father from his mind, determined to savor this gathering, if not the food. It helped that the marquis was his usual exuberant self, and even when he was being serious, he made Ad smile. Lafayette was beginning to recognize the extent of the whispering campaign against Washington, and he was outraged.

He drew Ad aside to say, "They 'ave lied about 'im! Even to the Congress they are lying. It is intolerable!"

"It is intolerable," he agreed, "and I am amazed by His Excellency's patience. I trust he will prevail over those who are lying."

Aside from the slight pause on Christmas Day, life at Valley Forge was work from sunup to sundown as the troops built huts as fast as they could, the task of housing eleven thousand men being more important than building fortifications. At the beginning of the encampment, Washington had offered a twelve dollar prize for the first well-built hut completed in each regiment, and the men worked so fast, one was finished forty-eight hours after the troops had arrived. By December 29, some nine hundred huts were going up. Addie was awed by the speed at which the log city grew.

Determined to keep the promise he had made to his soldiers "to share in the hardships and partake of every inconvenience" with them, Washington stayed in his tent, poorly heated by a fire outside, until construction of the log city was well along. Only then did he make his headquarters in the Isaac Potts house, which he rented from the widow who lived there. The house was better than a tent, but it was cold and so small, Ad and the other aides slept crammed together upstairs, and a new dining area had to be added to the house.

Addie and Silas found rooms at a farmhouse near the main artillery encampment. They were in better quarters than Washington and his aides for they did not need to choose a place as secure as headquarters had to be. As usual, Tullia had lodgings with them, but it wasn't the same as it had been before. Now Tullia missed being together with Prince Freedom. It had been much easier to spend time, often including the nights, with him in the warmer weather when they had slept under canvas or whatever shelter was available and had maintained at least some illusion of privacy in their affair.

Addie would not have minded had Prince joined Tullia at the farmhouse, but knowing Tullia as well as she did, she did not suggest it. As much as Tullia loved Prince, she was too strait-laced to live so openly with a man not her husband. Addie doubted Prince would consent, anyway. He wanted Tullia as his wife in reality, not in pretense, and to live at the farmhouse under everyone's scrutiny would not be to his taste. Addie thought it was a good thing that Tullia might finally be forced to make a definite choice.

When she discussed it with Silas, he teased, "You are so happy to be married, you want everyone else to be in the same state."

He looked so proud of himself, Addie laughed. "You are right, of course, but you needn't preen so obviously."

"Preen? In these fine feathers?" he asked in mock innocence, and that set Addie off again because his uniform was as ragged as most in the army, despite her efforts at repair, efforts that included reinforcing the crotch of his breeches lest he inadvertently disgrace himself.

"Ah, but I know my husband's inner beauty," she gasped, staring at his breeches.

He grabbed her, tumbling her on to the bed. "It's your fault. All that wear is due to thoughts of you." He planted wet, smacking kisses on her neck, as the shared laughter shook both of them.

"Oh, my goodness! Ad is coming for supper!" Addie struggled to get the words out and pushed at Silas, managing to shove him off only because he was as weakened by laughter as she.

"Ad? Is he someone we know?" Silas turned his head, his grin wide, his face so young and full of mirth, Addie's heart gave a little skip.

"Even if we don't know him, we must be courteous. He's on the general's staff."

"I am more concerned about my own staff than the general's."

Addie was still giddy with laughter when Ad arrived, and her joy spilled over when she saw that Justin was with him. He hugged her in greeting, and she clung to him for a moment, infinitely relieved to see him.

Harry Lee and his men had been recalled from New Jersey. Their present camp was only six miles away, yet Addie seldom saw Justin or their cousins. Their days were spent in foraging for the army and harassing enemy patrols. It was dangerous work, and Justin continued to thrive on it, but as they shared a simple meal, he confessed to some regret.

"Like other foraging parties, we're much better fed than the rest of the army, and so are our horses. We're doing our best to bring in what we can. There is no shortage of food and fodder in the countryside, there are just too many farmers who would rather sell to the enemy for hard coin than to us for Continental dollars."

"Perhaps the farmers would be more cooperative if they knew how many are near to starving," Ad said, "but the general dares not make the full extent of our plight known for fear of the encouragement such knowledge would give to our enemies."

None of them had a solution to this dilemma, and there was a lull in the conversation as Addie's brothers sought a way to broach the subject of Silas's impending trip to New England with General Knox. Silas had to go this time, not only because his superior officer ordered it, but also because the Valencourts needed him to see to their business affairs. Justin and Ad wanted to discuss final details with him, but they were uneasy, knowing how much Addie disliked having Silas away from her and wondering, since she seemed uneasy, if she were pretending he wasn't going.

Addie made short work of their hesitancy. "If the two of you keep tiptoeing around me like this, you're going to fall on your faces or something else. I know Silas is going. I don't have to like it to see the need for it. And he's not going into battle." She smiled up at her husband, who was sitting beside her. "For that, I am very thankful."

Seeing that she meant it, her brothers relaxed, and Ad said, "Well, we're thankful you're going north, Silas, because neither of us would dare ask the general for permission to go. His temper is growing rough over the number of officers who have already left, either with permission or through resignation, and he's beginning to refuse requests for leave."

"We follow the British in too many ways," Silas complained. "Most officers think the only time they have any obligation to their men is when they're in battle. Otherwise, it's all left to the sergeants. That's hardly a way to forge a united army."

Justin agreed with his brother-in-law, but he also had sympathy for the officer corps. "Many of the officers are older and have far more extensive business and familial obligations than we do. But we are all, like British officers, expected to provide for our own needs—uniforms, arms, food, whatever—but we receive only a third as much in pay as the enemy, when we are paid at all. At least the common soldier is due his necessities along with his pay."

"It's a moot point in our army where what is due scarcely ever matches what arrives," Ad said, and since none could dispute that, the talk moved to specifics of their business. They still had a reserve of silver for hard money, but the rents from the house and Addie's farm were now being paid in Continental dollars, which daily lost value. The renters had no choice, since money in specie was in such short supply.

There was also the matter of the commercial interests left to Darius. Darius was notorious among the Americans now, even in New England, for the leadership of his Tory regiment. The Valencourts and Silas were still loath to tamper with the disposition made by Marcus, but at the same time, it seemed ridiculous to let the properties go to ruin, or to some other owner, for the sake of stubborn virtue. Silas was to make a new arrangement if the authorities would allow it.

"You have so much business to conduct, it's a good thing Mistress Knox will be keeping your general occupied," Addie noted. The formidable Lucy would be cross that she had missed another Christmas with her husband, and no matter what the needs of the artillery, Henry was sure to spend as much time as possible with his spouse.

Silas thought of the long list he would take with him, all of the items on it necessities he would try to purchase. They hoped that prices would be reasonable in Boston, but Silas was skeptical. Addie and her brothers trusted him to deal with all their business from important to trivial, and he had doubts about that, too, but he was resolved to do his best.

Justin stayed the night at the farmhouse, and he and Silas departed at the same time the next morning. Addie was very proud of herself for seeing them off without tears, though it was hard to let go of Silas as she stood for a moment wrapped with him in his cloak.

"Travel safely, my love," she murmured.

To Justin she said, "Don't you, our cousins, and Harry Lee get in too much trouble."

"We're too fast to get in trouble." He gave her a jaunty wave as he rode off.

Despite his casual leave-taking, Justin thought of Addie often during the next week. He appreciated her gallantry, but the smile she had fixed in place for him and for her husband had not hidden the shadows in her eyes. He thought of Addie and Silas as one, so much so that when Silas was with her, he did not worry. But when Silas was gone, Addie was alone as she had never been before her marriage. Justin knew that Ad recognized this, too. And while neither he nor Ad could make up for Silas's absence, he was resolved to visit Addie more often if Harry Lee could spare him. They were sure to be sent on detached duty again before long, and then he would probably be too far away to visit.

Before he'd opened his mouth to ask Harry's permission, there was a warning shout as a sentry scurried into the house. A huge party of British cavalry was advancing on them. It was still early in the morning, so the enemy must have moved through the night from Philadelphia. They barred the doors, and everyone was remarkably calm considering that there were only eight of them in the house, not even enough to guard all the windows.

Harry flashed a grin at Justin. "We should be flattered that the enemy finds us worthy of such attention."

Harry was being generous, for he was certainly the quarry due to his growing reputation as the scourge of enemy outposts and foraging parties.

Despite the odds against them, Justin felt no fear, just grim determination that Harry not be taken.

The winter sun reflected gaily on the bright uniforms and the metal gorgets, buttons, and sabers as the enemy came on, plumes of frozen vapor marking the breath of men and horses. But when they opened fire, their shot bounced against the walls, and the Americans fired back at the easy targets they made, for the open yard offered little cover. The shooting from the house caused the redcoats to fall back, and when they advanced once more, again they were vulnerable.

Harry, Justin, and the others retaliated with lethal aim when one of their own was wounded in the hand as he fired from a window. Justin saw a ball from his carbine knock a sergeant from his horse, others were hitting their marks too, and the enemy faltered. There was as much fear as fury on their faces, for they had not expected such resistance, and they could not know how few were in the house.

Then the British turned toward the stables to drive off the Americans' horses. There was a collective groan and a string of curses inside the house, for their horses were vital to them and nigh impossible to replace.

"Time for reinforcements," Harry announced, and there was as much mischief as purpose dancing in his eyes.

Standing at the end window that looked out on the barn, he directed his men to fire, as he called out at the top of his lungs, "Fire away, men, here comes our infantry. We'll have them all!"

He sounded so exultant, the British did not wait long enough to see that there were no soldiers approaching; instead, raking their horses' sides with their spurs, they fled back the way they had come.

The men inside the house watched in wonder as the force, which they estimated to be about two hundred, disappeared from view. And then they started to whoop and laugh.

"That was well done! You might consider going on stage," Justin suggested.

But Harry shook his head. "And give up leading my invisible troops? Never!" And they fell on each other, pounding each other's backs like schoolboys who had gotten away with a tremendous prank.

When the excess energy was spent, Harry said, "I give you leave to go tell your sister that no harm has befallen you. There will be wild rumors at headquarters before the hour is out." The mischief returned to his eyes. "Hart and Reeves are going to be damn sorry they missed this!"

It was as if he had conjured the Castletons, they appeared so soon after he spoke of them. They came in with others of Lee's men from their various quarters in the surrounding countryside, all of them bemoaning the fact that they'd missed the action, none more loudly disappointed than the Castletons.

"When you're old men, you can always ask me to tell your children how it was at the 'Battle of the Invisible Infantry'," Justin offered, earning his cousins' matching scowls, but under the jesting, they were all infinitely relieved that Harry and the others had not been killed or taken prisoner.

By the time Justin left to go to Addie, the British wounded had been taken off as prisoners and the few dead were consigned to a burial detail. The arms and cloaks of the wounded and the dead had been confiscated; even such limited spoils of war would be put to good use among the tattered troops.

Addie had already heard the rumors by the time Justin sought her out, and she was jubilant to find him unharmed.

Though he was more restrained in showing it, Ad was as happy as his twin, but he was also frankly envious. "I would give a great deal to have heard Harry Lee yelling and to see those redcoats flee."

For once, Addie understood their battle fever, and more, she understood how good for the morale of the troops the tale of the rout would be. Indeed, it was possible to trace the passage of the story through the encampment by the sound of laughter and by the sight of the gestures of small knots of men. Ad claimed the story had been so embroidered, it had the British fleeing with such speed, they had had to carry their horses to safety. It was with pleasure that he transcribed the letter of praise from General Washington to Harry Lee. To be singled out in such a way by the general was considered an honor by most, but it was even more special to someone like Harry whose family had long years of friendship with Washington.

It was less pleasant for Ad to contemplate how vital those friendships were to the general with his rivals still whispering against him to Congress and elsewhere. But little by little, the general's enemies were losing ground, not only because of his powerful friends, but also because of his immense dignity and integrity and because it grew more impossible by the day to imagine any other officer taking his place and keeping the army together under such harsh circumstances.

When the malcontent Thomas Conway visited Valley Forge in his role as Inspector General, Washington had treated him with every measure of courtesy, but so coldly bestowed as to leave no doubt about how the general felt about having Conway underfoot. Washington also made it clear to him that many officers in the army would protest Conway's promotion over them, for Congress had passed over twenty-three brigadier generals who were senior in rank to the Irishman.

With that, Conway's peevishness and ambition got the better of him, and he became more open in his machinations, writing to Washington that the cold reception he had received at Valley Forge indicated that the commander in chief would not support his work as Inspector General. To Washington, ever insistent that civil government as embodied by the Congress be superior to the military, this was a terrible insult. Though Congress had created the office of Inspector General and had appointed Conway, it was Washington himself who had suggested the need for this office.

The situation was made nearly intolerable for Washington because Conway had injudiciously committed his complaints and jealousies to paper, in letters that had been forwarded to Washington by loyal officers. One of these letters was to General Gates and one damning sentence in it read: "Heaven has been determined to save your country, or a weak general and bad counselors would have ruined it."

When Washington wrote to Gates to rebuke him for being party to such business, Gates made a major mistake in trying to shift the blame to Washington's staff, specifically to Hamilton, claiming that he had spied on Gates's correspondence while visiting Gates's headquarters. None of the aides escaped, but the attack on Hammy was the most direct, and Gates could not have chosen a man of more prickly pride.

Hammy had rejoined the staff in December, still pale from his illness, but soon he was burning with rage, not fever. To have his honor so impugned was not to be borne, but he used his pen, not his sword, for revenge, helping Washington to draft what protests the general allowed himself.

Even without pistols or swords at dawn, they continued to slowly win the day. The congressional delegation that visited Valley Forge saw for themselves that Washington was doing the best he could for the army in face of impossibly bad conditions. Conway's supporters seemed to be fading away into the shadows, as Gates backed down from his bluster.

But Ad, Tench, Hammy, and John Laurens, the French-speaking aides, were worried about Lafayette. They had no doubt of his great loyalty to their commander, but they were troubled by his lack of understanding regarding American politics. He was leaving Valley Forge, the prize offered being the command of a new campaign in Canada. To the marquis, the idea of taking back the territory France had lost to the British held great appeal, but to Ad and others, it seemed more likely that the project was being held out as a bribe for Lafayette's support of a faction that might not be loyal to Washington. Lafayette had made his own place by the force of his character and enthusiasm, but nonetheless, he remained more than an individual; his powerful ties to the French court became increasingly important as American representatives in France urged an open alliance.

Ad tried to talk to him, as did others, but he had to remember that no matter how cordial their relationship, Lafayette was a superior officer.

"I really do not believe there is enough support for our cause in Canada to offer you success. Our previous attempt ended in disaster," he cautioned.

"But I was not in command," Lafayette countered, so straightforward that it didn't seem like boasting. "And why, if there is no chance of a *victoire*, would such a venture be proposed?"

Ad found he could not voice his sinister thoughts to the marquis, and if anyone else had done so, it had made little impression, for Lafayette set out in high spirits.

Addie was among the many sorry to see the marquis go, for his lively presence would be missed, and more than any other officer, he had the ability to lift Washington's spirits.

Addie thought that perhaps only General Greene might have been glad to see the Frenchman leave, and that not from any personal dislike for the man, but because Mistress Greene flirted so outrageously with him.

Addie couldn't fault Kitty Greene for her hardiness. Kitty had left her two children with relatives, and when she had first arrived to be with her husband, she had lived in a hut until suitable quarters were found. General Greene adored his vivacious wife, and Kitty seemed to return the affection. But she also seemed incapable of resisting the allure of anyone in breeches. And when the occupier of those breeches happened to be from France, she became quite animated, prattling away in schoolgirl French, batting her eyelashes, and generally fluttering so much Addie wondered she didn't rise into the air like a bird.

The odd thing was that, while Addie felt staid in comparison to Kitty, though the woman was a couple of years older than she, she couldn't dislike her. Kitty's flirtatiousness was sometimes so overdone as to be embarrassing, but she had a true gaiety of spirit so that even other women were entertained by her company. Still, Addie did feel sorry for General Greene, noticing that he reverted more often to the "thees" and "thous" of his Quaker upbringing when his wife was misbehaving. She thought if she herself fawned over other men in Silas's presence, it would hurt as well as anger him. She looked forward to the arrival of Mistress Washington, who, in her quiet way, set the standard for the wives of other officers.

After Lafayette left, Addie noticed that Kitty was singling out Ad for her attentions, but when she asked him if it bothered him, he stared at her blankly before he said, "I hadn't noticed," and then to Addie's further amazement, he blushed and muttered, "But Mistress Greene's regard would be better than…" His color deepened.

"Than what?"

His sister's curiosity was fully engaged, and he wished he hadn't said a word, but Justin had gone with Lee's men on duty to Delaware, Silas had not yet returned, and Ad was becoming more anxious about his problem.

"Do you think I am manly?" he asked abruptly.

Addie would have laughed had he not looked so serious. Instead, she picked her way carefully. "I don't suppose sisters are very good judges, particularly when they are twins with their brothers"—she saw how he winced at that and decided not to belabor the point—"but if I try very hard, I can see what Kitty Greene and other women see. They see a strong, comely man with wit and intelligence."

Because the resemblance between them was so strong, with their golden eyes and sun-touched hair, it was odd and uncomfortable to try to view him objectively as a man. But when she made the effort, she did manage for an instant to see him as a stranger. They would be twenty-one this year, but three years of war had matured Ad beyond that measure. He was tall, and though slender, hard-muscled, and though he had blushed like a boy moments before, his steady gaze and the easy pride of his carriage were the marks of a man, not an adolescent.

Something was definitely amiss to be causing him such unease, and it struck her that he might have formed an attachment for an unsuitable woman. There were a few families with daughters in the sparsely populated area around Valley Forge, and some officers' wives had brought their daughters with them when they joined their husbands. These young women were enjoying having flocks of lonely young officers call on them. Addie wouldn't worry if Ad were courting in that quarter but there were women whose purposes were not so innocent, women from Philadelphia who were coming to the encampment on the pretense of visiting friends but were in reality intent on enticing men to desert the Continental Army. Washington was so concerned, he was issuing orders to keep them out.

Before Addie's speculations became any wilder, she said, "I'm lost. What are we speaking about? Is it a woman?"

Ad's shoulders slumped and his mouth twisted in distaste. "If only it were! But it's a man, a boy really. He is driving me mad! He's underfoot all the time. I can't leave headquarters without the wretched little urchin jumping to offer help with my horse. His eyes follow me everywhere. It is hideously embarrassing, and I cannot understand what I have done to attract such unwelcome attention."

"Oh, my heavens!" Addie gasped, and she hid her face in her hands, trying to get control of the mirth bubbling up inside her. Compared to a liaison with a corrupting hussy from the city, a young boy's hero worship seemed tame.

Ad regarded her sourly. "It may seem amusing to you, but it isn't to me. Far better he be infatuated with you than with me."

"But I am no hero," Addie protested, "and that is surely how he sees you."

"If that is what he wants, he has the general right before him," Ad snapped.

"Ah, but who can judge the course of true affection?" She had to apologize as her laughter spilled over. "I am sorry, I am! I know this is vexing for you, but against all the sorrows of this place, it is diverting."

Ad conceded the point with a reluctant smile. "I am glad to provide you with entertainment, but I hope young Matt recovers from his infatuation very soon."

Matt was the brother of one of Washington's Life Guards, the soldiers whose special duty was to guard the commander in chief. They were required to be native born, and they were chosen for their marksmanship, for loyalty, for being physically taller and more fit than the average man, and a considerable number of them were Virginians. But Luke McKinnon was from western New York, had distinguished himself in the campaign against Burgoyne, and had been recommended to the Life Guards by General Schuyler. Matt was Luke's shadow, always nearby. And usually near Ad, too, since the Life Guards were posted close to headquarters and had their huts within hailing distance.

Now that Addie knew who the child was, she realized she had seen him quite often, a quiet presence in raveled clothing. The boy appeared to be twelve or so, with no beard yet. He was fairly tall for his age, but very slight, with the same dark-auburn hair and dark-blue eyes as his brother and a sprinkling of freckles across a straight little nose. And it didn't take Addie long to observe the validity of her twin's complaint because the minute Ad was in sight, the boy's eyes were upon him, his face shining with such youthful ardor, it was almost painful to witness, making Addie understand why her brother was so disconcerted. But Addie still saw no harm in it. Young boys often developed great attachments for their tutors or such, attachments that ebbed away with maturity, and in war a soldier like Ad would be a likely object.

Having solved that problem in her mind, she was more concerned about Matt's general wellbeing. It was hard enough that adults be hungry and cold at Valley Forge, but the children tore at her heart.

At least Matt had shoes of a sort, though they were little more than stitched hide, but he could have used more layers of clothing and certainly more to eat. Many officers shared what they could with the sentries at their doors, and in the same spirit, Addie brought a small packet of food to Matt.

The child looked at her in some alarm as she approached him, but he stood his ground.

"I am Addie Bradwell, Colonel Valencourt's sister," she said.

After a moment's hesitation, the boy grinned impishly. "Of course you are, ma'am, t'would be hard to mistake the blood between you. I am Matt McKinnon." His voice was low and husky, but then he made a sound of dismay, and Addie looked down to see that he had dropped a splotched scrap of cloth that had been clutched in his hand. Without thinking, she took his hand in hers, and his blood smeared on her skin.

"Oh, beg pardon, ma'am!" He tried to tug his hand away, but Addie held it firmly, looking at the chilblains from the cold that had caused Matt's hands to swell and split.

Measured against all the other miseries of the encampment, the boy's inflamed hands were a small matter, but they pulled at Addie's heart, and she felt frustrated that she hadn't so much as an extra pair of gloves to give the child. But she did have the food, and she offered it forthrightly.

"This is for you because young boys need adequate nourishment. I know that firsthand, having grown up with three brothers and Silas."

Addie could see Matt's hunger vying with his pride, and she was relieved when hunger won, and he took the food and thanked her. But then he asked, "Three brothers? I know you have one with the dragoons and the colonel here with General Washington." The color deepened in his weather-chafed cheeks and his eyes slid away for a moment at mentioning Ad, but his curiosity persevered. "But where is the third? Is he so young that he must stay at home?"

"I thought he was too young, but he didn't," Addie said, blinking back sudden tears. "Quentin died at the Battle of Long Island. He was sixteen years old."

"I'm sorry, ma'am. I know what it is to lose kin." He did not elaborate, and Addie did not press him.

"Is he troubling you, ma'am?"

The deep rumble of the voice behind her startled Addie, and she swung around to see Luke McKinnon looking at them with a worried frown.

"Not at all. It is I who sought him out," Addie assured him, and Matt made the introductions.

But though Luke was polite, the anxiety remained in his eyes, and when Addie left the two of them, she could hear the chiding tone of Luke's voice as he spoke to his brother. She couldn't distinguish the words, but she could tell he was more concerned than angry. She sighed inwardly, guessing that Luke was worried about this contact with an officer's relative. Even knowing the necessity for such distinctions, she was impatient with them. However, she would have to go carefully with her impulse to play mother to Matt for fear of putting him in an awkward position. But that did not stop her from giving him more food and a little jar of ointment the next time she saw him.

"My friend Tullia made this," she explained. "I hope it will ease the pain in your hands, though the true cure will come with warmer weather."

At first, she thought Matt was going to refuse to accept it, but then the thin, sore hands, both wrapped in rags today, came out to cradle the offering as if it were gold, and Addie felt the already familiar rush of emotion that came to her when she dealt with this boy.

Ad noticed her growing involvement with Matt and grumbled, "Are you planning to adopt him?" And then he said softly, "He's not Quentin, you know."

"I know he's not. He pulls at my heart in his own special way. As he's watched you, I've watched him. He works so hard to be useful. He hauls the water and the wood, does the cooking and tries to keep their hut clean. But for all of that, he's a child still, and he ought to be able to play like a child now and again. But I doubt he remembers how to do that anymore. And that would make me sad for any child in his situation, even for one who has such a pronounced tenderness for my brother." She smirked at Ad, lightening the mood for both of them. They were both aware of how difficult it was to find even small moments of humor or joy these days as conditions in the encampment continued to worsen, with food and clothing for the men and fodder for the animals in shorter supply than ever.

When Mistress Washington arrived, the men who recognized her coach saluted or waved, and one group found the energy to raise a cheer as she smiled at them. The word passed swiftly that the general's lady had braved the winter storms to join them at Valley Forge, and having her there heartened them.

Ad, with the other aides at headquarters, welcomed her, and his throat tightened when the general, taking no notice of his onlooking staff, swept his wife into his arms for a long embrace. Martha looked so small compared to her husband, but Ad had no doubt that it was the general who was drawing more comfort from the reunion.

The general escorted her and her enslaved maid Oney upstairs to the bedroom, but once she had had time to refresh herself and change her clothes, she reappeared for the supper the aides had arranged for her. They had managed to gather a hard lump of cheese with fresh bread to go with it, nuts to be picked from their shells, and best of all, two bottles of fairly passable wine. This was a feast by Valley Forge standards, and Martha added a currant cake brought from Mount Vernon. As usual, she had brought with her as many provisions from home as her coach would hold. These welcome offerings would be savored in small bites at headquarters for weeks to come.

It was amazing, the effect this one small woman had on the heretofore bachelor establishment at Valley Forge. She made the place seem instantly more like a home, and she had a kind personal word for everyone.

After assuring herself that Ad was in suitable health, she inquired after his siblings and cousins, and upon learning where they were, she said, "I trust we will all see your brother and the Castletons soon enough, and please tell your sister that I look forward to visiting with her as soon as is convenient for her. Your aunts have sent a package, and I will deliver it into your keeping as soon as Oney and I have gotten the baggage sorted."

She was as good as her word, and by the next day, Ad had the parcel to take to Addie—knitted scarves and stocking and lengths of cloth, some of it homespun, some of it fine enough to be made into uniforms.

"I never thought to be concerned over such, but now I look on good strong cloth with eyes as greedy as any tailor's," Ad confessed.

As precious to Addie were the letters from their aunts, letters that conjured the old magic of days at Castleton, except there was no way to avoid mention of the war, not with all their men away to the north and with Sissy's husband gone forever. There was no direct word from Sissy, but Aunt Catherine wrote that she was getting stronger and that little Randolph James Fitzjohn was a delight to his mother and everyone else. Addie wondered if Sissy would stay at Castleton or return to Bright Oak, her dead husband's home. She was grateful that her aunts wrote as if it were perfectly natural for Addie to be with the army.

The aides had set aside a downstairs sitting room for Mistress Washington's private use, though it further cramped their already tight working quarters, and Addie was received there when she came to call.

Mistress Washington had never, in Addie's hearing, made any overtly political remark, but that did not mean she was not aware of or interested in every facet of her husband's world. After initial pleasantries had been exchanged, she asked, "Has the general been well? He seeks to spare me and tries to keep distressing news from me."

Addie had the uneasy feeling that Martha was asking about more than the general's physical health. This woman was too quick of mind to be ignorant of the Conway and Gates affair, even if the general had not spoken of it to her. Addie was sure Martha had her own sources, and it appeared she herself was considered one of them.

She chose her words carefully. "The general is always better for your presence, but he has remained strong through *all* the vicissitudes of these past months. And I do not think his character has ever been higher in the hearts and minds of the country than it is now." She did not feel she was exaggerating in this judgment. Washington seemed to be triumphing over his domestic foes, and there were fewer and fewer making the suggestion that someone else should command in his stead.

Martha nodded in satisfaction, the lace of her cap fluttering delicately, and then she began to ask about conditions at Valley Forge. In her drive through the camp to headquarters, she had taken note of the desperate condition of the troops and animals, and her compassion and concern were clear.

"The Old Man cannot do this alone," she said softly, using her nickname for her husband. "If the people want him and our army to win this war, they must provide what is needed to fight it."

Even now, Martha's hands were busy with mending, and Addie knew that she and the other women who would come to visit would be expected to lend their hands and needles to the task of returning the officers' wardrobes to at least minimal decency. Mistress Washington would also visit the sick. She would do so with grace and kindness, despite knowing these were small efforts against the enormous need at Valley Forge.

Martha was as true a Virginian as her husband, and the plight of the horses distressed her nearly as much as that of the humans.

Addie told her, "I sent my Nightingale off with Justin as a remount because she will have a better chance of being fed with them than here."

There was also a much greater chance the mare would be taken by the enemy, but that was better than having her die of starvation. Justin had taken her other horses with him, too. They would be useful to the cavalry, and would be fed. "Personal" horses were now prohibited in the encampment, and even the officers' fine mounts were growing thin. Addie either walked or borrowed the old nag that resided at the farmhouse where she and Tullia were living.

"I'm visiting the artillery horses," she confessed to Mistress Washington. "I know it is foolish. They need hay and grain, not my attention."

Martha patted her hand in comfort. "It is the best you can give them for the present. And horses are like children, they flourish with attention."

Addie had another motive for visiting the horses. They made her feel closer to Silas. Despite her resolve to be patient in his absence, she missed him more every day. She knew how saddened he would be by the condition of the horses that had so faithfully pulled the artillery wagons and gun carriages. Silas knew many of the horses by name and maintained that they were as important as the guns themselves. Now they were scarcely recognizable as the animals that had dragged the cannon into battle. They had reduced their shelters to shambles as they gnawed at the wood, having nothing else to eat for too many days. Their rough winter coats hung tented on their large bones, and some of them had already died.

This day, Addie found a big brown horse named Whiskey lying down. His eyes were sunken deep in their sockets, the heavy lids closed, and his breath rasped harsh and slow.

"Oh, Whiskey, I hoped you would make it," Addie said as she settled down beside his head and began to stroke his rough face. He was a favorite and accustomed to her. She had brought him little shavings of sugar and the parings from winter vegetables. "I'm so sorry I couldn't bring you enough to eat."

Whiskey tried to open his eyes, but he was too weak.

The day was mild for the season, mild enough so that the scent of death, stronger than the acrid smoke of green wood that hung over the camp, came to Addie from horse carcasses nearby. She wished that spring and fresh grass had come. She wished at the very least that there was ammunition enough to shoot the animals when they got this low, but that kindness was denied. The men were forbidden even to hunt for small game for their empty cooking pots.

She watched her hand stroking the bony head, heard her voice, low and husky, saying, "Go to sleep now, Whiskey, just go to sleep." Tears rolled down her cheeks, blurring her vision, so that her hand lost its shape and then regained it when she blinked.

With one last long breath, Whiskey died a little while later. The temperature was dropping, and the light was fading by the time Addie returned to the farmhouse to have Tullia fuss over her.

"You and Prince, you're mourning every creature in this place," she scolded, but her tone was kind, and she made Addie sit close to the fire in her room while she brought her some supper.

Addie looked at her hand again as she picked up a piece of bread, and so softly that Tullia didn't hear, she said, "Dear God!" The elusive thought took hold and blossomed until it hit her with stunning clarity. Those hands, those sore hands wrapped in rags, they were the hands of a girl, tapered fingers, fragile wrists, and all. And that low, husky voice was like her own, not that of a twelve-year-old boy who was more apt to speak in squeaks. She, of all people, after her long experience of masquerading as a boy at Ad's side, should have recognized it right away. But people, including herself, saw what they expected to see.

Matt was female and probably a few years older than twelve. No wonder Luke was so protective of her. No wonder she gazed at Ad with hopeless longing.

Addie's first impulse was to laugh aloud as she imagined Ad's reaction when she told him, and she nearly blurted out the secret to Tullia, but in an instant, she sobered. She did not doubt her discovery, but the secret belonged to Matt and Luke, not to her. If she were to tell, their lives would change radically. There could be no official duplicity charged because Matt was not enlisted in the army, but she would lose the safety of her disguise. Addie assumed that there was no one besides Luke to care for Matt.

The memory of running with Ad through the streets of Boston on the night of the Tea Party came back so sharply, she could smell the cold sea air. The heady excitement, the fear of the redcoats, all of it flashed through her. And the homespun cloth, yards and yards, of her women's garments felt as heavy and confining as the iron bars of a prison.

It was Matt and Luke's business, though it was going to be difficult for Addie not to betray that she knew. Discovery would come at some point, she was sure. If the pair stayed with the army, someone else would see the truth, but it was not her duty to expose them.

"Whatever are you thinking about?"

Tullia's question startled her, but Addie managed to smile and tell part of the truth. "I was thinking of the days before the war, when life was not so complicated as it is now."

To her surprise, Tullia did not question her further but only nodded in agreement, her face reflecting memories of her own.

Every night since Silas had left, Addie had dreamed of him, sometimes catching just a glimpse of him, sometimes speaking with him and seeing him in so many ways, it was incredible it could all be dreamed in a night. But this night she dreamed of Matt and others like her, women and girls disguised as soldiers, legions of them, and only chance revealing who they were.

Chapter 11

The efforts of the various foraging units had eased the want of food during the latter part of January, but conditions worsened steadily in February, with meat and flour for bread in such short supply, the men went for days without and had little else. Even when supplies arrived at the encampment, they were often unusable, teamsters having poured out the brine from the barrels of salted meat and fish in order to lighten the load on the snowy roads, with the result that the contents had rotted by the time they arrived.

Washington was always mindful of civilians' rights, but he would not let his army starve, so foraging became confiscation with promise of future payment in Continental dollars. The needs of the army were so great, Washington even complicated his life at headquarters by sending some of his aides out on foraging expeditions. Earlier Tench had been successful in New Jersey, and Ad went out with his own detachment, determined to do well, though he found the duty unpleasant as he dealt with sullen farmers who were resentful having their livestock and their stored crops appropriated. Ad was torn because he did have sympathy for them, but not as much as he had for the starving soldiers and draft animals at Valley Forge.

It was galling to know that, by all reports, the British in Philadelphia, far from suffering any shortages, were enjoying plenty of food, spirits, and lavish entertainments, including plays, dances, concerts, gaming, and a general licentiousness with the Tory population participating with great abandon.

With her brothers on foraging missions, Addie was thankful that at least Valencourt's Rangers were not part of the occupation of Philadelphia, Darius and his men remaining in New York and thus not a threat to Justin or Ad. But Traverne's Highlanders were there, and Addie thought of John Traverne now and then. She judged him to be an astute, worldly wise man, but there was also an austerity about him, and she doubted that he would approve of the debauchery of the British forces. As the Hessians had lost reputation as fighting men, so Traverne's men and other Highland units had gained it, becoming known for their steady ferocity in battle, so much so that the wailing of their bagpipes was enough to send chills down the spine from far in the distance. Addie did not want any harm to come to her family from Traverne, but she did not want him hurt, either. She pushed the thought away, reminding herself that it was all out of her control.

She felt equally helpless regarding a matter nearer to hand. As soon as she had seen Matt again, she had wondered how she could ever have believed her a boy. Despite her efforts at disguise, everything about Matt was feminine, from the crown of her head to her slender feet in the awful shoes. Addie lived in daily fear that someone else would see the obvious and make trouble for both of the McKinnons, and, for her part, she found it exceedingly difficult to maintain the pretense that she didn't know Matt's secret. It made her behave more formally around Matt than before, and she could see the hurt in the youngster's eyes but could think of no safe way to alleviate it.

Even knowing she could not tell Silas about Matt, she longed for his return; everything was immeasurably better when he was with her. And just when she was contemplating setting out for New England to join him, he was back.

Silas was so glad to see Addie, a great shudder went through him as he wrapped her in his arms and murmured her name over and over again. He was exhausted, as much mentally as physically, and needing to confess all, he did not spare himself when they were alone.

"I proved myself undeserving of the trust all of you placed in me," he said flatly. "I didn't purchase so much as a paper of pins. Prices have gone so high, I could not make any sense of them, and my nerve failed. And though our properties are still intact, the rents being paid in paper are nearly worthless. As for Darius's holdings, well, Knox put in a good word for us, but nothing has been decided beyond the fact that no one else will be allowed to take them over for the present." He flexed his shoulders to ease their stiffness.

"Tell me, do you plan to shoulder the blame for British stubbornness and the depreciation of our currency? Or is there more?" she asked, and at his puzzled frown, she said, "You did the best for us that anyone could do, if you would only recognize it. You are not to blame for the confusions of the war!" She smiled at him mischievously. "And you give us ladies too little credit for invention. Thorns in place of pins are all the fashion in camp now, and they work very well." Time enough to tell him that they were once again recipients of the largess of Castleton. "And speaking of ladies—Lucy, how is she?"

The strain of the past weeks had been steadily draining away from Silas, and amusement rippled through him. "The formidable Mistress Knox is in fine fettle and more than a match for Henry. She will be here soon, for she refuses to be separated from him any longer. If I seem a trifle deaf, it is because I was the unwilling witness to one of their rows. No wonder Henry's voice carries so well on the battlefield; he has good practice at home. It was quite remarkable. They roared at each other like two lions, and in the next moment, they were laughing together, as loving as any couple could be."

Addie could easily picture the scene, for the Knoxes' rows were the stuff of legend, with Henry, despite the rigors of war, still weighing close to three hundred pounds, Lucy of considerable girth herself, and both of them possessing volume to match. But no one worried about their altercations because they never came to blows and always made up immediately.

"I could yell at you occasionally if you like," Addie teased, but then she realized that Silas had fallen asleep.

The dim light from the fire was the only illumination, but it was enough for her to see that even in sleep, his face was haggard. But he was with her, and contentment welled through her so strongly, she wanted never to forget how she felt at this instant. The riches of her father's house, even the security of having the family all together—all of it could not equal the joy of being with Silas.

They had been curled together in a chair before the fire, she on his lap, and she awakened him only enough so that she could guide him to the bed, then undressed him just enough so that he would be comfortable. He was swiftly sound asleep again. She was not disappointed; they had the days and nights ahead to share.

In the ensuing days, Silas came to feel less dejected about his performance in Boston. Ad was in and out of Valley Farge, and when he saw Silas and heard his report, his reaction was the same as. his sister's—an assurance that no one could have done better given the circumstances.

Silas was shocked by the conditions at Valley Forge, for he had expected that they would be much improved in the weeks he'd been gone. Instead, he saw hunger and want everywhere, and he shared Addie's grief over the state of the remaining artillery horses.

"You had the harder part, staying here," he told her. "The enemy prisoners at Cambridge are not in such straits as our soldiers."

"Ah, but there is a profound difference. Those prisoners have lost; the men here still believe they can win," Addie reminded him. "And they believe the right man is leading them."

The affection in which Washington was held was evident in the efforts made to celebrate his forty-fifth birthday on February 22. Martha and the headquarters' staff had gone to great lengths to collect fowl and parsnips for dinner, and there was rum mixed with water to drink in toasts to the general's health and good fortune. And while the meal was being eaten, the fifers and drummers of Knox's artillery paraded to headquarters to offer their music as a gift to the general. Though it was snowing and the wind was cutting, the musicians played as if it were a fine spring day. And when they were finished, Mistress Washington went out to thank them, to give them fifteen shillings, and a little rum.

"They were as warmed by her kindness as by the rum," Silas told Addie. "And I know how they feel. It is what you do to me. By the merest smile, you make me very warm indeed."

"I trust the musicians were not leering at Mistress Washington as you are at me," Addie giggled, pretending to dart out of his reach and then falling willing captive. Though Silas had fallen asleep the first night, he had been as attentive as a newly married husband since then.

He flopped down on the bed with her in his arms and began nipping and licking at her neck and earlobes, making her laugh harder until the sound changed to a long purr in her throat as his mouth grew more seductive and his hands wandered.

A long while later, so utterly content she could hardly move, Addie murmured, "The other women know."

"Who knows what?" Silas obliged when he had gathered enough energy to form the words.

"The other wives. When I join them with Mistress Washington I try to look very serious about the mending and to follow the conversations, but too often I find myself thinking about you and losing track of everything around me. And since I've only been doing this since your return, there isn't any doubt about the cause. But it doesn't matter. The ladies indulge me because they, too, have good marriages, else they would not be here. Winter quarters must be the best measure of a marriage. Those who do not love stay at home."

Silas drew her closer, pressing his lips against her temple. That she was so proud of loving him, of being loved by him, touched him deeply.

There was something he had meant to discuss with her, but he was too sleepy to remember it at the time, so it was not until the next morning that he asked, "Is Tullia all right?"

Addie instantly felt guilty, for she had been so absorbed first with missing Silas and then with his return, and with her worry over keeping Matt's secret, she hadn't noticed anything amiss.

She said, "I know she continues to fret over whether or not to marry Mr. Freedom, but that isn't what you're talking about, is it?"

"Perhaps it is. But she is thinner than when I left, and though she has welcomed me back most kindly, she does not seem quite herself." Addie's distress was so plain, he hastened to say, "I have been away, not with her every day as you have been, so it is easier for me to see a change."

Addie did not doubt his perception, but still, she was dismayed to have it confirmed the moment she saw Tullia again. It was just like the situation with Matt; once she saw the truth, she wondered how she could have been so blind.

It wasn't just the weight loss—many of them had been fined down by the past months. It was the gray cast to her skin and the look in her eyes—haunted, abstracted, not at all like her usual sharp focus on matters at hand.

"What is it? Are you ill?" Addie could not keep the frantic note out of her voice.

Tullia was so surprised by this sudden attack of concern that her face convulsed in misery and she opened her mouth, but then she shook her head, a sharp little jerk of self-admonition, and her expression was so blank, Addie felt as if a door had been slammed in her face.

"I am worried about Prince. He has a bad cough and won't take care of himself," Tullia said, but her eyes did not meet Addie's.

Addie suspected this was part of the truth, but she was not deceived into thinking it was all of it. Yet she was helpless before Tullia's dignity and the old habit of deferring to her.

"I must visit Mr. Freedom and see if there is anything Silas and I can do for him. But I know there is something more, something that is making you ill yourself. Perhaps it is about marrying Mr. Freedom, perhaps not, but whatever it is, please remember we all love you, and there is nothing that could ever change that."

Tullia's mouth quivered, then firmed, and she said, "Thank you," volunteering nothing more, her reserve intact, her eyes still bleak. It made Addie feel lonesome to have Tullia so shut away in herself.

It did not clarify matters to discover that Prince Freedom was, in truth, ill, though he insisted he was far better off than most in the camp, a claim belied by his hacking cough and the obvious loss of flesh from his big frame. Even harder to witness than his physical condition was the misery, a good match for Tullia's, in his eyes, but Prince was more forthcoming because he was desperate to understand what was happening between him and Tullia.

"She visits often, she brings me soup and her physicking remedies, but she's gone away in her spirit, and I don't know why. I swear to you, I love that woman, and I don't know what I've done to offend her. I'm not making her choose your family over me. I've told her I'll wait forever if it takes that long, or I'll leave her alone if that's her want. I just don't know."

"I don't either, Mr. Freedom, but I don't think it's anything you've done," Addie said. "Tullia keeps her own counsel, she always has. But I hope she decides that her future is with you. It would be best for her, I'm sure of it."

He brightened momentarily at this pronouncement, but when Addie and Silas left him they carried the image of his sorrow and the sound of his coughing.

"Damn! The situation in Boston is complicated, but this is worse! I would like to shake some sense into Tullia. That man is perfect for her, and I believe the health of both of them would improve if she would just decide to marry him," said Addie.

"I agree, but what we think Tullia ought to do and what she will do aren't the same. She is very stubborn, particularly when she thinks she's doing the right thing," said Silas.

Within a few days, it seemed that Tullia would not have to make any decision, that death would make it for her. Prince's illness worsened into pneumonia that had him struggling for every breath. Silas helped carry him to the farmhouse because they could not bear to see him turned over to the rough care that was all the rudimentary hospitals could offer. Such places were death warrants for most patients. The couple who owned the farmhouse had no objection to this new arrangement once they were sure Prince didn't have smallpox and after they had been assured of additional rent.

Prince himself was horrified by the move, protesting, when he was conscious enough to be aware of his surroundings, "Not right, it's not right."

"You foolish man, you think it's right for you to care for others but not for them to care for you," Tullia scolded.

Any reservations Silas and Addie had had about what Tullia felt for Prince were entirely gone. While she scolded and fussed over him, her face was so full of love, it hurt to look at her. There was no trace of the blankness she had turned on Addie.

Silas helped keep watch when his duties allowed, as did Ad, who had returned to headquarters the second day of Prince's stay at the farmhouse, and Addie did everything she could to help. But Tullia left Prince's side only when absolutely necessary, fearful that while she was away, he would die.

"Just keep breathing, one more breath and then another," she coaxed as his massive chest heaved with his struggle to draw air into his fluid-filled lungs. She held him tightly when the paroxysms of coughing racked him, and she listened to the words he babbled in delirium, low, grating words because not even the high fever gave him the strength to speak loudly.

She heard him speak to his dead wife and to his children; he praised his daughters and told his son how to make an anchor, how to turn a horseshoe just so. And she listened while he said her name, over and over, speaking it with love, with sorrow. She was listening when he said, "Can't ask, can't ask no more for her to leave her family, should have known that."

The reality of Prince consumed her. Here was a beautiful Black man who had established himself as a respected citizen of property in the white world. And then he had left his comfortable home to do what he could to win an independence that would surely be shaped by white men for white men. And he had chosen to love her.

She felt her heart break under the weight of her cowardice. She had found great satisfaction in running Marcus Valencourt's household, and most of all, in raising Lily's children as Lily would have wished. None of that was wrong. But Quentin was gone, and the rest of those children were grown, and they had seen Prince's worth more clearly than had she. They had urged her to risk a new life with him, but in the most secret chamber of her heart, she had relished the safety of her old role as mother to them and had not wanted to change. She had been as stubborn as Marcus, refusing to admit that the world as they had known it had been altered forever when the war began. Lily, Marcus, and she had done the best they could. Now she had other responsibilities; they had seemed like burdens, but she finally recognized them as gifts.

Looking at Prince, Tullia saw he was growing weaker, maybe even giving up. Addie, who was there too, saw the same signs.

Ignoring Addie's presence, Tullia leaned close to him. "You cannot leave me, me and your child. Do you hear me? You are going to be a father again, and I am going to be your wife. I love you."

When Tullia looked up, Addie knew her shock was plain, but all the pieces dropped into place as she began to understand why Tullia had been looking so poorly. Close on the heels of shock came rejoicing that after all these years of raising other people's children, Tullia was to have a child of her own. But there was concern, too, because childbearing was always a hazard and to have a first pregnancy this late in life could be very dangerous to mother and child.

"You are sure?" Addie asked softly.

Tullia's smile was wry. "That this old woman got 'caught' like the greenest girl? Yes, I'm sure. And I'm sure I want the baby and Prince and a different life than the one I've had." As she talked, her hand stroked Prince's face. "You hear me, Prince? I need you to come back to me." And then she told him about the baby all over again, and she kept telling him, as she and Addie labored to bring his fever down and ease his breathing.

Addie had to make an effort to breathe normally instead of following Prince's jagged rhythm, and her heart raced with fear that he would be stolen away in spite of all their efforts.

It was near sundown when his fever broke and his breathing quieted, but neither woman was sure these were good signs at this point. Addie shivered, thinking that most people died in the dark hours and hoping that Silas would return to the house soon because she needed his warm presence.

Prince's eyes opened as if it took great strength and concentration to lift the lids, but his words were audible. "You and our child need rest." A slow smile curled his mouth until he was gazing at Tullia with such tenderness, Addie looked away from the intimate moment.

When she looked back, Prince's eyes were closed again, but only in sleep, and his big hands were holding one of Tullia's against his heart.

Silas froze when he arrived on the scene to discover the two women weeping, but Addie sprang up at the sight of him, and her smile eased his fear.

They left Prince and Tullia in peace, and because Ad arrived close on Silas's heels, Addie only had to explain what had happened once, a good thing since the telling was drawn out by the men's interruptions.

"Is that possible?" Ad queried, and he flushed and stammered, "I mean not that I didn't know that she and Prince... I meant because of her age."

"Could she be mistaken?" Silas asked and looked as embarrassed as Ad.

"Another woman might be mistaken, but not Tullia," Addie assured them.

"Well, when is the baby due?" Silas persisted.

"I don't know, but I'd guess Tullia's only two or three months along."

A silence fell over them, and then Ad said, "I am glad for them and for us as well. It's reassuring to know that life can begin even in the midst of such hardship as this war. But Tullia will be gone from us for certain."

"We could not wish better for her." Addie meant it with all of her heart, but she shied away from facing how much they would miss Tullia.

Though Addie would have liked for her twin to stay a little longer, especially because he looked so tired, Ad insisted he had to return to headquarters. "The baron's language problems have become ours. His English is negligible, so he writes in French and one of his aides, Du Ponceau, translates the orders into very proper English. Then Hammy, John, Tench, and I translate further, into 'American', so the men will understand. It is a tedious way to establish a code of drill, but we haven't any other means." He rolled his eyes at Silas. "What we wouldn't give for a printing press!"

Baron von Steuben was yet another European recently arrived in camp, having been sent along by Congress. A Prussian, he claimed to have served under the renowned Frederick the Great, and he proposed to volunteer his services to teach the Continental Army how to fight as a cohesive force.

No one knew if he deserved either the title of "baron" or the claim of noble blood indicated by "von." And despite the fact that Washington had done him the honor of riding out to greet him, most American soldiers had had their fill of prinked up Europeans. The baron's initial appearance, clad as he was in an elaborate uniform of scarlet and gold with an enormous jeweled medal bedecking his chest, and mounted on a high-stepping horse, might easily have set him at odds with everyone. But so far, the reaction had been quite positive.

"You like him, don't you?" Addie asked her brother.

"I do. He's nearly fifty years old, and yet he reminds me of Lafayette in many ways. He has a charm that is irresistible, and it seems he is truly concerned for our cause. When he reviewed the troops, he treated them with great dignity, though God knows he cannot have seen a more seedy lot."

Though he was physically weary, Ad returned to headquarters with a light heart. Prince was going to recover, and he and Tullia were going to have a baby—the more Ad thought of it, the easier it was to imagine Tullia holding a little one. And he did not mind that there were hours more work to do before he could seek his rest. For the first time in a long stretch, he was excited about the words flowing from his quill. A standard code of drill, so basic to European troops, so foreign to the American army—if the baron could devise one that the army could follow, the result might climb to the miraculous. A standard cadence to the march and columns that responded in unison to commands, Ad could see all of it, although he had more trouble believing that such a transformation could be accomplished in the time remaining before the new campaign season was upon them.

He gave the countersign automatically as sentries challenged his passage back to headquarters, but he was startled when Matt, rather than one of the orderlies, appeared out of the darkness to hold his horse as he dismounted.

Still in high spirits, Ad felt more patient than usual with the boy, and his voice was kind. "It's too cold for you to be out this late, youngster. I'll see to Ember."

He heard Matt mutter under his breath, "It isn't fitting," and he smiled, knowing that the boy thought an officer of his consequence ought to have at least one servant.

Matt trailed along as Ad led the bay mare to shelter, and Ad listened as he made several starts before he managed to ask, "Your sister, is she well? I heard there is sickness."

"Addie is in good health, and I will tell her you inquired. It is a friend of ours who has been ill, and he is recovering, so we are much relieved."

It occurred to him that Matt had been missing Addie, and though he still wanted to keep his distance from this strange child, something about him pulled at his heart, and he began to understand why his sister was drawn to him. Matt wasn't like Quentin in demeanor or physical appearance, but in the essentials, he was too young, too tender, despite his determined participation in camp life, to be at war. He wished he'd had the foreknowledge and the chance to tell Quentin that the war was going to last for years and that there was time for him to grow, to play his music and paint his pictures, before he had to march away with the army. Then a tremor of sorrow went through him as he accepted that even such prescience would not have stayed Quentin from his choice any more than it would have stopped the rest of them. The best he could do for Matt was to ask Addie to continue her contact with him.

For now, he thought of practical things. "Have you had enough to eat today?"

It was too dark to see much, but he felt Matt stiffen before he heard him say, "Thank you, but there is no need for you to worry. I have eaten as well as any in camp." He slipped away before Ad could tell him he meant no offense.

"Damn bothersome little urchin!" Ad swore under his breath, but he could hear the lack of conviction in his voice.

He sighed, thinking the last thing he needed was to feel any duty toward Matt McKinnon. It made him feel somewhat better to blame Addie for getting both of them more involved with Matt than they should be, and he intended that she take on the responsibility he was feeling.

Chapter 12

Baron van Steuben proved himself to be as much a diplomat as a master of the drill, forsaking his Prussian background of expecting blind obedience from soldiers and taking into account the independent American character that demanded reasons for commands and respect from officers toward their men.

Washington's aides wrote out the drill in American English, and the pages went to specially appointed "brigadier inspectors" from each of the fourteen infantry brigades, who in turn copied them, and so on down the line until all the officers and drillmasters of every company could make copies. But the baron did far more than oversee paperwork; he taught the drill to the Life Guards and then to an additional hundred men, so that they might teach it to others. And in teaching, he added theatrical talent to his laurels, for he was quick to realize his difficulty with English could be turned to his advantage.

It was no use to give the troops German commands, so the baron memorized the key words in English and barked them out. But his exhortations and oaths were far more creative, a blend of German, French, and broken English. He cursed freely and with great good humor so that the soldiers had all they could do to keep from answering his laughter with their own. He amused them as he instructed them, lifting their spirits.

Ad observed the process and wished he had time to attend the drills every day, for they were as entertaining as theater. And in the atmosphere the baron created, the men learned so fast, Ad began to believe a miracle *was* possible.

Florid-faced, the baron had bright eyes, a prominent nose, and a mobile mouth. He was three years older than Washington and under six feet tall, but his boundless energy made him seem younger than his years, and his stout figure and erect military bearing made him seem much bigger than he was. But his most endearing trait was his genuine admiration for the American soldiers who had stayed with Washington in spite of all the hardships. The baron had conceived an affection for them the first time he reviewed them, that affection had grown by the day, and it was as visible to the officers as to their men. By his example, the baron was teaching American officers that the British model of having no concern for the troops until the moment of battle was not an example to follow. He was not above demonstrating the drills himself, not above showing the men how a musket should be loaded and fired.

He raised the morale of officers as well as that of the common soldiers, and Ad was pleased to be invited, along with some others, by one of the baron's French aides to dine at the baron's headquarters. All the guests brought their own rations to contribute to the feast, and beyond that the only requirement for admission was that no one wear a whole pair of breeches. Since most officers were as threadbare as their men, this was a simple condition to meet and one that put at ease men embarrassed by their appearance.

The spreading knowledge of the drill and the willingness of officers and men to learn and practice it were not the only cause for rejoicing. The spring thaw was coming early this year, easing the distress the cold had caused. Edible greens were appearing along the rivers and streams and wherever a little sun could reach, though those who were accustomed to meat and bread as staples at home were not often willing to add "salats" to their diets. But provisions in general were becoming more plentiful in comparison to the lack of the preceding months, and there were enough cattle being brought in so that the cries of "no meat!" ceased.

The Bradwells and Ad had a special reason to celebrate when Justin and their cousins returned to camp with Harry Lee.

"You look disgustingly fit," Addie teased Justin as she threw her arms around him, and then she pulled away and clapped her hands in delight as she heard a familiar whicker and saw Nightingale. The mare was as sleek and muscular as the men and a different creature entirely from the surviving camp animals that were just beginning to regain their strength.

As Nightingale nuzzled Addie's shoulder and made little snuffling noises, Addie said, "Thank you, thank you all!"

But Harry Lee countered, "It is we who thank you. She proved herself as worthy a warrior as her mistress, and more than one of the enemy has cause to regret her speed and bottom. Your other beasts also served us well and are even now performing their volunteer duties by bringing in supplies."

Although he paid tribute with his usual quick smile and courtesy, Addie noted that Harry Lee did not seem to share the high spirits of his band. As soon as she, Silas, and her brothers had time to themselves, she queried Justin about it.

Justin looked to Ad, and there was admiration, not condemnation, in his glance. "Our brother knows, but he would not betray our general's confidence, not even to you. Harry has been invited to join His Excellency's staff. It is an honor for anyone, but for Harry it is especially so. His father is a longtime friend to our general—to refuse such notice would be very difficult."

Silence fell as they all tried to imagine Harry Lee's voracious energy restricted to staff duties, and Addie had the courage to voice their doubts aloud. "It is ridiculous! Harry would run mad and make all around him mad were he so confined! And what would happen to you and the rest of his troop?"

"Someone else would take command, perhaps Hart or Reeves. They are good men and much in Harry's confidence. But it would not be the same without him. He is a dragoon of dazzling skill. The enemy seeks him out for the challenge of it. And yet, I sympathize with him for being in such a quandary. I still feel some guilt for leaving the general's family, though I know it was the right choice for me," Justin said.

Ad thought of having to cope with Harry Lee at headquarters, and he shuddered in mock horror. "Addie is right. Please, do what you can to dissuade Harry from accepting this post! Hammy is excitable enough for three men. If Harry were added to the mixture, there would never be another peaceful moment at headquarters."

Justin regarded his brother with affection, grateful that Ad had never made him feel any guilt for leaving the staff, but then he admitted, "I wish I could stay out of the matter entirely. My position is nearly as delicate as Harry's, and I don't want to do a disservice to either him or the general. I hope this is settled soon."

Though there was less chance for skirmishing with the enemy, Justin was content to be at Valley Forge for a while. He had missed Addie and Silas, but most of all Ad. There was a quiet steadiness about his brother that gave strength to those around him, and Justin knew it was a good thing for all of them that he remained at the commander in chief's side, for Ad, like Tench and one or two others, could always be trusted to put the general's needs above their own.

Justin was pleased that Tullia had waited for his return before marrying Prince Freedom. Justin, too, was initially stunned by news of Tullia's pregnancy, but like the others, he quickly shared the joy of it, and he was relieved that Tullia's condition was reason enough for the couple to leave the army. Prince was out of danger, but his illness had taken a dreadful toll, and it would be a long time before he was strong enough to work at his trade again; far better for him to be at home with his family and for Tullia to be there with him. Prince and Tullia were neatly caught in the trap of their love, for though each might ignore his or her own health, neither would neglect the welfare of the other.

The couple was married by a preacher-soldier, with the Bradwells and Valencourts standing as witnesses to the beauty and worth of the woman who had had so much to do with raising them.

Addie swallowed hard against tears and held tightly to Silas's hand. She had no misgivings about this marriage, but it signaled that very soon Tullia would leave, and no matter what preparations they made, parting would be difficult.

After the brief ceremony, they shared a meal. They refused to allow Tullia to help, and she was nervous at being treated as a guest until Prince spoke softly to her. "These are your children, and you must let them do for you."

Justin proposed the toast, "Tullia, all our lives you have guided us. As much as our father, you taught us all we know about honor and truth. You made our lives in Boston joyful when they might have been sad. You banished our nightmares and supported our dreams. You soothed us when we wept, and you gave us laughter. No children on earth could have had a better mother. But now, we are grown, and at long last, it is time for you to live your own dreams.

"Prince, we could not choose a better man for this beloved woman. We trust you to care for her, to allow her to care for you, and to love her for all the years you will have together. Your child, boy or girl, will be most fortunate to have such parents."

Addie didn't mind then that the tears were rolling down her cheeks, for no one else was doing any better.

And then Tullia, despite her own tears, raised her glass and declared with her old fierceness, "Don't any of you think I regret a minute of my time with you! No woman could be prouder of her blood children than I am of you."

Beyond any more words, each of the four hugged Tullia in turn, and all of them thought of Quentin, the other child who should have been with them.

Prince's enlistment was up by April, but the couple stayed until Tullia settled everything to her satisfaction. Addie felt as if she were attending a special school for housewives as Tullia drilled her on every aspect of cooking, cleaning, sewing, doctoring, gardening, and managing domestic staff, as if Addie were the mistress of an establishment as complex as the household in Boston had been.

"You must be concerned for those who work for you and polite to merchants, but you mustn't let them take advantage," Tullia warned. "You can be too sort-hearted."

After days of instruction, Addie protested, "You have taught me continuously since I was a little girl. I promise, I won't forget what I've learned over the years."

But it was Tullia who had the final say on the selection of a cook and a laundress who would also do simple maid's work. Both of them were army wives, hardworking and thankful for the chance to earn extra for their families. They were eager to please, but Addie had no illusions that anyone could ever take Tullia's place.

Addie began to realize that she and Tullia were acting out a ritual. Had there been no war, in the normal course of things, she would have left her father's house upon marriage, and she would have left with words of advice from Tullia ringing in her ears. The circumstances were altered, but not the heart of the matter.

The constant attention to details served another purpose, leaving little time for either of the women to be overcome with sorrow. Nor were sessions with Tullia Addie's only obligation, for Lucy Knox had arrived, and other ladies were coming to join their husbands. Visiting with them and being part of the mending parties and the like were the duties of an officer's wife, and beyond duty, Addie discovered she enjoyed the women and admired most of them enough so that she would have been as glad of their company in peacetime as in war. Even Kitty Greene was proving ever more entertaining than annoying, for the better one got to know her, the more persuasive was her charm. She was easily amused, and her ready laughter was infectious.

Addie particularly admired women like Kitty and Lucy because they were never free of worry about their children. The infants they brought with them, but the older ones, sometimes only a year or two old, they left with relatives or friends rather than expose them to the diseases and privations of camp life. It was a sensible routine, but it left these mothers constantly torn between the pleasure of being with their husbands after long months apart and the worry and sorrow of being separated from their children.

As the straitened circumstances of the American army were steadily weeding out the unfit men, so it was with the women. Little was said about it, but those officers' wives who were physically able to join their husbands and yet chose not to were judged wanting.

The return of the Marquis de Lafayette to their society added to the uplift of spirits, for though he was disgusted with the failure of the Canadian venture to materialize, he refused to allow that to diminish his optimism and energy. And perhaps he had accomplished something more important than a military expedition when he had been at York, where the Congress was still in exile. There, during a meal that Lafayette had shared in all innocence, toasts had been offered—toasts to victory for the American army, to various military and Congressional figures, but none to General Washington.

The men who had invited the marquis to dine had made a grave mistake in underestimating his intelligence, for he was instantly aware not only of the insult to Washington, but also of the attempt to draw him into the company of those who opposed Washington's command of the Continental Army. With increasing effort by American agents to draw France into open support of the American cause, had those against Washington been able to claim Lafayette and thus his powerful French relatives for their side, they would have gained much ground against the general.

Lafayette had stolen the chance from them when he had stood to propose his own toast to Washington, thereby telling everyone in the room that whatever influence he had with the French Court would be used for Washington's benefit and against his enemies.

At the swift pace of army gossip, the story had reached Valley Forge before the marquis, confirming the high opinion his friends had of the Frenchman.

Addie suspected Mistress Washington had heard the tale, too, for she was open in her delight at her first meeting with the marquis and was soon seen to share her husband's affection for the young man.

Addie couldn't resist teasing her twin that now Lafayette was back, Kitty Greene was not flirting as much with Ad.

"I confess, a little less of Mistress Greene's attention will be welcome, but that doesn't help me with the problem of Matt, does it?" Ad asked, neatly shifting her jest to his own use. Despite the boy having taken offense at Ad's concern about whether or not he'd eaten, Matt had not ceased to be his shadow. Ad had told his sister that he thought Matt was missing her and had asked if there was a reason that her visits with the boy had grown less frequent.

Addie hated to lie to Ad, and she was bad at it. She'd said, "I'm just so busy with Tullia, and I want all the time I can have with Silas, and then there are the hours spent with the other wives. I don't mean to neglect Matt, truly, but there just doesn't seem to be time enough for everything." She hadn't needed Ad's skeptical look to tell her how rushed and false her reasons sounded, but he had dropped the matter at the time.

Now he picked it up again. "I don't want to worry about the child, but I do. Luke McKinnon is so involved in the baron's training, he hasn't as much time to watch out for Matt. Damn! I wish I'd never noticed him at all! But I did, and I would appreciate any help you can offer. For obvious reasons, Matt is more comfortable with you than with me."

It was all Addie could do to keep her expression serene. He was absolutely right in his judgment and absolutely wrong about the cause of Matt's unease. She wanted to suggest he reread Shakespeare's *Twelfth Night* wherein it is finally revealed that the page Cesario is really the girl Viola. She felt dizzy with all the twists and turns. Most of all, she wished she had never "seen" Matt so clearly, never become part of the secret. When she herself had masqueraded as a boy at Ad's side, she had always been able to return to her home and her identity. Matt did not have this option, and that made Addie feel obliged to protect her. But rather than getting easier, each time she saw the girl, it was harder to behave as if she believed the lie.

"I'll keep a closer watch on him," she promised reluctantly. She couldn't tell him that poor Matt was less comfortable with her now, surely a reflection of her disquiet.

After hard deliberation, Harry Lee had written an eloquent letter declining the staff position offered to him by Washington, and to his relief, the general had been more than gracious to him in his reply, assuring Lee of his understanding and continued support. Now Harry was being promoted to major, and there was the possibility of more troops being attached to his command, which would make his force stronger and more independent. And that meant that Justin, Hart, and Reeves, who were among the officers closest to Harry, would have even more duties than before.

Addie was as proud of Justin as of Ad and Silas, but she worried more about him because his was a more active role. He had spent most of the winter in the saddle harrying the enemy, and it obviously suited him. He was physically strong, but more than that, his smile was quick, and he showed none of the heaviness of spirit that had weighed him down while he was on Washington's staff. Addie admired his ease with his companions, for most of the Virginian officers, including the Castletons, were far wealthier than he, though even their uniforms, too, were showing signs of wear. Some had servants or slaves with them. Harry Lee often rode into battle with his hair fully powdered, and he drank from a silver cup even when they were in the field. None of this mattered to Justin, nor did his lack of riches or his Massachusetts birth matter to the other men—as far as they were concerned, his mother's family made him kin, his skills made him their equal, and they were all bound together by their daring and their dedication to chasing the British from their shores.

As hard as they fought, they also caroused with a will whenever they had a chance, favoring the same pursuits—gaming, performing feats of horsemanship, drinking, and dancing—they had enjoyed at home.

There was a massive run of shad coming up the Schuylkill River, and Addie watched as Justin and some of the other dragoons used their horses to "herd" the fish toward shore. The fish were of practical use, but Addie laughed in delight at the expression of pure enjoyment on her brother's face as he drove masses of fish toward waiting nets. He saw her watching and saluted her with a wide grin.

That night they feasted on the fresh catch, not minding the many small bones. The fish were a welcome addition to the camp's diet and were plentiful enough to provide fresh meals for days as well as being dried and salted for later consumption.

It was a special meal not only for the bounty of the river, but also because they were all together, including Tullia and Prince. On the morrow, the couple would leave to go home to Massachusetts.

"We may not be able to serve you fresh shad when you visit, but we will feast whenever you come," Prince announced.

It was the perfect offer, for it made it seem likely that they would all be together again someday.

Tullia eased the situation further by reminding Addie of all the ways there were to prepare the fish and reminding her, "I know you turn up your nose at the roe, but it's good food."

She then began to list all the ways to use it until Addie said, "I'll eat it, I will! I'll just pretend it's not fish eggs!"

Ad rolled his eyes. "She's lying. She won't eat it. She'll feed it to us or"—he looked at his brother, Silas, and Tullia, and they chorused together—"she'll feed it to the cat!"

"You all knew!" Addie gasped in disbelief, remembering the elaborate stratagems she had employed as a child to make the roe disappear from her plate after Tullia had put it there.

"Oh, child, it was a wonder to watch you hiding it, though putting it in your pockets wasn't the best of your ideas. It was better when you gave it to that old cat. I kept thinking someday you'd like it as much as he did."

"Never!" Addie's face so exactly mirrored the mutinous expressions she had oft worn as a child, Prince laughed with the others, having no difficulty in imagining the very young Addie.

The supper was merry to the end, but Silas still worried, and when they were alone, he asked Addie, "Are you truly at peace about Tullia leaving tomorrow?"

"I am. So much so that I wish they had already left. Prince is trying hard to deny his weakness, but he is frail. He needs to be home with Tullia. And she is a clever woman. In these past days, she has reminded me that all she had to teach me had already been taught, that if not for the war, I would have left her care long ago to establish my own household. And so I will, with you, anywhere you are, Lieutenant Colonel Bradwell." She was proud of his new rank, his promotion from major a mark of his value as an artillery officer. General Knox had congratulated him heartily, and Lucy had told Addie how much it meant to her that Henry had the support of such a proficient officer as Silas.

"I am still trying to decide if colonels are as amorous as majors." Addie's words vibrated against Silas's throat as she nuzzled his skin, and the languorous slide of her body against his convinced him better than any words that she was resigned to Tullia's leaving.

He ran his hands down her back to the curve of her hips and pressed her against the proof of his desire, rotating his pelvis in a slow circle.

"Oh, yes, a goodly promotion in every part."

The mixture of laughter and lust in Addie's voice was as much an aphrodisiac to Silas as her caressing hands. He gritted his teeth, fighting to keep control, but Addie granted him no mercy until they lay panting in blissful exhaustion.

"Don't ever become a general," Addie gasped. "I don't think either of us could live through it."

They dozed in each other's arms, awakening to savor each other gently, slowly, sleeping again for a while before renewing the old dance, and so through the night until the first faint light of dawn, as if they had all the time in the world.

Silas was proud of Addie's and Tullia's composure as they bade farewell to each other.

He did not hear the words Tullia whispered to Addie, "You and Silas keep on loving each other like you do. Nothing else matters as much."

Addie blushed, sure that Tullia could read the activities of the night on her face, but the look the two women exchanged was one of mutual understanding, each knowing that her place was beside her husband.

Justin, Ad, and Silas kissed Tullia and then the cart, built by Prince and pulled by one of Addie's horses given as a wedding gift to the couple, rolled away on the rutted track. Addie leaned against Silas as they watched the wagon until it was out of sight.

Addie was so content this day, she noticed little of the bad of the camp. The easing of the cold was bringing its usual problems. The ground was muddy, and the odors from unwashed bodies and clothes, badly buried horse and cattle carcasses, other offal, and from the "necessaries," combined to form a miasma so strong, taking a deep breath in many parts of the encampment caused eyes to burn and stomachs to turn over. But this day Addie saw the green of spring beginning to sweep the land, saw that many of the soldiers were showing more animation than they had in months, reclaiming their youthful energy now that they had enough to eat. Addie saw one group running foot races and another playing at "long bullets," bowling with cannon balls.

She knew the advancing season meant that campaigning would be renewed as soon as the roads firmed, but for now this mattered no more than did the drawbacks of the camp. For now, she was young, in love with her husband, and equal to any problem, even the problem of Matt.

"I mistrust that look. What mischief have you in mind?"

Silas's words startled her, and for a moment, she wondered if he could somehow read the secret on her face, but she realized the impossibility of that, and she smiled up at him. "I am considering promotions and how much I enjoy them," she told him, and her smile widened at the flare of heat in his eyes. She didn't feel remorse for the diversion, for as much as she was considering Matt, no one was more important to her than Silas.

Later in the day, she called at headquarters, visiting with Mistress Washington and some of the other ladies, all of them busy stitching as they chatted. Addie hadn't caught sight of Matt on her arrival, and she didn't see the youngster on her departure either. If Ad challenged her, she could virtuously claim that she had made an effort, but it had come to naught. Still, Matt's absence bothered her because, since their first meeting, she could not remember a time when Matt had not greeted her when she was at headquarters. She checked again the next day and was further troubled when Matt still made no appearance. She speculated that she had become so aloof in her fear of betraying the secret, she had offended the girl to the point of Matt's avoiding any contact. That in turn made Addie feel even more reluctant than before to seek out Matt. It also made her feel guilty, sad, and as ineffectual as a kitten tangled in yarn.

It didn't help when Ad reported his own lack of contact with Matt over the past days. "It's as if he's disappeared! Maybe he has. Maybe his brother sent him home. I'm afraid to ask."

"I am, too," Addie agreed, and she told him of her futile efforts. She felt none of the satisfaction she had anticipated. "A fine pair we are! We have gotten what we wanted. We seem to be free of the… boy"—she barely prevented herself from saying "girl"—"and neither of us can stand it. This situation is degenerating into such a farce, soon we will be able to sell tickets for the camp's amusement."

They found no solution to the puzzle by the time Ad left, and it was all Addie could do not to confide in Silas. But she recognized that that would be selfish, serving no purpose beyond burdening him with the secret that was causing her such distress.

And then Luke McKinnon sought her out, and she knew immediately that something was wrong with Matt.

"Mistress Bradwell, I am bold to come to you, but I don't know where else to turn. It's Matt... he's... that is, he's ill. Perhaps it is nothing, but it has been several days now, and..." He shrugged helplessly, and his eyes avoided hers as he searched for further explanation.

"And he can't go to the hospital because he's a she—your sister," Addie said very gently.

Relief and embarrassment were equal in Luke's face when he asked, "How did you know?"

Clearly he expected Addie to say that his sister's unwonted fascination with Ad had betrayed her, but instead, Addie told him part of the truth.

"It was a dying horse, you see, an artillery horse named Whiskey. I held Whiskey's head, and he died, and later I saw that my hands and Matt's were the same. I heard my voice, and Matt's was the same. So I knew." She looked up at him and saw his complete bafflement, which was exactly the reaction she wanted so that no blame could be attached to Matt.

She quickly gathered the medicinal supplies organized for her by Tullia, but she warned Luke, "You understand, do you not, that if she is too ill, it may not be possible to keep her secret any longer."

"I do. The purpose of her disguise has been to keep her safe. I would not allow it to harm her now."

"Her name, may I know it? I assume it is not Matthew."

Some of the tension eased in Luke's face. "Her name is Matilda."

"Matilda McKinnon, it's a charming name." She smiled, thinking of Ad's reaction should he ever learn it.

But all levity fled when she saw Matilda. The girl looked small and terribly fragile in the shadowy confines of the hut, and she was stuporous with fever.

"What about the others who live here? Do they know?" Addie asked.

Luke shook his head. "They moved in with others as soon as she got sick. They're fond of Matilda as Matt, but they don't pay 'him' much mind. Matilda has been careful to stay out of their way. Now they just want to be away from the fever. So many have sickened and died in this camp, everyone fears contagions."

Even as she coaxed the girl to drink the brew of willow bark designed to lower her fever, and as she bathed her hot skin with cool water, Addie felt her newly discovered independence tottering, and she wished for nothing so much as to have Tullia beside her, making the decisions. But Tullia was gone. She straightened her shoulders. Luke was entrusting her with Matilda's welfare. She tried to consider all the ramifications of the situation, but in the end there was only one acceptable course.

"It is too dank here with the earthen floor, and the air is too smoky. I need to take Matilda back with me, to the farmhouse. She will have a better chance there than here."

Despite his reservations, Luke wrapped his sister in the thin blankets and lifted her in his arms. Both he and Addie knew the masquerade must end with this action, but Matilda's life was at stake.

"We will think of something," Addie assured him, determined that he not be punished for protecting his sister.

Their first bit of luck was that no one impeded their progress, and Ad did not emerge from headquarters, though Addie had no doubt that someone would tell him eventually that she had been nearby.

At the house, the farm wife, once again assured that smallpox was not being introduced, agreed to a fee for the new boarder. Overhearing the exchange, Luke insisted that he pay whatever costs there were. As one complication after another occurred to him, his growing distress was plain.

Addie waved away any discussion of money. "You and I have nothing to consider except Matt's... Matilda's recovery."

"But what of your husband and your brothers?" he persisted. "Surely they will object to your taking Matilda in."

"They won't, not when I explain. They will see there was no choice. The war has taught all of us a great deal about that. And you must not neglect your duties. Your sister is proud of you, she would not forgive herself if she judged herself guilty of making you a poor soldier."

Luke looked so forlorn, Addie wished she could put her arms around him and comfort him like a child. He would never have asked help for himself, and he was having a very hard time accepting it for his sister.

"We're doing the right thing for her, and that is all that matters."

It was not her words as much as the competent, gentle work of her hands that reassured Luke, for even as Addie spoke to him, she was ministering to Matilda.

He leaned close to his sister, stroking her face very carefully, as if afraid his big hand would do damage to her delicate skin. "Tilda, you'll be safe here, and you'll get well. Mistress Bradwell is with you, and I'll be back as often as I can."

The quaver in his voice made Addie's throat tighten, but it also stiffened her resolve to give Matilda the best possible care.

Once Luke had gone, Addie stripped off Matilda's rags and bathed her until she could feel the heat in her skin abate. She coaxed her to drink, tiny sips at a time. She saw no rashes on the girl's skin, no signs of measles or pox or such, and though her breathing was a little rough, it did not sound like pneumonia. She sighed in frustration. There were so many fevers in the camp, some easy to identify, if not to treat, and others with no names and unpredictable courses. The only thing she was certain of was that Matilda was better off here than subjected to the rough care offered elsewhere.

"Addie, what the...?" Silas's voice trailed away as he took in the scene before him.

Addie was surprised he was home so soon, and then she saw that it was late in the day. She drew him away from the bed before she spoke.

"I'm not sure how much she can hear. She hasn't awakened since we moved her." And then she tried to explain the whole business, as Silas's expression grew more and more incredulous.

The girl was in the same room Tullia had inhabited, and Silas wished, as Addie had earlier, that Tullia was still with them. Recognizing the futility of that wish, he tried to sort out the story Addie had just told him.

"You've known she was a girl for quite some time, haven't you?" he asked slowly, noting the way her gaze slid away from his.

That was the part she had glossed over, and she chastised herself for hoping he wouldn't notice. "Yes, and I wanted to tell you as soon as you came back with General Knox, but I couldn't!" Again she went through the tale of discovery, thinking she was going to have to repeat it to her brothers, too. "Don't you see? It wasn't my secret to tell!"

"Not even to me?"

She rested her head against his chest, her heart twisting at the hurt she heard in his voice. "Silas, I love you with all my heart. My own secrets will never be hidden from you. But this one belonged to Luke and Matilda McKinnon. In truth, they remind me of Ad and myself. I have so much because I have you! And I have my brothers and the Castletons. I even have Tullia still, for I know I could go to her in need. But I believe the McKinnons have only each other. And if Ad and I were so isolated, I know we would not be separated. We would do whatever was necessary to stay together."

"Just as you did the night Justin and I helped to make tea in the harbor," Silas conceded with the wry humor and acceptance that was overcoming his anger and confusion. Of all people, he should be able to understand this situation. Not only had he been witness to Addie's adventures in her disguise as a boy at Ad's side, but he had been taken in and cared for by the Valencourts as Addie was now enfolding Matilda McKinnon.

He focused on practical considerations. "You have two servants. Can't they help with the nursing?"

"Perhaps later when Matilda is better, but they weren't hired for the task."

"And you won't ask them to risk contagion, though you will risk it for yourself."

"I don't believe I or anyone else is at risk. We are strong and healthy. I think Matilda is just worn out from trying to hide her identity and be a good soldier."

Silas hoped she was correct, not only because he didn't want some illness spreading through the household, but most of all because his wife, in spite of the odd circumstances of her meeting with the girl, had obviously developed a deep affection for her. Along with the rest of them, Addie had seen enough death at Valley Forge without losing Matilda, too.

"There is little I can do to help you here," he told her, "but I can spare you having to explain to your brothers."

"Thank you! I have dreaded it. Justin will be amused, but I expect Ad is going to be furious."

"Not when I'm finished with him. He's the one who got you involved in the first place."

Matilda stirred restlessly, murmuring unintelligibly, and Addie went to her.

"Her fever is rising again," she said, beginning to bathe the hot skin, so intent on her patient, she did not turn as Silas left.

Hours had passed, and night had fallen. Addie looked up to see Ad staring down at Matilda. The room was dim with only a low fire on the hearth and two smoky tallow candles burning, but there was enough illumination for Ad to see the pale oval of Matilda's face and her shoulders above the sheet.

"How could I not have known?" He wasn't angry, he was stunned. "I couldn't believe what Silas was telling me, and now I cannot understand how I could have believed otherwise. She is beautiful, isn't she? Even her name is beautiful. Matilda McKinnon."

There was such tenderness and awe in his muted voice, a frisson of alarm shivered down Addie's spine. She had never heard him sound like this, she had never seen quite this expression on his face.

He picked up one of Matilda's hands, cradling it in his. "You will get well, and then you will have a place with us."

Addie raised her eyebrows in silent question, and Ad looked at her as if he had heard her speak. "I think it was all decided a long time ago. She's mine, Addie. She's too young now, and I have my duty to the general, but the war has taught me patience."

His voice was low, but she knew she hadn't mistaken what he'd said. She had always known that he would love and choose a wife someday; she wanted him to have the same fulfillment she had with Silas. But she would never have imagined such a strange course as this. For all their sympathy with her, they hardly knew Matilda. They didn't even know her age. Ironically, it had been much simpler when Ad had believed her disguise and done his best to avoid her.

"You go eat something and get a little rest. Silas should return soon, after he has found Justin. I can stay a while before I must go back to headquarters. I will watch over her."

Addie started to tell him that it wouldn't be proper and then thought better of it. She was hungry, weary, and propriety had little bearing on this affair.

She stood up, stretching cramped muscles. "Call me if there is the least change. And it is on your head if Luke McKinnon finds you here."

"Luke has duty tonight, but I will talk to him when I go back, to assure him that everything possible is being done," Ad told her, but he did not look away from Matilda, and when Addie left them, he was bathing her face and neck, speaking softly to her.

Silas and Justin discovered Addie at the table before the kitchen hearth, her head cradled in her arms, and for an awful moment, they assumed Matilda had died. But when Silas touched Addie's shoulder and spoke her name, she roused and blinked up at them, her eyes fogged by exhaustion, not tears.

She gestured vaguely toward Matilda's room. "Ad is with her. He promised to tell me if there is any change. He thinks he's in love with her. He plans to marry her when the war is over." These last words were muffled by a jaw-cracking yawn. "Perhaps I can pry him out so that he can return to duty before he is court-martialed for desertion." She yawned again. "I don't know why, but I am utterly certain that she is going to recover. Ad will not allow anything else. He has run mad."

"Trust the quiet ones, they always have the most adventurous lives," Justin said. "Trust Ad to find his bride in such a manner. Oh, I shall torment him forever about the boy who loved him enough to become a girl! I tell you, it has mythic proportions." Justin's smile was broad, but he grew serious as he studied his sister, trying to gauge her temper. He knew how difficult it would be for her if Ad courted a woman of whom she did not approve. Ad had had the advantage in his twin's choice, for he had known Silas for as long as she had. Matilda McKinnon was an unknown quantity. But for Justin, it was enough that his brother was interested in her.

"One bride lost and one found, is there not symmetry in that?" he asked his sister, and for a moment, he allowed her to see how much he still mourned Sarah.

Looking at Justin, Sarah's image came vividly to Addie. She remembered her kind heart, her adoration of Justin, her wish to learn everything that she might still hold him even when the years had worn away the beauty of youth. Then death had stolen all—her youth, the promise of age, the hunger of her mind, everything except the memories they had of her, and those would surely fade with time until it would be impossible to call her back as Addie was doing now.

"Not symmetry, Justin, never that! It is too benign a word for your loss. But hope for Ad, yes, I see that. If Matilda can bring joy to him, then I will love her like a sister, as I loved Sarah."

"You have a good heart," Justin said, and the betraying brightness in his eyes touched her more than his praise.

Ad heard the arrival of the men, but the sounds were muted, far away. His world had narrowed to the slight figure on the bed. He knew he had to leave soon, but he was transfixed, at once numb and enlivened by emotions he could hardly comprehend. He had never felt this way before, so certain of something that was at best doubtful and illogical. In spite of their political differences, he was as much a man of order as his father. He believed in calmly assessing a problem from every angle and deciding how best to solve it in the most scientific manner with no clouds of superstition or whimsy obscuring the process. As close as he was to Addie and Justin, until today he would have been quick to judge that they were far more apt to act out of passion than he. Yet now he was having an experience that spoke of passion, not of reason. His mind told him that he could not feel so deep an attachment with so little knowledge of Matilda, while his heart declared what his mind refused.

Matilda moved fretfully, and then as Ad murmured words of comfort, her eyes opened.

"Dreams," she said, and Ad understood that though she recognized him, he seemed no more substantial than a fever ghost. A little smile curved her mouth as her eyes closed again. His heart soared because she had welcomed the dream.

When his sister returned to the room, Ad knew it was time and past for him to return to headquarters. He did not have leave to be gone overnight, and he would not strain the other aides with his work. But it was physically wrenching to go.

"She seems cooler, doesn't she?" he asked anxiously.

Addie was relieved she could confirm his observation. "Did she awaken at all?" she asked.

"She opened her eyes, and she saw me, but she thought she was dreaming. She really is going to recover, isn't she?"

"I believe she will, and Tullia trained me well in this. Matilda is not as sick as Prince was, nor does she have pneumonia. Trust me. I will take good care of her for you." She resisted the temptation to plead with him, to consider the situation sensibly. There was no sense in this. She had never seen such yearning in him, but she knew he had seen it in her, in her love for Silas. And he had never been anything but supportive of her choice.

"Thank you," he said, and he looked away briefly before he asked, "Do you think Papa ever felt as I do—so compelled?"

It was another gift she could give him. "Of course he did! His courtship of Mary was prudent, for all the happiness she's brought him, and I don't know about his English wife, but you cannot have forgotten the stories about Mama and Papa! Uncle Hartley, our aunts, Tullia, and Papa himself, they all told us how Papa took one look at Lily Castleton and was determined to marry her. And Mama, according to all the stories, was no less eager. So you must see, this is just part of our parents' legacy to you."

Ad put his arms around her. "No matter what comes of this, nothing will ever change between you and me."

She knew it wasn't entirely true. Things had changed with her marriage to Silas and could change again if Ad pursued his courtship of Matilda. But the essential bond of love and loyalty between them that had existed from the earliest memories, that still held, and she could imagine no circumstance less than death that could break it.

"Nothing will change; we will make sure of it," she assured him. "And Matilda will love you because there is no finer man on earth."

Ad was so moved, he teased to blunt the force of emotion. "Will you write that out for me, so I can give proof to Silas and Justin?"

Addie fell in with the play. "I was not specific enough. I meant you are the finest among those men who are available to love. Silas is in love with me, and Justin is enamored of his saber and horse, so that leaves only you and millions of others. A paltry number, indeed, with Silas and Justin removed from the equation."

Ad sighed dramatically. "I suppose I will have to settle for that."

After he had gone, Addie could still see the bright life in his eyes. Her doubts about his enchantment with Matilda faded, and suddenly she was nearly as keen as he to know Matilda now that she was no longer hidden behind "Matt."

Chapter 13

As Addie had hoped, Matilda recovered swiftly under the simple regimen of warmth, rest, and food. And as soon as she was conscious and understood where she was and how she had gotten there, she was touchingly grateful, but she was also so embarrassed her skin glowed with a deeper blush than fever had caused.

"Luke must have been very worried to so burden you," she murmured, "but I am fine now." She made a feeble attempt to get up.

"You are not a burden! And we're all happy that you are so much better and getting stronger every day," Addie told her, gently pressing her back onto the bed. "But you are not going anywhere yet. And when you are well enough to be up and about, you'll still be Matilda, so you'll have to make your plans accordingly. Matt is gone. Too many people know, including my husband and brothers."

"Your brothers!" Matilda gasped.

Addie decided that subterfuge had little place anymore. "Yes, and particularly Ad. He sat with you the first night, and he's been back to check on you as often as he could, as has Luke."

Matilda buried her hot face in her hands.

"Ad likes you much better as a girl than as a boy," Addie told her.

"I never meant to have him notice me, never! But he is so kind and so... so... I made a complete fool of myself." The words were muffled by her hands.

Addie put an arm around her thin shoulders. "No, you didn't. You have been very brave under trying circumstances. And though only time will reveal the measure of it, I think there is some special affinity between you and my brother. Life seems to find its own course, like a river." Addie kept talking, shifting subjects to put Matilda more at ease. "I used to dress as a boy to go on adventures with Ad."

"You?" Matilda asked in disbelief, her hands dropping away from her face.

"Yes, and I enjoyed it mightily. I even disguised myself for most of the journey from Boston to New York to join my husband and brothers two years ago." She pulled away so she could see Matilda's face. "Will you mind very much that you can't be Matt any longer?"

Matilda considered that for a moment, and then she smiled shyly. "No. It was very hard work to be a boy for so many days and nights."

It was plain to Addie that Matilda was also thinking that since Ad liked her as a girl, she was happy to be one.

Matilda cocked her head, studying Addie. "You knew before this, didn't you?"

Addie nodded, explained, and apologized. "I know I neglected our friendship, but once I knew you were a girl, I didn't want to betray you." And then she asked a question of her own. "Are there others disguised as you were?"

"I've been with Luke and the army since August, and along the way I've seen a soldier or two I suspect are female." An elfin grin transformed her face, making her look very young. "I did not ask them. Just think how awkward it would be if I inquired, and they weren't female at all. But I am sure I am not the only one. If one hasn't much of a shape"—she gestured ruefully at her slender body—"or if one is large and rawboned, well, either way, it is possible to fool people."

"It alters one's perspective, doesn't it, imagining women behind the muskets?" Addie mused, and then seeing that Matilda was tiring, she patted her shoulder. "Enough talking for now. Time for you to rest." She did not have to repeat it, for Matilda curled up like a kitten and fell asleep in an instant.

With each exchange, Addie's affection and admiration for the girl grew. Matilda was seventeen, not a child, but still young to be as mature as she was. Beneath the quick humor and lively spirit, there was a stoicism that had undoubtedly served her well in her years of growing up on the frontier of New York.

When Addie asked her about her family, she was tender in her memories but also matter-of-fact. "Da was a minister's son in Scotland, but he did not share his father's piety. He became a tutor instead of a preacher. He was employed by an English family that lived near the Borders. He taught the sons, but he fell in love with the daughter. That was unacceptable to both families, so my parents came away together to America. My mother had jewelry, including pearls from her grandmother, and that's how they paid their passage and started trading on the frontier." She smiled at Addie's look of surprise. "Oh, Da kept his hand in with the books, teaching us and other children in the settlement how to read and cipher, but he had grand plans for a new life in a new country. He liked the challenge of living at the edge of civilization, of dealing with other adventurers and with the Indians. He was proud that McKinnon was the name of the post and of the little settlement that grew up around it. He dealt honorably with every man and woman, red or white.

"Life was harder for my mother because of the babies. She had one every year or so, but only Luke and I survived. The others—some died when they were infants, and some lived for a few years before illness or accidents took them. Our mother loved our father very much, but she mourned each one of those children. I think death stole a little of her spirit each time, and three years ago she died giving birth again. The new baby perished, too."

She paused, looking inward, before she went on. "I know it is not the same as you and your twin, but there was a real Matthew. He was called Matty until he was three, and then he announced that Matty was a baby name and he wanted to be called Matt. He was *my* twin, you see, but he was bitten by a snake and died before our fifth birthday. I don't know how much I truly remember about him and how much is from stories Luke and my parents told me. But I think of him often and wonder how it would have been had he lived. It is why I took such notice of you and your brother. You are so close to each other. It made me think that Matt and I might have been so. Luke is a splendid brother, but he is five years older than me and must always play the elder."

Matilda was in control; it was Addie who had to swallow tears. People, particularly mothers and their children, died in the cities, but the scale of the losses in Matilda's family was a jolting reminder of how much harsher life was on the frontier, and she could not imagine her own life without her twin.

She feared the answer, but she could not resist asking, "And your father?"

For an instant, Matilda's calm fled, and her face twisted with grief still raw, but when she spoke, there was only the slightest quaver in her voice. "Da said the war was about the commerce of coastal merchants and had naught to do with him. But he understood that Luke felt obliged to go. So Luke went off to fight, and Da and I stayed home. McKinnon is near Fort Stanwix."

Addie's heart froze at the mention of the fort. It had been saved only by a rumor of reinforcements from being overrun by Colonel St. Leger's force of Indians, British regulars, Hessians, Tories, and Canadians. St. Leger had not made the planned rendezvous with General Burgoyne's army. But though the defenders of Fort Stanwix had not been taken, some other inhabitants of the region had not fared so well. Even children had been scalped.

Matilda read the knowledge in Addie's eyes and nodded. "Da didn't go to the war, but it came to him. We had a hiding place. He sent me there. But he stayed behind. He believed he would not be harmed because he was known far and wide for his honesty. He was ever a canny man, but not in this. They killed him. They plundered the post and burned it. I heard the Indians shrieking, and I smelled the smoke. But I couldn't help him. I stayed hidden for days. Then I stayed near the ruins of the post until Luke came for me. I wasn't alone all the time. There were a few others from the settlement who came out of hiding, too." She looked into a distance far beyond the room. "In a way, the Indians honored my father even when they killed him. They did not torture him or take his scalp."

"My God! How you must hate them!"

Matilda's gaze came back to Addie's face. "I hate the ones who killed him. But I don't hate all Indians any more than I hate all white men, though it was the whites who loosed the Indians on us. There were often Indians at the settlement. They knew Da would give them fair trade for their furs and that he would not addle their wits by selling them rum or other spirits. Most of them were good people, some of them not, just like the rest of us. I will never believe any who had traded with my father killed him."

She watched Addie closely as she continued. "My father did not die alone. A woman stayed with him. We knew her as Marie Rambeau. Her husband was a French trapper, but she was an Oneida Indian. She and her husband came to McKinnon every year until a year before my mother died. Then a year after Mother's death, Marie came alone. Her husband had died, she had no surviving children, so she came out of her loneliness to my father, and he, in his loneliness, was comforted. They were of near age, and they appreciated each other. Luke and I were glad of her coming, for after Mother died, Da became a dark, miserable man. He was one who needed a woman in his life. Marie made him smile again and look to the business. And she was kind to Luke and to me. She stayed with Da at the end, knowing what must happen. He could not make her leave him. She made it possible for me to run and hide. People will forget or choose not to remember that there were Oneidas with our troops."

Addie did not mistake the cause for the defiance in Matilda's voice—many people had nothing but disgust for white men who consorted with Native American women—and she managed to say, "It is good that Marie was with your father and that they loved each other." But then the images that attacked her mind were so lurid, she clapped her hand over her mouth as her stomach heaved. She thought of Jane McCrae and how easily Matilda could have met the same fate, and she thought of her own father.

All this time she had mourned the loss of him, had seen the ocean and the ideas that separated them as being as vast as death. She had acknowledged the idea that it would have been unwise and unsafe for him to remain in Boston when the British left. But she had never faced the reality of what might have happened had he stayed. Now she saw in graphic detail how it might have been, saw his spirit and body subjected to the indignities of the rabid Patriots, the ones who were still active in the towns but were so reluctant to serve in the army.

Tarring and feathering and being ridden on a rail were punishments meant to humiliate, but they also caused severe physical harm. When the tar was peeled away, skin and hair went with it, and being jolted about astraddle a thick plank of wood could cause permanent damage to a man. Marcus was not young, and Addie doubted he would have long survived such abuse. And any harm done to Marcus would have hurt Mary, too.

"My dear, you make me more grateful than I ever thought to be that my father is far away, safe in England. He's a Loyalist, you see, and he, my stepmother, and their little ones left Boston with the British two years ago." She told Matilda about Darius and about the Castletons, explaining how differing loyalties had divided the family.

Matilda was grateful for Addie's acceptance of Marie, and she was too polite to admit she had already heard that the Valencourts had Tory connections. Instead she observed, "I can think of few choices more difficult than deciding one's loyalty in a civil war. And the consequences of the choice can last long after the war is over. Da told us that there were those in his family who turned out for Bonnie Prince Charlie in the '45 and those who fought with the government against the Prince. As far as Da knew, even though they were kin, the survivors of that bloody time kept the line drawn as sharply as it had been during the fighting and never spoke across it." She saw the sorrow in Addie's face and hastened to say, "Of course, I am sure it is not the same for all."

"Don't fret. You are not telling me anything I haven't considered already. I do not think Papa will ever forgive us for the choice we made. But that doesn't matter as much to me as it did. What matters is that Papa is safe in England, and he has Mary and the children with him. You have made it possible for me to see that."

Addie also saw how that pleased Matilda.

It was hard for the girl to accept aid, and she insisted on helping with the chores before Addie thought she was strong enough. Luke and Ad came to see her as often as they could, but with the pace of camp life quickening, neither had much free time. When they were at the farmhouse together, Addie had to work to control her amusement, for though they were polite to each other, Luke clearly considered himself Matilda's protector and parent, while Ad was her suitor.

Addie had expected that Matilda would be shy with Ad; instead, Ad was so gentle and charming in his pursuit, Matilda blossomed with his attention. But it went beyond that. There was a sureness about the couple, as if they had known each other for long years rather than months.

Sometimes Ad couldn't recall everything he and Matilda had talked about, for the topics ranged from the progress of the war to books to ideas discussed just for the fun of it. Matilda had a lively mind, and her father had taught her well, though his library had been far more limited than Marcus's. But the overall feeling Ad took with him when he left the farmhouse was of a contentment he had never known before. Each new thing he learned about Matilda convinced him further that even if they had decades together, they would still rejoice in each other every day. Finally he understood the well of sorrow that was part of Justin because of losing Sarah, and he understood the river of joy that flowed between his sister and Silas because they were together.

Soon he would ask Matilda to marry him, though he planned to speak to Luke first, out of courtesy. Feeling perfectly confident of his plan, he nonetheless discussed it with Justin, as he would have discussed it with their father had that been possible.

Without embarrassment, he stated how much he loved and wanted Matilda and explained, "I know it will be difficult for us for a while, but we will be much better off than many young couples. And I believe a new Valencourt's can rise up in Boston. I haven't asked Matilda yet, but I'm sure it won't be long before the way will be clear."

Justin listened to him, but instead of the approval Ad expected, he frowned and asked, "Are you planning to leave the general's service?"

"Of course not! My duty to him comes before all else!"

"Then do you have some intelligence the rest of us lack? You speak as if the war will be over in a month or so, setting us all free to return to civilian life."

"More supplies are already arriving from France, and I believe, as do Tench and others, that a French alliance is very close," Ad said. "In

England, there is much disagreement over the war, and once France joins us, I cannot believe the war will last much longer. The enemy has little to show for so much expense and effort, and with France taking up arms, Britain will be threatened that much closer to home."

Like the rest of the family, Justin was more impressed with Matilda McKinnon the better he came to know her, and he wanted Ad to be happy. But he also expected Ad to behave with his customary good sense, and to see him so abandon it made Justin so afraid for him that his temper flared.

"Love has muddled you entirely. Your mind seems to have been destroyed by the bulge in your breeches. We have no confirmation of a French alliance, and even if it comes, do you think that alone will make England surrender? Gather what wits you have left! Do you think the enemy will forget that they have once before beaten France on this continent? We need men, arms, supplies, and victories! Hell, we even need shoes, and do you forget that the ones we just got from France are so inferior as to be useless? What if all the aid France offers is of the same poor quality? And you might ask Silas and others like him what they feel about fighting side by side with the French. There are many men who have good reason from the last war not to trust them. It is one thing to have visiting officers such as Lafayette and the engineers. It will be quite another matter if French troops and ours are required to march and fight together. Perhaps it will work, perhaps not, but no one knows. No one knows! Least of all you with your head up Mistress McKinnon's skirts—or breeches, as the case may be."

Justin heard his infuriated words echoing in his ears a second before he saw Ad's fist coming toward his face. He ducked before the fist connected, and he embraced his brother with all his strength.

"I'm sorry! I am so sorry! I like Matilda, I do, I swear it! I think you and she will fare well together. But I cannot bear that you forsake all sense. A soldier who does that is a dead man."

Ad jerked away, his anger so high he didn't hear Justin's concern for him. "Maybe you have gotten to love war so much, you cannot bear the thought of peace."

The moment the words were out, he was ashamed, and his shame deepened with his brother's reaction.

Justin bowed his head. "Perhaps you are correct, for I can scarcely imagine life without the war."

He looked so defeated, Ad couldn't bear it, and belatedly he heard the love that had fueled Justin's fury.

"Or it could be that you are right," Ad conceded. "There could be no sense in letting anything or anyone, even Matilda, come between me and you. And logic is on your side when I consider the duration of most European wars. I just hope we can find a swifter finish."

The tension in Justin's face eased. "Truly, I share that hope with you." A sudden smile stripped years from his face. "I confess, had you ever been as disrespectful of Sarah as I was of Matilda, I would have thrashed you."

This time their embrace was mutual, both of them infinitely relieved not to be out of sympathy with each other. And a few days later, on May 6, Ad's optimism seemed to be validated when the whole camp turned out in formal celebration of the official confirmation of the signing of the Treaty of Alliance with France back in February. This document left England with no choice except to declare war on France. England now had two enemies to fight, and the United States had the promise of troops and supplies.

General Washington had been moved nearly to tears by the news that at last his army would have help, and though his face was solemn as he reviewed his troops at the celebration, Ad and the other aides could see his joy and pride.

At 9 a.m. the brigades had assembled to spend the next hour and a half offering prayers and listening to their chaplains. Then at 10:30, a signal was fired from the artillery park, and the men fell in for inspection. An hour later, another cannon shot set them marching to their parade positions where they formed two long ranks. Washington trooped the line, and with his aides and the Life Guards took a position on a slight rise from which he could not only watch the proceedings but could also be seen.

Addie stood beside Matilda, viewing the spectacle with such a full heart, she had to struggle against tears. In the past weeks, enough clothing had come in so that the soldiers looked less like scarecrows. But the change went far beyond that. Baron von Steuben had indeed worked a miracle.

Fieldpieces on a hill boomed a thirteen-gun salute, and then a "feu de joie" of musketry crackled down the ranks. The men raised a cheer, "Long live the King of France!" The big guns spoke again, and the muskets, and another cry went up, "Long live the friendly European powers!" And yet again the ritual was repeated, and the men roared their praise of the American states.

The army that hadn't been able to march except in single file, that hadn't been able to march and reload their weapons with any rhythm, were now performing the baron's drills with precision. Now they knew how to march and wheel in unison, in measured steps and cadence with or without the beat of a drum. Now they loaded, fired, and reloaded their muskets with the same exactitude that measured their march. Now they had bayonets, and they knew how to use them to kill in close combat.

It was not the baron's miracle alone. The first men he had trained had trained others, and the new recruits who had been arriving during the past weeks had been introduced quickly to the drills.

The officers were as changed as their men. The baron had taught them to be as concerned off the battlefield as on about those under their command, and officers and men alike shared the pride in what they had accomplished. It showed in the erectness of their bearing, in the fierce readiness in their eyes. They were still short of men and officers, but they were more ready than ever before to face the enemy. They were finally more than a collection of men from separate regions; they were soldiers in the Continental Army.

Addie couldn't see Silas, who was with the artillery helping to direct the cannon fire, and Justin and their cousins were out on patrol, lest the enemy take advantage of the celebration to attack. But she could see Ad, sitting on his horse with easy grace among the other aides, and Luke McKinnon, keeping his post among the Life Guards.

"They both look very handsome, don't they?" Matilda whispered.

Because Matilda was obviously glad she had come, Addie didn't feel guilty for insisting that she attend. And though the gown of homespun had been made quickly and was very plain, she looked so feminine in it, she bore little resemblance to the quiet boy who had been Luke's shadow. The change was so radical, they—Addie, her brothers, Silas, and Luke—had decided the best stratagem would be to tell the truth, or at least part of it. She was to be introduced as Luke McKinnon's sister and Addie's companion. And for those who had noticed Matt and had inquired about his whereabouts, the answer was that Matt had gone home due to illness. There was no question of desertion since Matt had not been enlisted in the army, and Luke and Matt had kept so much to themselves, few knew any details of their background.

They were counting on the tendency of most people to have little interest in anything that did not directly affect them, and on this outing with Matilda, that was proving to be the case, except for a few of Luke's fellow Life Guards who eyed Matilda closely when they thought no one was looking. But Addie judged that most of the interest was because Matilda was a beautiful young woman, and even if the cause were otherwise, she doubted there were many men willing to admit they had been fooled.

An arbor had been built, and commissioned officers and their ladies had been invited to partake of a cold collation with the Washingtons. Matilda would have hung back, but Addie tucked her arm through her own, and flanked by Ad and Silas, they presented a charming spring picture and blended with the other couples.

Matilda was so pleased to be with Ad, her nervousness eased. She was able to answer sensibly when addressed, and she was grateful that the other women greeted her cordially when she was introduced to them. But her heart pounded wildly when she was presented to General and Mistress Washington. This was quite different from observing them from afar.

They smiled kindly at her, and Martha said, "It means a great deal to me that men such as your brother hold the general's welfare so dear."

Washington played the gallant, saying to Ad and Silas, "There are no more fortunate men than we today and no beauty that could surpass that of our ladies." Then he said to Matilda, "I believe a younger brother was with us until quite recently but has left the camp. Will we see him again?"

Matilda was paralyzed by the intensity of his gaze, but then she realized there was no censure there, only amusement, and she answered, "No, Your Excellency, I do not think young Matt will reappear."

He smiled and nodded his approval, and they continued on their way.

"He knows!" Matilda gasped, still so stunned she wasn't sure she knew what had just occurred.

"He knows most of what happens with his army," Ad said. "And as he has not condemned you, no one else will dare." The soft warmth and brightness of the May day, the festive atmosphere, and the general's tacit approval of Matilda combined to make Ad feel as if all good things were possible.

Rum had been issued to the soldiers, and liquor flowed in plenty for the officers, too, so that patriotic toasts were offered with increasing fervor, and when Washington rode away to return to headquarters, he raised his own "Huzza!" several times, leaving no doubt about the satisfaction the day had brought him.

The general had reasons beyond the French alliance for rejoicing. Ad and the other aides spent more time with the general than anyone else—even his wife—but only now, when his spirits were so high, did they realize how heavy the problems of the winter and the campaigns by his American enemies had weighed on him and on them. And though there was more work to be done with each passing day, they felt less burdened because their hearts mirrored his.

For Ad, this was yet another sign that it was time for him to settle his future with Matilda, and when he sought out Luke, he made it clear that he was on personal, not official, business. Luke nodded his compliance, but the still way he held himself said otherwise.

Ad forged ahead anyway. "I want your permission to marry your sister."

Luke relaxed a little at this proof that Ad's intentions were honorable, but he took his time before he replied, "I appreciate all you and your sister have done for Matilda. I believe she would have died without Mistress Bradwell's care. But the war has tangled things. In

normal times, you and my sister would never have met. I am proud
of my family, but they were very different from yours."

"They aren't, especially our fathers," Ad protested. "Don't you
see, they were both well educated and both came to this country to
make new lives. And while it was unusual that my father married a
woman from Virginia, now people from different regions are coming
together as never before. The war has changed things forever. There
are no longer separate colonies; we are the United States. The old
divisions must surely vanish in an era when the daughter of a frontier
merchant and the son of a town shopkeeper can meet. Matilda and
I have had the good fortune to find each other in this new age, and I
will be ever grateful for it."

Though Luke felt responsible for his sister, he was not foolishly
possessive of her. In truth, the best he could wish for her was that she
marry a good man who would treat her kindly. He liked what he knew
of Adrian Valencourt and the rest of his family and he was gratified by
Ad's earnest attempt to place the McKinnons on an equal social footing
with the Valencourts. But despite Ad's enthusiasm, Luke was uneasy.

"Do you mean to leave His Excellency's service? Marriage does not
seem compatible with your position as an aide."

"My duty to the general comes before all else," Ad said, and he
explained, as he had to Justin, his certainty that the war would end
soon and his plans for a new bookstore even if the old properties in
Boston remained out of reach.

He saw that Luke shared Justin's skepticism, though Luke was
more polite about it.

"I hope your confidence is well placed," he said before he fell silent,
pondering what Ad had said.

Luke felt a touch of pity for him, judging that his blind optimism
must spring from his affection for Matilda. His view was quite different, for it seemed to him that their army was still very small, that
it would take some time before French help arrived, and that the
British and their hirelings weren't likely to surrender just because
the odds had shifted a bit. He was a little envious of Ad, too, and
wondered if he himself would ever again believe in the possibility of

happiness. The world had turned into a dark place for him the day he had returned to find his home burned down, their father dead, and Matilda waiting patiently for him. But somehow she had been able to keep the darkness at bay, and all these months she had been a steady companion, always willing to do the tasks that made his life easier, never complaining despite the hard conditions and the added strain of keeping her identity secret.

Suddenly he understood the truth of Ad's claim that the social divisions that would have kept Matilda and Ad apart before the war had no validity now. Any man would be blessed to have Matilda at his side. And if she and Ad could dream of better days when so many, including himself, had lost that power, then so much the better.

Ad grew more nervous as the seconds ticked by, for he could not tell from Luke's impassive face what the man was thinking. Then Luke smiled and looked so much like his sister, Ad was startled.

"You have my permission to court Matilda. And I will glory in the day you marry, for it will mean we can all go home and begin life anew."

Ad blinked at him stupidly for a moment, unable to comprehend this wholehearted approval of his plans, and then his smile stretched as wide as Luke's. "Neither you nor she will ever regret this. I swear it!"

Ad remembered how amused he'd been when Justin had been so daft over Sarah that he could hardly speak of anything other than his passion. Now he wished he'd paid more attention. Despite the uniqueness of their situation, he didn't want Matilda to look back down the years and feel that she had been cheated of the fuss and excitement of a formal courtship. With little effort, he persuaded Addie that there would be nothing improper about him taking Matilda for a walk in the daylight with no chaperone.

"I wish you luck, though I don't think you'll need it," Addie said without Ad stating his intention to propose to Matilda.

In his head, he practiced all the things he wanted to say, to at least make the words memorable, but in the end, the best he could offer was a rather wilted bouquet of wildflowers and his heart. Matilda looked up at him with such trust, he lost himself in the deep blue of her eyes, and his usual ease with words fled.

"I love you, Matilda McKinnon. I am bound to the general's service until the war ends, but as soon as it does, I want to marry you, if you'll have me, if you'll risk my uncertain prospects."

"Of course I will marry you. Today, tomorrow, or a thousand days from now—it doesn't matter, for there isn't going to be anyone else for me. I think I've known that since I first saw you." A sly smile curved her mouth. "And that was shockingly inconvenient for 'Matt'."

Even in the shelter of the trees near the farmhouse, the sounds of the encampment reached them, and troops passed to and fro nearby, but for the moment, it was as if they were the only people on earth.

Ad cradled Matilda's face in his hands. Her skin was soft and warm, her hair glowed deep cinnamon in the sunlight that filtered through the spring leaves, and Ad trembled from the force of tenderness and desire that swept through him in equal measure. He meant the kiss to be gentle, but the first taste of her and her untutored welcome vanquished his good intentions. He kissed her until both of them were breathless, and still he would have gone on except that a hardy cheer penetrated his consciousness, reminding him that they were out in the open and scarcely alone. He shielded Matilda with his body until the men had gone on, but before he could apologize for losing control, Matilda spoke.

"Oh, my! I do hope the war ends very, very soon." She smiled up at him, her expression dreamy.

"So do I!" he said with such vehemence, both of them laughed, and he was grateful for it because it eased the spur of passion.

In the next days he became increasingly familiar with that spur. He had never before understood how sharp the longing for a woman could be. Serving with the army had taken all of his energy during the years when, had there been no war, he would surely have been preoccupied with the fair sex. It took all of his concentration to keep steadily at work when his mind wanted to wander away to contemplate all the attributes of Matilda that delighted him. The other aides knew of his preoccupation, but beyond some good-natured banter, they did not worry him about it, except for Tench, and Ad could not resent that because it stemmed from Tench's concern, which was the same as Justin's.

"No matter how much better trained the army is now, we are still too small a force to attack the British in Philadelphia or New York. As usual, we must wait for them to move before we can," Tench reminded him. "It is not the best of times to make domestic plans."

"I know," Ad conceded, "and Matilda and I are being sensible."

Tench nodded, but he did not look convinced.

For his part, Ad paid more attention than ever before to every report regarding the enemy, hoping to discern some pattern of disintegration. There was to be a change in the enemy's command. General Howe was going home for good, and General Clinton was to take his place. Once in England, Howe would certainly be called upon to explain why he had not pursued General Washington more avidly, and there was a chorus of voices raised on both sides of the Atlantic, claiming that General Howe, like his brother, Admiral Howe, was too fond of Americans to fight them as he ought. Ad tried to put the best light on the change, tried to believe that such problems at the highest level boded well, but when he was honest with himself he suspected they were losing a subtle ally with Howe's departure.

And however the angriest Tories regarded Howe, he was immensely popular with his officers and men, and they did not mean to let him leave without a proper fanfare. Accordingly, after a series of lesser celebrations, on May 18, all of Philadelphia was treated to the most ostentatious public display they had ever witnessed. Loftily titled "Meschianza," meaning medley, the production seemed to include most of the officer corps, their women legitimate and otherwise, and many common soldiers who took part in everything from a mock medieval joust to barging on the river to feasting, dancing, and fireworks. The spies' accounts were as incredulous as they were disdainful of such extravagance in wartime.

Ad had not shared his shifting opinions of the command change with Matilda and Addie, but he felt no such reserve in discussing the Meschianza, for he was as fascinated as they.

"Is it true that even the buildings along the waterfront were dressed for the occasion?" Addie asked.

"For more than a mile, the houses were draped with yards and yards of bunting," Ad confirmed. "There were also flags and pennants on the ships at the wharves and decorative arches on the land. And there were boats of musicians to play for the officers and ladies on the barges."

"The food, is it true about the food?" Matilda asked.

Ad nodded. "Lamb, veal, chicken, Yorkshire pies, puddings, pyramids of cakes, jellies, syllabubs, on and on."

"I didn't know there was that much food left in the world." Matilda sighed wistfully.

"I would have liked to have witnessed such a day and night," Addie confessed. "But I believe the enemy has been less than wise to stage such an extravagant event now, and in Philadelphia of all places! The Friends may allow good food to eat and fine cloth to wear, but theatrics, gambling, and dancing? Even the Tories who aren't Friends must wonder if the British are willing to put as much effort into defending their interests as into this frivolity." She and Ad exchanged a look of satisfaction—anything that distressed the Loyalists was good for the American side.

Addie had a sudden vision of John Traverne in the midst of the festivities. She doubted he would approve of such excess under the circumstances, and she could picture how well he could express his disdain without crossing the line into obvious disrespect for his superior officers. She blinked, banishing his image, but she acknowledged to herself that the Scotsman seemed to have stolen an odd corner of her mind, for she often caught herself trying to imagine how he was judging the progress of the war—from the other side.

Shortly after the enemy's lavish Meschianza, there was a much more modest celebration in the American camp at Valley Forge. Major General Charles Lee, he who had been captured at a tavern in dubious circumstances after having delayed sending his men to help Washington's army two years before, had been exchanged, and since it was an exchange, not a parole, he was free to rejoin the army on active service, and General Washington was paying him the honor of riding out to welcome him.

Ad was not the only one who had misgivings about General Lee's return.

"I care not that the Congress chose him to be second in command. The beginning of the war seems a long time past, and Lee has been away more than a year and in British custody. He has had no hand in the changes His Excellency and the baron have wrought," Ad complained to Tench.

"I would give a good deal to know the full story of why he did not bring reinforcements to the general when asked and what really happened when he was captured at Basking Ridge," Tench admitted.

The two men stared at each other, realizing how close to treason they were. But despite their trepidation, Ad and Tench, uniforms neat, horses groomed, every piece of metal shining, rode four miles out with the rest of General Washington's escort to greet General Lee.

From the first sight of Lee, it seemed the man had suffered no adverse effects from his detention by the British. His pack of dogs yapped at his horse's heels, and he sat in the saddle as if he were a ruler coming to visit his subjects, except that he was so odd looking, his attempt at majesty appeared as nothing more than arrogance in face of Washington's cordiality. Lee's great beak of a nose, his barrel-shaped torso, and spindly legs made him a bizarre figure, even on a horse, which was a pose that gave most men stature. He looked like a vulture incompletely transformed into a man.

The day was warm, but Ad felt a chill trace down his spine. General Lee might appear a ludicrous figure, but beneath his pretensions and his irascibility, there was cunning intelligence. It showed plainly in his bright eyes that darted, measured, judged. Ad could only hope that that intelligence was going to be used for their cause.

Two miles from the camp the general officers waited to honor Lee, and soldiers lined both sides of the road. Nor did the tribute stop there, for that night there was a supper and music for his entertainment, and he was given a room at headquarters.

In attendance at the meal, Ad's stomach twisted in disgust at Lee's slovenly manners. Food dribbled down from his mouth, staining and sticking to his clothing, but he didn't bother to brush it away. Ad admired Washington's restraint and the gentility that allowed him to treat others with grace, but in this instance, he found it difficult to observe the general's deference to Lee, particularly because Washington knew how disdainful Lee had been of his leadership.

"If you lock your teeth any tighter, you are going to break your jaw," Tench muttered to him, and Ad reminded himself that if the Washingtons could behave so politely, then so could he.

But the next morning reinforced every bad thing he thought of Lee, for the man not only kept Washington waiting very late for breakfast, he was filthy and disheveled when he did appear, and it was no secret that he had smuggled his doxy in by a back door and that she had stayed the night. Lee had spent the past weeks with the enemy in Philadelphia, and the woman he had brought with him from there was reputed to be a sergeant's wife. Ad wondered what else the British had given him.

If the aides had to pretend to be glad that General Lee had returned to them, there was no pretense in their joy that Lafayette had escaped capture by the British. With three thousand men, the marquis had been sent out seven miles to Barren Hill to keep watch on the British and perhaps to entice a small force into action. Instead, the enemy had turned out in strength, and but for Lafayette's quick thinking and a race to a ford the British could not see from their position, Washington would have lost men he could ill afford and would have suffered the personal hurt and political repercussions from having Lafayette captured or killed.

Though the Frenchman had prevailed, the incident, coupled with Lee's arrival, had a dampening effect on Ad's optimism. Whatever Howe's departure meant to them, the enemy still had fangs. The new campaign loomed more important than ever, and while Ad tried to hide his growing preoccupation, both Addie and Matilda noticed it. But they were experienced campaigners and knew the futility of complaint.

It wasn't just Ad, all the men were growing restless. Silas had less and less time to spend with Addie, and privately she mourned the passing of the long nights of intimacy they had shared. But she could not ignore the fact that the better prepared he and his artillerymen were, the better their chance of survival. By now, she knew many of the soldiers personally, and she cared as much as Silas about their welfare. Often when Silas returned late and exhausted, she simply held him while he slept, thankful that at least she did not have to leave him. Many of the officers' wives were packing to go home and would not see their husbands for months to come, would not know for days upon days were their men wounded or killed.

Kitty Greene was the first to go. Not only had she been parted from her two small children for months, but she was also expecting another before too long. Addie was sad to see the fluttery creature go. They embraced warmly, with promises to meet again after the coming campaign was finished.

Addie's heart went out to Mistress Washington, for Martha would have delayed her departure if she could, but it was important for her to be out of harm's way before the enemy was on the move and could cut off the route to Mount Vernon, or worse, capture her. Addie knew her well enough now to see the sorrow in her eyes, despite the unruffled facade she presented. But despite the press of her affairs, Martha made sure that Addie felt free to send letters to Castleton with her and assured her she would also contact the Castletons to give them news. When her coach rolled out of Valley Forge early in June, Martha wore a smile for the sake of the troops, and they waved to her as she passed.

Lucy Knox was not among those leaving. She and Henry had lost their infant son, but two-year-old Lucy was flourishing with her parents at Valley Forge. Lucy was determined to stay with Henry until the British had quit Philadelphia and the Americans could repossess the city.

Addie was happy that Lucy would remain with them, for she was less retiring than Mistress Washington and had a special knack for bringing people together and putting them at their ease. The Knoxes' house was the liveliest place in the encampment. But Addie admired them for more than their social skills. The loss of their son had hurt them, but they were a couple who expressed their sorrows, their angers, and their joys openly and went on together, no matter what. And they were both completely devoted to General Washington. That had long been an important quality, but with General Lee back in their midst, it was doubly so.

Addie did not need her twin's confidences to make a judgment about Lee. Without committing any overt breach of manners toward her, he managed to convey a lascivious interest that made Addie's flesh creep, and the feverish glitter in the man's eyes, his slovenly habits, and his complete self-absorption made her wonder about the stability of his mind. She was as worried as Ad about his role in the coming campaign.

Regarding that, new rumors sped daily through the encampment, but certain things seemed clear. With the promise of a French fleet due to arrive at any time, it would not serve Clinton to stay in Philadelphia where he might be cut off forever from his base of power in New York. Before, with no American navy to speak of, the enemy had had little fear of interference when moving troops by water under the armed support of their fleet. But now they might run into heavily armed French ships. In addition, sailing down the Delaware River to the Atlantic and then north again to New York was a far longer journey than going overland until they could be transported across a short stretch of ocean to their strongholds in and around New York City. There was an obvious risk in traveling by land where the Americans might have a chance to get at them, but few believed the British would fear that more than going the long way around and possibly meeting the French on the way.

With Matilda's help, Addie had everything packed and ready to go when word came that the enemy was on the verge of evacuating Philadelphia. The spies' reports came in with more and more details. The British were rounding up every horse and wagon so they could haul their baggage to New York. Redoubts were being built on the Jersey shore, and the three hundred vessels in the river would probably be used to get the army across the Delaware River to New Jersey. Then the ships would begin the long journey to New York by water, and they would be loaded with what the army was not taking with them and with the Loyalists who were filling the streets with their possessions and with the same panic that had seized those in Boston when the British left. There was little General Clinton could do to quiet their howls of outrage and fear.

Part of Addie thought it served them right to be so punished for their welcome of the enemy, but because of Marcus, another part of her was sympathetic to their plight. At least the French would have little interest in such refugees should they come upon the ships.

On June 18, word came that, beginning at three in the morning, Clinton had gotten his entire force across to the Jersey side of the river in just seven hours.

One division of the Continental Army was ready to move out of the encampment before the sun set, and the next day, precisely six months since they had arrived at Valley Forge, the rest of the army moved out. They bore little resemblance to the ragged force December had seen. These men marched in easy cadence, heads up, and weapons carried with authority. These men wanted their chance at the enemy.

Addie glanced back for a last look. Much had happened in Valley Forge, so much suffering and so much triumph. And on a personal scale, too, here she and Silas had discovered new depths to their marriage; from here Tullia had left for a new life; and here Matilda had been found for Ad.

Addie wondered how long it would take for the land to heal its wounds, to replace the thousands of trees that had been cut down, to dissolve the huts, and to absorb the refuse of thousands of humans. Already the land was so green, perhaps it would not be long before all trace of the past winter was gone. She wondered if, in a generation or so, the loyalty and courage of the men and women who had stayed with General Washington through the months of hellish want would be remembered and honored.

From beside her on the wagon seat, Matilda said, as if in answer to her thoughts, "None of us who were here will ever forget how it was. And each of us will tell others down the years, so that even when every one of us is gone, the story will be remembered. People yet unborn will want to know how this nation was begun, and Valley Forge is part of that beginning."

Matilda spoke with Ad's certainty of victory, and Addie's doubts eased as she let the full import of the day sweep over her. The enemy had failed to hold Philadelphia, and Congress could return. And now Washington was on the march against the British commander in chief and his army. Suddenly all good things seemed possible. She did not look back again.

Chapter 14

A force led by General Arnold entered Philadelphia on the heels of the British. Arnold was still hampered by the leg wound received during the campaign against Burgoyne, but he was fit enough to accept the position of Military Governor of Philadelphia.

While the transition in the city went smoothly, the pursuit of Clinton did not. Washington believed that Clinton intended to draw him into battle on ground of his choosing, and the general was ever cautious about that. But he was also anxious to engage the British if the advantage was the Americans'. Determining that meant having accurate troop returns and details about every aspect of the enemy's movements. There was no difficulty in tracking Clinton's progress as it was very slow, hobbled not only by the hot weather, but also by a baggage train more than twelve miles long. Clinton's troop strength was estimated to be about equal to Washington's—nearly twelve thousand.

Ad and his fellow aides believed that at last they had a chance to thoroughly trounce the enemy, but to their growing horror, the opportunity seemed to be slipping away piecemeal, and it was hard to understand the general's plan, for he kept detaching troops, trying to test Clinton here and there, instead of keeping his army together. And worse, he continued to defer to General Lee.

Even before Clinton had left the city, Lee had argued against a full attack on Clinton when Washington had suggested it, and his continued reluctance seemed to have infected Washington in a way so profound it was causing him to work against his own interests. More than ever, Ad believed that the British had served their own interests in their exchange of Lee.

"General Lee does not believe we can stand against the British, or perhaps he thinks we can and does not want it to happen," Ad said to Tench. "I swear to you, whatever virtue brought him to our side in the beginning has fled. The man will ruin us!"

But there was grief rather than anger in Tench. "His Excellency is a noble man, and he expects nobility in others. It always strikes him hard when he finally finds it lacking. Though in truth, I do not know why he continues to suffer General Lee's insolence or his faint heart."

They were doing double duty both as secretaries and riding aides, going from pen to saddle and back to pen again in the dark hours. But they realized that their exhaustion was more from tension than from physical effort.

Ad had little time to see Addie or Matilda, and he thought it just as well that they not witness his increasing apprehension. But he wished Justin were at hand instead of still being off in the countryside with the cavalry. He wondered what his brother would make of this erratic campaign.

The one thing that gave Ad some hope was that Lafayette was to be in command of one of the forward detachments. Again deferring to General Lee, and because of Lee's seniority, Washington had offered him the post, but for whatever peculiar reasons of his own, he had declined. And in this case, Washington had made known his preference for Lafayette. Unlike Lee, the marquis was eager for battle; however, even this arrangement was not without its hazards because Lee then changed his mind, saying he would like to command after all. Then he declined it once again.

The army had moved north from Valley Forge, crossing the Delaware about forty miles above Philadelphia. From there Washington had begun sending out the detachments to test Clinton's intention while he himself moved the main force from one hamlet to the next. Then word came in that Clinton was pressing toward Monmouth Court House. With that, Washington sent yet another detachment, this of a thousand men under the Pennsylvanian General Anthony Wayne, and Lafayette went with them in order to take command of all the forward troops.

On June 26, at headquarters, they received messages from the marquis that enemy stragglers were being captured and many deserters were coming in, and that he believed Clinton's army could be struck. Ad and the other aides scarcely had a moment to enjoy this news before General Lee presented himself to Washington. Lee had changed his mind again, deciding he wanted Lafayette's command after all. Lafayette had graciously written a letter stating that if General Washington wished him to serve under Lee, he was willing.

"I am senior to the Frenchman," Lee pointed out, as if Washington were not well aware of that.

Ad felt the particular torment of being one of the aides recording the meeting, and it was all he could do to control his quill. So much anger was coursing through his body, his hands wanted to make fists, and he wanted to shout his protest. But his duty was to write down the words of others, not to speak his own. He wrote them all down, including those spoken by Washington to give command of the forward divisions to Lee.

Just for a moment, Lee's eyes glared at Ad, bright with triumph and scorn. Despite Ad's attempt to appear impassive, Lee had read something of his thoughts, and Lee was not the sort of officer who believed those beneath his rank should have opinions of their own.

Ad had had his own revelation, for beyond the obvious in Lee's look, he had seen the flicker of something else, and for the first time, he wondered if those who whispered that General Lee might be unstable were right. Heretofore, he had discounted such rumors, judging the man sane though treacherous. Now he thought that insanity and treachery mixed must surely be a lethal brew.

General Washington was not like Lee. He was not above consulting with the junior officers on his staff, and Ad gathered himself to explain his reservations if given an opening. But this time the general simply thanked and dismissed him. And the next day Lee, with orders to attack the British as soon as possible, left with two brigades to take command of a force that included nearly half of Washington's army.

Addie and Matilda were as aware as everyone else of the shifting of various brigades, but their main concerns were domestic. To their mutual delight, they were proving to be good traveling companions, and while the army was on the move, their challenge was to set up camp at the end of the day, always making sure that they cooked enough of whatever they had so that if Ad, Silas, or Luke could join them, they would not go hungry. They bargained for vegetables, fruit, poultry, eggs, and whatever else the farmers along the way would sell to them. The prices were much lower than they would be in Philadelphia, and there was plenty on the land now, in great contrast to the starving months.

They saw little of Ad, and Luke, too, had trouble getting away from whatever temporary camp represented headquarters, but Silas spent each night at Addie's side. The weather was so warm, even at night, and they were traveling in such close confines with the army, privacy was impossible. Despite the mosquitoes and other insects, they often didn't bother to rig a tent, but slept under the wagon while Matilda slept in it.

The Knoxes had entered Philadelphia just as Lucy had wished, but the city was so dirty and malodorous in the wake of the enemy's departure, General Knox had had to find lodgings for Lucy outside of the town. Knox was with Washington now, as was Silas, but one of the new skills the army had acquired during the months of training was the ability to send artillery wherever it was needed. Silas knew that he could be detached at any moment to a position where it would not be feasible for Addie to follow, and that made him savor his time with her even more than usual.

They whispered in the dark, mixing nonsense with the subjects closest to their hearts, speaking honestly of the battle to come.

"The men are ready, and I'd match them against British gunners any day."

"I'd add their wives to the match," Addie said. "They are the most formidable women I've ever met!"

They laughed together, but there was fondness in their humor. Many of the wives who were accompanying the gunners were as brawny as their men—women built wide in body and appetites, women who smoked their pipes, spat, cursed, joked, ate, drank, and brawled as heartily as their husbands. But they were loyal wives and as tender as any with their infants. Though they weren't likely to become close friends, the women and Addie treated each other with mutual respect, and they all shared the worry when their men went to fight.

"Some of the women stay beside their husbands in battle," Addie said.

"Do not even consider it!" Silas's voice was sharp. "Were you there, I would not be able to think of aught else."

They were accustomed to the sounds of the army, and usually slept before long, but this night the camp was so restless, Addie began to wish that they had found a room at a farmhouse. She could hear dispatch riders coming in and going out long after darkness had fallen. Neither Luke nor Ad had showed up for supper this evening, and Addie supposed her brother was writing messages and riding in the dark to deliver them.

It was not only those closest to the general who were astir; it was as if an odd current, a river of energy, were flowing through the whole army. Addie wondered if the same was flowing through the enemy's ranks. If there was to be a battle, it must be soon, before the British escaped to their lair.

Ignoring the heat and the whine of mosquitoes, Addie curled closer to Silas. Tomorrow would be a Sunday, but Addie doubted that would silence the guns.

By dawn, those at headquarters knew that Lafayette, although still deferring to Lee, was worried about what action Lee was going to take and had gone to Lee's headquarters to speak with him the preceding evening and again at four this morning. Then the report came in that the British had begun to move out at daybreak, heading toward the sea. Washington immediately sent word to Lee "to attack the enemy, unless very powerful reasons prevented." Washington also assured Lee that the main army was advancing to support him.

Von Steuben had taught the army well, and Washington's soldiers were swiftly on the march, even the sick wanting to take a turn at the enemy. Blanket rolls and anything else that might slow the men down were left behind.

Addie hugged Silas hard. "Godspeed. I love you."

Silas kissed her, not caring how many people watched. "I love you, too. Keep safely to the rear. I'll find you when the day is done." He mounted his horse and rode off looking so confident that Addie's fear eased.

The day was already very warm despite the early hour, and it was going to be miserable to trail behind in the dust, but Addie and

Matilda were resigned to it, for neither of them wanted to stay too far in the rear.

Ad rode with the general and those aides who were not carrying messages. Like most of the others, Ad had gotten no sleep at all during the night and little the previous nights, but rather than feeling exhaustion, he was enveloped in a strange calm. It was hot, growing hotter by the minute, and dust and flies swirled around the horses. He noticed these things, but they did not cause him any special discomfort. All his senses were concentrated on the battle ahead. If they carried this day, the war must end soon. Then he and Matilda could marry and begin a new life together. He had never wanted victory so much. It made him understand Justin better than ever before, and he wished his brother and cousins were riding beside him.

By the time they passed a meetinghouse not many miles from Monmouth Court House, they had heard the distant rumble of cannon and crackle of musketry, and when the road forked, Washington sent General Greene's wing to the right to avoid any chance that the enemy could turn his army's right flank.

They hadn't proceeded very far beyond Greene's departure point before a roughly dressed man on a chunky farm horse came toward them saying he had heard that the Americans were retreating and close on his heels came a fifer, so frightened by what was behind him that he didn't realize he had been brought before his commander in chief until Washington asked him quite patiently if he was with the army and if he was, why was he coming this way?

The young man looked up at the man on the tall white charger, and for an instant, he swayed as if to faint, but then he croaked, "Our soldiers, Your Excellency, them that was gain' forward, they're retreatin' now." He glanced back the way he had come.

To Ad's amazement, the general seemed more exasperated than apprehensive at this news, telling the youngster that if he spread the rumor any further, he would be flogged. And he ordered the civilian on horseback to be kept in custody.

Some fifty yards farther along the road, they met three more men, one of them in uniform, and all of them in a hurry. Their stories matched the fifer's. But still, Washington was not convinced, particularly because they could no longer hear cannon fire and because in every battle there were those whose nerve failed even when things were going well.

Ad exchanged a look with Tench and saw that he shared his dread, and that gave him courage. "Your Excellency, this account is being given by different persons. Perhaps it is worthy of investigation." There were already aides in the field, but so far there had been no useful reports from them.

As soon as Ad made the offer, other aides spoke up, and the general dispatched him and two others to gather what information they could. They rode forward, separating to cover as much territory as possible.

Though reports had the terrain fairly flat, that was deceiving, for the land flowed over small hills and was cut by ravines, and the footing varied from firm, to sandy, to swampy. Nor was it an entirely natural landscape, for the area was well farmed. Wild patches of trees and bramble gave way to planted fields and lush orchards. Ad wished he had enough information about the topography to know if there was a lookout that would let him see all. The chance of finding a local to guide him seemed remote, as civilians were prudently making themselves scarce in the wake of two armies. And even were they not, it would be as likely to find a Tory and thus treachery as to meet a Patriot.

He saw more men coming this way, and he recognized a captain in that regiment. "What is the cause of this retreat and is it general?" he inquired. "Or is only part of the army involved?"

The captain regarded him owlishly for a moment before he said, "Yonder are a great many more troops in the same situation, but I know not the cause." He appeared to be more baffled than frightened.

Ad went on and recognized another officer in a different troop. Again he asked the cause of the retreat, telling the man that he was after information for General Washington. But this man knew no more than the first except that his unit had lost only one man, so heavy casualties were not the reason for quitting the field.

The heat was growing more stifling by the minute. Ad could see its effects in the red, sweaty faces of the foot soldiers and in the lather on his and other officers' horses. But he felt a growing chill at the strangeness of the situation. These were not men fleeing in terror as American troops had in the past. Everything was backward, for the farther he went, the more confusion and frustration, not fear, he discovered. He could see no other course except to keep going to the rear of the retreating troops because someone there must surely know what was happening.

When he asked his questions of another officer, the colonel spat, "By God! They are flying from a shadow!" and Ad wondered if some heat-induced madness had seized their army.

But then he saw one of Lee's aides. "For God's sake, what is the cause of this retreat?" he demanded.

The man took exception to the rough urgency in Ad's voice and answered haughtily, "If you will proceed, you will see the cause. You will see several columns of foot and horse."

Ad stared at him. "I presume there are no more of the enemy than left Philadelphia. For what purpose did we come here if not to meet foot and horse?"

The man glared at him but offered no further explanation, and Ad pressed on, continuing to question officers he knew, but nothing they said lessened his apprehension. General Lee had called a meeting of his staff the previous evening, though he himself had not attended it. And though he had set his army on the march this morning, it had been with muddled orders and without his going with them, so that the advance had been halting and confused. Nonetheless there had been at least three major skirmishes with the enemy, and by the last one, the Continental Army had seemed to be winning. Then had come the order to retreat. Though the men were confused about why, they were all certain that the retreat had been ordered, though they had been given no direction beyond that, a circumstance that was making the confusion complete.

Suddenly Ad was face to face with General Lee, and this was the strangest of all the encounters, for the gulf in rank yawned between them, and Ad had no choice but to answer the general's question and refrain from asking his own. All Lee wanted to know was where

Washington was, and all Ad could tell him was that the general was advancing. Ad wanted to demand he explain the disaster that was unfolding, but instead, he wheeled his horse around, intent on getting back to Washington to report the extent of the retreat. He carried with him the image of General Lee's darting eyes and the muscle that had been twitching in his cheek—the man appeared to be quite unhinged.

Other aides were bringing the general the same news, that the day that should have been theirs was instead providing Clinton with a perfect escape. Ad opened his mouth to say that he thought General Lee had lost all reason, but then he marked the growing fury on Washington's face, and he heard him mutter, "Damn the man!"

Ad swallowed convulsively, looked away, and heard the yapping of dogs before General Lee appeared, riding in no great hurry toward them, so busy yammering at his aides he didn't see his commander in chief until Washington had ridden up beside him and shouted, "What is the meaning of this?"

Washington was shaking with rage, but incredibly, Lee's reaction was one of surprise, and he stuttered, "Sir? Sir?" as if he had no idea anything was amiss.

"What is all this confusion and retreat for?" the general bellowed.

Lee found his tongue, though not any sense, and launched into a rambling discourse about bad intelligence, disobedience of some officers, the impertinence and presumption of individuals, and about how he had saved the day by getting his army away from a vast plain where his soldiers would have been helpless against the enemy horse. He would have gone on, but Washington interrupted him, snarling that there was good information that it was but a strong covering party of the enemy.

Ad listened in reluctant fascination as Lee chattered on, his tone one of injury because he had averted such a disaster and because, after all, the attack on the enemy had been carried forward against his own opinion.

"All this may be true, sir, but you ought not to have undertaken it unless you intended to go through with it!" Washington roared, and Ad saw even steadfast Tench flinch at the volume. They had seen the general's temper before, but never like this. The skin of his face was stretched so taut, it was as if the bones and muscles were swelling beneath it.

And still Lee had the temerity to keep talking, insisting that everything would have gone well had his orders and thus his plan of attack been followed.

While Lee continued in full spate, Washington rode away from him, intent on bringing some order to the troops that had already filed past him. But before he could get very far, Colonel Harrison, one of the aides who had gone out with Ad, came galloping up to report that the enemy was advancing and were not fifteen minutes away from the general's position.

Momentarily, Washington and his staff were frozen. The unthinkable was happening. Clinton had turned the enemy withdrawal into an advance. This day that should have brought victory could well see the destruction of Washington's army.

Ad could hear the rush of his blood through his body, and the only coherent thought he had was that he hoped that Matilda and Addie were far enough to the rear so that they would be out of the range of enemy guns.

He looked to the general, awaiting further direction, and before his eyes he witnessed a remarkable transformation. Washington's back straightened, his shoulders squared, and the fire in his eyes was no longer rage. Utterly resolute, the general took control of the situation, asking questions and issuing firm orders. Tench told him he had found an officer close by who knew the ground; within minutes Washington was asking the man about the terrain and receiving the best news possible—the ground sloped in the enemy's direction, giving the Americans the advantage, and, in addition, there was cover for Washington's troops and a narrow swampy passage the enemy must traverse to attack.

The general deployed troops as surely as if this were the plan he had had from the beginning. And the soldiers obeyed willingly because he commanded them. The imposing figure on the white horse owned the soldiers' hearts. When they looked up at him, they saw their courage, their belief in their cause, their hope for the future magnified a thousand times.

More and more of Lee's troops came in, and Washington continued to rally them and to order them into position. Lafayette appeared with his detachment and made no secret of his joy that Washington was now commanding the action.

Most of the troops were so eager to turn and fight, they re-formed very quickly, but two regiments came in so disorganized, the general wisely sent them to the rear to regroup. There had been enough confusion this day.

With every minute, the enemy was getting closer, and when men became visible far to the left of the corridor the general was preparing to defend, he sent Tench and another officer to identify them. If they were enemy troops, they were bent on turning the American flank. Ad let his breath go in an audible rush when he saw Tench cheerfully waving his hat in the distance, signaling that the troops were more of their own.

Washington still had most of his force behind him, and they were fresher than Lee's, but they too would have to take up the best defensive positions. And meanwhile, the commander in chief was, with every passing second, coming closer to being exposed to enemy guns, a circumstance that seemed to worry him not a whit, while it was agonizing for his aides.

General Wayne's men had just been placed when the humid air rumbled with the thunder of British cannon from across the marsh. Red-coated infantry swung into view flanked by the cavalry so feared by Lee. And though no Highlanders were yet in sight, the distant moan of their bagpipes warned of their coming.

Looking at the general, Ad saw an expression of such yearning he knew how much Washington wanted to ride forward into combat with no regard for anything except this chance to turn defeat into victory. Ad was so torn between compassion and alarm, he didn't know whether to offer to ride forward with him or to drag him to safety. Just when he thought he must do one or the other, the general bowed his head for a moment and then turned his horse toward the rear.

Washington's party hadn't gotten far before they came upon General Lee, but to Ad's relief, this encounter was brief. Instead of his earlier fury, Washington now treated the man with icy control, asking if Lee would take command of this defensive position while he himself organized the troops in the rear. When they rode on, Lee was still babbling about his willingness to remain on the field despite the enemy's "great superiority in cavalry."

The eagerness of the troops awaiting his disposition confirmed Washington's belief that they could stand against the enemy when the forward troops fell back, and he issued his orders accordingly. Generals Greene and Stirling were with the main body of troops Washington had led out this morning, and he trusted both of them. He also had Lafayette and his men. If all went well, the British were going to feel as if the army of the morning's flight had vanished, replaced by a completely different one.

Ad saw his brother-in-law pass by with his cannon, and his mouth curved in response to Silas's ferocious grin. Ad knew how much Silas wanted to get the enemy within range of his guns.

The heat he had not felt earlier began to stifle Ad as he rode with messages from one unit to another. He guessed the temperature must be climbing toward a hundred degrees. He could feel it in the laborious effort his mare was making to answer his commands, and worse, he could see it in soldiers who collapsed as if dead without a mark on them. But short of being rendered unconscious, this army was not quitting. Even when the front defensive position gave way, it was done with order. As those men retreated, the fresher troops, many of them sheltered behind a fence, let them pass by, and waiting until the last possible moment, they fired on the British horse that came galloping toward them.

Ad was so close, his ears were filled with the screams of men and horses as they fell in bloody heaps, cut down by the steady fire of the Americans' muskets. Some of the wounded men and beasts tried repeatedly to regain their footing, only to be knocked down by the continuing hail of musket balls, while some of the luckier men and their mounts, those who had not been hit, fled the scene, disappearing through the heavy smoke of gunpowder.

The enemy infantry came on doggedly in the wake of the cavalry, but they met with the same murderous fire until they veered off, trying to turn the American left flank and then the right, each motion being met with American infantry and cannon. The ground shuddered with the blast of artillery from both sides. And the British infantry, in their heavy woolen uniforms, with their heavy packs, and with bodies made unfit by months of inactivity in Philadelphia, were suffering even more than Washington's men from the heat. Unwonted pity stirred in Ad as he saw men swooning, their faces stained every strange hue from white to red to black.

When he felt the thump against his right knee, Ad thought a stone had been kicked up to hit him, but when he looked down, he saw the blood just above where the top of his high boot ended. There was so much battle fever flooding through his veins, the pain was there, but blunted, and he decided the wound didn't seem that serious and wouldn't hamper him too much as long as he was riding, not walking. The general needed every man, and Ad was determined to keep going as long as he could. He wanted to see the enemy—the British and the Hessians, all of them—driven from the field as the Americans had been so often. He believed they could do it; his hope had begun to flood back the moment Washington had taken charge, and it was at full tide now.

Silas, too, saw victory within their grasp. All the drilling they had done at Valley Forge was proving its worth this day as his gunners fired one volley after another with such skill that when they enfiladed the enemy infantry, the redcoats toppled over one another like ninepins in a deadly game.

Then suddenly, the odds changed, and they were facing both horsemen and foot soldiers coming at them in numbers too great to stop with even their best efforts. And the enemy was sweeping toward them so fast, there was no way they could all escape, let alone take the guns with them.

With only seconds to act, even as Silas gave orders to retreat, he grabbed Tim, the drummer boy, and gave him a shake.

"Can you ride?" he snapped.

"Yes-s-s, sir, but…" As the boy protested, Silas threw him up into Blaze's saddle.

"Get out of here! Ride to the rear! If you don't, I'll shoot you myself!" He turned Blaze and sent the pair off with a slap on the horse's rump. The boy was no more than thirteen, and Silas had seen how the heat and carnage of the day had worn him down. But it wasn't this boy who was clear in his mind, it was Quentin who was riding off to safety.

Addie, please understand.

He had hardly completed the thought when enemy fire hit him. The musket ball that creased his left temple spun the screaming havoc of the battle away into dark silence.

Ad was cold again. Vaguely he marked that that couldn't really be true, not with more and more men falling over from the heat, not with Ember, lathered from head to tail and sucking air like a blacksmith's bellows.

"That's my girl, just a bit farther, and I'll give you a rest."

Trying to pat Ember's neck, he nearly fell out of the saddle, and that was certainly as odd as being cold in the middle of an inferno. It made him cross because he prided himself on having a good seat on even the most spirited horse, let alone one slowed by exhaustion. If he could find Addie, he could exchange Ember for Nightingale. But first he had to deliver the latest report to the general. For some reason, this simple plan seemed complicated, and he was relieved when he caught sight of Washington with Tench. His right leg was beginning to throb like a bad tooth, and dimly he recalled that he had a wound. His boot was uncomfortably tight and clammy, too, so all in all, it might be better if he didn't dismount until he found Addie and Nightingale.

When he tried to report to the general, his words sounded muffled even to him, and Washington and Tench stared at him in such consternation, he tried once again to form the words.

Tench caught him as he pitched from the saddle. "My God! How long have you been riding around with your leg like this?"

"He must have aid immediately! You there and you, take this man…"

The words faded in and out for Ad, but he could hear the scolding concern in Tench's voice and the urgency in the general's, and this coupled with the pain that had streaked through his leg as he came out of the saddle focused his mind long enough for him to croak, "Get Addie. Don't want to lose my leg."

The one clear thought he had was that men with severe arm or leg wounds had those appendages hacked off with alarming frequency, and most of them died anyway.

"Get Addie! Promise? And Ember, my horse, take care, she..." There were other things he wanted to say, including that he didn't want Matilda to see him this way, but the power to speak slipped away with his consciousness.

Addie and Matilda were close enough to the battle to hear not only the guns, but also the bugles and trumpets of the cavalry, the fifes and drums of the foot soldiers, and the bagpipes and drums of the Highlanders. The women were close enough to have gleaned news of the initial confusion and retreat and to know that now their army was reorganized and well engaged with the enemy. They were helping tend the wounded who were being brought to the rear. The training at Valley Forge had not been entirely for the men; during the spring preparations for the new campaign, Washington had encouraged the employment of camp women as nurses, and they were proving their worth today.

The heat was stifling, but the stench of blood, sweat, vomit, urine, and excrement was worse and too strong to be covered by the acrid smoke of gunpowder.

Addie was proud of Matilda, who, though she was short of nursing experience, was doing her best to be useful. Despite the heat, Matilda's face was bone-white with strain, but she managed to find a smile and soft words for the men, and her hands were steady.

Her soft gasp of distress caught Addie's attention as they worked side by side. They were out in the open, and Addie followed Matilda's gaze. The instant she saw Ad's mare and Tench, her heart tripped on its beat, and when she saw the two men bearing a third on a litter she didn't need to see his face to know it was Ad. She called to another woman to see to their patient, and then she was on her feet and running with Matilda at her side.

"He's alive!" Tench told them, dismounting at the sight of the pair. "But he's losing a lot of blood." There was the slightest hesitation before he said, "He doesn't want to lose his leg."

"He won't," Addie proclaimed with such determination that Tench thought Ad had a better chance than most to survive this, but still, his heart was heavy, and he felt helpless, wishing he could stay with his friend, knowing he could not. One thing he could do was to give very specific instructions for the care of Ad's horse, and then he remounted his own.

Addie tore herself away from Ad's side long enough to go to Tench. "Thank you for bringing him to me, and pray, thank General Washington, too, for allowing you to do it." Even in the chaos of the moment, she recognized the honor that had been paid to her brother by the general's sparing of Tench for this duty in the midst of a battle.

Tench looked down at her standing at his stirrup, at this feminine version of the young man he had come to value as a friend as well as a compatriot, and his throat tightened, making his voice gruff. "Your brother is well loved by all of us. His Excellency's family will be much diminished until Ad returns to us."

Though he said the words, he rode away sadly convinced that considering the blood Ad had lost, it was doubtful he would survive the night, and that if he did and even kept his leg, he would be so debilitated, they would never again see him on active duty at headquarters.

When Addie saw that Ad's wound had bled so much that blood had leaked down into his boot and was seeping out again, and when she saw the gray tinge to his skin, her vision blurred, but the choked sounds coming from Matilda focused her attention. Matilda's eyes were wide and blind, her skin as ashen as Ad's.

"If you faint, you won't be any use to him at all," Addie hissed. "He needs us, and we are not going to fail him." She dug her nails into Matilda's hand until Matilda drew a deep breath and nodded.

The most seriously wounded were being carted off to nearby buildings, any place that could provide shelter, and the women went with Ad when he was taken to a church and laid on straw that had been hastily spread on the floor.

It was as stifling inside as out, but at least there was less dust here, and it was out of the sun. Addie was resolved that they would transport Ad to better surroundings as soon as they could, and not to some pestilential hospital. She did not allow herself to consider that he might not live long enough to be taken anywhere else.

When Ad's high boot and the tight cloth of his breeches were cut away, the surgeon inspected the ruin of Ad's knee and shook his head. "This knee is no more use to him. Better if the leg comes off."

"No," Addie said flatly. She knew the harried man was only doing his duty, knew he might be right, but she had to speak for Ad when he could not speak for himself.

"Please, just remove the ball if you can and stop the bleeding, then we will care for him." Her eyes locked with his, and it was the surgeon who looked away first. He knew who the patient was and how Washington valued him. Beyond that, he wanted to do his best for the young man, and he had to admit to himself that he didn't think this patient had a chance, no matter what treatment he received; he was sure the wound had been too long ignored. Having come to that conclusion, he was tempted to do nothing at all, but he could not resist the plea he saw in the women's faces. At least he found the flattened musket ball without too much trouble, picked out a few slivers of bone and cartilage, and got the bleeding controlled to a slow ooze. He was good at what he did; the war had given him far too much practice.

That Valencourt had not stirred even when his wound was probed was further proof to the surgeon that he had already slipped beyond help. He moved on to other casualties, but he carried with him the sound of the women's voices, thanking him, and the image of their eyes, one pair so golden, the other so blue, eyes filled with horror and dread, hope and love, all in equal measure.

Addie wanted Silas, though she knew he could do nothing for Ad; she wanted Justin to come back from wherever he was; she wanted Tullia here beside her showing her how best to care for Ad; but most of all, she wanted Ad to open his eyes and tell her he was going to live. They were parts of a whole, bound together by their twin birth and by the love that had grown every day since that birth. Addie could not imagine the world without Ad, and she was terrified that if she so much as looked away, his barely perceptible breathing would cease altogether.

"I need my medical supplies. I left them near our last patient. Will you get them?" she asked Matilda.

"Of course," Matilda said, though she no more than Addie wanted to leave Ad's side.

"And if you can find someone who will carry the message, we should let Silas and Luke know where we are." Addie fixed on practical tasks, piling them up as a barrier against panic. But she was glad when Matilda returned to her side, because with Ad so still, she felt lonely even in the middle of the constant activity in the crude hospital.

News filtered in from the battle. The Continental Army was winning the day, stopping one enemy advance after another. But as much as blades and guns, the heat was proving a lethal weapon, striking down men on both sides and diminishing the strength of those who remained standing until the conflict didn't end in a definitive way, but rather wound down in mutual exhaustion, leaving the victory to be decided on the morrow after a night of rest.

It took Addie a while to realize that she hadn't heard the boom of cannon for some time, and she looked up at every new entry into the church, expecting to see Silas at any moment. But it was Luke who found them first, and his shock at Ad's condition was plain on his face before he could conceal it. He nodded at Addie and sat down beside Matilda, putting his arm around her shoulders.

"I can stay the night in case you need to shift him or whatever else I can do to help."

Matilda's eyes filled with the tears she'd been holding back for hours, and she hid her face against her brother's chest.

Addie thanked him for his offer of help, and then she asked, "Any news of Silas?"

This time Luke was braced against betraying too much. "I have no news of him, but things have been very confused today. It will take time for everyone to get sorted out." All of that was true, but he had heard that though relatively few of their troops had been captured, some artillery had been overrun by the enemy, some of the men killed or taken prisoner. He had no intention of worrying Addie with that information when her husband might walk in at any minute.

But it was Timothy, a drummer boy of Silas's unit, and his parents, not Silas, who found Addie. Addie knew the Chepman family. The father had lost toes from both feet to frostbite during the winter at Valley Forge and was too lame to be of any further use in his former role as an infantryman. He and Mistress Chepman could have gone home, but they stayed with the army to watch over Tim. Silas was fond of Tim, and Addie and Tullia had helped Mistress Chepman care for her husband when he was ailing.

Addie wanted to believe that they were here out of concern for Ad, but she knew it wasn't so even before Mr. Chepman said, "Tell her, son, tell her just how it was."

Tim's words poured out with his tears. "We was doing so good! But then too many of the enemy came at us, too many to shoot. Colonel Bradwell, he made me get on his horse, ma'am. He put me up there and sent me off to be safe. I shoulda stayed with him, with all of 'em. I looked back, but I couldn't see nothing, the smoke was that bad. But they didn't have a chance, not against so many."

It was peculiar, Addie thought, how small the Chepmans appeared, very small and far away. "Silas, my husband, he is dead?" She framed the question with great care, as if she were trying to speak a foreign language she had never heard before.

Mr. Chepman's throat flexed visibly as he struggled with his answer, and she thought that he had somehow lost the sense of things, too.

"Ma'am, his... as much as I know, he has not been found among the dead or wounded, nor a few others who were with him. Things are in a terrible mess out there; it will take time to know what's what."

What he wasn't saying raced through Addie's mind, and that silent language was much too clear; time to find the bodies of those who had crawled away or fallen into brush; time for the severely wounded to die without care; time for the enemy to cart off the living who might be of use to them as prisoners. She grabbed the last thought and clung to it; if the enemy had him, he wasn't dead, not yet.

Mistress Chepman's soft voice reached her. "Of all the babies I've borne, Tim is the only one living. And today your husband saved his life. I pray to God that he and your brother, too, will be spared to you."

"We owe a debt that can never be repaid," Mr. Chepman said.

But it was the boy's grief and his repeated, "I shoulda stayed," that pierced Addie's heart and gave her voice power.

"No, you did exactly what you should have done. You are a soldier, and your commanding officer gave you an order. It would have done no good for you to remain behind. You know Colonel Bradwell would not have left his men. And had you been lost, it would not have been the saving of him. Do you understand?" She held his gaze until he gave a little nod. She could not ease his grief, but she hoped his feeling of guilt would lessen.

Promising to return quickly, Luke left with the Chepmans so that he could see to Silas's horse.

Addie stared blindly at Ad, and then she said, "Silas cares about Tim, but it was Quentin he saved today."

She felt a scream working its way up from deep in her gut. She wanted to open her mouth and howl in rage, pain, and terror, most of all terror, howl away the nightmare of this day. She closed her eyes and bit her lower lip until she tasted blood. Her loyalties had long set a steady course. She had chosen the Patriot cause over her father; she had chosen Silas over other men; she had chosen to follow the army rather than be apart from Silas and her brothers; but now she was faced with a choice that was the Devil's own—to stay by Ad's side or to go in search of Silas.

Squeezing her eyes more tightly shut, she gave up her hold on Ad to wrap both of her arms around her body, trying to control the shudders that racked her.

"You're not alone, Addie. We're here with you."

It took a moment for Addie to understand that Matilda was talking to her and to feel Matilda's hand touching her shoulder. She opened her eyes and saw that Luke was back and both McKinnons were staring at her in concern, their sense of helplessness plain.

"I must go look for Silas. I can't leave him out there with night falling. You stay with Ad." The urge to go to Silas was suddenly so strong, she had started to get to her feet before Luke's firm grip stayed her.

"You cannot go out there! With the light going, you're as apt to be shot by our soldiers as by the enemy's. The battle isn't over; it is only suspended until tomorrow."

Addie started to shake again, thinking of the wounded lying out there, seeing Silas among them.

"I have learned much from you, but not enough for this, not enough for what Ad needs!" Matilda said, and her voice quivered in acknowledgment of the cruelty of her next words. "We don't know where Silas is, but Ad is right here."

Luke joined his logic to hers. "The story of Silas saving the boy is being repeated, and you, he, and your brothers are well known. If anything is discovered, the news will be brought to you here."

There were other stories of the day's battle spreading through the camp, and among them were stories of the gunners' wives who had gone into battle beside their men, of one who had carried water to the men until her husband had been wounded, at which point she had helped to load the gun. When a cannon ball had passed between her legs, taking part of her petticoat, she had laughed, saying it was a good thing it hadn't hit higher, taking something more important. And she had gone on helping.

The story was being passed around with great humor and appreciation, but all Addie could think was that she should have been with Silas. That being there was unthinkable for an officer's wife; that Silas had specifically forbade her to be too close to the battle; that she most probably would have been unable to do anything to save him—none of this made any difference to her.

She looked down at Ad, still so deeply unconscious that the only way she could make him swallow precious liquids was to feed him a tiny amount at a time and stroke his throat. He was utterly helpless.

"I will stay until dawn, but then you will have to watch while I search for Silas, battle or not."

She and Matilda exchanged a look, both of them knowing that these first dark hours were the most critical for Ad.

In spite of the prospect of renewed fighting looming in the morning, throughout the night, the aides came to check on Ad. They came singly and could not stay long, but their love for him was manifest. Tench and Hammy came, and the others, trying to walk softly to keep their spurs from clinking. Each bore General Washington's command to bring him word of Ad, and their sorrow was matched by their frustration at being unable to help their friend.

John Laurens was the exception; he came with a pledge of assistance. "I have sent word to my father and to your uncle. They will know where Ad should be for the best care and how to take him there."

Congress was on its way back to Philadelphia from York, and express riders had gone out with the news of the day's action. And since John's father was the President of Congress, the message from John would reach him without delay.

When Addie thanked him, it was as much for his belief that Ad would survive to be transported as it was for the dispatch he had sent.

Messages came from the generals, too, not only from Washington, but from Lafayette, and from Knox, who inquired after Ad's welfare and promised that everything possible would be done to find Silas.

"I wish I could tell you how many people are awaiting good word of you," Addie said, stroking Ad's face. And then she heard Tullia's voice telling her that no one knew why, but often people who had been insensible could, when they regained consciousness, repeat every word that had been spoken near them.

"Perhaps you can hear us and are just too weary to answer. It is all right; you rest now. But you must not leave us, you must not! We need you to stay here with us. And I need you to help me find Silas. He is missing."

Following Addie's lead, Matilda chimed in, ignoring any disquiet that might have come from having others listen, telling Ad how much she loved him, how much she longed to be his wife.

Ad stirred and moaned once, and even so little meant much to the watchers, but he did not awaken.

Finally Luke had to return to duty, and Addie and Matilda waited out the time to dawn, braced to hear the army moving out to renew the battle. But instead, they heard the news that swept through the camp—during the night, Clinton had stolen away to safety, using darkness and stealth to cover his retreat as General Washington had in the past. It was a victory of a sort that the enemy had quit the field, but Clinton's army was still largely intact.

The heat promised to be punishing again, and Washington's troops were feeling the bad effects of the previous day's hot-weather fighting. Even if they did march out in pursuit of the enemy, there was too much of a chance that by the time they found them, the British would have the cover of their fleet or reinforcements from the New York garrison, or both. The Battle of Monmouth was over.

"I have to go look for Silas now. I must!"

In counterpoint to Addie's rising panic, Matilda was calm. "Ad and I will be here when you come back." She knew what an act of trust it was when Addie left her with Ad.

Taking medical supplies with her, Addie rode Nightingale, heading for the position where Silas's battery had been overrun. It was a landscape horrific in the aftermath of war. Burial parties were hauling away corpses of both armies, and the wounded being collected were from both sides, too, men who had lain helpless and in pain throughout the night. But for Addie, the women were the worst sight. Some were searching as she was for their men, but others were efficiently stripping bodies of all their valuables, including shoes, boots, and other articles of clothing.

She saw a group of women she knew, women she and Tullia had nursed when they or their families had fallen ill. All restraint fled, and she scrambled off Nightingale, screeching like a fury.

"Stop it! Stop it, all of you! How can you do this? Are you pigs come to root at the corpses? Filthy, filthy, all of you are filthy robbers of the dead! Perhaps you rob from the living, too. Do you, do you take all they have while they yet breathe? How will anyone know who they are if you have taken all from them? How will anyone know?"

Some of the women looked away from Addie, but none answered her anger in kind, and with shock, she recognized their pity.

One of the women said, "Mistress Bradwell, we know your colonel. If he's out here, we'll find him for you."

Then another spoke up, still without anger, but not mincing words. "Ma'am, what we're takin' will be put to good use. Dead men don't need it no more."

Over the long months, Addie had gotten used to these women, had come to admire them, but now it was as if she were seeing them for the first time. She saw how threadbare was the homespun they wore, how cracked and broken their heavy shoes, how some feet were clad in wooden clogs, some in leather, and some with no shoes or stockings of any kind. She saw the weathered skin and the missing teeth, even in some of the youngest women. She saw bodies made lumpy and heavy or whittled down to the bone by years of bad or inadequate food, by ceaseless toil, by the trials of childbirth and the familiarity with graves soon dug for too many of those infants brought forth with such labor and risk.

A pair of boots, a shirt, a few coins—any of these could make an enormous, if fleeting, difference in these lives. Never had she felt the privilege of her life more acutely. Even in this time of sorrow and loss, her lot was infinitely better than that of these women, for if he lived, Ad would have far better care than these women could expect for their men; and Silas—

One of the women spoke the thought before Addie had fully grasped it, "Your husband, if the redcoats 'ave 'im, 'e'll be a prize to 'em, wot with 'is rank an' all."

This practical judgment was offered as comfort, and Addie accepted it as such.

"I'm sorry for the things I said." The apology seemed woefully inadequate, but it was accepted.

"No matter. 'Tis the worry, takes some of us the same, in temper more'n tears."

One of the group cupped her hands so that Addie could remount Nightingale, but that was the only break in the routine. When Addie rode away from the women, they were again busy at their grisly task.

This day was already another inferno. Bluebottle flies, sunlight catching in the vivid ultramarine of their abdomens, buzzed through the air in a frenzy to enjoy the vast meal of rotting flesh spread before them. The sweet, metallic odor of death was so overpowering, Addie gagged on it, the smell becoming a loathsome taste in her mouth. Nightingale skittered and protested with every step, but Addie forced herself and the mare to go on.

She saw that there were other scavengers, not just the women from the American camp and some from the enemy who had lagged behind, but men as well, men who bore no arms for either side but skulked along the fringes of both armies, stealing whatever they could from the living and the dead.

Then she saw two dead Highlanders, their tartan stained but recognizable, identifying them as Traverne's men. The sound of the bagpipes from the previous day echoed eerily in her head, and she knew that John Traverne had regretted leaving his dead behind. Black hatred rose in her that he should fight against the Americans, but then it was gone, and she could not quell the hope that he had survived the battle.

When she recognized two bodies as men from Silas's regiment, she nearly turned Nightingale around to flee, but she had come too far. She made herself look, and she saw that the enemy had not taken this position easily. Grotesquely bloated horses lay dead, some with their riders crushed beneath them. And red-coated infantrymen lay in careless knots, as if a giant hand had tossed them away.

Yesterday's stirring martial music that had called the men to war was today replaced by the incessant drone of flies, and the sound battered Addie's eardrums in ever increasing volume.

"You oughtn't be out here, ma'am."

The gently spoken words startled Addie, when they finally pierced the buzzing, and she looked down to see a man from a burial detail gazing up at her.

"No one should be out here, not the living nor the dead," she said. She ignored his puzzled look, but she turned Nightingale to ride back.

She heard the cries of the wounded still being carried in, but she could not help them. She had to get back to Ad, had to find that he still breathed.

Matilda's cheeks were wet with tears, but the instant she saw Addie, she smiled and said, "He opened his eyes just a while ago, and he knew me!" Then she sobered and asked, "Silas?"

"I could not find him." Addie settled down beside her brother and took one of his hands in hers.

He did not open his eyes, but first Addie felt a slight pressure from his hand against hers, and then she heard the low whisper of his voice.

"We will find him, wherever he is."

The tight band around her heart eased. Ad would not leave them; if not for his own sake, he would stay alive to help in the search for Silas.

Chapter 15

Philadelphia and New Jersey, 1778–1779

Addie was grateful for the speed with which her uncle and Henry Laurens had arranged for Ad to be transported to Philadelphia, but she knew she would hate the city for the rest of her life. Each day offered a new misery.

It was as if the enemy occupation had soiled the once fair city beyond repair. Broken bits of Loyalist goods left behind and plunder discarded as unworthy by the enemy littered the chessboard streets along with garbage and waste. In the smothering summer heat, the stench was overpowering. It was no surprise that Lucy Knox had not lingered in the town.

But for Addie, the human refuse was worse. Despite the fact that the Congress had made the city the center of the government, it remained a stronghold of Tory sentiment. Of the Tories who had stayed, many of them were less than discreet in expressing their disgust at the British departure and the American reoccupation.

Uncle Hartley had arranged for Ad, Matilda, and Addie to lodge with the Birdsalls, and there was no doubt about their loyalties. The three had been welcomed so warmly, Addie felt remorse for her negative thoughts about the city.

Mr. Birdsall had been a prosperous merchant with extensive British contacts before the war. He and his family were Anglican, and though his wife was native born, he had been born in England and had come to the colonies with his parents and siblings when he was seven years old. He was well read and a man at once kindly and shrewd.

He was like Marcus Valencourt in many ways, but not in his politics. Thomas Birdsall was an outspoken Patriot. He had served in the Congress, and he continued to work unceasingly to aid in the financing of the Continental Army. Two of the Birdsalls' sons were in the army, on General Wayne's staff, and there were sonsin-law and nephews in the Pennsylvania militia. Two older sons held civil offices in the state government.

Thomas was tall and growing heavy with the years, but his wife Chloe was short, slight, and so energetic, she made Addie feel like a sluggard in comparison.

Thomas might have been head of the family, but Chloe was in firm control of domestic affairs. When her guests had arrived, she was still in the process of removing all traces of the enemy, for the Birdsalls had fled into exile when the British took the city, and their house had been occupied by an officer and his staff.

"I suppose we can count ourselves fortunate that he was a gentleman," Chloe conceded reluctantly to Addie when the household inventory was at last complete. "He didn't pilfer the linens or anything else, except for a few bottles from Mr. Birdsall's cellar, and Colonel Traverne left a note and payment for those."

"Colonel Traverne?" Addie could hardly get the name out.

"Yes, a Highlander and, according to my husband, a good soldier for all that he is on the wrong side." Chloe cocked her head to the side and peered at Addie. "Do you know the man?"

"I've met him," Addie admitted and explained how John Traverne had been recommended to the Valencourts by Callista in England. She did not, however, mention how compelling she had found the man during their brief contacts, nor how often she had thought of him in the ensuing years. And now it seemed a most peculiar turn that she should be in the house that Traverne had just vacated.

But she had little time to brood on it, as caring for Ad demanded every ounce of energy both she and Matilda possessed. For the first couple of weeks they had never left him alone because they were terrified he would yet slip away from them. He had not regained full consciousness, but he was growing more restless by the day, thrashing about in fever, which threatened to tear open the wound, so finally they had had to tie him down, a process that brought both of them near to weeping.

Addie also had to contend with the well-meaning physicians her uncle and Henry Laurens sent to consult on Ad's case. To a man, they advised that a surgeon be called to remove the leg. Seeing the ugly, festering wound every time she renewed poultices and bandages, it was hard for Addie to stand fast against the medical counsel, but Matilda helped with her insistence that what Ad wanted was the most important thing.

Every day that passed was a victory over death, and finally Ad opened his eyes, and they could see that he recognized them, though he didn't speak. The next time he was conscious, his voice was little more than a rasp, but the words were too clear.

"I don't want you here. Go away," he said, staring at Matilda.

Matilda gasped and backed away from the bed, still clutching the cloth with which she had been bathing him, and then she bolted from the room.

Addie stared at her brother in consternation. He closed his eyes and turned his head away. And Addie understood as if he were explaining it to her.

"You are ashamed to have her see you like this!" She grasped one of his hands, needing the contact. "You are foolish to mind. She has cared for you as tenderly as if you were a babe, but she has done so because you are the man she loves. And I cannot do without her help."

She was sure he heard her, but he said nothing, and his lips were tight against the waves of pain that radiated from his leg. She hadn't the heart to scold him further, and she waited until he had drifted off again before she dared to leave him to be watched over by one of the Birdsall servants while she went in search of Matilda.

She found her huddled on the bed in their room, looking all the more woebegone for the lack of tears. Addie put her arm around the thin shoulders.

"You mustn't mind what he said. He feels miserable, and he's embarrassed, that's all. He's wanted to protect you from the first, and it's hard for him to do that when he's so helpless. As he gets stronger, his temper will improve."

Matilda nodded wearily, but she said, "Ad is right, I don't belong here." She gestured at the spacious, well-appointed accommodations they had been given. "It was different with the army, but here I can see how your home in Boston must have been. Every minute I fear I will make some mistake that will disgrace you and Ad."

Addie had noticed how nervous Matilda was in the house, but she had thought it was all to do with Ad's condition. Now she felt stupid for being so blind. Of course Matilda had never been in such surroundings; her life on the frontier would have offered nothing equivalent to a city mansion. She hated seeing Matilda's self-confidence so diminished.

Addie gazed about the room and made a confession of her own. "It's true, we grew up in a house much like this, and Mr. Birdsall reminds me of my father. But Boston and our lives there seem a lifetime ago. I swear to you, I feel as out of place here and miss being with the army as much as you do. None of us will ever be the same as we were before the war, and if I can grow attached to traveling about and sleeping on the ground, then you can adjust to a house like this, if you must. Surely Ad is worth that." She resisted the impulse to point out that as sick as Ad was, Matilda was not separated from him, while she herself was tortured every waking hour and in her sleep by Silas's absence, by not knowing whether he was alive or dead.

After a long silence, Matilda said, "Da would be cross with me. He tried to teach Luke and me that as long as we were honest and hardworking, we were as fine as the finest in the land. I'll try to remember that. And don't worry, I would not leave while Ad is so in need." She hesitated, and then she said, "But even when he is better, he may still want me to go. He has changed. I can see it in his eyes. More than his body was wounded at Monmouth."

Addie wanted to deny it, but as the days passed, she saw the truth of it. Ad apologized to Matilda as soon as he saw her again, but the words were perfunctory, a gentleman begging pardon of a woman he scarcely knew.

He was as careful to thank them both for their care of him, and he did not complain even when they were causing him great pain, but instead lay with his jaw so clenched against sound that Addie wanted to scream for him. Yet he would not take the opium or rum that could have eased his agony. He wanted his mind clear, but he did not share his brooding thoughts with either woman.

Justin arrived, shaken out of his usual self-command by his frantic concern. Grimly, he had carried on his duties after word had reached him about Ad and Silas but, finally, Harry Lee had sent him off in mock disgust.

"There won't be a thing you can do to help, and you'll be in the way, but go," he told him, and he added, "Give them my best regards. It is good that Addie has Mistress McKinnon with her."

Harry Lee was right. Justin found there wasn't much he could do beyond listening to his brother. But having feared that Ad would die before he reached him, he was infinitely relieved to have Addie's assurances that slowly, slowly their brother was mending.

"Though I don't know about his leg. Even if he keeps it, the knee is so badly damaged, it will never be right. But as ill as he's been, I'm more worried about his mind. His thoughts seem to be causing him as much pain as his wound, and I can't tell what he's thinking."

Justin understood her panic; she was accustomed to closeness with her twin, and Ad was deliberately shutting her out.

Though the situation was better than he had anticipated, Justin was shocked by how thin and pale Ad appeared. He gripped his hand for a moment, his throat working, before he trusted his voice.

"For Christ's sake, you are one of Washington's best aides! You are supposed to be writing a steady hand and speaking French, not stopping enemy fire with your body."

Until Ad saw his brother, he did not know how much he wanted to talk to someone who would understand. "It's always a risk, and I accept that. But that day... that day the confusion was unbelievable! And all because His Excellency could or would not see how unfit General Lee was to command the forward troops."

"But General Washington turned the day around," Justin protested.

"He averted a disaster caused by his bad judgment. We could have taken Clinton, his highest officers, and the army with them. We might have ended the war that day. Instead, where are we?"

"We are much further along," Justin answered without hesitation. "Despite General Lee, Monmouth proved that our army can fight as well as them. General Lee is being court-martialed. And now the Comte d'Estaing has arrived with the French fleet. Yes, I would say we are much further along."

"As for General Lee, a court martial can hardly undo the damage he did, and as for the French, it depends on what use they prove to be," Ad countered. "Silas said little about it, but we both know how much he doubted the wisdom of being allied with them." He moved restlessly, grimacing as he jarred his leg. "He paid far more for the mistakes at Monmouth than I. Addie goes on trying to believe that he lives, but he could just as well lie dead somewhere."

Justin had feared that Ad's spring euphoria would exact a high price were the war not to end as soon as he had hoped, but this was more profound than that disappointment. He recognized the heart of the matter and felt immeasurably sad for his brother.

"General Washington did make a serious mistake at Monmouth," Justin said. "But I beg you remember who he is, and you and I know that far better than most. He gained some military experience in the last war, but he was no soldier when this war began. He is a planter, a farmer who has not been able to go home to the land he loves for more than three years. He has had to learn not only to be a warrior, but also to be the commander in chief.

"He has made mistakes before; he will probably make them again. But he does not falter. He goes on against an enemy commanded by professional soldiers. And he has to deal not only with our army but also with a Congress that is often disorganized and recalcitrant and has too often refused to listen to him and has burdened him with incompetent officers. A lesser man would have quit long since. And I cannot imagine another who could have held our hearts and given us courage for so long. But you have lost faith in him, and you cannot continue to follow him without it." He did not mention the possibility that Ad might be too lame to continue serving at all.

He saw that his brother was tiring, but he went on. "I cannot make you believe in him again, only you can do that. But remember everything he has done for our cause, not just the errors of his command."

Ad's eyes were closed by the time Justin finished, and the brothers did not speak of the matter again in the short time Justin was there. Nor did Justin confide his thoughts about Ad to their sister. His time with her was spent in trying to reassure her about Silas.

"Silas is not a common soldier. He is an officer of high rank, and he has powerful friends—General Washington, General Knox, and Uncle Hartley—who are most interested in his safe return," he reminded her, but he found it difficult to meet her steady gaze or to listen to the flat logic of her words when he could hear, with equal clarity, the pain shimmering through her.

"We do not know whether or not the enemy has him. If they do not, then he is surely dead. If they do, his case is little better. He would not be an easy prisoner. He would never give his oath not to fight in order to obtain parole. And the exchange of our prisoners for theirs is still a disordered, uncertain business, and it may be murderous, too, because the one thing we know from every report is that the British treat their prisoners abominably because, after all, those prisoners are Rebels, not fellow soldiers. At least the enemy is consistent in injustice. Now, tell me again about my husband's powerful champions."

With the sarcasm still bitter on her tongue, Addie glared at Justin, but then she saw how dismayed he looked. "I am sorry! None of this is your fault, and I know how much you love Silas. I will make you regret having come to us when the truth is that no one could be more welcome."

But Justin was unconvinced. "I am the eldest, and yet there is so little I can do for you or for Ad."

"No matter how hard you try to fill Papa's place, no matter how hard I try to fill Tullia's, we can't do it," Addie told him. "And really, we shouldn't want to. We're different; our family is different now; and we're doing our best."

As Addie intended, Justin was comforted, but he rejoined his unit still wishing he could do more for his siblings and missing their father more than he had in a long while. And he could not banish the image of how fragile Ad seemed, mentally and physically.

Addie had sent Blaze, Silas's horse, with Justin for a remount, reminding him, as if to persuade herself, that it was only a loan until Silas had need of the animal again. But she had kept Ember with her stock, explaining, "I don't want Ad to have the slightest doubt that I believe he will ride again." Justin appreciated Addie's decision, but it was difficult for him to imagine their brother recovering enough for that. He regretted what he had said to him, condemning himself for doing no more than lowering Ad's spirits further.

At first, Ad felt exactly that, more heartsick than before Justin had visited. Then he was angry that his brother read him so well. But finally, when all the layers had been peeled away, he had to admit to himself that the fact that Justin had seen the truth did not alter it. Though on occasion, he had questioned some decisions, his basic loyalty to the general had been a constant ever since Washington had arrived at Cambridge to take command. It had remained intact after the disastrous losses on Long Island and Manhattan Island; not even Quentin's death had shaken it. It had only grown stronger when the general's enemies had plotted against him. More than once, Ad had feared so much for the general's life, he would have given his own instead without a second thought. One day had changed all.

Images raced through his mind, faster and faster. He saw the general enraged, amused, depressed, elated, impatient, patient, harsh, and tender. He saw him still strong in the saddle when his aides were faint with exhaustion. He saw him so ill, it seemed he could not survive. He saw him on the way to Trenton, the big man on a big horse, the man whose mere presence had inspired his soldiers to keep on despite their cold and hunger. But nowhere in his mind did he see the general afraid for himself.

The general had pledged everything he was, everything he had to the cause, and he had kept the army together and in the field against impossible odds. Yet, for one day's indulgence of an unfit officer who was not Washington's choice, who had more than once whispered against the commander in chief, Ad had forsaken him. It did not matter that only Justin suspected the betrayal. The pain in Ad's heart was more acute, more unmanageable than the steady throb of his leg.

Then relief swept over him. It was arduous to confront his lack of steadfastness, his breach of faith, but it was, even with his brother's knowledge, a private affair that need never hurt the general. And the remedy for the inner treachery was obvious; he need only renew the vow long made by returning to the general's service to remain there until Washington had no further need of him.

"Is your leg hurting you very badly? Can I do anything for you?"

He opened his eyes to see Matilda peering down anxiously at him. He saw her more clearly than he had in days, saw that even as she tended to him, she was wary, as if she expected him to order her away again at any moment.

He caught her hand and brought it to his mouth, kissing each knuckle. "You can forgive me, if you will. I have behaved like a spoiled child, angry because things have not gone my way. I want to return to His Excellency as soon as I am able." He paused, gathering courage. "I intend to walk and to ride again and soon, but I am not so foolish as to think that I will ever be as I was. I will not hold you to our engagement if—"

"If what, if you are not perfect?" Matilda spat at him, snatching her hand away. "How dare you think so little of me! That bullet did worse damage to your good sense than to your knee. You are very pretty to look at, Master Valencourt, but I do not love you for your beauty alone. Were something to happen to me, were I to be lamed"—she used the word deliberately—"would you cast me off? I think I ought to know if you are of such a mind."

It was the first time Ad had seen her in a high temper.

"My beauty, eh?" he teased, but then he grew serious. "I would never cast you off, not ever! I will be thankful every day of my life for you. But we can't know how long the war will go on or even how it will end, we—"

Again she forestalled him. "I promised that I would wait. You were the one, not I, who sought to see into the future." She chose not to tell him that she dreaded adjusting to living in such surroundings as this house far more than traveling with the army anew, even if the latter meant their marriage would have to wait. It was enough that

Ad was so sure he would be fit enough to reclaim his life; her doubts seemed pale beside his certitude.

The change in Ad was as welcome to Addie as to Matilda, but it was not without its perils. Ad was no longer stolidly enduring; now he wanted to test the limits of his strength and to increase it. He wanted to see how well his leg would hold him and what mobility he had in it before Addie thought it should bear any weight at all.

"You will not undo all the good work Matilda and I have done," Addie warned him, insisting he take it slowly.

His body helped in the compromise, for he was still so weak, just sitting up and flexing his muscles in bed took enormous effort. But he kept at it doggedly, ignoring his dizziness and the sweat that drenched him, working until he could feel his body coming under his control again.

When his sister and Matilda finally helped him to stand, he managed it only because they were supporting him, but in spite of the pain in his leg, he was reassured when he could feel his foot and toes as well as ever. The knee was still too swollen and tender to allow any bending, but he vowed to himself that that would come in time.

The other sign of his recovery was his avid pursuit of war news. He wanted to know every detail, questioning Uncle Hartley and other visitors, reading and rereading letters from Justin, his cousins, and from Tench, Hammy, John, and other aides. He was particularly frustrated that he was not on hand to assist in Washington's dealing with the French, for the arrival of Comte d'Estaing and the French ships had greatly increased the work of the French-speaking members of Washington's staff. Though in the end, translations or lack of them had had little effect.

When d'Estaing had arrived off Sandy Hook, he was too late to stop Clinton from getting his troops to Long Island and New York City. Then the lack of any pilot who believed the deep draft French ships could safely get across the bar into New York Harbor to attack the English ships had left d'Estaing with no effective mission against the main British garrison. Therefore, the Americans and French had decided on a joint action at Newport, Rhode Island, a port that gave the enemy easy access to the waters and coastal towns of both New England and the Mid-Atlantic states.

The operation was a disaster that left American troops scurrying to safety after the French fleet abandoned them. The French had put out to sea to meet the British, but a huge storm had battered both fleets. The French then sailed for Boston for repairs, though some rumors had it that only one of d'Estaing's ships was badly damaged. Further, d'Estaing made no secret of his intention to move for the West Indies as soon as possible, to protect French interests there, and also to be out of American waters before the storm season began.

Feelings against the French ran so high in Boston, several Frenchmen were killed by rioters while the fleet was in port. The best that had happened in a bad situation was that when British ships had come prowling after the French, a second ferocious storm had driven off the British, clearing the way for d'Estaing to head for the West Indies as planned. Still in possession of Newport, but thwarted in their attempt to defeat the French, the British contented themselves with raiding and burning several seacoast towns known to be ports for American privateers.

It was not only New Englanders who thought it was good riddance when the French sailed away; many Americans, ignoring the financial and material aid that had already proved vital, were reaffirmed in their conviction that the French alliance had been a bad idea from the start.

The summer also brought news that the enemy and their Mohawk allies had ravaged Pennsylvania's Wyoming Valley and would undoubtedly continue their raids. Ad could hardly bear Matilda's sorrow when she learned of the killings, and she was equally saddened by the demands that Native American towns be destroyed in retribution.

In the midst of all these dire reports, Ad was grimly satisfied that the court martial of General Lee had found the man guilty of disobeying orders, of "making an unnecessary, disorderly, and shameful retreat," and of disrespect toward Washington. Lee had been dismissed from the service for a year. It was ironic that while Washington would probably have been willing to forget the whole sorry business at Monmouth, Lee himself had caused the court martial by demanding vindication of his actions. Ad thought the punishment disgustingly light and would have preferred that the man be hanged, but he knew that General Lee would be stung by the judgment, and at least he would be out of the way for a year.

Though it took some weeks after the event for it to find its way to them, one piece of news brought pure joy. Tullia had been safely delivered of a healthy baby boy in August, and he had been named George Washington Freedom. More than once, Addie had been tempted to write to Tullia to tell her of the misfortunes that had befallen them at Monmouth, but now, she was very glad she had not. George Washington Freedom was living proof of Tullia's new life, and Tullia did not need to fret about problems she could not solve.

Addie didn't begrudge Tullia her happiness, but it underscored her misery. At first, Ad's critical condition had taken so much of her attention and energy, sheer exhaustion had dulled her worry about Silas, but as Ad grew stronger, so did Addie's obsession with her husband's fate. She was tortured by the thought of his being badly wounded or sick, in the hands of the enemy with no one to care for him. She tried not to dwell on the likelihood that he was dead and buried in an unmarked grave. At night she dreamed of him, sometimes horrific images, but it was worse when she dreamed that he was beside her, dreams so vivid that she could feel his warmth, his touch, and could smell his scent, only to awaken to mourn his absence.

She despised the enemy for being so inhumane on the subject of prisoner exchange, as she had learned that were Silas imprisoned his case would be made more complicated by the fact that the British did not have many of his rank serving in America, which made a direct exchange, rank for rank, even more difficult.

Nor did it help that well-meaning people like the Birdsalls found it uncomfortable to address the subject of her husband and so avoided it until she had the perverse impulse to mention him often, as if speaking of him would keep him alive. It made her more conscious than ever of how much a part of army life she had become, of how alien civilian life was, for the aides who wrote and the officers stationed in the city who came to visit never failed to mention Silas. He was one of their own, and they shared his family's concern about him.

It was especially inspiring for Ad when General Arnold paid a visit. Arnold had also resisted amputation, despite the seriousness of his leg wounds, and though he still needed a walking stick, at least he was ambulatory. His visit was a special gesture from a man who had a reputation for often being brusque in his dealings with people and who had his hands full in his capacity as Military Governor of Philadelphia.

They had had little contact with him before this, and Addie was surprised at how charming he was toward her and Matilda.

"If the army could just recruit more nurses like the two of you, our wounded would be in much better condition," he assured them.

When General Arnold had taken his leave Addie said, "He is quite the gentleman."

"And a good soldier," Ad reminded her, judging that that was the most important thing. "But I think he would do well to be less charming with some of Philadelphia's residents. He is being very accommodating, perhaps too much so, to prominent Loyalists here."

Thinking of how kindly Arnold had inquired after Silas, Addie dismissed the subject with a shrug. "Maybe it is simply his way of keeping the peace."

By December, Ad was up on crutches, and his knee was growing stronger by the day, though it was still extremely stiff. Justin managed a brief visit, and he returned to duty encouraged by the extent of his brother's recovery, and yet haunted by the deep sorrow in his sister's eyes. He would never admit it to Addie, but the more time went by, the more he doubted they would ever find Silas or learn what had happened to him.

On December 17, Mistress Washington arrived in Philadelphia from Mount Vernon, and five days later, General Washington came in with Tench, Hammy, John Laurens, and General Greene accompanying him. On the following day, John, having issued a challenge, and with Hammy acting as his second, met General Lee in a duel, wounding Lee severely enough so that Lee was unable to answer a similar challenge from General Wayne.

Lee had been unable to keep his mouth or his pen still since his court martial. He had called Hammy a son of a bitch, accusing him of committing perjury at Lee's trial, and he had attacked Washington in letters to Congress, and to the public in the *Pennsylvania Packet*.

General Washington did not sanction dueling, particularly not in his defense, and he was angry with his aide, but John was unrepentant, bolstered by his father's approval. John had been nicked by Lee's pistol ball, but his only regret was that he had not called out the man sooner. "Damned scoundrel! It is a marvel that he got away with so much for so long," he declared.

By the avid look on her twin's face when he heard about the duel, Addie was thankful that he hadn't been involved, though he did concede that it was probably better that John hadn't killed General Lee. Even Tench, older than the others and always sensible, found little to condemn in John's action, but he found some mitigation regarding Lee.

"I doubt the man is in his right mind. After the duel, he said, 'How handsomely the young fellow behaved! I could have hugged him!' I ask you, is that the utterance of a sane man?"

Ad could not claim that it was, especially because he had long since come to the conclusion that Lee was unstable. But that didn't make him feel any more kindly toward him.

Having three aides in the city and often at the Birdsalls' brightened this Christmas season for the twins and Matilda, although Matilda wished her brother could be there, too. But all of them were aware that Washington was the reason for the aides' presence in the city and for their attendance at various social functions, and that under the surface gaiety ran the constant stream of politics. The Congress needed to exhibit the hero who had kept the army in the field and saved the day at Monmouth, and the general needed to convince the Congress that more—and more dependable—support of the army was essential.

But whatever the complications, there was no doubt that Mistress Washington, at least, was delighted with the receptions and celebrations being given for her husband. It was the first time since the war had begun that the general had been so publicly and lavishly honored, and though Martha had never complained about the discomforts of the various houses used for winter quarters, it must have been a welcome respite to be lodged in the luxury of the city.

As usual, Martha brought letters and gifts from Castleton for Addie and her brothers, and this year, for Matilda, too. There was much-needed homespun and delicacies from the plantation's larder, and to Addie's singular delight, there were little packages of cooking and healing herbs for her particular use, as if her aunts were telling her in a concrete way that they expected her to be back with the army soon. The aunts and Sissy had been kept well informed of Ad's progress through Uncle Hartley, and they were pleased, though they wished there were some news of Silas.

Mistress Washington was as straightforward and warm as always when Addie visited with her, but the general was so reserved, Addie could not ignore it, not when she understood its cause.

"Your Excellency, I know everything possible is being done to find my husband."

These were hard words to say when she wanted to plead that he suspend his rules of seniority and everything else regarding prisoners, beg that he use all his power to find Silas. But she knew she was following the right course when the general's expression eased, and he spoke gently to her.

"Your husband is a fine officer, one we cannot afford to lose."

Addie could have hugged him for using the present tense, as if he were certain that Silas still lived. And the general endeared himself further to her by treating Ad as if there were no doubt that he would soon be back in his service.

It was the best medicine Ad could have had. The general's faith in him coupled with his need to make amends for his mental lapse of loyalty made him resolve that when the general and the others returned to the army, he would go with them.

Though it was not a problem during the intimate visits of old friends, with Silas's status so uncertain, it would have been awkward for everyone had Addie attended the social events to which she, Ad, and Matilda were invited. The invitations came for a variety of reasons—because of Uncle Hartley, because Ad was one of Washington's aides, because the twins had known the Washingtons before the war, and because of the genuine liking for the twins and Matilda by people who had met them through the Birdsalls and who wanted to honor the sacrifices they had made for the cause.

"I think it is most civil of them to include me," Addie told her brother when the invitations started to come in, "though it would not be fitting for me to accept. But that is no reason for you and Matilda to hide away."

Ad grinned at her without a trace of self-pity. "No, that is no reason for it, but my clumsiness is. I am still knocking against things at an alarming rate, and I have no intention of doing that in front of a large gathering." He hesitated before he said, "This is all so strange for Matilda. She has adjusted very well, but I do not want to overwhelm her. Of course, she is a match in beauty, wit, virtue, and heart for any woman I have ever met, but that is my view of her, not her own."

As the days passed, Ad was more and more grateful that he had an excuse to refuse the invitations, for even Tench's normal good temper was wearing thin under the social demands, and he longed to return to winter quarters at Middlebrook. "Philadelphia may answer very well for a man with his pockets well lined, whose pursuit is idleness and dissipation. But to us who are not in the first predicament, and who are not upon the latter errand, it is intolerable. A morning visit, a dinner at five o'clock, tea at eight or nine, supper, supper, and up all night is the round," he grumbled.

Ad looked forward to Tench's visits for something beyond the close friendship they enjoyed. Tench remained convinced that the French alliance would prove successful, and he was persuasive enough to make Ad begin to hope again.

"It is hard for many of our countrymen to see it, but what the French do elsewhere can be as important as what they might do here. Now, everywhere France and Britain come upon each other, they are at war. That will certainly make it difficult for Britain to commit more troops here. And with Lafayette returning to France to plead more and speedy aid for us, it must be forthcoming, for who could resist the man?" Tench paused, and then he said, "That is, if his sovereign forgives him for having left in the first place. The truth is still a bit obscure, but I doubt the young marquis had royal permission to come to America."

"He wrote me a charming letter of farewell before he left for Boston to take ship," Ad said. "I cannot imagine that even the King of France is proof against him. I hope his departure from Boston is not delayed; we need whatever help he can obtain for us. However, I am sorry that we and His Excellency will be deprived of his company."

Neither of them minded that Lafayette had become such a favorite of the general, easily able to make him smile and even laugh aloud. And Martha was equally fond of him.

"So Lafayette will not be with us at Middlebrook, though there was a room set aside for his use at headquarters." Tench hesitated and then asked directly, "And you, will you be with us? I doubt you'd merit the room—we aides are too lowly for that—but I and the rest of the family would give you warm welcome and a deal of work."

"I want that more than anything," Ad said. "There is nothing wrong with my hands or my mind. I can do the work of a secretary as well as ever. But an aide who must be transported in a carriage or wagon or borne on a litter place to place is of no use. I have not been on a horse since Monmouth; I do not know whether or not I can ride."

"You have moved from bed to crutches and now to a stick—a horse should require less effort than any of those. Your mare is an enviable animal. If you can bear the discomfort, I think she will bear the shift in your balance. If you return with us to Middlebrook, you and the mare will have time to make the adjustment before the new campaign."

When Ad asked his sister and Matilda what they thought of Tench's suggestion, their instant acceptance of the idea did much for his confidence that he could return to active duty. And when he proposed his return to Washington, the general was voluble in his approval, saying, "It cannot be soon enough!"

The tide of affection Ad felt for his leader flowed through him, even stronger than it had before Monmouth and as important as the strength returning to his leg. In his heart he had broken faith, but he had the chance for his private redemption in public service.

Ad teased his sister that she should demand a commission, for she organized their removal from Philadelphia as efficiently as any general, and when Washington's party left the city on February 2, they were with him. They bid farewell to Uncle Hartley and the Birdsalls, with gratitude for how kindly they had been treated but with no regret for quitting the town.

Tench was not with them, having gone to visit his family in Chester, Maryland, his first leave in more than two years, but he was soon to rejoin them and, in the meantime, there were many other friends who welcomed them to the encampment, which stretched some miles over the New Jersey countryside.

Justin and the Castletons were lodged, with Harry Lee and others, in the home of a family named Van Horne. The Van Hornes had five bright daughters who were keeping the bachelors busy vying for their attention.

Kitty Greene was living in a brick house on the shore of the Raritan River with all three Greene babies, including the infant Cornelia born the previous summer. The Knoxes had a new baby, too, also a daughter, Julia, and they were at Pluckemin, where General Knox had established the Artillery Park. Baron von Steuben, General Wayne, and a host of others were present as well, reinforcing the cohesiveness of the army.

As usual, Ad would stay at headquarters, but Justin had secured lodgings for Addie and Matilda in a house not far away, a place made more attractive in that it had room in its stables for Addie's horses.

"I know if Silas were here, you would want to be closer to the Artillery Park, but—" Justin started to explain.

But Addie stopped him. "You made a perfect arrangement." She looked up at him, cherishing having him healthy and whole before her. She put her arms around him and leaned against him for a moment. "It is so good to be back with the army! It is like coming home."

Justin hugged her, and his voice was unsteady when he said, "You and Matilda did a wonderful job taking care of our brother."

Addie stepped back so she could see his face. "We took care of his body, but he took care of the rest. I don't know what demons he fought, but he won." She searched his eyes and saw that he was privy to the reason for Ad's struggle, but she didn't press him, turning instead to the immediate problem. "He drove the wagon, but he hasn't been on Ember yet. He needs to be able to ride."

"Who better than a cavalryman to help him with that?" But Justin's smile faded as he remembered how badly wounded Ad had been, and the doubt he had felt in Philadelphia returned full force. "Can he do it without damaging his leg further?"

"I believe he can, but I know he will try to do too much too soon. It will not be comfortable. The knee joint is still very stiff and probably will always be. But he is determined."

Justin left her, his mind testing various ideas for making riding easier. So natural was riding to him, as it had been to Ad, it was like thinking about breathing instead of just doing it.

Matilda had her reunion with her brother, and at his first sight of her, Luke's usual reserve vanished in a big smile. He grabbed her up in his arms and swung her around, ignoring her giggling protest.

He set her back on her feet, saying, "It seems you survived your time in the city without coming to harm."

"It was so grand at the Birdsalls'! Mirrors, so many of them, furniture, porcelain, silver, all of it gleaming in elegant rooms with ceilings so high! And at night, fine spermaceti candles everywhere, so the shining just went on. I was overwhelmed at first, but the Birdsalls were wonderful to all three of us. They treated us as if we were part of their family."

His little sister had matured a lot in the past months, and now Ad was the most important man in her life. That was exactly as it should be, but that did not prevent the twinge of sorrow Luke felt.

He pulled an exaggeratedly long face to cover his emotion. "While I am happy that you and Colonel Valencourt found each other, it reminds me that I will probably be too old and enfeebled to go courting by the time this business is over."

"Never! You will be a handsome war hero, and all the ladies will swoon over you," Matilda assured him.

She was glad she had not confided the misgivings she still harbored about her fitness to be Ad's wife. As the days passed at Middlebrook, she discovered that she was not nearly as shy with the officers' wives as she once would have been. While the sojourn in Philadelphia had shaken her confidence in one area, it had strengthened it in another. But she was wise enough to know that it was also the leveling effect of the war that was easing her way into a society a frontier trader's daughter would not normally encounter. And none of these considerations were as important as Ad's wellbeing. She rejoiced that he was as content as she to be back with the army.

The hardest thing of all was controlling her panic when Ad began to ride again. "His wound, it won't split open again, will it?" she asked Addie.

"No, it is healed well beyond that," Addie told her, not voicing her fear that the true danger was that Ad could be thrown and badly injured due to his lack of balance. "I think it best that we not watch, at least not in the beginning. We'll have to trust Justin and the others."

Initially, Justin rode Ember until the mare had gotten over her skittishness from long months without a saddle. It helped that the weather was milder than it had been during the winter at Valley Forge, so there were many fair days for riding. Justin took Ember on patrol and found her as steady a beast as his own Colonel and as Silas's Blaze, which was what he expected from Castleton stock. But there was no doubt Ember was Ad's. When Ad was near she whickered softly and nuzzled him so affectionately, Justin told his brother that Matilda was bound to be jealous.

Ad had good reason to be grateful for Ember's responsiveness, for during the first session, a less forgiving animal might have sent him flying, despite Hart's steadying hand on the bridle. Justin and Reeves helped boost him into the saddle, and Harry Lee stood ready to help on the other side.

On his first attempt, Ad slipped backward when he tried to throw his stiff right leg over the saddle. Justin and Reeves pushed him up again, and this time, he overcompensated, making such an effort with his bad leg, he would have plunged over the other side had not Harry braced him back into the saddle.

He sat there, feeling utterly humiliated by his clumsiness, seeing how anxious his companions looked. Then Ember made a soft, protesting sound, and Hart loosened his hold enough so that she could turn her head to look at her rider. Though she was standing quietly for this ungainly performance, she was clearly puzzled.

"Truly, it is I," Ad managed, patting her neck.

Ember snorted and bobbed her head as if in agreement, and suddenly the hilarity of the scene struck Ad, and he started to laugh.

"This will work," he gasped, "all I need is four strong men and one intelligent horse."

Justin peered at him uncertainly, but then he realized Ad was genuinely amused. "Well, as long as you don't need four intelligent men."

Exhilaration eclipsed mirth as Ad savored the pleasure of being atop a fine horse, all the hot life and power of the animal ready to do his bidding. And when Ember was led forward, her gait was fluid, sweet substitution for his halting steps. His knee ached like fury, but it didn't matter, he knew he could do this. It was unlikely that he would ever be proficient enough to serve again as a riding aide, but his main talent had been as a secretary, and he would be able to move with the army and to follow the general into battle when he had to, and that was enough.

There were adaptations to be made. Mounting and dismounting required special effort and concentration, and because his knee had little flexibility, his right stirrup had to be longer than normal, but every day riding got easier.

When Tench returned to camp, he became part of the riding parties, and he was unabashedly proud, and frankly relieved, by Ad's progress.

"While you were absent from headquarters, my work more than doubled, which says much for your efficiency and my lack of it."

It was a generous compliment from the best secretary of all of them.

It was a special day when Ad felt confident enough to invite Addie and Matilda to ride out with him, and the women pretended they had never had any reservations about his return to the saddle.

The only thing that could have made the day more perfect for Addie would have been to have Silas riding with them. But life in camp was eased for her because Lucy and the other wives did not shy away from the subject, but rather mentioned Silas quite often and always as if it were certain he was in British hands. If they had their doubts, they did not express them in Addie's presence.

Lucy was growing stouter with the passage of each year and the production of each new baby, but her energy seemed to grow apace. When the Knoxes gave a ball to celebrate the anniversary of the signing of the French alliance, Washington opened the ball with Lucy, who, in spite of her bulk, danced as lightly as a girl.

It didn't surprise Addie that the Greenes had a dance not long after the Knoxes—Kitty Greene was not one to be outshone. She had fully recovered from the birth of her last child, and, slim and laughing, she declared she could dance forever without respite.

"Forever is a long time," General Washington reminded her.

"I will dance as long as you," she challenged, and with a bow, the general led her out. His face was alight with the smile of purest pleasure, as if he had no other care than to step to the music, and other couples followed.

Harry Lee appeared before Addie. "We were very good at this long ago," he said, instantly conjuring images of the dance at Castleton.

Addie hesitated and heard her brothers urging, "Go on," and she allowed Harry Lee to lead her into the dance. It was different here from how it had been in Philadelphia; here she was comfortable.

General Greene, whose infirmities, including asthma and a stiff knee like Ad's, barred him from the dance floor, took a seat beside Mistress Washington, who seldom danced. It was reassuring to Ad, who shifted to alleviate the strain on his own bad leg, to note that neither Nathanael nor Martha seemed to mind not dancing with their spouses. With a broad grin, General Greene pulled out his watch to time "forever."

They danced the minuet and country dances, and Addie lost herself in the motion and the music, feeling young and carefree for the first time since Monmouth. But she and Harry Lee were no match for the general's endurance, and finally even Kitty surrendered to a stitch in her side, leaving Washington, who showed no signs of fatigue, the victor after two hours of constant dancing.

Matilda was persuaded by Justin to join in a country dance before the night was through, and although Ad would have preferred to be her partner, he delighted in watching her, her cheeks rosy as much from her shyness at performing in such company as from the exercise. To his eyes, there was no more graceful woman in the room.

But no matter what amusements they designed in camp, the war intruded. News came that the enemy had taken Savannah, Georgia, on December 29. In a way, it was tribute to Washington's skill that the British were turning their attention southward once more, away from the general's reach. But it was also undeniably an ominous development. The Continental Army's presence was minimal in the South, and though there was militia there, there were also many Loyalists, a factor of great importance to British planning. Loyalists had not turned out to fight in the expected numbers in the North, but the enemy believed they would in the South.

John Laurens had what had long seemed to him a reasonable answer to the troop shortage in the South, particularly in his native South Carolina, and that was to raise battalions from the slave population. He did not understand how a fight for freedom could overlook the plight of the enslaved. He was willing to argue for hours with those who claimed the slaves hadn't enough humanity inside of them to aspire to freedom. Despite much opposition, he gained enough support from his father and other prominent members of Congress to carry a resolution to Charles Town that he would present to the Assembly of South Carolina, recommending Georgia and South Carolina raise three thousand Black troops to help with the Patriot campaign. All men who served faithfully would gain their freedom.

When John left Washington's family his fellow aides pretended that he would rejoin them soon, but none of them believed it. Loyal as he was to the United States, John was a Carolinian to the bone, and the enemy in Georgia was too close to his home state. If war came to South Carolina, John intended to be there.

"Take good care," Ad said when it was time to bid farewell.

"I would that you and the rest of the army were going with me." John's smile was wry. "But failing that, we must manage on our own."

Ad had nothing to say to that, and his throat knotted. So close had he grown to John and the other aides, he felt as if he were losing a brother. It did not occur to him that the next farewell would be to his sister.

Chapter 16

Spring 1779

Early in April, General Arnold married nineteen-year-old Margaret "Peggy" Shippen. Though Arnold was twice the age of his new wife, and was a widower with three sons, Addie could understand how the young woman could be enamored of him. In spite of being rather thick and squat, he had a dark handsomeness, was a war hero, and as she and Matilda had experienced firsthand, he could exude a powerful appeal.

Nor was it hard to see why Arnold would be attracted to Peggy, for she was from one of the best families, blond and vivacious, and she was fully aware of her worth. Unfortunately, her branch of the Shippen family was Loyalist, and whatever personal benefit there was in the match, the political repercussions were severe for General Arnold.

He was already in bad repute with both military and civil authorities, accused of using his office as Military Governor of Philadelphia for his personal gain and, possibly more damning, there were accounts of his "discouragement and neglect" of patriotic persons and an obvious favoritism toward Tories. It was conduct particularly galling to the more radical Patriots, who fumed that Arnold had indulged the very people who had lived in luxury with the British while the Continental Army was starving at Valley Forge.

The whole situation was made more volatile by the mix of Pennsylvania authorities and the military because no one was sure where the jurisdiction of state power ended and military or national influence began. This conflict was a reflection of the nation's thorniest problem, for it was the states' reluctance to yield individual power that made it so difficult for the Congress to act as a national government, even in something as vital as providing for the army.

Ad thought General Arnold had been less than wise in his actions, but he was more concerned about the effect on General Washington than anything else. Arnold's court martial was set for late April but had been postponed, and while General Washington would have liked to have kept clear of the whole business, he was loyal to Arnold as a good soldier, and Arnold had always treated Washington with the greatest respect. There were also uncomfortable parallels with the criticisms of Greene and the troubles Washington had had with Conway and his bunch, but there was also a great difference—Washington had not been involved in increasing his personal fortune at public expense.

Ad would have liked to discuss the situation at length with Tench, but it was not an easy subject with him because Peggy Shippen Arnold was his first cousin, and he was too much of a gentleman to condemn her new husband or her, despite her Loyalist sympathies. Still, to Ad's mind, although there were difficulties in having an appreciable number of Loyalist connections in the country, Tench was in an enviable position because he remained in contact with his father, who was living in Maryland in placid exile from public life. Father and son shared a deep bond of affection that had not suffered for their political differences and Tench was willing to speak openly about that, saying ruefully, "I think we have become like two musical instruments playing a set piece. I speak of freedom and the rights of man, he of loyalty and duty to crown and country, and there is a certain odd harmony in it, though I will never cease to try to change his tune, nor he mine."

Tench had changed in one way during his trip home. He had met his cousin Anna Maria Tilghman, and he praised her so highly, there was no doubt of a special attraction. Ad was so unabashedly in love with Matilda, it was natural for Tench to confess to him that he was captivated by the intelligence, amiability, and beauty of his cousin. "Though it would be better were it not so, for now I understand your impatience with this business," he allowed.

Ad was twenty-two this year, Tench would be thirty-five in December, but in matters of the heart, there seemed to be no difference. That realization made Ad feel more charitable toward General Arnold. Perhaps Arnold had overreached out of his passion for his pretty Peggy and his desire to keep her in the same style to which she was accustomed. Were that so, it was bad luck that Arnold had not succumbed to the charms of someone like Matilda, whose worst fear seemed to be that she might someday have to live the luxurious, urbane life to which Arnold aspired.

If headquarters was preoccupied with Arnold's problems, Addie cared only about a meeting between British and American representatives regarding prisoner exchanges. Since one of the Americans was Colonel Harrison, an aide of Washington, Addie would have word of the outcome without delay.

Just seeing Ad's face, she knew it had not gone well before he confirmed it. "The enemy wanted an exchange, one for one, but their troops are trained soldiers, many of ours are barely competent militia. If the exchange were made on that basis—"

"Enough! Don't say any more!" Addie raised her hands as if to fend off the words. "I know there are good reasons, scores of them, but what it means to me is that I am no nearer to finding Silas."

Ad's heart ached for her, but he had no comfort to offer.

On the second day of May the whole camp participated in a military review to honor the visit of Monsieur Gerard, the French Minister. The activity was held on a broad green field, and a stage had been erected for the spectators. Addie and Matilda sat there with Kitty, Lucy, Martha, and other ladies.

Addie was filled with pride as she watched Harry Lee's troop lead the procession. Justin, the Castleton cousins, and the rest looked splendid in their bright-green coats and their cavalry accoutrements. General Washington followed them with his aides, next came the foreign visitors, and then the general officers and their aides. Washington, the dignitaries, and the general officers passed in front of the army, reviewing the troops before retiring to the stage.

Baron von Steuben's training was evident in the precision with which the troops displayed their skills, but none performed better than Harry Lee's light horse. The riders seemed to be part of their horses, and the horses went through their paces with such spirit and willingness, it was as if they knew they were on exhibition. Addie felt the thunder of their hoof beats in place of her heart. And it moved her no less that Ad had ridden in with the rest of Washington's suite. If his dismount was still stiff and his gait uneven, it didn't matter, for he bore himself with confidence.

An idea that had seemed too extreme when it had first occurred to Addie months before had started to appear more reasonable by the day as she considered every aspect of it. Especially since the failed prisoner exchange meeting. Ad, Matilda, and Justin would protest, but they did not need her now. Silas did. She waylaid Justin immediately after the reviews.

"I want you to talk to Ad for me," she said, and Justin refused instantly.

"You want me to talk to your twin? Oh, no! You never, never need me to speak to Ad, and he doesn't need me to speak to you for him. The two of you hardly need words between you." He stated the truth without jealousy and with the certainty that this was not like the secret crisis of loyalty Ad had been suffering when Justin had gone to see him in Philadelphia; Addie looked too resolute for that. "If you are asking me to intercede, it is because you are planning something wholly unacceptable, and I want no part of it."

"I am going to do what I must, no matter what. But it would be better for everyone were it done in an orderly fashion."

Justin knew this version of his sister. This was the same person who had chosen Silas and would not be deterred; who had pledged to the cause as firmly as any man who had survived the siege of Boston, and had not fled with their father to safety; who had been following the drum for three years; who had saved their brother's life; the list went on and on.

"What am I to propose to Ad?" His reluctance to be part of this dragged every word.

"I am going to New York to find Silas. It would be easier did I go under a flag, but if not, I will find my way there without sanction."

Justin stared at her. "Your wits are rattled! You are sister to one of Washington's aides and to one of Harry Lee's men; you are cousin to others and niece of a member of Congress; and you propose to put yourself in the enemy's hands?"

"I am not going to present myself as a hostage. I am going to search for my husband. And I am going to use a relative to help, if he will. Darius is my brother, too—at least we share the blood of our father,—and he is a prominent Tory. Loyalist," she corrected herself, already practicing the least offensive language to use in New York. "Darius spared your life when he could have taken it. I have to believe he will help me find Silas. And you cannot claim I would be the first to go on such a quest. Some enemy officers' wives have come through our lines to minister to their husbands, and a few of us have gone through theirs. These have been among the rare civilized 'exchanges' of this war."

When Justin showed no sign of yielding, Addie abandoned logic. "I am dying a little each day without him. If he is alive, he must be in great distress, otherwise there would be some word of him. I have to go."

Justin closed his eyes for a moment. Then he said, "I will speak to Ad for you."

Ad was as resistant to her plan as she had anticipated, but she had not only Justin to argue on her side, she also had support from Matilda. In most circumstances, Matilda would not intervene between the siblings, but in this case, she did not hesitate.

"Addie stayed with you when you were wounded. She stayed all night fighting to save your life, and she only allowed herself a brief search for Silas the next day before she was back at your side. Had you not been in such need, you know she would have sought him without ceasing."

Ad had no defense against this truth, but even under pressure from Justin and Matilda, he could not agree with his sister without argument.

"You will be surrounded by the enemy. Have you truly considered how that will be?"

"Better than you have," she said. "I have not forgotten being in Boston under British rule."

He winced at his stupidity for having momentarily forgotten that her experience of the siege of Boston was radically different from his. It was a reminder that each of them—including their father, and Quentin, and Silas—had had to choose their own way in this war since the beginning.

Suddenly her plan did not seem as farfetched as much as it seemed necessary. Addie needed to learn Silas's fate, and if Darius were willing to help, he would be just the one who could. Undoubtedly he could also send Addie back to the American lines, too, if he thought it best, and Ad found comfort in that. Though Darius was their sworn enemy, Ad did not believe he would harm Addie or allow anyone else to do so.

Having gotten her family's cooperation, Addie was not worried about obtaining General Washington's. Whatever personal reservations he might have, his public policy was based on justice, and as Addie had pointed out to Justin, there was precedent for her to go to New York. But there were details to be discussed, and she did so forthrightly in the private meeting she was granted with the general, after he had already given his permission for her journey.

"Your Excellency, perhaps I will spend but little time in New York, but if I tarry there, I may learn things that could be of use to you. Is there a way for me to send you word?"

The general was a master at hiding his reactions when he wished to, but for an instant, his shock was plain. However, Addie was encouraged that he did not reject her offer out of hand. Instead, he let the silence stretch between them.

In the British Army, the adjutant general usually served as the "intelligencer" or "scoutmaster" in addition to his other duties. But in the Continental Army, General Washington was indisputably in charge of intelligence gathering. Because of her twin and her closeness to headquarters, Addie knew that confidential information came in and went out in a steady flow, and that the aides kept careful track of locked boxes, trying to keep the other side from gaining access to vital information regarding troop returns, battle plans, and the like. She also knew that more than once, Washington had not only made sure false information was left in open view so that suspected spies might pass it along, but had dictated the composition of the falsehoods. It was an exercise that afforded the general pleasure and amusement, despite its serious intent.

"It is dangerous work." Washington broke the silence abruptly. "And many say it is dishonorable."

"Your Excellency, I mean no disrespect, but I think it must be men who would judge it so. Perhaps women do not have so fine a sense of honor, but I believe that most of us who have men at risk are not so delicate about something that might speed the advantageous end to this war."

She won a brief smile of approval for that, but then she felt the full force of the man as the gray-blue eyes studied her as if he could see far beyond the words exchanged.

"Allow me time to consider your generous offer," he said, rising and giving her a slight bow to signal the end of the interview.

"Of course." Addie resisted the impulse to plead that he decide right now because she had already delayed too long, but she could not forgo saying, "Whatever you decide, I pray you do not tell my brothers about this business." She managed a smile of her own. "They do have too fine a sense of honor, and they would not approve."

His nod of agreement made her feel as if he had even now accepted her offer. But two days later, she had a caller who proved that the process was not to be so simple. General Washington had sent her a message to expect Major Tallmadge, and he left the difficult questions to his deputy.

Major Benjamin Tallmadge of the Continental Dragoons was only a few years older than Addie, and they had been introduced in the past at headquarters, but the gravity of his bearing put her on her mettle. Today he was all business.

"General Washington made it clear that this is to be a private meeting?" Major Tallmadge asked after they had exchanged greetings.

"As you see." Addie gestured to the empty room. She had told Matilda that Washington was sending someone to help with arrangements for her trip behind enemy lines, and Matilda had not questioned her. If Matilda suspected the meeting was taking place here to avoid Ad's scrutiny, she had given no sign.

"I do not doubt your loyalty, Mistress Bradwell, and it is obvious that the more we know about the enemy's plans, the better it is for us. But those who are giving us information from New York are, for the most part, undistinguished to British eyes, people able to move about without attracting notice. You are a different case. You will be noticed wherever you go. Do you plan to claim a change of heart and mind, to disguise yourself as a loyal subject of the King?"

Addie shook her head. "No. I plan to go exactly as I am, a Patriot wife searching for her husband. The truth can be very disarming—the truth and the enemy's arrogance."

He considered this thoughtfully, and then he asked the hardest question of all. "Your half-brother, Darius Valencourt, is not only an eminent Tory, he is also an effective leader of his troop. Would you betray him to us?"

It was a question Addie had considered at length before she had gone to see General Washington, but she still had no easy answer to it. "I do not know. I assume there will be those around him who could inadvertently provide valuable information, but intelligence regarding his actions—I am not sure I would report that to you."

"Fair enough. I would judge you an unnatural creature indeed had you answered otherwise." His eyes searched her face. They were as piercing as General Washington's had been. "Do you think you have the nerve for this? A slip may endanger not only yourself but others. It is a great responsibility."

"I was in Boston before the war began. My brothers and Silas were working with the Sons of Liberty while my father's house was frequented by British officers. I did not betray my brothers or Silas. I know that was different, but I can only tell you that I believe my nerve will hold."

"I believe it will, too," he said slowly, and then he proceeded to give her concise instructions about what she would and would not do in New York. She had had notions of being required to memorize ciphers, to use invisible writing fluid, or to write on tiny scraps of paper that could be easily hidden, but Major Tallmadge dispelled these ideas. All initiative would be left to the agents already in place; it would be up to them whether or not she was contacted at all. Tallmadge entrusted her with an address, but even at this establishment, she would not know who the agent was unless he approached her.

The name of the place sent a jolt of shock through her, but she kept her expression calm, and when Tallmadge said, "Well done," she knew she'd passed a test. Nonetheless, at the end of the interview, Addie was humbly aware that she was like the rawest recruit in the army and would have to step very cautiously to avoid disaster.

As he took his leave of her, Major Tallmadge said, "Remember, your first task in New York is to find Colonel Bradwell. I hope you accomplish that and a safe return to us so swiftly that none of what we have discussed today will be necessary. But if that is not to be, I beg you remember, no matter how courteously the enemy might treat you, none of them are to be trusted, not even your brother. I doubt your sex would prove defense against their vengeance."

"I will not forget," she promised him.

The second test of her nerve came in the following days as she waited for final arrangements for her passage to New York. For all her efforts toward secrecy, it was a terrible strain to resist confiding in her brothers and Matilda. She loved them so much and was so afraid of what awaited her in New York, she nearly gave in to the urge to cancel the journey. And then she saw Silas's face as clearly as if he were with her. She had to know if he was in New York; it was the only place where she could hope to find him alive.

It also gave her strength that Martha, Lucy, Kitty, and other officers' wives wished her well, not one of them telling her she was foolish to go.

When she bid farewell to Matilda, Addie told her, "I have faith in you to take care of my brothers and your own while I'm gone."

Matilda embraced her fiercely. "You take care of yourself, I'll take care of them." Addie's last sight of Matilda was of her scrubbing away tears as impatiently as "Matt" would have done.

Both General Washington and Harry Lee were generous in allowing Addie's brothers to be relieved of their duties long enough to escort her to the enemy, and Washington made a special point of wishing her a safe journey, his facade of impassivity back in place so that he gave no hint of the business between them.

General Knox gave her a message for Silas as if he were utterly certain that she would find him. "Tell him his command is anxious for his return, as I am."

But Addie was most moved by a brief encounter with the boy Silas had saved and his parents. Though she had tried to banish it, she knew the Chepmans still carried a heavy burden of guilt that made it difficult for them to face her. But they had mustered their courage to come wish her good luck in her search, news of her going having spread through the encampment.

Tim held a bouquet of wildflowers, and his hand shook as he offered the flowers to her. But his voice was steady when he said, "Mistress Bradwell, I hope you find the colonel and bring him back."

"So do I, Tim, but whatever happens, what he did, and what you did at Monmouth was right. Don't ever forget that." She meant every word. A year had made a great difference. Though only fourteen now, Tim had grown some and filled out, his voice had lowered, and it was easy to see the man he would be, horrible to imagine that, except for Silas, all the promise might have died at Monmouth.

"You have a fine son," she told his parents, and the Chepmans' faces glowed for a moment with pride.

Justin, Ad, and an escort provided by General Washington rode with her all the way to the sea, spending a night on the road that they might arrive very early where the British party would meet her. Only once on the way did Ad break down enough to say, "You can turn back. No one would think less of you," though he knew his twin well enough to hear her answer before she said, "I would think less of myself."

In the pale dawn light, when they were in sight of the enemy, it was Ad who saw him first and exclaimed, "Good lord, Addie, it's your Scotsman! Darius must have arranged for him to come." Neither he nor Justin had met John Traverne in Boston, but they had seen him in battle and knew the look of him and his men and their uniforms.

Addie was so stunned by the sight of him, she didn't make her old protest of Traverne not being "her" Scotsman. She blinked, but he was still there, looking even taller and broader than she remembered, familiar, yet utterly foreign because he was clad in his regimental uniform, and unlike her brothers, she had never seen him in this guise. Over a snowy shirt and a waistcoat, he wore a red coat faced in the same dark-blue, green, and black tartan of his belted kilt. A band of the same pattern trimmed his bonnet, and his plaid, a length of tartan, flowed down his back, pinned at his shoulder by a heavy silver brooch. Silver also framed the badger-skin sporran that hung in front of his kilt, and there were silver buckles on his black shoes. The intricate hilt of his sword gleamed silver and gold. Patterned stockings were held neatly in place by garters below his knees, while the kilt ended above his knees, leaving them bare.

Two of his men were with him, also in this military version of Highland dress, though they were less richly bedecked, and the three should have looked outlandish in comparison to the soldiers with them who were dressed in standard uniforms of coats and breeches, but instead, the three Highlanders made the others look enfeebled.

"Big brutes, aren't they," Justin muttered. "Highlanders seem to come in only two sizes—very large or very small. Addie, I judge you will have safe passage to New York."

Addie knew he was trying to lighten the mood and reassure her, but she was grappling inwardly with the strange emotions arising at the sight of Colonel John Traverne. It had been four years since she had last seen him, yet her mind had carried such a clear image of him, she would have known him anywhere. Good and bad memories stirred from that time. The war had just begun, and with the British penned in Boston, it had seemed possible that the King and Parliament might make some settlement acceptable to the colonies without further bloodshed. Quentin and Sarah had been alive. Marcus had been at home. And she herself had been so in love with Silas and so worried about him—that had not changed.

She remembered Traverne's sorrow that his wife and child had died in his absence. And she remembered that though he had gone home to Scotland, he had returned with a body of fighting men who were, by now, well known for their skill in battle. A shiver went down her spine as she heard the bagpipes in her memory, skirling through the dust and heat of Monmouth.

When they were close enough so that she could see Traverne's face clearly, she saw that she was not the only one trying to appear calm at this reunion. For a moment, his dark-blue eyes searched her face intently, as if only the two of them were present. Then polite distance covered his emotions. He made a slight bow.

"Mistress Valen— Bradwell, your brother Darius has arranged that I be part of your escort to New York. He awaits your arrival, and we are ready to sail."

"Thank you, Colonel Traverne," she replied formally and introduced her brothers.

He inclined his head politely, acknowledging them with "Colonel, Captain," ignoring the sullen looks of some of the British regulars who did not think Rebels should be granted the courtesy of rank.

It took only minutes to transfer Addie's meager bundles and the routine diplomatic and domestic correspondence aboard the small coastal schooner that would take them to Manhattan Island.

Addie stroked Nightingale's velvety nose, and the mare snuffled affectionately.

"Take care of her for me. Make sure she doesn't get too fat and lazy while I'm gone." She bowed her head, fighting for control, and then she looked from one brother to the other. "You may have to care for her for a long time. Silas will never accept parole, so I will stay with him until exchange is possible. But I will hold both of you in my heart every minute of every day."

She allowed no doubt that she would find Silas.

She was so resolute and yet so vulnerable, Ad wanted to grab her and carry her back with them. But the searing pain in his leg reminded him that though he knew Addie had not wanted him to make this ride, she had not tried to dissuade him. He had to respect her choices as she respected his.

He put his arms around her and held her close. "We'll be waiting for you and Silas."

Justin hugged her, too.

She heard Colonel Traverne say, "No harm will befall your sister. You have my word on it," but her attention was fixed on watching her brothers remount their horses, Justin with lithe grace, Ad with dogged strength. From the deck of the schooner, Addie watched until she saw a final wave from her brothers before they rode away. Gradually the creaking of the ship and the sounds of the crew and soldiers intruded on her consciousness, and she realized that Colonel Traverne was standing beside her.

"It is startling to see the three of you together, so alike. In my family, there is also a marked resemblance among us, but one ceases to notice what is familiar." His voice was gentle as he sought to distract her from the sorrow of parting, and she found his presence comforting, allowing her to speak openly.

"It is the Castleton blood from our mother's side. Quentin looked like Papa, as Darius does, probably even more now that he is older." She made no mention of Justin's confirming that after his encounter with him. "He and I have not seen each other for five years. I am grateful that he has allowed me this journey. I know he could have prevented it had he chosen."

"Darius was saddened to learn of Quentin's death, and so was I."

Even having assumed that Darius and Marcus would correspond regularly, it was jarring to have it confirmed. News of Quentin's death would have come to Darius the long way, from Marcus in England. The familiar longing to see her father, to speak with him again, swept over her, but Traverne's next words reclaimed her awareness.

"I think you will find Darius somewhat changed. You couldn't know, I suppose, but his wife died in childbed last winter. I know he misses her."

"Poor Darius! I met his Harriet just once, on that brief visit five years ago, but she was most kind to us, and Darius seemed very happy with her." She remembered Harriet as a slender, brown-haired, brown-eyed woman possessed of a lively wit and ready smile. She had been connected to some of the most prominent Tory families in New York, but Addie was sure that Darius had loved her for her own sake. She thought of how ironic it was that Justin and Darius had such sorrow in common, but because they were on opposite sides of the war, they could be of no solace to each other. She wondered if their parallel losses formed a special bond between Darius and Traverne.

"Despite all, your brother looks forward to seeing you. He would have come to escort you himself, but he thought that under the circumstances, it might be easier if he awaited you in New York."

This had been a formal meeting under truce flags, and the soldiers on both sides were required to appear in uniform. Imagining Justin and Ad in their Continental Army uniforms facing Darius in the uniform of his Tory regiment, Addie gave Darius credit for his circumspection.

Aside from this oblique reference, Addie and Colonel Traverne did not discuss their political differences or even her determination to search for Silas. Addie was glad of it, knowing she would be speaking of little else once she arrived in New York. But it was hard to ignore the fact that she was sailing into enemy territory, particularly because the fair day allowed a long view. The flag on the schooner and on every vessel of any size was British. And redcoats and Hessians could be seen in their encampments on Staten Island and Long Island. Ad had warned her, but the reality made her feel like a fox caught out in the open. Still, she remained on deck although she was offered accommodations below. If she flinched from the sight of the enemy, she was going to be of little use to Silas or to General Washington in New York.

Traverne had introduced the two Highlanders with him as Angus and Duncan, and Addie noted that though they gave their colonel some privacy when he was speaking to her, they remained watchful. They were both big, brawny men, considerably older than Traverne, and Angus was red-headed while Duncan was dark. When they spoke to Traverne or he to them, it was in Gaelic and caused some muttering among the English sailors and soldiers.

"They can speak a little English, but they prefer it not foul their tongues," Traverne explained with a wry smile, though Addie had not asked the question.

"I do not think they approve of me. They watch as if they fear I will push you over the side." Addie resisted the childish impulse to make a face at the men.

"They are my nursemaids. They have known me since I was in leading strings and refuse to notice that some years have passed since that time." There was as much affection as resignation in his voice.

"But you are their chief, are you not?"

"Here, perhaps, but my brother Rob is the true chief of the clan and thus of all of us." He searched for the right words. "I do not envy him his power or his responsibilities, for they are equal. Clan means 'children,' and while my brother may own the land and all upon it, he is responsible for every man, woman, child, and beast there. He is a good father, far better than I could ever be."

She wanted to ask him how he and his men could fight for the government that continued a policy designed to destroy the Highland clans forever. Instead, she asked him to tell her more about his home. He obliged with descriptions of the ragged cliffs and waterfalls, the green glens and quiet lochs, and with fond tales of Rob and Rob's children, who now numbered five, the last one having been born during the three years that Traverne had been in America.

"Rob's wife, Caitlin, is a good woman, and Rob is a fond father to his brood, as he is to the clan, as he was to me, for he is fifteen years older than I. He always includes tales of the children in his letters. We have two sisters, but they are married, live some distance away, and neither is a good correspondent."

His deep voice soothed as he told stories as fair as the day, and Addie appreciated his efforts, though she doubted that all was as idyllic as he presented it. The Highlands of Scotland were a notoriously troubled part of Great Britain.

She listened to him, to the sounds around them, and to the occasional exchanges between him and his men. She had heard Scottish Gaelic only a few times before, and it was so exotic to her ears, so mellifluous, that it was difficult to discern where one word ended and the next began, to imagine capturing the unique sounds with the English alphabet. But after a time she recognized the names.

She sounded them out carefully. "*Aonghus* is Angus. Duncan is *Donnchadh*, and you, but of course, you are *Iain*! That name I know. It sounds not so different from the English of your name."

"It is a world of difference!" His voice was suddenly harsh. "To my family, to the men who follow me, to myself, I am Iain. To the English and in the British Army, I am John, and all my men bear names hammered from their own tongue into English because the Gaelic is still officially forbidden."

"But you speak it openly here," Addie protested.

He smiled without humor. "The army is ever practical. That the men are allowed to speak here the language they must whisper in their glens is a small price to pay that they might fight as boldly and tenaciously as they are expected to. So, too, are we allowed to play the pipes and wear the kilt." He took a deep breath and deliberately lightened the conversation by describing another of the childhood adventures he had shared with Rob.

Addie listened politely, but she was considering the flash of anger she had witnessed. It had seemed more intimate and telling even than his revelation those years ago of the death of his Jeane. Under his urbane manner, there was a man of passion and compassion; he might claim his brother was better suited to be chief, but surely no one could care more deeply for the men under his command. He would now be forever Iain in her mind. John belonged to the enemy, but Iain belonged to his people.

Wind and tide favored them so that there was daylight left when they docked. Everywhere Addie looked there were redcoats, and then she saw no one except the tall man striding toward her. He was dressed in civilian clothes, and he looked so much like Marcus her heart jumped. When he caught sight of her, Darius's warm smile appeared instantly, and Addie knew he was genuinely glad to see her. The tension of the past days eased so abruptly, she swayed, but Darius was there to steady her as he said, "Welcome, Addie, welcome," and Colonel Traverne said, "She's had a very long day."

Addie didn't mind that they were treating her as if she were a child; she felt like one, weary and willing to allow others to take charge for now. She was bundled into Darius's carriage with him, and Colonel Traverne said he and his men would be along later.

"They live with you?" she managed to ask her brother, though she could hardly keep her eyes open, let alone think coherently.

Darius nodded. "When John is in the city. His regiment is garrisoned at Jamaica on Long Island, but he is here quite often, and Angus and Duncan are his shadows. John is an admirable man, and I value his friendship. I am thankful that our sister recommended him to us."

"Are Papa, Mary, and the children still with Callista?" Addie was too tired to control the quaver in her voice.

"They have an establishment close by in the country; they visit London quite often; and by Papa's letters, life seems to be going well for them. But…" Darius hesitated and then continued, finding no delicate way to frame the truth. "Papa made his fortune in *this* country, and he is beginning to understand that he is more a part of the New World than of the Old. When the rebellion is over, I believe he will return to Boston."

Addie was too tired to soften her response. "Then he will never return. It is not a rebellion. It is a war for independence, and we will win."

In that brief exchange, they had established the immense gulf between them, and Addie's fatigue was pierced by the fear of what she would do if Darius changed his mind about helping her. She was here under the condition that she reside in his house, under his protection—under his supervision. Yet, she could not step back from the truth.

"I do not want to deceive you. I am here to find Silas, but my heart and my mind are wholly committed to my country. Nothing can change that."

Darius surprised her by conceding. "I suspected as much. If not, you would have come here long since with other refugees, or you would have gone to England. But it is difficult not to hope."

"As it is for me. Were you, Papa, and I loyal to the same cause, life would be much sweeter."

"Agreed," he said softly, "but since we are not, a truce would seem in order that we not worry each other with arguments we cannot win."

"Truce," she concurred, and she thought he was right—Darius had changed. He had always been kind enough to her and her brothers, but he had also been rather stern and aloof. Now there was not only a melancholy about him, there was also a warmth Addie had felt since he had greeted her, as if nothing about the war could be more important than her presence.

"I am sorry Harriet died," she offered, needing to acknowledge his loss.

"And I am sorry that Quentin is gone," he said.

Grief flowed between them, as close a bond as shared blood.

Then guilt slithered through her as she considered her dual purpose in being in New York, and she admitted to herself that it would be infinitely easier if Tallmadge's agents never made contact with her.

Chapter 17

New York City, Spring 1779

When she awakened the next morning, for a moment Addie was confused about where she was. Then she remembered the voyage with Colonel Traverne and the carriage ride with Darius, but the rest of the details of how she'd come to be sleeping in this gracious room were clouded. Once she'd gotten to the house, she had let Darius's housekeeper take her in hand and tuck her in, again the child.

As she became more alert, the urgency to find Silas returned full force, and she was up, washed, dressed, and heading downstairs so swiftly, she startled a squeak from a maid who was on her way up.

Addie found Darius and Colonel Traverne just sitting down to breakfast. The smell of food made her stomach growl, reminding her of how little she'd eaten the day before. There was freshly baked bread, butter, thin slices of smoked beef, and steaming pots of coffee, chocolate, and tea. But when she would have served herself, Darius motioned her to sit.

"Pray, allow me. And I assume you would prefer chocolate or coffee to tea?"

His smile met hers when she said, "Chocolate, please."

She was taken aback when she saw the amount of food he heaped on her plate. He set it before her with a flourish, resumed his seat, and he and Traverne watched eagerly, as if they expected to see her consume it all forthwith.

When she reached for a piece of bread and buttered it, she saw her hands as they must seem to them—long-fingered and very thin with short broken nails and calluses from riding too often without gloves and from chores most gentlewomen seldom performed. Freckles dotted the skin of her hands and marched across her nose, though she had tried to shield her face with hood or hat. But no amount of caution could have prevented the effects of having followed the army for three years. At this moment, she had more in common with Matilda and the other camp women than with any civilian lady.

She nibbled at the bread and meat and sipped the chocolate, which, even with milk and sugar, was bitter, and she wished tea did not have political implications. When she had eaten her fill, more than half of the food remained on the plate, and both of the men were so clearly disappointed, she chided them.

"You cannot expect to fatten the goose with one meal." They looked so abashed at being found out, she laughed. "Colonel Traverne, you have your nursemaids, and now it seems I have mine." Then, abruptly, all levity fled from her, and she asked, "How do I search for Silas?"

"I have already made inquiries," Darius said, but his eyes shifted away from hers. "You must understand, the situation is as complicated as the city is at present. There are not only a great number of prisoners here, but refugees as well. There is a shortage of lodging and everything else for both civilians and prisoners, and—"

"And?" Addie's soft question seemed to echo around the room.

"The overcrowding is acute. Oh, hell! The prisoners are kept in horrible conditions. It is inexcusable, but it is the reality. Finding one man when there has been no word of him…" His eyes questioned and her curt nod answered. "You must understand how great a task this is."

"I have no proof that Silas was brought here, but if he was not, then he died nearly a year ago." She forced herself to say the words. "Or perhaps he was brought here and died here. Before I accept either of these possibilities, I will search every corner of this place." Her heart pounded at the thought that Darius had allowed her to come this far only to thwart her efforts out of misguided concern.

But he said, "We will take you around today, and you will see what you are facing. And you must never go out without an escort—if not I or Colonel Traverne, then one of the servants."

Within moments of beginning the tour, Addie understood Darius's warning. They went on foot, and everywhere there was glaring evidence of the changes the war had brought. Addie had noticed very little the previous day, not even how close the fires that had broken out after the American withdrawal had come to Darius's property. Between four and five hundred buildings had burned, and few had been rebuilt, so great stretches lay in rubble. But many of the ruins were inhabited by people who had made rude shelters of blackened timbers and bricks or had stretched canvas across boards. Children ran in packs, approaching passersby with their hands out, begging for coins in their high-pitched voices. Darius and Colonel Traverne shooed them away automatically, but Addie could scarcely bear to look at them, so guilty did she feel that she could not help them. And it was not only the white refugees, Loyalists who had left their homes in American-controlled areas to seek the protection of the British Army; there were also thousands of runaway slaves. Slavery was still practiced in New York, but the British had no policy of returning runaways and, further, had incited slaves to desert their masters. The comparative freedom they found in the city was coupled with terrible deprivation that made them the first to succumb to want and disease.

The day was mild, but the stench of refuse, excrement, and unwashed bodies hung over everything. And yet, in the midst of such grim conditions, there was also wealth and ease.

Most of the British troops were quartered on Staten Island and Long Island, but to Addie's eyes, they were everywhere, particularly the officers, riding or strolling by, many of them with female companions. There were richly dressed civilians, men who wore high-crowned hats in repudiation of the Rebel preference for cocked hats with three corners formed by a rolled-up brim, and women who tripped along under towering edifices of powdered hair, theirs and what they had purchased, topped by feathers, ribbons, other ornaments, tiny hats, or profuse combinations of various decorations, as if they were in London or Paris.

Coffee houses were doing a brisk business, and broadsides advertised theatrical performances, concerts, dances, cockfights, horse races, gambling clubs, and myriad other amusements, as if these frivolities could recreate European capitals in the midst of a war thousands of miles away from the originals. Addie felt no physical danger. Not only were Darius and Traverne with her, but the colonel's men had fallen in behind them when they left the house, and she was conscious of the solid presence of Angus and Duncan at her back. Her spirit was not so safe. Everything she was seeing was evidence of how atrocious the conditions of the prisoners must be, for if so many citizens could indulge their appetites while their fellow Loyalists suffered, what comfort would they offer to their captured enemies?

She felt as dazed as if someone had struck her on the head.

Numerous people hailed her escorts, and she acknowledged introductions automatically, hardly noting the faces, but seeing that both Darius and Traverne were accorded respect. She understood why Darius was wearing the uniform of his rangers—however elaborate was the costume of civilians, military uniforms earned the highest regard.

Then she saw other uniforms, tattered and faded, but still marking the wearers as Continental soldiers. She froze in her tracks, staring at the men.

Darius followed her gaze. "They are on parole, free to wander the city during the day, but not to leave it. Poor fellows, it is a bleak existence, and they are hard pressed to find enough to eat or to see to any other needs." There was sympathy in his voice, but also acceptance.

"I wish to speak to them."

Her escorts' surprise at the suggestion made her impatient.

"They are not ghosts! They are soldiers who might have news of Silas."

"As you will," Darius said, but when their little group approached, the three men began to move away, obviously not wanting any attention.

"No, please wait!" Addie called. "You stay here," she ordered Darius and the others.

They halted, Colonel Traverne muttering, "Command comes easily to her. She would be useful on the parade ground."

Addie wasted no time telling the Continentals what she wanted. "I am looking for my husband, Lieutenant Colonel Silas Bradwell. He is an artillery officer, under General Knox. He was taken at Monmouth, and I think he was brought here. Have you heard anything of him?"

The soldiers glanced from her to the men, and the tallest and thinnest of the trio said softly, "Seems as if you're keeping strange company, ma'am."

"I'd keep company with the Devil if it would help me find my husband," she snapped.

The men blinked at her. Then the tall man nodded as if he'd just completed a silent conversation. "I have seen you before, and you have a brother on General Washington's staff."

"Yes, I do. And Colonel Valencourt is our half-brother. He is loyal to the King, and I am loyal to the United States, but he has agreed to help me find Silas."

Addie could see the men relax as they digested this information; families divided by the war were familiar to them. They conferred in low voices, and the tall one again acted as spokesman.

"I am sorry, Mistress Bradwell, but we don't know your husband. If he were on parole here, we'd know him. But the prisons and the hulks, well, there are thousands of men in them." His hat was much the worse for wear, but it still had a white cockade on it, indicating his rank.

Addie said, "Thank you, Captain…" She looked at him inquiringly. Though he paused for a moment, he gave his name, Daniel Trumble, and she told him where Darius's house was should he have information for her. She resisted the impulse to ask where and when he and his companions had been captured and why they had been offered parole and had agreed to it. She knew parole was as uncertain as exchange, offered to some, mostly officers, but not to others, and carrying with it the demands of good behavior and a promise not to fight against the British until the term of parole had expired or an exchange had been arranged. Addie remained convinced that Silas would have refused parole had it been offered.

She wished she had money to give him, but her supply of coin was so meager, she could not. All she could do was thank him again and walk away.

"They have no news of him. They will bring me word if they discover anything, but I cannot wait for that," she told Darius and Traverne. "I need to visit the prisons."

"Then we begin," Darius said. He was prepared for this and did not try to turn her aside from the very purpose that had brought her here, but his expression betrayed his distaste for the exercise.

The first place they visited was a sugarhouse. It was five stories of dark stone with small windows, and the windows were crowded with faces. A high wooden fence ran around the building, and within the space between fence and walls, British and Hessian sentinels patrolled. However, when Darius displayed the paper signed by Sir Henry Clinton, his party was admitted and allowed to see the records. But scrawls, blotches, and great water stains made much of the lists illegible and gave clear proof of how little the authorities cared for the inmates.

"I must talk to the prisoners," Addie said.

The officer in charge gaped at her as if she'd demanded to be thrown into a den of lions. But Darius was grimly in accord with her, convinced that a good dose of reality would undermine her determination. Whatever Colonel Traverne thought, he kept to himself, but any of the guards who let their eyes wander too freely in Addie's direction received such a withering scowl from him, they quickly shifted their attention.

The gloomy cellars were used as dungeons and each of the above floors were divided into two chambers. No trace remained of the sweet substance once stored in the warehouse; now the misery of hundreds of men filled the place. Some lay or sat on dirty straw, while others slouched against the walls, their legs too weak to hold them upright. Those pressed against the windows were desperately trying to get a breath of fresh air before their ten minutes were up and they had to relinquish their places to others in the system of rotation they themselves had created. The men were filthy, emaciated, and many were so ill the stench of disease and the sounds of hacking coughs and fevered groans filled the air. There was a constant rustle from fingers scratching against the lice and other vermin that infested straw, clothes, and bodies.

Addie's stomach did a somersault, and it took all her willpower not to cover her mouth and nose against the fetid air. While the sentinels had viewed her with a mixture of contempt and lust, those prisoners who were conscious enough to be aware of her presence whispered their shock among themselves. But eyeing her companions, they did not approach.

"Please, stay here."

She heard Colonel Traverne's exasperated sigh at being ordered about again when she motioned him and the others to stay back as she stepped forward.

"I am looking for my husband, Lieutenant Colonel Silas Bradwell. He was taken at Monmouth…" She listened to her voice reciting the litany; already it seemed as if she had said the lines a thousand times.

More whispers swept the shadows, then a voice called out, "He isn't among us."

She heard another say, "Lucky man to have you lookin' for 'im."

Then someone else volunteered, "Never served with Colonel Bradwell, but I heard tell he is a good officer." It was so little, and yet this acknowledgment gave Silas substance.

"Thank you," she said and moved on to the next room, unwilling to leave until she was sure every group had heard her.

There were a few more comments of recognition of Silas's name—he was, after all, one of General Knox's best officers—but nothing about where he might be. When Addie left the building, she was hardly aware of her escorts following on her heels. She drew a deep breath when she got outside, but the smell of despair was inside her now.

"Have you had enough?" Darius asked gruffly.

Rage boiled up and spilled over before she could stop it. "Enough of seeing how your government treats honorable prisoners of war as if they were the lowest felons? Oh, yes, more than enough of that! Enough of searching for Silas? Never. Not until the day I find him! It is unpleasant to visit hell, but how much worse to be held captive there. Where next?"

Darius's face was tight with the anger that had risen to meet hers, but then the anger faded, and he shook his head ruefully. "You are so like your mother. Had Papa been in such need, Lily would have been no less resolute than you are."

It was a weapon, the blood they shared through their father and this affection he still had for her mother, and a weapon that would allow her to stay in New York as long as necessary. Her calculation was cold-blooded, and welcome. The suffering she was seeing this day was tempering some part of her soul into steel. She had thought the war had changed her as much as it could, but not even the want at Valley Forge or the gore of battle was as bad as this. It was harsh enough that the men had lost every vestige of the freedom they had been fighting for, far worse that their captors were holding them in conditions designed to destroy the health and spirit of all, from the weakest to the strongest man. To Addie's eyes, every prisoner was Silas.

The next place they visited had been one of the dissenting churches. Every stick of wood, including pews and pulpit, had been stripped and burned by the prisoners for warmth. It was overly cool even now in spring, and Addie wondered what they would do when winter returned. Again the conditions were appalling, and again there was no direct word of Silas, though two men knew of his reputation and Addie was once more recognized for her close resemblance to one of Washington's prominent aides, and from another quarter, for her obvious kinships with two men who rode with Harry Lee.

When they left, Addie said, "I see Provost Marshal Cunningham's work everywhere. Brutal, bestial man! His treatment of prisoners in Philadelphia will not be forgotten. It is reported that more than two thousand men died of starvation and disease there because of him, because he sold the food and everything else meant for them. Others he hanged for imaginary offenses. And now he is killing more."

"Cunningham is still Provost Marshal, and Joshua Loring is Commissary of Prisoners, both good positions for dishonest profit." Darius's disgust was plain. "I will not defend every action of the government, and they are two very bad appointments. But there is nothing I or you can do about it."

"Of course not," she said evenly, but she did not believe it. If enough men of Darius's prestige protested, there would be changes; it was just that they didn't care.

She heard a ripple of Gaelic from Angus, answered by Colonel Traverne, and when she glanced at Angus, she caught a look of approval before his face settled into stern lines again.

"He says you are almost fierce enough to be a Highland woman," Colonel Traverne translated, his expression bland, but Addie thought she saw approval in his eyes, too.

Addie braced herself to visit another prison, but this time Darius was firm, and before she knew it they were standing in front of Valencourt's, which in New York combined a bookstore, stationery store, and a printing office under one roof.

"You will go mad if you fill every minute with misery. You have been long away from Papa's library. Surely you can spare a few moments to reacquaint yourself with old friends."

She knew he was offering her a kindness, sharing his special domain with her, but she felt as if all the blood had drained out of her body. She had intended to come here, but not yet. This was the place where one of Tallmadge's agents would approach her if he chose. It was her lack of reaction to the mention of Valencourt's that had convinced Major Tallmadge she had the nerve he was looking for, and it was that conversation that had told her the store had not burned down. But her nerve was faltering now.

"Are you all right, Mistress Bradwell?" Colonel Traverne's voice seemed to come from far away, and then she heard her brother's anxious inquiries.

Shame stiffened her knees and sent energy coursing through her. "Pray forgive me! So many memories came all at once, I was overcome," she lied. "But I do want to see the books and everything else! I am so glad the fire did not come here."

She fixed a smile on her face as they entered the store, and in the instant, her claim of nostalgia became the truth. The subtle scents of leather bindings, of ink and paper, were overlaid with the perfumes of turpentine, linseed oil, and the other ingredients of artists' alchemy. Beautifully made musical instruments awaited human skill to make them sing, but the shop had its own sound—the murmur of voices as men and women used the store as a meeting place for discussing not only the books and other treasures therein, but also the events in the town. From an adjoining chamber came the steady thump of a printing press turning out handbills, announcements, invitations, and other papers designed to sustain the business and social life that went on despite the war.

Writing, blotting, drawing, and foolscap music papers; parchment; wax wafers for seals; ink powders; quills; pounce, the fine powder to keep ink from spreading, and pounce boxes to keep it in; ledgers; delicately tooled Moroccan leather etuis, the little pouches made to hold bodkins, needles, toothpicks or the like; playing cards; ivory game markers; sheet music; prints; engravings—everywhere she looked, Addie saw more neatly displayed treasures that bespoke a cultured life upon which the war did not intrude. Everywhere she looked she saw her father's shops in Boston. Marcus had had other investments and properties, but the book and stationery store and the printing office had been dearest to his heart. She knew it was the same for Darius: whatever his other business interests, this place was his pride.

"It is just as I remember." She knew Darius understood she was speaking of more than her immediate surroundings.

"You must come here whenever you like," he said, and he tucked her arm in his and introduced her to each of his clerks, there being two in the store and three more who ran the printing business.

She acknowledged each of them, hoping all the while that Darius could not hear the pounding of her heart. The innocent memories fled. One of these men must work for Tallmadge, but to her relief, none of them betrayed any particular interest in her. And seeing how busy the store was, she wondered how contact could ever be made without discovery.

She made a show of examining the books and merchandise, praising the variety and quality, feeling as if she were being wound tighter and tighter into an immense spider's web. She wondered how she had ever had the temerity to believe she could tolerate being so surrounded by the enemy.

Silas. The sharp scent of printer's ink drifted to her, and she saw Silas not as a soldier, but as he had been when he worked at the printing office—so quick and competent as both compositor and pressman, so enthralled by the power of the written word that he gave as much care to handbills as to philosophical tracts.

The thought of him steadied her. Any deception, any risk, was worth the smallest chance of finding him.

She looked up to find Colonel Traverne studying her, his dark eyes intent on her face, his expression giving little away. Since their first meeting, he had been kind to her, but he was still the enemy and an astute man, and she would do well not to forget that. It was a small victory when he looked away before she did.

They returned to Darius's house for a late afternoon dinner, though even the men had little appetite after what they had witnessed at the prisons, and they did not press Addie to eat. For her part, she wished she could pack up all of the food and take it to the prisoners.

Darius's house, though it offered ease and comfort, did not provide sanctuary from the enemy. In addition to Traverne and his men, there was a steady stream of military visitors. Addie supposed the traffic might not have been so heavy had Harriet still been alive, but without her, Darius's household had taken on the aspect of a London gentleman's club where visitors were assured of good food, drink, and conversation. And now they had another reason for coming to call—curiosity about Darius's sister who had just come in from the Continental Army.

It was tempting for Addie to hide in her room, but every visitor was a potential source of information. She was nervous, but she was also touched because her brother and Colonel Traverne planted themselves nearby as if she were a young girl in need of protection, but they made it clear they considered her the lady of the house and deserving of respect. She was shameless in her use of their presence, and she began as she meant to go on. When challenged, she did not apologize for her loyalties, nor did she feel there was any cause to, for under the surface good manners of those few who did confront her were antagonism and disdain for Americans and their army.

"What is Mr. Washington's true nature?" A horse-faced major asked the question as if he were inquiring about a strange beast, but

Addie answered as she had all evening, as if there were no denigration intended in the question.

"*General* Washington is a man so noble by nature, he does not need a king to give him title. He has great strength of spirit, of mind, and of body. We are the most fortunate of peoples to have found such a man to see us through start to finish. It must be so very difficult for you to have to accommodate yourself to one general after another." She assumed an expression of deepest sympathy, though she wanted to laugh at the high color rage had painted on his face.

He gave her a sharp bow and moved off.

Colonel Traverne murmured, "Very neatly done."

Addie was exhausted by the time she went to bed, but her mind refused to rest. She had been dueling with words for hours, but the old frustration was sharper than her wit. Nothing she could say to any of the enemy would change their minds, nor could they change hers. And worse, there was nothing she could do to ease the lot of the prisoners.

The next day, they went to the "New Jail," one of only two regular prisons in the city and a facility now known for housing American officers and eminent Patriots whose activities or sentiments had run them afoul of the British. Most of these men had been accustomed to some degree of comfort before the war, but at the New Jail they had none and were under the direct supervision of Provost Marshal Cunningham.

Cunningham was a man whose appearance fit his nature, a lout with beady, weasel eyes. But his voice had the lilt of his native Ireland, a soft mockery. Here, each prisoner was introduced formally to him, each having his name, age, size, and rank recorded. And then the prisoners' hell began when they were confined in gloomy cells or in upper chambers where they were so overcrowded that when they lay down to sleep on the hard plank floor, they had to change position in unison at the command "right" or "left."

Addie assumed she had not been taken here first because Darius had had some small hope that she would turn faint-hearted at all the misery she had seen the previous day and thus would not have to encounter Cunningham. Though it was still morning, the man was already well in his cups. His gestures were too broad and his voice slurred, but he was focused enough to want no invasion of his domain.

"Ye got no business 'ere," he snarled after Darius had stated their mission. His eyes swept over Addie, and she felt as if his grimy hands were grabbing at her.

"Oh, but we do, my good man." Colonel Traverne's voice was silky. "And Sir Henry has granted his consent." He gestured to the paper Darius held. "He has even been so kind as to put it in writing. If you refuse to recognize the authority of the commander in chief, it will make interesting conversation when next we dine with him."

"Rebel bitch an' a Scots skirt," Cunningham mumbled.

In the instant, Traverne's hand was on the hilt of his sword and Angus and Duncan were flanking him, while Cunningham's henchmen backed as far away as the room allowed.

"You've grown so accustomed to dealing death, you've forgotten it can come for you. And you've forgotten why the British Army values its Highlanders. It is not our fine plaids they love so well. It is our talent for killing." Traverne's voice was even smoother than before, and pitched low, but everyone in the room heard each word as if it were a thunderclap.

In Boston, Addie had seen how easily Traverne commanded the respect of other men, but for the first time, she saw him as he must be in battle—hot violence barely leashed. He, Angus, and Duncan seemed warriors more ancient and dangerous than the other men. It was no wonder all the monarchs in Europe welcomed Highlanders into their armies.

"What Sir Henry commands." Cunningham was still surly, but he had lost the battle, and no one there believed it was because he was afraid of General Clinton.

Addie felt that the defeat of Cunningham was such a good omen, they would surely find evidence of Silas here, but when they searched the records, they did not find his name. It meant little, for these records were no better than the others they'd checked. Many names had been inked over so darkly, the letters were illegible, and others had cryptic notations, marks that they interpreted to mean that the prisoners had died or had been executed.

Contact with the prisoners was as wrenching as it had been the day before and as fruitless. And here there was an added element, for though most of the men were so starved and weakened as to make their movements slow with effort, hatred glowed in their eyes, hatred for Cunningham and his minions and, by association, for the soldiers with Addie.

Addie hoped their hatred would keep them alive, and that the same flame burned in Silas. She was humbled by their courage, for they had an option not available to the deserters from the British Army and the common criminals also imprisoned. Exchange was uncertain, parole offered on a whim, but every one of the American soldiers could end his imprisonment by swearing loyalty to the King and by enlisting in the British Army. The rarity of this action and the enormous number of American soldiers crowded into the prisons gave testament that they were willing to die like animals caught in traps rather than forswear their loyalty to the United States.

When they were clear of the noxious environs of the New Jail, Darius released his breath in a sigh. Seeing her growing resolution, he no longer entertained the foolish idea that his sister would give up her quest.

"It is time you met the commander in chief." He was not aware that the tone of his voice betrayed his lack of affection for Sir Henry.

Clinton's headquarters was in a house at Number One Broadway, though he also frequented a country estate outside of the city, as Washington had done. The Union Jack flew atop the house, and inside hallways and rooms were crowded with members of Clinton's staff going about the work of war. For Addie, it was like being in a distorted version of Washington's headquarters where everyone was wearing the wrong uniform, but the brisk tap of boots and jingle of spurs, the rustle of paper and scratch of quill pens were achingly familiar.

Sir Henry was middle-aged, short, with a plump form that belied his passion for vigorous riding and fox hunting. He looked more like a clerk than a commanding officer. Addie knew quite a lot about him, because as well as his time in Boston during the British occupation, he was a frequent topic of conversation in the American camp, and deserters who came in to the Continental Army were often anxious to demonstrate their value by claiming special knowledge of him. Generals Burgoyne and Howe had been popular with their men; General Clinton was not. He was said to be haughty, morose, and churlish, and he was often at odds with senior officers in his command, preferring to favor younger men whose standing was much less than his.

From Addie's point of view, it was a decided advantage that the Americans had Washington while the British had Clinton. But that did not lessen her apprehension at appearing before the man. The last time she had been so close to him had been during the Battle of "Bunker Hill" when she and Sarah had watched from Copp's Hill, as had Generals Clinton and Burgoyne. She wondered if he would ask questions about the Continental Army and General Washington, and how she would answer if he did. She must withhold any useful information while appearing to be courteous; this was the man who had allowed her to come to New York and could send her away again if he pleased. She needed to remain in his good graces.

As it turned out, it was an easy thing to do. After she was introduced to him, he accepted her thanks for letting her come to New York to search for Silas, but then he deliberately shifted his attention to Darius and Colonel Traverne, speaking to them of inconsequential things such as the prospects for summer amusements on Long Island where it would be more pleasant than in the city once the heat began.

"Did you acquire that mare you had your eye on?" he asked Darius. "By your description, she might be fit for the races."

"I did, sir, and she's a good animal, though I fear she is too fractious for competition."

When Sir Henry addressed Colonel Traverne, his manner was particularly warm; he went so far as to inquire if Traverne had had recent news from home and seemed genuinely pleased to hear that letters had come on the most recent packet and that all was well.

Addie had been dismissed as effectively as if she had been led from the room. Patriot women would not be among his favorites, but beyond that, it seemed he simply did not want to discuss any details about the prisoners. To do so would be to admit that there were injustices that cried out for redress. It made her angry, but it also amused her; General Clinton was afraid of her, afraid she would cause embarrassment. It was so absurd, she tipped her head down, fighting to hide a smile.

But her amusement faded as she became aware of Captain André's scrutiny. John André was Clinton's current favorite aide and a man of many talents, if the gossip in Philadelphia was valid. André had been prominent among those British officers who had played the suitors to the Loyalist belles, including Peggy Shippen, now General Arnold's wife. André had earned a reputation as a man who could turn his hand to a clever drawing or poem or could produce a credible theatrical production from a cast of amateurs. His had been the guiding hand in the "Meschianza" that had bid such an elaborate farewell to General Howe.

Addie could see why he appealed to women. He was handsome, slender, with olive skin and dark hair and eyes. His features were somewhere between the cherub and the satyr, an intriguing combination. Addie guessed he was still in his twenties, but it was difficult to tell. His face was smooth, young, but his eyes were far older, bright and shrewd. She was sure he had sensed and measured every current in the room.

To her astonishment, when she met his eyes directly, he winked at her. It was not salacious, but rather, an invitation to share the drama of the meeting and an acknowledgment that she knew as well as he what was transpiring. Addie managed a little nod in response, but inwardly she marked André as a dangerous man for his potent combination of charm and intelligence. She was far safer with someone who would ignore her presence as Sir Henry was doing.

Once they were outside of headquarters, Colonel Traverne said, "Captain André certainly took note of you."

Addie grinned at him, thinking he was behaving even more like a protective brother than Darius. "And General Clinton certainly made much of you."

To her delight, he blushed as he muttered, "He has a strange fondness for Highlanders."

"It is better to be liked than disliked by him," Darius pointed out. "The man shifts his favor so erratically, one cannot be sure of his goodwill from one meeting to the next."

"Ah, but you forget, neither of us is a threat to his position or his power, and if we continue to sing his praises, we should be able to keep our places in the ranks of sycophants." Traverne sounded more resigned than resentful, as if he expected nothing better from an English commander.

The next day brought more fruitless searching, and more visitors to Darius's house, and this time, among them were officers who had been friends of Captain Byrne in Boston. They had not forgotten Addie's care of Paul Byrne nor her kindness toward them. Seeing them again was awkward because they had known her as a Loyalist's daughter, not a Patriot's wife, but nonetheless, they approached her with respect and pleasure in seeing her again, no matter what the circumstances. They were a buffer of kindness against those redcoats who judged her in a much less flattering light.

Though she had been in New York only a short time, she was already adjusting to the pattern of witnessing terrible desperation for part of the day, of hoping each prison might be the one to yield Silas to her, and then of returning to the ordered luxury of Darius's household. But the pattern proved fragile, no match against marching orders from General Clinton. The illusion of gentlemen at their ease vanished in the quickened pace of soldiers readying for battle. Colonel Traverne and his men returned to their regiment on Long Island, and Darius's house was busy with the traffic of the men of his Loyalist troop.

Addie had known a new campaign would begin at some point, but she had hoped she would have more time, enough time to find Silas before the armies bestirred themselves.

"You are not to go to any of the prisons until I or Colonel Traverne return," Darius ordered. She had no choice but to obey him; she needed the men's authority to gain admission.

Darius and Colonel Traverne were going out to fight their enemies, and for that reason she wished them failure. But she did not want them harmed any more than she wanted them to harm Justin, Ad, or their cousins.

"You will take care, won't you?"

Darius's smile was sad. "It must be difficult for you, having concern for men on both sides."

"It is. Justin told me how you spared him, and I will always be grateful for that."

"I would pray that we do not come face to face again." The harshness of his voice left Addie with no doubt that quarter would not be so instinctively given a second time.

Addie missed Darius acutely as soon as he left, though she was surrounded by comfort that exceeded even that of the Birdsalls' Philadelphia residence, and the servants had been instructed to treat her as mistress of the household and displayed no animosity in dealing with her. It was yet another complication of the war that she felt closer to him than ever before.

Chapter 18

General Clinton took his troops across the Harlem River, north of Manhattan Island, and then across the Hudson River to seize the American outpost of Stony Point on the last day of May. Stony Point was well named. Surrounded on three sides by water and connected to the mainland by ground so low it was flooded at high tide, it rose to a flat, rocky summit one hundred and fifty feet above the river. It was important to the Americans because it commanded King's Ferry across the Hudson, a vital route for troops and stores to pass between forces in the state of New York and those in New England.

Clinton's purpose was larger than the outpost; he hoped the attack would tempt Washington into a major battle. But Addie began to breathe easier as word filtered through New York that, once again, Washington was refusing to be baited into risking his army at the pleasure of the British.

Addie did not have to make any special effort to glean the news; the city buzzed with it and with every sort of rumor, and James Rivington's *Royal Gazette* gave news, rumor, and outright lies equal weight. The lies were scurrilous attacks on Washington, on various other American officers, and on Rebels as a whole, and Addie wondered if the British really believed them.

Rivington had been prominent in newspaper publishing and book-selling before the war, and Marcus, Darius, and others such as Henry Knox had known and done business with the man. He had started out being fairly even handed, but then had become stridently Loyalist. Like Marcus, Rivington had been born in England, and he had returned there, but he had come back to New York once it was under British control again. Now there was no more zealous Loyalist than Rivington.

Addie dreaded seeing him. He had been a guest at the Boston house; he knew her. She was sure he was aware of her presence in New

York; his paper was so full of the gossip of arrivals and departures, he could scarcely have missed her coming. But as long as she was under Darius's protection, she knew Rivington would not attack her in his newspaper. Her fear concerned her own reaction, not his. She hated him for his calumnies against General Washington, and she hated the idea that she would have to treat him with some semblance of civility should they meet. In the meantime, even detesting what he wrote, she was driven by curiosity to read the paper as avidly as anyone.

Though she could not visit the prisons in Darius's absence, she refused to become a prisoner herself in the house. Accompanied by one servant or another, she went out most days, and sometimes, if she concentrated very hard, she could see the city as it had been when the Continental Army had occupied it. But the British presence was so pervasive and the city so altered, she could only sustain the illusion for brief moments.

She did not want to cause any undue attention to fall on Mistress Chaffey, but the woman had been so kind to Tullia and the Bradwells when they had boarded with her, Addie couldn't resist going to the house. She meant to pay only a brief visit, but not even that was possible. The house was a burned-out shell with people living in the ruins, but no one knew anything about Mistress Chaffey.

Hoping the woman was safe with her brother, Addie swallowed her tears. She could not shut out the boom of guns and the sound of martial music filtering through the town. It was the fourth of June, and the King's birthday was being celebrated. Addie cut her walk short and returned to the house, too depressed to make what had become her usual visit to the bookstore. She wished someone could give the King some common sense regarding the United States.

The next day she returned to the routine she had established, taking a leisurely stroll to the bookstore, listening to the snatches of conversation as she went, and looking for any paroled American soldiers whom she had not yet questioned. She did not consider speaking to these men a breach of her promise not to visit prisons, and she didn't care that it was boldly improper to approach strangers on the street. Most of them promised, as had Captain Trumble, that they would bring her word if they discovered anything, but Addie was losing hope. She was also beginning to doubt that Tallmadge's agent, whoever he was, was going to reveal himself to her. Without Darius and Colonel Traverne, and with only a disinterested servant acting as chaperone, she had made herself as available as she could in the busy shop, and still, she had not been contacted.

She was more numb now than nervous while she was in the bookstore, but at least there was the pleasure of the books themselves. Darius also had a subscription library, and the wide range of old and new titles was proof that the war had not hindered his trade with England. For her, there was guilty pleasure in reading books that had been published since the war had begun and Patriot trade with Britain had ceased.

She was reading and laughing at *The School for Scandal*, a comic play first performed in England two years before, when she heard the soft words, "Sissy Nightingale sends her best wishes."

Her blood seemed to cease to flow in a sudden freeze. There was no mistake; she and Tallmadge had decided on the code, nonsense but explicit, her cousin's nickname and her horse's name cobbled together to form an imaginary acquaintance.

Just when she thought she could not draw enough breath to remain upright, her blood began to race again. Even with voice so low, she recognized the speaker as one of the clerks, Robert Moore, a small, drab man, a Quaker, though he did not use the "thees" and "thous" of their pointedly informal speech. With her knowledge of the Pennsylvania Quakers who, for the most part, preferred the security of British rule, she would have judged Mr. Moore a most unlikely spy. But then she thought of General Greene, whose Quaker origins had been no stop to his sword.

The decision was still hers. If she did not answer the line, there would be no further attempt at communication.

"I hope Sissy and her son are well." The response was out before she was conscious of forming the words.

She could feel Mr. Moore relaxing as he replied, "They are both in the best of health," completing the exchange.

She breathed easier, too, realizing that she had not startled in fear or dropped the pages she was reading, or betrayed herself in any other way. She glanced around casually, seeing that neither the servant-chaperone nor anyone else was close by or paying any attention to her and Mr. Moore.

"I may not be much good at this," she said, not wanting him to expect too much. "Even when my brother's house was overrun with soldiers and I knew something was about to happen, I had no idea what it was."

He carefully aligned the spines of several books. "It will often be like that. Most of what we learn is by chance— a conversation overheard, a carelessly unconcealed movement of troops. All you have to do is to listen and watch. Remember, you are just one of many. Sometimes, even when we have the best information, we cannot get it out of the city quickly enough, or our army cannot act on it anyway. You must accept that, or this game will drive you mad."

She was reassured as much by the calm confidence of his quiet voice as by what he was saying. In his guise as a clerk, he appeared diffident to the point of shyness, but there was no trace of that now. Though she still doubted her abilities to be an effective spy, she left the store feeling much less lonely knowing there were truly others in the city who were loyal Americans.

General Clinton traveled up and down the river between Stony Point, where he had ordered extensive work to improve the fortifications, and the city, but many of his troops remained in the field. Darius was still on the west side of the river, hunting for a chance to skirmish with American dragoons, but Colonel Traverne returned to the city in the third week of June. His men were encamped in Westchester County, north of Manhattan Island, but he came back to the city out of concern for Angus, who was suffering the effects of a rattlesnake bite.

Angus was feverish, and his leg was horribly swollen, but Addie reassured Colonel Traverne. "He has lasted this long, and he is a strong man. With proper care, he should recover swiftly."

Colonel Traverne had intended to take Angus to one of the hospitals, but he had been pulled to Darius's house as if by a magnet. As soon as he saw how gentle and efficient Addie was in her care of his man, he knew he had made the right decision. But he did not fool himself. He had come to the house because she was there. He had been attracted to her from the first time he had met her in Boston, but it had not mattered. He had been married and faithful to Jeane, no matter how far from her he was. Even when he had received news of Jeane's death, he had still felt married, had felt so until he had returned home and seen the grave where she was buried with their infant.

But when he had sailed once more for America, this time with his troops, he had discovered that Ariadne Valencourt was so fixed in his mind, he could not think of her country without thinking of her. It was disquieting, for he was not given to romantic fancies. Even his marriage to Jeane had had as much logic as passion in it, the match pleasing both families, despite the fact that Jeane's people were far more Anglicized than his. He and Jeane had known each other since childhood, though he had been gone for long periods of time once he had reached adolescence. They had married when he was twenty-two, she twenty-one, and two years later she was dead.

On his return to the colonies, he had learned that Addie had married and was firmly on the Rebels' side; news delayed by the roundabout way of its passage from Marcus to Darius. He had not expected to see her again, and given the lingering effect she had had on him, he had thought it just as well.

Now it was the war that had brought them together anew, and he was more drawn to her than before. The hardships and losses of the war were visible. She was as finely drawn as if a fire were consuming her from the inside, and even when she was cloaked in her most decorous manner, her golden eyes burned with a ferocity that was never quenched. She was a Rebel in heart and mind, and she made no secret of it. But that mattered less to him than that she was married. While he knew many men who would see that as an added spur to the chase, he was not one of them. His best course was to do everything possible to find Silas and to push for a swift exchange so the couple could leave New York, and he himself would have no further contact with Addie. In the meantime, he needed to maintain the brotherly pose he had adopted when he and Darius were escorting her about the city.

To Addie, it was natural that Colonel Traverne had brought Angus to her. No matter how well run, hospitals were foul places. Far better that Angus be treated in the common sense way Tullia had taught.

The only thing that had taken her aback on the party's arrival was that though Angus was in a wagon being driven by Duncan, Colonel Traverne was on horseback, and because of that, he was wearing trews instead of his kilt. Made of tartan, they fit as tightly as breeches but extended into his short boots and presumably to his ankles. They were as flattering to him as was the kilt, showing the strong muscles of his legs to perfection. She almost made a teasing comment as she would have to one of her brothers, but she checked herself in time with the realization that, in spite of his kindness, he was no relation.

He stayed for two days, to make sure Angus was truly mending, before he returned to his troops. During his time in the city, while Duncan stayed with Angus, he accompanied Addie to more prisons, but the search was fruitless.

By unspoken agreement, they tried to avoid discussion of the war, but it was difficult because the city was humming with reports that a British force from Savannah, Georgia, had gone north and had taken Charles Town, South Carolina. Charles Town was one of the few major cities in the South, and its loss would be a hard blow to the Americans, but Addie's concern was more personal—she wished John Laurens had not left Washington's staff to return to his home state. And, quite irrationally, because of him she refused to believe the city had fallen.

During their forays to the prisons, Addie willed herself to patience as officers who knew Colonel Traverne stopped to speak with him. Most of them knew who she was, and it obviously gave them pleasure to mention "the good news from the Carolinas" and the "good work done in the Chesapeake." It helped that Colonel Traverne did not seem to share their pleasure at her expense, and she remained aloof until one of them, a man she had met at Darius's house, addressed her directly.

"These developments must be most distressing for you," he said. His voice oozed with false sympathy, but his eyes glittered with malice.

"How very kind of you to be so concerned about my feelings." She smiled at him and had the now familiar satisfaction of seeing how disappointed he was that she had not risen to the bait. But it was wearisome to deal with his sort, and she breathed a sigh when he was out of earshot.

"Being here must be like running a continual gauntlet for you."

Addie recognized Colonel Traverne's sympathy as sincere, but the anger she had controlled boiled up anyway. "I know the Chesapeake raids happened. Part of the plunder has been unloaded in this city. And even without that proof, I understand as well as anyone that it cannot be very difficult for an army well supported by its navy to attack civilians, to burn and pillage and sail away.

"Your army has been making war on civilians since this war began. But as for Charles Town, that is another matter entirely. I do not believe you've taken it, not so swiftly and easily as the rumors have it. You've tried and failed before, and I wager you've failed again." She stopped abruptly, glanced around, and was glad no one seemed to be paying special attention to them amidst the bustle and noise of the city.

Guilt quenched her anger. She meant every word she said, but she had lashed out at the wrong person. He was the enemy, but he had also become a friend, and he was willing to use his authority to help find Silas. She looked up at him, expecting to suffer his temper in return for hers, but instead, his face was impassive, giving nothing away.

"I am sorry. You did not deserve that."

He shrugged. "Better that you express such thoughts to me or to Darius than to others." He thought he'd phrased that well, invoking the absent Darius as an invisible chaperone. Far easier for him had her anger sparked his, but instead, it moved him to pity. She was so gallant, but that would not change what must surely be the truth about Charles Town and, ultimately, about all the Rebels' efforts—they simply could not prevail against the British Army and Navy.

It was both a relief and a trial for him to leave her to return to his men. No good could come out of caring too much about her, and yet, he was perturbed that neither he nor Darius was with her.

On her account, Addie was frustrated by his departure because she had to curtail her search until he or Darius returned. But she felt sorrier for Angus than for herself. Duncan went with the colonel, and that left Angus with no Gaelic speaker nearby. But when she had suggested they find a translator for him, Colonel Traverne had said, "Angus is stubborn, not stupid. He has enough English to survive your tender care."

Addie quickly discovered the truth of that and was amused. Angus doled out English words as if they were precious coins he was reluctant to spend, using the barest minimum. And yet, he understood everything said to him and was careful to thank her and the servants for their attentions. She got into the habit of speaking to him as if they were having a normal conversation, and if he didn't participate much verbally, at least he seemed to be listening closely, and his expression was less forbidding than it had been before he had fallen ill.

"The weather is already overly warm, and there is still so much of the summer to go. It must be very different from summers in the Highlands of Scotland."

The usual pattern was for Angus to follow along, nodding or even saying something in Gaelic now and then, but this time rather than acknowledging her innocuous prattle, he stared at her so intently, she shifted uncomfortably and asked, "Are you all right? Have you sudden pain?"

At first she thought he had answered her in Gaelic because the words were unintelligible to her, but then he repeated them carefully spaced apart, "Dinna hurt him."

"Don't hurt you?" she asked, still confused.

He shook his head violently. "No! Dinna hurt Iain."

It was such a bizarre idea that she could harm Colonel Traverne that she reached out to touch Angus's face, fearing his fever had risen suddenly, but he was only slightly warm, and his blue eyes were clear and piercing. There was no confusion of languages; he meant what he said.

She kept her gaze steady, unnerved by the thought that he might have some suspicion that she intended to pass information to the

Continental Army had she the chance. It was the only thing that made sense to her, and yet, there was no way he could know such a thing.

"Colonel Traverne has nothing to fear from me," she told him firmly, deciding, despite his improved condition, to mark down his strange fancy to the lingering effects of the snake's venom. She was glad he did not pursue the subject further.

On July 4, the distant rumble of cannon marked the American celebration of the third anniversary of their Declaration of Independence, and Addie remembered the soaring excitement generated by the reading of it in this very city. Now, frustration and anxiety overrode joy. Every minute of every day was precious to Silas if he lived, if he was here, but she was no closer to finding him.

Captain Trumble and his companions came to the house late one afternoon, and Addie went out to them.

"We believe we have news of your husband," Trumble said without preamble.

"He's alive?"

The captain's eyes shifted away from hers and back again. "He was when he was brought here from Monmouth. But he had a head wound. He was put in one of the hospitals, not a regular prison. Then he escaped, tried to get out of the city, but he was caught. It angered the redcoats that he had so abused their 'hospitality'."

Addie closed her eyes and swayed, and the captain said sharply, "No, ma'am, no, they didn't kill him for it! But they put him where… where he would have a harder time getting away. They took him aboard the hulks, and now he is reported to be on the *Good Hope*."

She had known what he was going to say before he finished it. She dug her fingernails into her palms to counteract the blackness sweeping over her. The prison hulks were reputed to be far, far worse than the prisons in the city. It was a bitter irony that one of the ships should be named "Good Hope."

"It may not be true, any of it. We asked everyone we know about Colonel Bradwell, and we got bits and pieces of a story, but no one knew the whole of it, and we may have put it together wrong." He couldn't bring himself to say that one account had had it that Colonel Bradwell had been executed for his escape attempt.

Captain Trumble's misery was so acute, it pierced the fog enshrouding Addie. He and his two friends had gone out of their way for her and had had the courage to bring this news to her when it would have been easier for them to have made no effort on her behalf or to pretend that they had never learned anything at all. They deserved far better than standing like beggars in the street.

"I am very grateful for what you have told me. Now, you must come in and share a meal with me." She saw their conflict, torn as they were between the prospect of food and entering the house of a Loyalist officer. "Please, it is little enough to offer you, and my brother is not here. If he were, he would welcome you no less than I." She wasn't sure it was true; what mattered was that they believe it.

After an exchange of glances that seemed to work as well as conversation, the trio followed Addie into the house. She bid them be comfortable while she left them to order the meal.

Seeing the scandalized looks of the servants whose tolerance toward her did not extend to ragged Continental soldiers, she warned them, "If this is not done generously, my brother will hear of it the instant he returns. He has met these men and wants their information as much as I do."

She returned to her visitors just in time, for they looked to be on the point of fleeing, so uneasy were they in Darius's house.

"Did you hear our guns today?" she asked, as if this were a Patriot, not Loyalist, stronghold, as if her mind was not tumbling with nightmarish images of Silas. "I expect there must have been a grand celebration at headquarters."

The tentative smiles they offered in response to her attempt at normalcy pulled at her heart. It was as if they had smiled so little since becoming prisoners, they scarcely remembered the mechanics of it.

Passing the time until dinner was ready, Addie described the festivities staged for the French at Middlebrook and told other stories of camp life, and the men listened as avidly as if they were hearing about their own families.

The servants did not dare defy her, so though the meal had been prepared at short notice and was limited to cold fare, it was lavish by any standard. There was bread, butter, cheese, chicken, beef, smoked ham, fresh greens dressed with vinegar and oil, and fruit.

It was painful to watch the men eat. They were trying so hard to behave like gentlemen, but they had been deprived of adequate food for so long, it was a struggle for them not to grab at the food and cram it down as fast as possible. Cheeks bulged as they took too-big bites, and the sounds of frantic chewing and the efforts to swallow large morsels without choking beat at Addie's ears.

She tried to ignore the situation, but finally fearing that what she meant as a kindness was going to make the men miserably sick, she said, "Please, I know how hungry you are, but you mustn't think you need to eat everything at once. I should have told you before that there will be food to take with you."

It was a transparent excuse, and the men looked abashed and stopped eating altogether.

Then Captain Trumble said, "Thank you, Mistress Bradwell. We will enjoy it as much as we have this."

Wanting to weep, Addie smiled at him. "You might try some of the chicken, Captain, it is quite good." She nibbled at a piece herself, though her throat was so tight, it was like swallowing a stone.

The men began to eat, but less desperately, and when they had finished, Addie prepared generous packages of food for each of them. They had to go because they could not risk being out after their curfew that came with nightfall, but Addie longed to beg them to stay, not only for the sake of their company but also so that she would not have to be alone with her thoughts. Instead, she thanked them once more for coming to her.

Captain Trumble turned back briefly as he was leaving. "Your husband has much to live for," he said, and then he was gone.

As if there had been no reluctance in the servants, Addie thanked them for their treatment of her guests. Then she looked in on Angus and found him sleeping peacefully. He had been getting up for short periods for the past several days and had been gaining strength, but his efforts still left him weak at day's end.

Addie maintained the illusion of calm until she was alone in her chamber. When she started to shake, she wrapped her arms around herself and held on, rocking, hearing her crying as if it came from someone else. Even when she was so exhausted she could weep no more, she did not sleep. By dawn, she was resigned; she could not get Silas away from the *Good Hope* without help from Darius or Colonel Traverne. She drifted through the next few days so dazed that she didn't notice that Angus and the servants were eyeing her worriedly.

On the third day after Addie had had news of Silas, Colonel Traverne returned. He had expected to find sly triumph in Addie, but at his first sight of her, he exclaimed, "Have you not heard? You were right! Charles Town has not fallen to us." He stopped, startled that because she looked so unhappy, he had offered the first comfort he could find, though it was news of a British defeat.

He studied her more closely. Dark smudges bruised the skin beneath her eyes, eyes that were pure gold and frantic, and her facial bones were too defined. This was nothing to do with a faraway military defeat, and mere unhappiness did not describe her state.

"Your husband? What news?" he asked, her urgency becoming his own.

Initially, Addie fought to say anything at all, and then the words spilled out of her so quickly, the colonel had trouble deciphering them, but he did not mistake the name of the hulk. The ships were used mostly for sailors taken prisoner from privateers, whaleboats, and other craft in Rebel service, but due to the overcrowding of the land-based prisons, there were also soldiers incarcerated on them. And though there had been a few escapes, they were not easy with the surrounding waters filled with British ships.

He knew the wisest course would be to wait until Darius returned, and he knew that Addie could not wait. Wisdom had no force against her need.

"I will make arrangements today and go to the *Good Hope* tomorrow."

Expecting that Colonel Traverne would demand more proof than rumor of Silas's whereabouts, Addie was moved by his instant willingness to act on Captain Trumble's information. She had thought she had no more tears to shed, but her eyes filled and overflowed. She wasn't aware of clutching at his coat sleeve.

"Thank you, thank you! I've gone nearly mad waiting for you or Darius to return." Belatedly it dawned on her that he meant to go alone to the *Good Hope*. "But I must go with you, I—"

"No!" he cut her off. "The hulks are no place for you!"

"The hulks are no place for Silas, nor for you, and this is no place for me, here in the middle of the enemy." She was sobbing openly now. "You do not know Silas by sight. I must be there; I must!"

Her loss of control was a painful blow to him. He wanted to hold her in his arms and promise her nothing would hurt her again. Instead, he ignored the nervous pulling of her fingers on his sleeve, the tears rolling down her cheeks, and his own good sense.

"All right, you may go with me, but on one condition—you will do exactly as you are told."

"I will, I promise." Addie became aware that she was holding on to him. She snatched her hand away and wiped her eyes, terribly embarrassed by the display to which she had subjected him. She backed away from him, head lowered to avoid looking at him. "You must want to know about Angus. He is growing stronger by the day. He was in the garden a while ago. Perhaps he is still there."

With that she fled, and Colonel Traverne let her go.

By the next morning, he had made all the arrangements for their journey, including hiring a boat to take them across the East River to Wallabout Bay, a slight indentation on the Long Island shore. The day was warm and cloudy so the ships and the water itself seemed formed of the same gray shadows, but that did not soften the ugliness. The derelict ships had been stripped of beauty, figureheads taken away, no sails unfurled in anticipation of dancing with the wind. Ports were closed, and square holes had been cut in the hulls for ventilation and barred against escape.

Having seen the city prisons, Addie had been trying to prepare herself for conditions aboard the hulks ever since Captain Trumble had brought his news, but her imagination was no match for the reality. The stench of filth, disease, and death made the dank fishy smell of the nearby muddy flats mild by comparison. The unkempt figures of the prisoners up on deck were more of scarecrows than of men; the soldiers and sailors guarding them appeared obscenely fat by comparison.

Small boats plied the waters between the hulks and the Long Island shore. Some were carrying water barrels to be filled and taken back to the hulks, but Addie squinted at one, puzzled because it seemed to be loaded with cordwood, an odd commodity for summer and odd to be going toward the shore. Her brain accepted the truth slowly. Not wood, but corpses of prisoners stacked like wood, and living prisoners doing the rowing, though God knew where they got the strength. Her eyes darted to the shoreline and away, but not quickly enough. There were bodies there, some half buried in the muck, others in careless sprawls on the surface, looking like discarded dolls. And there were bones, dull white under the clouds. Whatever burials the authorities allowed were no match for the tides.

She was dimly aware that their boat was coming along the side of the *Good Hope*, the oars changing rhythm to stop their craft.

"You will stay here with Duncan and not come aboard unless I send for you."

The snap of his voice fixed Addie's attention on Colonel Traverne. His face was without expression, as forbidding as if graven in stone. She nodded, not tempted to defy him because she did not think her knees would hold her to stand, let alone to climb up the ship's ladder. She looked up and saw men peering down at her. The sight of a woman near the hulks was so rare, the men, both guards and prisoners, appeared more surprised and curious than anything else, but she quailed inwardly from the look on some of the prisoners' faces—as far as they were concerned, she was contemptible because of the company she kept. But she didn't look away; she kept searching for Silas among them.

Traverne was hardened to the blood and suffering of battle. He did not allow himself to feel anything until the fighting was over. But the conditions aboard the *Good Hope* filled him with such revulsion, it writhed inside him like a living thing. He had seen the bodies and the bones, and the chance that Addie's husband was still alive seemed so remote.

When his inquiry was met with recognition of the name of Lieutenant Colonel Silas Bradwell, his mask of calm slipped for a moment as he demanded, "He's alive? He's here?"

The officer scratched nervously at his neck, uneasy at having this big Highlander towering over him. "Well, alive maybe, but not 'ere, not anymore. Sent 'im to the *Hunter* a few weeks back. Stubborn bastard, kept trying to escape. Last time 'e made it into the water and nearly drowned, weak as 'e was. Then 'e was insensible with fever, so off 'e went." The man's busy fingers moved to tug at his ear. "Damn Rebels, stubborn fools, the lot of 'em. Could join 'is Majesty's Navy and be off the hulks quick as you please."

"As you would undoubtedly join their forces were the situation reversed."

Colonel Traverne turned on his heel and left the man sputtering, "No, not so! I'm loyal to the King, I am!"

Addie's face was as white as the bones on the beach.

As Traverne lowered himself into the boat he explained, "He tried to escape, and they transferred him to another ship." He directed the oarsmen to row for the *Hunter*.

Traverne unconsciously braced his shoulders, expecting Addie to recognize the *Hunter* as a prison hospital ship, but she said nothing.

It was Duncan's Gaelic that came to his ears, saying, "The English lie with the Beast, and now, see their get."

And he answered back in the same tongue, "We lie with them to gain their favor. With them, we have become the Beast."

Duncan had no reply for that; he had never heard Iain speak so.

Addie heard the sharp notes in their soft language; she heard the slap of water against the boat, the gulls' cry, the human voices sounding on the heavy air, but she heard all of it at a distance. They would find Silas now or never. Silas was on the *Hunter* or he was gone away forever, gone in the bodies and bones on the shore, or perhaps gone more than a year ago after all, undiscovered but dead at Monmouth.

When they reached the *Hunter*, Addie made no protest when Colonel Traverne again left her. And then a blanket-wrapped body was being lowered into the boat. Even as she opened her mouth to say this could not be her husband, she saw his face and knew it was. This skeletal, stinking wreck of a human being was Silas.

Traverne looked down at Addie with Silas cradled in her arms, and rage raced through his veins until his temples pounded with it. The medical officer had released Colonel Bradwell into his keeping with a casual shrug, saying "You're wasting your efforts. He won't last any time at all." Traverne wanted to throttle him and everyone else connected with this infernal business. And his rage was directed as much inward as outward; what he had said to Duncan was true—they shared the blame for being part of the British Army. His men who had been taken prisoner by the Americans in the waters off Boston three years before had been well treated, and through good fortune as much as by his efforts, they had long since been exchanged. The contrast between his returned men and Colonel Bradwell was unbearable.

For Addie, everything and everyone except Silas ceased to exist.

"You're safe now, safe, my love," she crooned, and she told him to keep breathing. She told him the same things over and over, and all the while, she kept her hand over his heart as if she could transfer the pulse of her life to keep his going.

She hardly noticed when they were back in the city, but when they arrived at the house, Tullia's training came to her automatically, and she directed that Silas be carried to the garden, and she asked for hot water and other items. She stripped the blanket and the rags away from him and cast them on the fire the servants built at her order. She bathed him from head to toe, shaved his beard, trimmed his hair, and rid his body of vermin. She saw the marks on him—the raw patches where the lice and other pests had feasted, the deep runnel the musket ball had carved in his temple, the angry lesions manacles had rubbed around his ankles and wrists. She dressed and bound his wounds with steady hands.

Colonel Traverne and Duncan had carried him to the garden, and they carried him inside, too.

"You must wash very thoroughly and brush your clothing and your hair, particularly you, Colonel Traverne, because you were aboard the hulks," she told them. "There can be no worse places of pestilence; the very air is poisoned. You both will have my gratitude forever for what you risked for us."

She turned her attention back to Silas, and Colonel Traverne had the curious sensation that he and Duncan had been rendered invisible in that instant. He feared her calm control as much as he admired it. He did not doubt the sincerity of her gratitude, but he had seen a flash of something else in her eyes—a fury even greater than his own and hatred to match any he had witnessed in the Highlands where hating the English was a way of life. He was not accustomed to feeling inadequate or cowardly, but he did now, and he hoped Darius would return soon. Despite his anger over the medical officer's pronouncement, he could not dispute it, and he wanted Darius to be here when Colonel Bradwell died.

Addie was vaguely aware of the quiet bustle of the house and that everything from broth for Silas and food for herself to fresh water for drinking and bathing were being constantly supplied, but she had no true awareness of anyone except her husband. Spoon by spoon she fed him liquids; she bathed his skin over and over to lower his fever; and as she had done with Ad, she talked to him constantly, trying to call him back from the great distance he had traveled away from her, trying to see him as he had been. But even when she closed her eyes, the image remained of his body so diminished that his bones protruded as if they would jut through the skin.

She waited for him to open his eyes. If she could just look into his eyes, she would know if he still dwelt in the ruins.

Chapter 19

For three days, Colonel Traverne left Addie to her vigil, but when the servants reported that she had scarcely touched the food they kept leaving for her and that they doubted she had slept at all, he took command.

"You are going out in the garden to eat and rest for a while. We will keep watch and care for Colonel Bradwell." His tone of voice was the same he used to give orders to his men, but her only response was to gaze uncomprehendingly at him out of eyes so dull and red with exhaustion, all the gold was dimmed.

His concern for her overriding his sense of propriety, he picked her up and carried her to the mirror that hung in the room. "Look at yourself!" he demanded. "How much longer do you think you will be able to care for your husband if you continue on this way?"

He watched her reflection in the glass, saw her dawning shock and, still carrying her, he strode out of the room, not breaking pace as he ordered the waiting Duncan, in English so Addie would understand, "Guard him. I will be right back,"

Addie, stunned by fatigue, by what she had seen in the mirror, and by Colonel Traverne's actions, offered no resistance until they reached the garden. When the sun touched her and she smelled the garden, the city, and the sea all mixed, she started to struggle in his arms.

"I must go back to him!" Her voice was hoarse.

He set her down but held her firmly by the arm, and she saw that Angus awaited her, and that in addition to a chair and a small table holding food and drink, a blanket and pillows had been spread out for her in the shade.

"You will do as I say for now. You owe me that much. I promise I will summon you immediately if there is any change."

Colonel Traverne was implacable, and Addie capitulated, lacking the energy to defy him. She bit back hysterical laughter at the thought that Colonel Traverne's unlikely nursemaids were now watching over her and Silas.

"Eat now, mistress, then rest," Angus dictated softly.

Addie obeyed.

Sitting beside the bed, Colonel Traverne studied Silas's face and thought he could discern some small changes for the better, though it might have been wishful thinking on his part. But the man's skin seemed less waxen and his breathing seemed deeper. For the first time, Traverne allowed himself to believe that Addie might win the battle for her husband's life. But it would be no victory at all if the man did not regain his senses. He found himself as compelled as Addie to speak to Silas, as if the human voice were a pathway back from the twilight.

"By all accounts, you made every effort to return to Addie. Instead, she has come for you. But you have to be strong enough to leave with her," he told the unconscious man. "And leave you shall. Darius and I will make sure of that. You must be anxious to see Addie's brothers again." He spoke of the house and the shops in Boston; he spoke of everything and anything that might stir something in Silas, and all the while, Duncan spooned broth into the man and sponged him with cool water as tenderly as if he were ministering to an infant. Nor did it trouble either of them that they were behaving so toward an enemy they would have killed without question in battle.

Hours passed, and it was Duncan who saw it first.

"The dead man is trying to arise," he said in his native tongue, and he made the sign of the cross.

Colonel Traverne saw the faint fluttering of their patient's eyelids and heard the subtle shift in his breathing, and he raced to get Addie.

She was sound asleep, with Angus keeping watch, Angus who frowned when Colonel Traverne called her name. In the excitement of the moment, he didn't realize he had been so informal.

"Addie, I think your husband is regaining consciousness!"

She opened eyes heavy-lidded from deep sleep and stared at him in bemusement as she sought to get her bearings. Then his words sank in, and she was up and running in a swirl of skirts, but not before the men had seen fatigue, sorrow, and grim resolution disappear in a blaze of joy. It stunned them both, and they followed slowly in her wake.

Addie stroked Silas's face, tracing the bones, touching his mouth. "You are almost here. I can feel you so close. Open your eyes now. Please, Silas, open your eyes."

She saw his eyelids tremble, still, and tremble again.

"Please, please, my love!" she begged.

And then he was looking up at her, his dark eyes so blessedly familiar, hers blurred with tears. Then his gaze wandered, and she realized how it must seem to him to see Duncan beside the bed and two more Highlanders at the door when the last thing he had known was being aboard a prison ship.

She explained quickly before confusion could take root. "They've all helped to bring you here. We're in Darius's house." She kept touching him as she told him of her search and assured him over and over that he was truly safe. "You won't ever go back to the hulks, not ever!"

His eyes closed again, but he seemed to accept what she had told him. She put her head down beside his, her arms around him, holding on, and when she lifted her head again, they were alone.

He did not awaken again until the next morning, but when he did, he knew where he was, and this time he managed to say, "Addie love…"

No gift had ever been more precious than those two words, but the effort it took for him to speak, and the frail, hollow sound of his voice, chilled her to the bone. She tried to convince herself that he had been so near death, it was only natural that his journey back to the living would be arduous. But she could not hold back the image of Paul Byrne—so far from home, wanting to live, dying in her arms because his body could not match his spirit. And she could not ignore the odd skip and stutter she felt in Silas's pulse. As she had so many times before, she longed to have Tullia beside her telling her that everything amiss in Silas's body would right itself.

She had thought she had considered all the possibilities before she came to New York; now she knew better. She had not imagined she would find him so debilitated that leaving the city, even if an exchange was arranged, would not be possible for a long time. When she had thought they might have to tarry for official machinations, she had pictured Silas as quickly restored to health after his imprisonment and impatient to rejoin the army.

It was hard for her to acknowledge that she could not care for him by herself, but that was the truth of it. And it was not as if she had to ask for assistance; it was more a matter of falling in with the cadence set by Colonel Traverne. He arranged for her letter to Ad and Justin to be delivered through the lines, so that her brothers would know Silas had been found but was too ill to be moved. He organized the household so that Silas was never left alone, but Addie had time to rest and to go outside for air and exercise. Her only worry was that he was neglecting his military duties, but when she broached the subject, he dismissed it.

"Save when we are on the march, I spend a good deal of time here, close to headquarters." His slight grimace said more than his words about the annoying necessity of paying political court to General Clinton and the rest of the British command. "I trust my officers and men; they do not fall into confusion or mischief in my absence. They are Scots, not English. Messengers are going back and forth, but there is little to do unless your General Washington"—he used the military title intentionally—"decides to confront us." His frustration at the deadlock the war had become was evident.

Addie refrained from pointing out that General Washington's plan, though dictated by necessity, seemed to be proving very effective. Since coming to New York, she had become more and more aware that despite the appearance of strength, the British were virtual prisoners here, controlling only Manhattan Island, Staten Island, and part of Long Island.

The single most powerful weapon the British had against their isolation was their navy. Addie longed for the day when their ships, loaded with troops, would sail away forever. And surely if General

Washington could keep General Clinton's forces so contained, that day would come soon. But when she tried to see beyond that event to a life without the war, she felt more fear than anything else because it had become even harder to imagine a "normal," peacetime life than when she and Silas had last discussed it. She remembered how they had lain together with the sounds of their army all around them, and she could see too clearly how diminished he was compared to the strong, healthy man he had been that night.

She came out of her reverie to find Colonel Traverne regarding her with a worried frown.

"Just old memories," she explained.

"I have sent word to Darius. I am sure he will return as soon as possible." He worried that in spite of his own best efforts, Darius would be better able to manage everything.

"There is nothing he could do that you have not done," Addie assured him, and his anxiety quieted.

Having received Colonel Traverne's message, Darius expected the order he found in his house on his return, but though informed that Silas was in a low state, he was stunned by his first sight of him.

Darius had been nineteen and still living in Boston when ten-year-old Silas had appeared and been taken in by Marcus. Far from feeling jealous, Darius had been as charmed as his father by the spirit and intelligence of the child. When Darius had left for New York two years later, he had been glad that Marcus had had Silas as his apprentice, for Lily's children were still a bit young—Quentin only four, the twins seven, and Justin ten—to provide much help to their father at the shops. Once he had left Boston, Darius had had little contact with Silas but enough to have respected the man who had emerged from the harsh beginnings of the orphan boy; had respected him until he learned that Silas, along with Lily's children, had thrown his lot in with the Rebels.

Darius tried to keep that in mind as he stared down at Silas, but somehow he could not view this man as his enemy. As Addie, since her arrival in New York, had seemed more his sister than ever before, so Silas was part of his family, more even than a brother-in-law.

Silas opened his eyes and smiled with such welcome, Darius was taken aback, then he saw the smile fade into confusion, and he understood.

"Don't worry about your sanity. I'm Darius, but I know that the older I grow, the more I look like my father." He had to speak past the lump in his throat.

Addie was sitting on the bed, beside her husband, and she patted his hand. "I'm sorry. I should have warned you, for I was startled, too, by my first sight of Darius when I came here."

"Thank you... for... all... your... help."

Seeing the enormous physical effort it took for Silas to say so few words, Darius felt the knot of sorrow growing inside of him until his chest hurt and his own voice sounded strangled.

"Consider this your home. You and my sister are secure here."

He left them abruptly, and that night, long after the rest of the household had settled to sleep, he and Colonel Traverne stayed up. They talked more personally than they ever had before, and they drank too much of Darius's finest Madeira, but the pain did not go away.

"Christ! He looked so happy to see me when he thought I was Marcus. I'd convinced myself, you see, that they didn't care about Father at all, that it was as easy as it was foolish for them to betray him. But I saw in Silas's face and in Addie's how much they love him, how much they miss him, how much they have sacrificed for their beliefs. It must be the same for Justin and Ad, it must have been the same for Quentin. I don't want to see that in my enemies! I don't want to see my brothers and my sister as my enemies!" Darius's voice slurred slightly as he followed his circle. "And enemies or not, they are my family. I've tried to pretend it made all the difference that they are Lily's children and a stray taken in by my father. It makes no difference. And Silas is going to die. How will Addie bear that?"

This was Colonel Traverne's grief, too private to confess, even now in this hour of darkness and drink, that he had dreaded few things in his life more than he dreaded bearing witness to the tragedy that was stalking Addie. He spoke the lie from his own hope, "He has not died yet, and if anyone can keep him from it, it is your sister. At least we can prevent further harm to him at our hands."

Darius did not question Traverne's indictment of both of them for being part of the army that had dealt so dishonorably with a fellow soldier.

The next morning, both men were uncharacteristically subdued and pale of face, but Addie, guessing they had overindulged, pretended not to notice. And then all such mundane considerations were swept away as news came into the city that the Americans had attacked and retaken Stony Point during the night, capturing the garrison of six hundred men. As if that were not enough, a rumor raced through the town that the Continental Army was on its way to attack New York City itself.

Darius and Colonel Traverne reported immediately to headquarters, but Angus was left behind to tend to the Bradwells. He gave no sign that he resented this detached duty.

Addie told Silas everything she had heard. "I doubt very much that General Washington is planning any action against the city, but the local Tories are ready to believe anything. After all, our soldiers waded through a swamp in darkness and took Stony Point; who knows what else they might do?"

"Stony Point?"

"But of course, you couldn't know." Addie explained, belatedly realizing that Silas had been in no condition to glean war news when Clinton had taken the position in May. "So you see, we've taken it back again!"

She looked so happy, as if she had taken Stony Point herself, Silas smiled back at her. For so long, he had existed in a thick gray fog, too ill to be aware of anything. Now the fog was lifting slowly, and he struggled to concentrate on what Addie was telling him, though he was more interested in her joy than the cause of it. He tried to keep his eyes open, but he drifted off to the sound of Addie's voice saying, "It's all right. You need rest more than anything now."

Addie was encouraged that Silas was more aware each time he awakened, and she treasured his smile, but she was terrified by the degree of his weakness. She willed herself to patience. It had taken a head wound and more than a year of maltreatment to so incapacitate him; it was reasonable that it would take time for him to regain his strength.

Bit by bit she pieced together how Silas had gotten so lost among the prisoners. When the musket ball had creased his skull, he had fallen unconscious, and had he remained so for any length of time, the enemy would surely have left him on the field. But he had regained his senses too quickly, looking up to find himself surrounded by redcoats. Despite the pain in his head, he had known who and where he was, and he had managed to stay alert for the first part of his capture, but when they had neared New York, his senses had fled again, and he had not known anything more until he had awakened to find himself in an enfeebled state, stored and forgotten in the wretched confines of a hospital for prisoners. None of his command were with him, and the only reason he still breathed was that other patients had fed and cared for him.

Even when they discovered he was conscious, the British attendants had seen no threat in him, and that had been enough for him to begin to plot his escape. He had eaten whatever was offered, no matter how foul, and he had exercised as well as he could without attracting the enemy's attention, and when he judged himself strong enough, he had slipped out of the hospital one night, intending to make his way to the Neutral Ground and from there to find some way back to his lines. He had not been offered his parole; it was no offense against honor to escape. And nothing was as clear to him as that he had to get back to Addie.

His body failed him, and he collapsed before he was out of the city. By then the nights had turned cold, and by morning when enemy sentries came upon him slumped in a doorway, he was shivering with fever. It was the beginning of his long descent into hell, of more severe confinement aboard the hulks, more futile escape attempts, and worsening physical condition. And never had he thought of trying to contact Darius to ask for help.

It was plain to him now that that was what he should have done, but when he tried to apologize to Addie, she could not stand it. "I did not ask his help either, not until far too much time had passed, and I was better able to do it from the first."

"But you no more than I could know he would be in such sympathy with us." Silas was willing to absolve himself if it would make her accept absolution for herself, too.

But nothing could ease Addie's guilt for waiting so long to come for him, not the fact that there were thousands of prisoners here whose families were not with them, nor the truth that she had not known his fate while Ad's need for her care had been relentlessly before her. It made it worse that Silas saw no wrong in her delay, only wonder that she was here at all, because the orphan child who yet dwelt inside of him believed that everyone else was more deserving of attention and affection than he. She could not fight that child; the best she could do was to accept him as part of the man she loved.

Though the household continued to run smoothly in their absence, Addie missed Darius and Colonel Traverne. She was on edge, considering that this might well be the beginning of a new campaign that would see the two armies clash once more on a large scale.

She needn't have worried. After holding Stony Point for two days, the Americans abandoned it, taking their prisoners with them, and thoroughly disgruntled, Darius and Colonel Traverne returned to the house.

"Your Washington is a clever man," Darius conceded reluctantly. "He managed to stir up a hornet's nest without getting himself stung."

"By all reports, it was General Wayne who actually did the stirring, but I'm sure General Washington won't mind sharing the blame. I take it that Sir Henry is not pleased?"

Addie's glee was so thinly disguised under her pose of innocence, Darius scowled at her, but there was no real anger in him; it was more the look of a brother impatient with his younger sister's teasing. Suddenly his scowl disappeared in a grin. "Sir Henry is behaving like a hornet indeed, a hornet in a bottle. He lacks a certain dignity at the moment."

This exchange, light-hearted though it was, seemed to make official the truce that already existed in the house. Notwithstanding the division of loyalties and whatever chaos the war might cause outside, in this house the bonds of affection and concern were growing stronger by the day.

Silas felt it, too, and it was the strangest of situations for him. For more than a year, his love for Addie, his determination to get back to her, and his hatred for the enemy responsible for the hideous conditions of his captivity had kept him alive. But now those straight lines of love and hate were blurred. Darius was the enemy, but he was also Marcus's son, Addie's half-brother, and a memory of kindness from the past, and he and Colonel Traverne had gone to great lengths to rescue him. They were honorable men, and they were offering not only physical care, but something more, an undemanding fellowship. He was being tended like an infant, the servants or Angus or Duncan helping Addie to shift and lift him, but Darius and Colonel Traverne did not condescend, despite his helpless state. They treated him with the same dignity they would have wanted for themselves had they been in his situation.

His body remained maddeningly inert, except for the jump and skip of his heart, but his mind was growing increasingly alert, and he began to look forward to the visits of the two men. He understood that there was a practical aspect, that when either of them was with him, Addie felt comfortable in being absent from the sickroom, but there was also pleasure in discourse that had been denied him for a year. During his term of imprisonment, the subjects discussed had been limited to war rumors and, more importantly, to how to survive on meager food and fuel supplies, and how to escape. Sometimes they had spoken of their families, sometimes of past battles, but they had rarely had the energy to consider more esoteric matters.

With Darius and Colonel Traverne, the situation was reversed, for though they found themselves comfortable within surprisingly wide boundaries, they spoke little of the war, but rather of ideas, of books and plays and of themselves.

Seeing the bright light of intelligence returning to his brother-in-law's eyes, Darius began to hope that Silas was going to survive, but he doubted he would ever be strong enough to return to the Continental

Army. He didn't need Addie's knowledge of illness to note the frequent breaks in Silas's breathing and the bluish pallor that lingered around his mouth and stole healthy color from his hands. It was as if an old man's heart now pumped sluggishly in Silas's body.

Darius didn't wish to be too blunt about it, but he was concerned enough about Addie and Silas's future to offer his help.

"With trade so disrupted, I know it must have been impossible for you to obtain adequate stock to reopen the bookstore and printing office in Boston, but perhaps I can recommend neutral sources to meet your needs. And the wharfage and other properties must be capable of producing some income even now. I think you must consider these matters, for it might be some time before you will be strong enough to return to military duty. But then, mayhap everything has been settled long since. As you might imagine, I have been in no position to ascertain anything about Valencourt affairs in Boston."

Silas answered slowly. "We have never tried to reopen the shops or the other commercial properties left to you. We have only tried to keep them from being sold into other hands. Marcus left the house to... us"—even now he had trouble counting himself a member of Marcus's family— "but the rest is yours."

Darius was so obviously nonplussed by this information, a flash of temper shot through Silas, giving him a burst of energy. "We are loyal citizens of the United States, not thieves! Under the circumstances, Marcus was most generous to us."

The flush of color in Silas's face alarmed Darius as much as the paleness it had replaced. "Please, I meant no offense! In truth, I judged you by my own poor measure. Were I in such a position, I fear my honor would not hold as well as yours. And what Father wanted three years ago makes no sense now. I think when you and Addie leave here, you ought to consider reopening the shops and seeing what use can be made of the other properties. I will do whatever I can to assist you. When the war is over, we can resolve the finer points."

Silas could not doubt his sincerity, but he still felt uneasy about going against Marcus's wishes. However, what Darius said was true. When Marcus had left Boston, he had thought the "rebellion" would be over swiftly and British rule restored. Darius believed in the same end, though he accepted that it was taking a long time to achieve it. But he was nonetheless willing to enter into dealings with the Bradwells for their mutual benefit.

"Thank you. Addie and I will consider your offer." Silas tried to keep his eyes open, but the brief energy his anger had given him had ebbed away.

Darius was so troubled by the exchange, he discussed it with Colonel Traverne. "I made no inquiries. I just assumed Lily's children were benefitting from the Boston properties. I'm sure they've had some aid from Lily's family in Virginia, but it must have been difficult for them with such limited resources."

"It is unsettling to find honor among your enemies, and even more complicated when the enemies share your blood. The Highlands are good proof of that. And I think we are in more danger from having these two Rebels here than they are from being in the midst of His Majesty's army." Colonel Traverne's sardonic tone was a mockery of what he felt inside.

He was accustomed now to the fascination Addie held for him, but he had not expected to like her husband. Daily he looked for signs of improvement in Silas, wanting him to grow strong enough to go away with Addie. And in the meantime, with every visit, he felt himself pulled deeper into a strange friendship that should not exist at all. He fought against it, but the more he considered Silas's situation, the more he admired the man.

"Was it your father who brought a regiment over to fight against the French and Indians?" Silas asked him one day. That war was safe ground, a time of unity between the Old and New Worlds, when most colonists had proudly identified themselves as English men and women.

Colonel Traverne knew that Silas expected nothing more than the simplest answer, but suddenly he wanted to offer more than that and wanted more in return.

"No, it was my brother Rob, though he was scarcely more than a boy and not by nature a soldier. But he commanded his men with respect, and they followed with the same heart. By then, he was all they had."

He paused, searching for the right words.

"In many ways, I envy you. For good or evil, you have chosen your cause. Rob and I have spent our lives trying to regain what our father lost for his choice. By all accounts, my father was a pragmatic man, less given to romantic passions than to practicality. Still, in the '45, he turned out to support Bonnie Prince Charlie, a man so flawed, he was not worth even one of the brave, foolish clansmen who perished for him. For all his early victories, the Prince could not prevail, no more than Highlanders could prevail over all of Britain. And neither could my father. He was wounded at Culloden, while many of the clan died around him and others were slaughtered after the battle was over, but some of the survivors managed to spirit him away. He, my mother, and their children fled to France, to the Stuart court in exile. I was born there four years after, and in that same year, in 1750, we all returned to Scotland. My mother's family had strong English connections, and my father had stronger guilt for leaving what remained of the clan to the mercy of the English, which was no mercy at all. My father thought enough time had passed that some accommodation could be made. He was beheaded in London before the year was out."

He nodded at Silas's expression of revulsion. "Ironic, isn't it, that Highlanders were called savages by the same people who lopped off my father's head. But after that, the persecution of the Travernes ended, and the lands were not given to others. For payment and service to the Crown, they could be redeemed. My brother began the process when he fought here, and my service and that of my men should finish it. Most of the indemnity has been paid. Rob is a good farmer. And we have more than fields and forests to harvest; we have men who make some of the best soldiers anywhere. We Highlanders have proven our mettle in battle. We are a valuable commodity."

Silas heard the irony, but he knew Traverne spoke the truth. The Highlanders were not like the Hessians, who had been rounded up and sold for soldiers by their princes, nor were they like the English regiments, with ranks so filled with men shaped by the desperation of poverty, ill health, and crime that it made it easy for their officers to regard them as little better than livestock. Highlanders were loyal not only to their officers, but to each other, many bound by kinship, and despite the fact that most of their ranks owned little of material worth, they were proud of themselves, of their strength, stamina, and skill.

Silas experienced the same astonishment as Traverne at the growing friendship between them, particularly because this was "Addie's Scotsman," a man he had disliked out of jealousy and insecurity without ever having met him. But now he understood why Addie had been not only impressed but worried that such a man would be on business for the Crown.

"Your reasons for fighting here are valid as any and not so different from ours. After all, it might never have come to this had Parliament and the Crown acknowledged our right to conduct our affairs to the best benefit of our lives. The miles between London and your home are not so many, but it seems the differences are. The pity is that we can be so much the same and enemies." He closed his eyes, gathering energy. "Do you like it, being a soldier?"

There was no challenge in the question, only curiosity, and Colonel Traverne answered without reserve. "Yes, I do. Rob was born to be a farmer, I to be a soldier. I was only sixteen when I returned to the Continent to begin learning the trade of a soldier. It is not raw killing that requires the most difficult training, it is learning to anticipate one's enemy, to use every weapon at hand, not just cannon and sword, but the land itself, the light or lack of it, the wind, everything. The worst we faced at Monmouth was not your guns, it was the blazing heat of the day. And at Stony Point, your troops used swampy ground and darkness to their great advantage. It was a bold, professional exercise." He made no attempt to disguise his admiration.

He saw understanding in Silas's dark eyes, but he saw something more—pity, there and then swiftly gone—and never had the divide between himself and the enemy seemed wider. He fought to restore and preserve his clan, but he also fought because he enjoyed it. People like Silas, indeed most of the Continental Army and the various militias, no matter how skilled they became under arms, would never regard themselves as more than citizen soldiers on temporary duty. He wondered how many would find, when the time came, that the transition from war to peace was not as easy as they anticipated.

"Having His Majesty's troops quartered on the populace gave many a distaste for professional armies. Of course, it was different in my father's house. We never had soldiers forced upon us, and those who came were welcomed by him." Addie's voice from the doorway startled both men. So intent had they been on their conversation, neither had noticed her arrival. By her comment, she revealed she had been listening to at least part of what had been said. But there was no rancor in her tone; she was simply explaining how it had been in Boston. He wondered if she, too, found him lacking in some profound way. And then to his chagrin, he realized she wasn't thinking about him at all; she was anxious that Silas had talked too long and overtaxed himself, but she did not want to unman her husband by being too obvious in her concern.

Only when he had left them did Colonel Traverne consider how disquieting it was that he had needed no words from her to know how she was feeling. He was growing far too attached to both of the Bradwells. He was relieved by the necessity of spending several days with his regiment while they moved their encampment once again, returning to Long Island.

Sir Henry was nervous about the Rebels' intentions and outraged that they had increased their activities both along the Hudson River and in the vicinity of Long Island, using whaleboats and other small craft to slip about, causing little material damage but much annoyance as they seemed to say, "You see how little you control," while avoiding any chance of open confrontation.

The Highlanders were neither an amphibious nor a mounted regiment, so their usefulness was limited in the present situation, but Colonel Traverne did not worry that his men would chafe at this lack of action. Their war cry was "Dìleas gu bàs," "Faithful till death," and when they roared the words in battle, the sound came from their hearts. But also to a man, they loathed the English. They were dedicated to the good of their clan, not to the good of the British Army. Colonel Traverne knew that as time passed, his men were becoming more in sympathy with the Rebels than with His Majesty's Government. They would continue to fight hard when required to do so, but they would not regret lack of action.

The usual summer amusements—horse races, cricket matches, bull baitings, boxing matches, and golf—were available, and Traverne was tempted to join the men who chose to ignore the war. Less intolerant than his men, he had a fair number of acquaintances among the English officer corps, as well as among Loyalist civilians, and there was no lack of invitations to various social and sporting functions. He had no illusions about his motive for considering these invitations this summer; it was sheer cowardice. He wanted respite from the spell the Bradwells seemed to have cast over him.

But it was not to be. He had left Duncan behind at Darius's house, but Angus had accompanied him, and Angus was determined that they return to the city as soon as possible. He had fallen under the spell, too. Traverne had sensed the man's reservation and even disapproval toward Addie in the beginning, and then he had seen his softening toward her and his concern for her husband, but he had not realized how deeply involved in their welfare Angus had become. It pricked Traverne's conscience because he was considering delaying his return, and guilt made his voice sharp.

"They can do without us for a while! Colonel Bradwell is growing stronger. And it doesn't do for us to forget he is the enemy."

Angus stared at him unblinkingly for a long moment, making him feel as if he were a child again.

Then Angus said, "It is not that he is getting well. The man has not left his bed, nor will he, not on his legs. He lives in his heart and his spirit; he stays only for his wife. He cannot stay much longer. He is not your enemy or mine, not now."

The low-spoken Gaelic was harsh to Traverne's ears, not softening the truth.

They returned to the city, and Traverne saw Colonel Bradwell more clearly than he had since the day he had brought him off the hospital ship. Silas could scarcely sit up in bed; there was no question of him getting out of it on his own. He had gained some weight so that he was no longer so skeletal, but it was a cruel gain, hinting at what a handsome man he had been, giving the illusion of improvement. But an illusion was all it was. Angus had seen the truth. Silas's body continued to decline while his spirit and his stubborn will burned, embers of the same fire that had sent Addie in search of him.

It made it even more painful for Traverne that the Bradwells were so pleased to see him and Angus. He had never felt more helpless in his life. He had the sensation not only of his inability to alter the situation, but also the nightmare it must be for Silas to be captive in an unresponsive body. He thought of him being trapped further by spending day after day in the same room. It was a small thing, but that, at least, he could change, and Darius gave his approval readily.

Traverne gave the Bradwells no chance to protest. He, his men, and Darius simply presented themselves, and Colonel Traverne announced, "Enough of being shut in this room. We are kidnapping you both to the garden."

With a minimum of fuss, Silas found himself transported outside. The scent of the garden and the touch of the sun were pleasures so acute, he had no words except his thanks.

A well-cushioned pallet raised against the damp had been fixed for him in the dappled light beneath a large elm. There was a chair beside it for Addie, and a table held food, drink, and books, refreshments for the body and the soul.

Addie had to hold back tears at the effort that had gone into this surprise, and then she wanted to laugh because Colonel Traverne and his cohorts looked as pleased as small boys who had just completed a successful adventure.

"We of the Garden Guard will perform our duties on every fair day," Traverne intoned with mock seriousness, and while Addie was still trying to express the depth of her gratitude, the four wheeled about and were gone.

Seeing the pure bliss on Silas's face, contentment flooded through Addie. She settled beside him and took his hand.

His eyes were closed, but a smile curved his mouth, and after a time, he said, "Of all the strange places we have stayed during the war, this must be the strangest of all. But I not only trust those men with my life, I trust them with yours, which is far more precious to me. You must trust them, too, no matter what happens. Your Scotsman is as valuable an ally as Darius."

Addie's heart skipped as unevenly as Silas's was wont to do, and then it seemed that it stopped beating entirely. Her jaws clenched so tight, she could not utter a sound, but Silas answered her anyway.

"I have no intention of dying, sweetheart. I hope that you and I will live together until we are so old, we cannot remember the war. But if that is not to be, if I must leave you here, then it is good to know I leave you with worthy men who will see you safely back to our lines, to Justin and Ad." His voice was calm and gentle.

Every conscious minute on the *Good Hope*, he had fought death and plotted escape. He had even begun to welcome the morning call of "Rebels, bring out your dead" because if he could hear the command, it meant he was not one of the corpses being hauled away for shallow burial in the mud. He had felt fever and vermin devouring him. He had thought he might never again smell air that was not rank with the stench of the dead and dying. Though every escape attempt had failed, he had gone on fighting, and his goal had remained the same—to see Addie again. Now he was with her. At night she slept beside him, touching him, and nightmares of the hulks were kept away. During the day she was gone from his side for only short periods of time. He had everything he had lived for, and he was satisfied to take each day as it came. The only thing he regretted was that the other prisoners had not also been redeemed.

Addie's head was bowed, and he heard her muffled sobs.

He reached out to stroke the curve of her cheek. "We do not need to speak of this again."

Addie wanted to weep without ceasing, but she regained enough control to mutter, "He's not my Scotsman!" and Silas was amused, as she had hoped.

"Indeed not," he conceded. "Despite the obligations that guide his actions, if ever a man belonged to himself, Colonel Traverne does. And even though I will never fully understand a man who seeks war, I wish he were on our side, in our army. We could use him and his men."

"We have someone like him. We have Harry Lee," Addie said. "And maybe Justin, too."

"Harry Lee was born a warrior, just like Colonel Traverne, but you needn't worry about Justin. He is doing what he must to keep on; when the war is over, he will change again. He won't be the same as he was before—none of us will—but he will find the way to a new life."

It reassured Addie, even more than what he was saying about Justin, that Silas was speaking as if he himself were also part of the future.

They spoke of many things, and she purposefully brought up the subject of Tim Chepman, the drummer boy, wanting Silas to see the future in the child.

"He is growing to be a fine young man. You made the right choice to save him," she said, and she could see his relief that she did not resent the risk he had taken.

"It was no choice at all," he said, and she understood without either of them mentioning Quentin.

They spent part of each day in the garden, except when summer storms kept them inside, and it was as if the green shady place were an island separated from the reality of Darius's household. Silas was aware that among frequent visitors were some of the most aggressive cavalry officers, including Lieutenant Colonel Banastre Tarleton of the British Legion and Lieutenant Colonel John Graves Simcoe of the Queen's Rangers. Tarleton and Simcoe were among the enemies of Harry Lee's legion and thus of Justin and the Castletons, but Silas did not have to meet them. Darius and Colonel Traverne made sure that no one intruded on the Bradwells' privacy, and if the visitors thought it amiss that a Rebel should be so kindly treated, none of them dared challenge it openly, particularly since that would mean a loss of access to Darius's generous table and cellar.

Unlike Silas, Addie had met Tarleton and Simcoe, and she detested both of them for the renown they were gaining for being as ruthless against civilians as they were against their military foes. Addie recognized the greater threat in Tarleton. At least Simcoe bore himself with dignity, but Tarleton, short, muscular, with an even-featured face, fancied himself the most dashing of cavalry officers and seemed to Addie to be posturing constantly, as if he were appearing on stage. He was extremely vain and viewed many of those around him with disdain, and Addie doubted that his sense of honor could bear much testing. She was not alone in this assessment, for he was not universally popular with his fellow officers.

Simcoe had simply avoided her after they had been introduced, but her first encounter with Tarleton was unpleasant.

"It is odd, but I have seen the like of your face before, though it was a man I saw. I shall look more closely the next time."

The barely veiled threat to Justin was so plain, for an instant, it was all Addie could do not to fly at him and claw out his eyes, this man who was gaining fame for killing those who tried to surrender. She stopped herself in time and peered at him with feigned innocence. "As you say, it is odd, for I have never known your like before."

She had the satisfaction of seeing color stain his face as he perceived her meaning.

"How fortunate you are to have seen such beauty in two different guises." Colonel Traverne's voice came to both of them, but there was no doubt about whom he was addressing. He was not wearing his sword, but his hand hovered where the hilt would be, warning Tarleton that there would be consequences for any further insult to Addie.

It was also a reminder to her that she could not afford to give offense here. But when she tried to thank Colonel Traverne later, he told her there was no need.

"The man is insufferable, but not so stupid that he wishes to deal too closely with me or with Darius."

His judgment was accurate, for though Tarleton continued to partake of Darius's hospitality, he treated Addie with rigid civility.

It did not matter to her that risk had been everything for so long; now safety was all that mattered. A safe place for Silas to grow strong was worth any compromise, even to treating Tories politely.

As for her preference for guests, she could not ask Darius that he invite Captain Trumble and his companions to the house as she had done in his absence, but during one of her brief forays outside, she saw the men and went to them to tell them that Silas had been found.

Captain Trumble nodded. "We know, Mistress Bradwell. Your brother told us." At her look of surprise, he added, "He seems a good man, for all that he's an enemy. He gave us a reward, ordered us to accept it." A small smile eased the stern lines of his face. "I see he didn't want you to know, but it seems to me a man ought to be known for his good deeds as well as for the bad ones. And your husband, how does he fare?"

"He is growing stronger every day," she said firmly, denying her doubts. "Perhaps you will be able to meet him soon."

"We will look forward to that day," the captain said, and Addie imagined the meeting quite vividly, with Silas recovered enough to walk about the city and to thank these men himself.

When next she saw Darius, she put her arms around him and kissed him on the cheek. "That is for your kindness to Captain Trumble and the others."

Darius looked embarrassed, then he smiled. "It seemed more appropriate for me than inviting them home for dinner."

It was Addie's turn to blush. She was certain that the servants' account of the hospitality she had offered the Rebels had been detailed, but Darius had made no mention of it until now. More than ever he reminded her of their father, for Marcus had been given to quiet kindness, too. But she did not relate this episode to Silas. He already felt such a burden of gratitude toward his brother-in-law, she did not want to add to it.

The sultry days drifted by, and then on August 19 there was a renewed flurry of alarm caused by another surprise attack by the Americans. This time they took the British strongpoint at Paulus Hook, which was nearly opposite New York across the Hudson. Again they traversed swampy ground during the dark hours, and they struck the fort at four in the morning. They had no intention of holding a position so close to the city, but they inflicted heavy casualties and made off with one hundred and fifty prisoners, while suffering very few casualties of their own. Only the British officer in command and some Hessians escaped capture because they barricaded themselves in the blockhouse from which it would have taken the Americans too long to extricate them.

It was a small victory, but a victory nonetheless, and another reminder to the British that they were vulnerable west of the Hudson. For Addie and Silas, it was a particularly pleasing triumph because Harry Lee's legion had accomplished the raid. Both of them could imagine the fierce joy Harry Lee, Justin, and the Castleton cousins were experiencing, as well as how pleased General Washington and his staff must be with the success. They wished they could be with their family and the others, but failing that, it was some consolation to know that the enemy had once again been thrown into high temper.

Darius did not try to conceal his rueful admiration of the raid, saying, "It was a hellishly difficult place to attack, but they managed it." He was departing with his men, but when he saw Addie's worry, he said, "You needn't fret. By the time we get across the river, I am sure your lot will be far out of reach."

He was so certain of that, he wished he did not have to go and was glad that Colonel Traverne would remain in the house. He did not want to leave Addie and Silas until Silas was strong enough to be getting about on his own. He had grown very fond and protective of both of them. When he was with them the boundaries of the war seemed to disappear.

Their visits to the garden continued in his absence, but Addie missed the reassurance of having Darius close, and Silas missed the conversations that were becoming increasingly congenial between them. But they expected him back shortly, agreeing with his assessment that Harry Lee would move away swiftly, not wanting to take the chance of having the British liberate his prisoners. Nor would the hunt be pleasant, for the weather had turned stormy.

The pouring rain kept the Bradwells inside, but finally the wind came about and drove the clouds off, and on the fourth day, they ventured out again. The sounds of the city seemed far away, muffled by the house and the garden walls. The air was hot and steamy so that even the bees were lazy. But every plant and stone looked new, washed clean by the rain, and Addie and Silas were cool in their shady refuge.

Silas lay with his eyes closed, listening as Addie read to him, and it seemed to him that he could hear the voice of every tiny creature in the garden, too, and the louder cries of the gulls passing over the land, and the humming of the tides running in the rivers and the sea. He felt more alive than he ever had and yet removed from it all, as if he were watching himself and Addie from some distance. Addie wore no hat or cap, and the beams of sunlight that slipped past the leaves were catching in her hair, making it gleam in shades of gold, brown, and amber. The light touched the clean bones of her face. Even with his eyes closed, he saw her so clearly. He could not remember another day in his life when he had felt so utterly peaceful and content.

His heart trembled, but he had grown accustomed to the strange dance, and he thought he would sleep for a while, and perhaps when he awakened, they would speak more of the days to come when the war would be over and people would be eager for books and music again.

Addie was reading aloud one of Sir Philip Sidney's romantic poems, and Silas remembered how he and her brothers had teased her for liking such fare when she was a young girl—it had seemed incongruous with a girl who dressed up as a boy—but now the words spoke for him, for her. A little sleep, and he would tell her... a little sleep and then...

Addie stopped reading, and it seemed for an instant that all the world inside and outside of the garden was silent. Silas's hand was held in hers, uncurled. She broke the silence deliberately, finishing the love song:

> *He loves my heart, for once it was his own;*
> *I cherish his because in me it bides;*
> *My true-love hath my heart, and I have his.*

She cradled his hand against her cheek, murmuring, "There, my love, there, now you can rest," unaware of the tears rolling down her cheeks and over both of their hands.

Chapter 20

Colonel Traverne witnessed Silas's death. He went into the garden to tell the Bradwells that a message had arrived from Darius promising to be home by nightfall. But he hesitated, arrested by the intimacy of the scene before him. He turned to go, but turned back when he heard Addie's voice stop midverse. He felt Silas leave the garden, and the sensation was so definite, he blinked in puzzlement at Silas still lying there. Then he heard Addie's voice soft as a lullaby, finishing the poem, and he knew, and he left her there, alone, while he went to tell Angus, Duncan, and the rest of the household. He took with him a pain so sharp, it was as if his beloved brother had died.

Darius arrived home to a house of mourning. Even some of the servants were red-eyed from weeping, having grown fond of the Bradwells despite themselves. Colonel Traverne, Angus, and Duncan looked as if they had lost a major battle. But Addie had not shed any tears since Silas's body had been carried indoors and she and Angus had prepared it for burial. It seemed as if she were far away, and when Darius took her hands in his, the chill of her skin shocked him.

"I am sorry, so sorry, Addie, that I wasn't here."

"It would not have made any difference. His heart was too weary. He could not stay." She shaped each word precisely.

As much as it unsettled Darius, it occurred to him that it was probably just as well that she was so dazed because maybe she could escape some of the grief, and he forced himself to go on with the dreary details that attended death.

"If it meets with your approval, Silas will be buried beside Harriet and our child."

"That is most kind of you."

"And I will send word to Ad and Justin."

"No, thank you. If you will see it delivered, it is better I write the letter so that they will know I am well," she said in the same careful tone. "And with your permission, I will tell them I am not yet prepared to rejoin them." She drew a deep breath, and Darius saw a brief flicker of light in her dull eyes. "Silas is gone, but our days together here were kind because of you and Colonel Traverne, and I would remember those days for a little time longer."

"For as long as you wish." Darius's voice was much less steady than hers.

When Silas was buried, the proper Anglican words read over his grave meant nothing to Addie, but the lament of the bagpipe grieved and wept in her silence, and she accepted the honor Colonel Traverne was granting Silas by having his piper play the mournful music. Captain Trumble and his companions were there also, but off to the side and in the shadows so that their presence would not draw undue attention, though Darius had invited them.

Addie felt as if she were in the shadows, too, in a deep, dark, hollow place. She had known Silas for most of her life and had loved him for nearly as long, and it was his love for her that had taken her from child to adult, had made her feel her value as a woman because a man of such infinite worth had committed himself to her, as he had accepted her commitment to him. The world without him was bleak. It would be unbearable to return now to the army, to Ad, Justin, and others who had also loved Silas, unbearable to witness their pain, unbearable to watch the other officers' wives return for their yearly reunions with their husbands. She must face them all eventually, but not yet.

There was useful work she could do. When Silas had been found, she had given up the idea of spying because it would have endangered him and because Darius and Colonel Traverne had been exerting such effort on his behalf. Those reasons no longer existed. Nor did the truce that had reigned in the house, not anymore, not for her. She wanted the war to end so that no more men like Silas could be killed, for the enemy had killed him; not cleanly in battle, but by slowly destroying his body while he was their helpless captive. No amount of kindness by her brother or Traverne had been able to heal the damage that had been done.

The ironies of her situation did not escape her. She had never spoken to Silas about this, but she knew he would have disapproved, not only because of the risk to her, but also because he would have considered it a dishonorable enterprise. And further, had not Darius welcomed her so graciously and allowed her to stay on, she would have had no opportunity to collect intelligence.

The question remained, the same one Major Tallmadge had asked during their meeting, whether or not she was willing to betray Darius. Silas's death had provided the answer. What she might be able to do here would be, at best, a small effort in the grand scheme of the war. But it was something to keep her from being entirely lost in the dark, hollow place.

There would be nothing odd in her visiting Valencourt's. She had gone there a few times recently for short visits when she had ventured away from Silas's side. Not even the tension of having Tallmadge's agent there had tarnished the familiarity of the establishment because it was so like her father's shops in Boston had been. She knew that old comfort would be gone once she began to pass information to Mr. Moore, but that didn't matter; there was no real comfort anywhere with Silas gone from the world.

The greatest obstacle to her plan was the solicitousness of Darius and Colonel Traverne. They treated her as they had when she first arrived in the city, as if she were a fragile child, urging her to eat, asking if she'd slept, asking if there was anything she lacked that they could provide. She felt smothered by their attentions, but she also pitied the men. They were the children. They trusted her, and she had every intention of betraying them for a greater loyalty. She was set on her course, but it did not prevent some last vestige of tenderness from stirring regret in her heart. And then she reminded herself that while not all the enemy were evil, what they were doing was, and her heart grew cold.

Her announcement that she wanted to go to Valencourt's was greeted not with suspicion, but with relief that she was showing interest in something. Darius had no idea that his plans had triggered her action. He escorted her, and because he always had business to discuss at the shop, she had no trouble in managing a brief conversation with Robert Moore.

"Valencourt's Rangers leave the city three days hence. They go for horses, to the Jerseys, I believe," she told him.

That she would begin by passing information about Darius brought the slightest gasp of surprise from Moore, but his reply was no more than a repetition of her words, to confirm that he had heard her correctly before he moved away from her.

She waited for remorse, or terror, or some other strong emotion to sweep over her, but the cold calm that enveloped her was unchanged. Like other Loyalist mounted troops, Valencourt's Rangers were often used against vulnerable civilian targets, although Darius's men did not have a reputation for the rape and murder that had become a common part of the terror inflicted by some. Attacking civilians and their property was a calculatedly brutal policy of the British. When Darius went after horses and whatever other plunder, innocent people would suffer losses they could ill afford. Even friends of the British lost as much in the raids as did their enemies. The brother who walked beside her was a different man from the one who led those raids to pillage and burn farms and hamlets. Addie knew that was a dangerously artificial separation in her mind, but she embraced it anyway.

When Darius left on his nefarious mission, she bid him, "Keep safe," and she meant it, though her message to Robert Moore could well bring harm to her brother. If Darius were two people, then surely she was, too.

Only at night when she dreamed did her resolve falter, for then in nightmares Darius became Marcus and Quentin and Silas, all of them strangely blended into one figure of loss by distance, by death, gone beyond her reach forever. And she would awaken with the cold all around her no matter how warm the night, sometimes waking to the sound of her voice calling for Silas.

Colonel Traverne watched Addie with growing concern. He had once thought he could understand her easily, but now she was hiding so deep inside herself, he could hardly catch a glimpse of her. She was polite to everyone, meticulous in thanking servants and anyone else who offered her a service or a courtesy, and she was competent in acting as hostess in Darius's absence. That made Traverne most nervous of all, her playing that role, as if it did not trouble her that most of the visitors to the house were deadly enemies of the Rebels. Not for a moment did he believe that her loyalties had shifted, nor did she claim that they had, and that made her behavior all the more puzzling. From their first meeting he had seen the passion in her for those she loved, for ideas, for life itself, the passion that had made her so vivid—but now the brightness was quenched. He knew it could scarcely be otherwise, she had loved her husband so, but that did not prevent him from missing the woman she had been.

He was becoming obsessed with Ariadne Valencourt Bradwell. He had known that for some time, but there seemed to be nothing he could do about it, which made him feel self-disgust for his lack of control. And circumstances were conspiring to keep him in her presence. It appeared that this campaign season was going to end without a major confrontation between the British and the Continental armies. While that left Colonel Traverne and his men little to do, it was the opposite for Darius. In the absence of a general action, Sir Henry was frustrated and was relying increasingly on quick raids to punish his enemies and to remind them that the war was not over. When Silas had been with them, Darius had not gone into the field as often as he might have done otherwise; now it was likely that Darius would have his troop out more frequently until winter came, particularly because he trusted Colonel Traverne to watch over his household and his sister.

On the surface, it was a good arrangement. The hospitality offered by Darius had made Traverne's sojourn in New York a pleasant experience, and their friendship had grown apace. But he wondered what reaction Darius would have if he told him he desired Addie. He checked the thought as soon as it presented itself. Desire was part of it, but so was the need to protect and to cherish, to bring light and laughter back to her.

They had both lost spouses, and remarriage was no oddity; after all, the Valencourt patriarch had married three times. But not only were he and she enemies, her husband had died from British maltreatment, and most of the males of her family were active Rebels. Their situation was impossible, and he did the only sensible thing; as she had withdrawn into herself, so he withdrew behind brisk propriety and limited his contact with her by spending more time at headquarters and by having Angus or Duncan, rather than himself, escort her on her excursions about the city. And he tried to think of her only in formal terms, as Mistress Bradwell, though he could not control the dreams wherein he called her by her given name, her nickname, and by Gaelic endearments, and spoke to her with an intimacy that embarrassed him when daylight came without banishing memory of the dreams.

At first, all Addie noticed was that it was easier to be with his men than with Colonel Traverne. The intensity of the colonel's blue eyes made her uneasy now that she had so much to hide. Sometimes he made her feel transparent, as if he could see far more than she wanted to reveal. But she had some guilt, too, for she had grown fond of Angus and Duncan, and she had come to understand that the privacy they allowed her at Valencourt's had to do with their own unease. Neither of them was literate—indeed, the written form of Scottish Gaelic was so new, few but poets and scholars commanded it—but that did not prevent their discomfort at being in the presence of so many books written in a language they despised. They regarded the rows of English books with the same suspicion they displayed toward English soldiers and held themselves aloof from both.

However, the apprehension about their colonel and the compassion she felt for the two men were faint emotions, far away and muffled. The fear she had expected would chase her once she had begun to pass information to Mr. Moore was still no more than an echo of true emotion. Even the knowledge that by her action she had put Darius's life in peril did not penetrate with any force. Everything was being filtered through a fog so deep, when she pinched her skin, she could hardly feel it. Her mind was as dull as her flesh, capable of coherent thought for little more than short spaces that did not connect. Only at night when she tried to sleep did the pain cut through, sharp and true with the knowledge that Silas was gone. Enduring each day and each night took tremendous energy, and the one thing that made the endurance worthwhile was the prospect of gleaning more information for General Washington.

She was in such a state that even facing James Rivington did not rouse intense feelings. He came to the house specifically to call on her, and she allowed the meeting because, though she still considered him a despicable liar, she was grateful he had made no mention of her or Silas in his newspaper. She suspected that Darius and Colonel Traverne might have had something to do with Rivington's restraint, but Rivington was powerful enough to have printed one of his snide, gossipy attacks had he so chosen.

The encounter was peculiar from start to finish, for he greeted her quite kindly, saying, "My dear, I regret that you are here under such sad circumstances. How I long for the world we knew before the war!" He chattered on about the past, about Marcus and the publishing and book importation ventures they had shared. Addie followed his lead, and not once did they discuss the war itself or the wide rift that separated their loyalties. She could assume only that the whole exercise had been his way of paying tribute to her father and to Darius by letting her know she would not be a subject for the *Royal Gazette*. It was just one more contradiction of the war that a man who circulated vicious lies about General Washington and other Patriot leaders could also behave honorably for the sake of an old friendship.

Colonel Traverne's reaction to the visit was less placid than Addie's. When he learned of it from one of the servants, he went to Addie immediately, his resolution to remain aloof cast aside in concern for her.

"Did Rivington insult you?" he demanded without preamble.

His outrage was so palpable, amusement stirred in Addie. It was an emotion she had not experienced in so long, her smile surprised her. Colonel Traverne was giving a good performance as an outraged father or brother.

"You are taking your role as Darius's substitute quite seriously, aren't you?" she teased gently. "But you needn't worry. Mr. Rivington was very civil to me. In fact, I think he visited to let me know that I am not to be one of his targets, in spite of my Patriot sympathies. I wondered if you or Darius had spoken to him, or mayhap it really is just because Mr. Rivington and my father have long been friends."

Colonel Traverne was so distracted by her smile, it took him a moment to recall the matter at hand.

"Perhaps Darius did speak to him. I did not. I cannot abide the man. He jabbers in print. With his copious notations about who has arrived and who is leaving, his newspaper must be useful to our enemies."

"*Your* enemies," she corrected him. Her voice was still soft, but her smile vanished.

Colonel Traverne cursed himself inwardly for his blunder. That it was safer that the line between them be clearly drawn was little solace, as little as having her see him in the role of brother.

"As you say. I did not mean to offend."

Addie saw the pain in his face before his mask of control was back in place, and it was her turn to regret, but he had left her before she could think of what to say.

She remembered Angus's plea. It was unsettling to imagine that she could hurt the colonel, more unsettling to realize that she was not sure what was going on between them. She had come to rely on his strength without questioning why he was so willing to involve himself in her affairs. She had assumed it was out of gratitude for the hospitality he had received at the Boston house and now enjoyed from Darius, but on reflection, that seemed an inadequate explanation. He had openly risked official censure and that of his fellow officers and had used his standing to search for and then shelter an enemy soldier. Darius had the burden of the familial affection he bore for her, but Traverne was not bound by the same obligation. Suddenly Addie had the disorienting sense that she and the colonel were engaged in a dance in which both steps and music were mysteries to her.

In the ensuing days, she wished she had never had such thoughts, for where she had taken him for granted before, now she was so aware of him, it was like having sensation flow too quickly back into a numbed limb, causing invisible flames to lick along the flesh. The fire spread, burning away the fog that had shrouded her, making her feel the pain of being alive despite her efforts to cling to the blessed insentience.

She began to notice far too much about the Scotsman. She noticed how careful he was in her presence—careful of what he said, careful not to betray his thoughts or emotions—surely far less at ease than he had been before. And she noticed that while he still kept watch over her in Darius's stead, he spent less time in her company, leaving her in Angus's or Duncan's charge as much as he could. With the new tension between them, it was just as well, but she missed him when he was not about, and that underscored how dependent she had become on him.

She began to spend more time at Valencourt's, enough time to send her escort away for hours before he returned to see her home, and she maintained cordial relations with all the clerks so that no suspicion could be attached to her occasional discourse with Robert Moore. Not that she had much to tell him. She listened assiduously to every conversation at Darius's house as she played hostess, and many of the officers were so accustomed to her presence, they no longer guarded their tongues when she was near. She was Darius's sister and a sad widow now; what threat could she be? But they seldom spoke of anything that interested her. She had expected spying to be hard on her nerves, but she had not believed it could be so dull. Most of what she heard concerned such inconsequential matters as the outcome of various athletic contests, the virtues and weaknesses of favorite racehorses, and details of the latest fashions being worn in London.

What war news there was had little to do with the New York garrison. Spain had declared war on England, but no one expected Spanish ships to sail into New York Harbor. Rather, it meant added danger for British ships in other waters, and it expanded the list of ports where American ships would be welcomed and protected. It also added further weight to the arguments of those in England who wanted the war to end. The stalemate was causing widespread frustration, and there was open talk of pursuing the war more vigorously in the South where, the British continued to believe, the Loyalist population was numerous and committed enough to substantially increase the ranks without the need of reinforcements from home.

Addie overheard two officers discussing it at Valencourt's. Each had a lavishly dressed woman on his arm, and both were strutting a bit and trying to impress the women with the heroics they would show were a Southern campaign to materialize.

"Of course, the summers in those colonies are unfit for white men, so we would have to take to the field before the heat sets in," one of the men said.

The other bolstered the claim. "So you should be kind to us in case we are soon to be shipped off to the wilderness."

"See here, we're kind enough as it is," protested one of the females, while the other one giggled.

Addie kept her expression bland and continued to straighten a pile of books, but inside she quailed at this talk of an expanded war. The enemy already held Savannah, and though there were various bodies of militia, overall there were few Continentals in the Southern states. And there were assuredly strong pockets of Loyalist sentiment, though it was impossible to predict how many men would be willing to serve with the British Army. She thought of her Virginia family and the peaceful acres of Castleton and hoped the war would never reach them.

When she arrived back at the house late that afternoon, she was still beset by images of redcoats swarming over Castleton's grounds, but she discovered that Colonel Traverne had more immediate concerns.

"I am certain that Darius does not require you to earn your keep."

She knew instantly that he was referring to the longer hours she was spending at Valencourt's and the work she had begun to do, just small tasks such as shelving books, rearranging displays of merchandise after customers had pawed through them, checking the proofs in the printing office for errors. She ignored the curious stares she still received from some customers. It was enough that the clerks seemed grateful for her help as she deferred to them, and Robert Moore thought a clever ruse to allow her further reason for being at Valencourt's.

"Have the clerks complained of my interference?" she asked, wondering if one of them resented her presence after all.

Colonel Traverne shook his head. "Far from it, they are no doubt grateful to have your expert assistance. But—"

"But it is hardly proper," Addie finished for him. "You are mistaken. I am the daughter of a merchant, a bookseller, a printer, but more than that, I am now among those termed 'women alone,' and as a widow, I have more freedom to do as I wish than I have ever had before, more than if I had never married, more than if Silas had lived. I could run a shop or a public house or a plantation or wear red petticoats or take a string of lovers, and few would object unless I took something, be it property or lovers, from them. It gives me pleasure to help at Valencourt's. It reminds me of much, much happier times. There I can almost see my brothers and Silas as they were before the war changed them all and killed two of them. Your idea of what is proper for me differs greatly from mine."

The flat, harshly spoken words rained against him like stones, but the blaze of gold in her eyes was as welcome to him as the sun after days of darkness. He could not explain to her that it was not for any notion of propriety that he had spoken, but because he could not bear having her observed as if she were an exotic zoological exhibit. He knew many of Valencourt's customers did just that, even Angus and Duncan had commented on it, not liking it any better than he. There was grudging admiration for her daring in coming to New York to find her husband and reluctant sympathy that the man had died, but she was nevertheless an oddity, this Rebel widow in their midst, and the more involvement she had in Valencourt's, the more chance there was for people to treat her unkindly.

He was miserable that she should judge him so rigid that he would demand she conform to his specifications. Then he was furious as the words "string of lovers" sounded in his mind because she was right about her new status; she could do very much as she pleased as long as she practiced a little discretion. Accepting that she had been married to Silas whom she had known and loved for so long was one thing, thinking of her in the arms of another man was intolerable.

"I beg your pardon. I have overstepped my bounds," he said stiffly.

His distress was so visible, Addie's anger faded. "No apology is required. You have taken as good care of me as would any of my brothers."

His patience slipped away before he could hold it firm. "I am not suited to the role. Remember, I was the youngest in my family; my siblings directed me, not I them. Darius is your brother. I would prefer that you consider me a friend."

They were both surprised by his words, but Addie recovered first.

"I would be a fool to refuse such an offer. I am in need of friends in this city, and friends are often more forbearing than brothers." She smiled at him tentatively. She was unsure about where all of this was leading, but she had never seen Colonel Traverne in this light. He seemed more uncertain than she and terribly anxious, as if her response was very important to him.

She barely heard his words acknowledging their new bargain. She watched him conjure a smile to answer hers, she watched him struggle to regain his customary control and the slightly aloof posture that kept everyone, except perhaps Angus and Duncan, at the distance he chose. As she watched him, she saw him more clearly than ever before. Because of his reserve and his responsibilities, she had come to think of him as Darius's contemporary, but he was, at twenty-nine, exactly between her and her brother, seven years older than she, seven years younger than Darius, only two years older than Silas. The figures spun around in her head as if they held some arcane magic.

Suddenly she saw him as a man, not as the questionable presence he had been in Boston so long ago, not as the confident commander of his regiment, not as one of Callista's acquaintances referred to the family in the colonies, and, most of all, not as Darius's substitute—not as anyone except himself. She saw a handsome man, as comely on the inside as he was on the outside, a desirable man.

She had been very sheltered because of Silas. She had loved him from such an early age, she had not looked on other men as desirable or not. She had seen the coy glances women cast toward her brothers, cousins, and Silas, and had observed the progress of various flirtations, but whenever a situation had moved toward involving her personally, such as with Paul Byrne, she had always managed to prevent it from going further than simple friendship. Despite having been married and having traveled with the army for years, and despite her foolish boast that as a widow she could take lovers, Addie knew herself to be as innocent as a green girl compared to someone as worldly as Colonel Traverne.

She did not want to view him as a man and was appalled that she could. There was no place in her life for this. It seemed a betrayal of Silas even though Silas was dead. But something had changed between her and Traverne, and they could not seem to regain their safe footing. They were more and more uneasy in each other's company, and it was a relief to both of them when Darius returned, though he was in a foul temper. Not only had his troop failed to procure horses or anything else of value, they had very nearly been captured by the Americans.

Contrarily, it was only when Addie saw her brother before her, unhurt, that the full terror of what she'd done finally hit her. The information she'd passed along might well have gotten him killed.

She ran to him and put her arms around him, exclaiming, "Thank God you're safe!" She knew her reaction was too strong, but Darius was pleased rather than suspicious and hugged her close.

"Such a welcome! You make homecoming worthwhile, but you needn't tremble so. I truly am safe, and I must add that Justin and your cousins are, too. There was no close dueling this time, but it was your Major Lee's legion that chased us off." He admitted this grudgingly, but Addie clung to him for a moment longer before she let go. It was logical that mounted troops should be sent after mounted troops, but that scarcely pacified her conscience, and she hoped beyond reason that Darius would not go out again, and most of all that he and Justin would never again be within pistol shot or saber's blade of each other.

Unlike Colonel Traverne, Darius was pleased when he learned of Addie's increased involvement in Valencourt's. He thought anything that distracted her mind from Silas's death was to the good, and he was not above furthering that aim. He understood that her Rebel pride would allow her to accept little beyond food and lodging from him, though her resources were severely limited. She was as lovely as her mother Lily had been, but her sparse wardrobe was growing so threadbare, sometimes it pained him to look at her when it would cause him no hardship to clothe her in the style he thought she deserved.

Feeling very clever, he put it to her as a business proposition. "I am grateful that you are taking such an interest in Valencourt's, but my dear, you need more suitable clothing." He forestalled her refusal by explaining, "I won't ask you to enrich the coffers of British and Loyalist merchants, but I have not yet disposed of Harriet's clothing. I could not bear to do so, and now my cowardice can pass as wisdom. Harriet liked you when she met you, and I know she would want you to have the use of her gowns, if it would not distress you that they were once hers."

She accepted to please him and because the war had taught her practicality. She cared little that her appearance had grown so shabby, but her brother cared, and Harriet's clothing was of no use stored away.

When Addie began to sort through the fine fabrics, everything from light silks and cottons to heavy wools, velvets, and brocades, she was startled by the spark of vanity that remained in her. She had gotten out of the habit of considering how she appeared to others and had been satisfied as long as she and her clothing were clean and neat. Now when she saw the colors Harriet had favored—the blues and greens, the shades of gold, ivory, and apricot—and tried on the garments, she saw herself as she might have been without the war and with her aunts' guidance, a well-dressed matron, as Harriet had been.

The scent of rose petals and lavender wafted from the clothing, testament to the care with which it had been stored. Harriet had appreciated quality, but she had disdained an excess of furbelows, choices that endeared her to Addie and made her wish she had known her better. The clothing also told Addie much about Darius beyond the fact that he had provided well for his wife; that he had, by his own admission, been unable to part with Harriet's possessions until now was proof of how much he had loved his wife and how much her death had affected him. Addie remembered Colonel Traverne telling her that she would find Darius a changed man, and she wondered if he would have allowed her to come to New York at all had his heart not been softened by love and loss.

From Harriet's clothes, Addie chose the quietest garments, as befitted a woman recently widowed, but still, the transformation in her appearance was dramatic enough to earn closer attention from the male patrons of Valencourt's and from the officers who visited the house. Though the intense scrutiny made her uncomfortable, it was also useful. Because she now looked more like the Loyalist women some of these men squired about the city, the men were even less careful in their speech when she was near, and she was able to pass more information to Mr. Moore, notwithstanding that none of it was what she would judge of major importance.

Addie could not ignore Colonel Traverne's reaction to her new wardrobe, and it both troubled and amused her. While Darius was pleased to see her in Harriet's gowns, Traverne did not seem to share his opinion and looked more stern than ever when other men were showing interest in her.

Colonel Traverne thought he was behaving with admirable restraint since his impulse was to knock a few heads together. Seeing other men lusting after Addie accented his growing desire. Nor could he escape to the Long Island encampment, for his regiment had been reassigned to city duty. It was such an admirable posting, he could not refuse it, particularly not on the ground that he was enamored of a Rebel woman. He was beginning to long for action as much as some other officers did. There were disquieting accounts of an American–French victory in Georgia, a retaking of Savannah, and he speculated that Sir Henry might make some response. But as morose and unpredictable as the man was, there was no way to foretell what he would do. Traverne counted himself well lost in that he cared more about Addie's reaction to the news than about General Clinton's.

He thought she would be jubilant but when he asked her directly, she replied, "There have been so many false rumors in this war, I will await confirmation of this."

What she would not admit to him was that Silas's doubts about the French alliance had become hers. That she could not speak honestly to him was another reminder that they were enemies. She wished that were enough to warn her away, but she could not banish the knowledge of his kindness to her and to Silas, to the men he commanded and their families.

With his regiment in the city, she met more of the soldiers and the women and children who accompanied some of them. While most English officers had little to do with the lower ranks, Colonel Traverne was concerned with every aspect of his regiment's welfare, from adequate provisions and weapons to new materials, including tartan, to refurbish or replace worn uniforms. Though he claimed that his brother was the true chief of the clan, it was hard to imagine that anyone could treat these people with more tenderness than the colonel.

She saw another side of Angus and Duncan, too, for when they were with their fellow Highlanders, they were much less reserved, conversing in rapid Gaelic and smiling often. She learned that though Angus was a widower, his wife having died some years ago in Scotland, he had two sons who were being fostered in Rob Traverne's household, and Duncan had a wife and four children waiting for him at home.

"Duncan's wife is a staunch woman and would have come with him had he allowed it, but he did not want to subject her or his children to the dangers of the New World," Colonel Traverne explained. "He thought this would be a most uncivilized, wild place with savage red men lurking behind every tree."

"In contrast to savage Highlanders lurking in every glen?" Addie asked, and won a smile from him.

It was dangerous, this human face she saw on the enemy, and so was the attraction she felt toward Colonel Traverne. The presence of Darius as a buffer became more important by the day.

Then he began making plans for another foray into the Jerseys, to be executed with Lieutenant Colonel Simcoe's Queen's Rangers. This was in response to the rumor that Washington was collecting boats preparatory to launching an attack on New York City itself. Addie overheard only snippets of the conversations, but they were enough when coupled with the heightened activity at Darius's house and his frequent trips to headquarters. Before she could lose her nerve, she reported what she knew to Robert Moore, holding to her courage by reminding herself once again that innocent people were going to be terrorized, even killed, their homes and shops burned.

But when it came time for Darius to leave for the embarkation point on Staten Island, Addie could scarcely bear to see him go and was mopping at tears before he was out of the door, despite his assurances that he would be back soon.

She was glad Colonel Traverne was not there to witness her outburst. Her emotions were no longer veiled, and she was torn by guilt and fear, yet sure she was doing the right thing. She wondered how much longer she could continue her duplicity without losing her sanity entirely. Nor did it ease her inner conflict that a reply from Ad and Justin had arrived, full of their sympathy and understanding, and innocently giving their blessings to her staying on with Darius. She was so worried about what might be happening to Darius, and to Justin if Harry Lee's men were on the hunt, that she couldn't eat or sleep. The strain was obvious enough for Robert Moore to warn her, "Betray yourself, and you will betray me and others."

It was Colonel Traverne who brought her the news less than a week after Darius had departed. He told her bluntly, before she could think even worse, "Darius, Colonel Simcoe, and a few others have been taken prisoner by your army. There is some concern that Colonel Simcoe might have been wounded, though no one is sure as yet, but no such report was made about Darius. Apparently your brother tarried to help Simcoe when they were fired upon. Their attackers were mariners and militia, not Continental dragoons." It was the only good news he could give her, that Justin and her cousins had not been involved.

Her face lost all color so that even her eyes seemed bleached of their warm brown tints and left an eerie pale gold like a cat's eyes. She stared at him as if he were unknown to her, and he caught her before she could crumple to the floor.

All thought of formality and distance fled as he cradled her against him. "Addie, listen to me, listen! Darius is not dead! He is a prisoner of your army, which is, in truth, far better than being held by the British Army."

"But he is a Loyalist, a Tory," she whispered, thinking of the mistreatment many Tories had suffered at Patriot hands.

"He is a high-ranking provincial officer in the British Army," Traverne reminded her patiently. "Your army treats our soldiers taken as prisoners honorably, there is no reason to think it will be different in Darius's case. And it will only help his cause that it is widely known you are staying here under his protection and that he has brothers who are close to your commander in chief. I'll wager both Darius and Simcoe will be exchanged quite swiftly."

"I must go to him, I must..." Her voice trailed away as the full weight bore down on her—she was the one who had sent warning of the raid.

It didn't signify that the same message also might have come from others; it had definitely come from her. She was responsible for his capture. From the beginning she had known that possibility existed, but that did not make the reality any more supportable. She had wanted to do the right thing for the American cause but without personal consequences. A few words to Robert Moore, and she had delivered Darius into the hands of his enemies, her compatriots. And in spite of Colonel Traverne's attempts to reassure her, all she could see was Silas diminished unto death by his months of imprisonment.

She felt the terrible secret of what she had done clawing to get out. She wanted to confess to Colonel Traverne and hear his soothing voice grant her absolution. She wanted to flee back to the time before the war or far ahead to a time when it would be only memory; she wanted anything except to be trapped here in the battle of her conflicting loyalties.

She did not fight. She welcomed the shadow sweeping over her until it blotted out sight and sound. She tasted the salt of her tears, felt Traverne's strength, and then she relinquished those senses, too, and let the dark come down.

Chapter 21

Colonel Traverne waited for Addie to wake. He did not know what else to do. When she had not regained consciousness for hours, he sent for a physician and then nearly threw the man out bodily for suggesting that a good bloodletting was in order.

"Bloodletting for someone who is already pale as a ghost? Are you mad?"

"No, I am not!" the doctor snapped in answer to the colonel's bellow. "But that woman might be, in which case she may never come back to her right mind."

The maids had undressed Addie and put her to bed, but it was Traverne who kept vigil, just as Addie had kept vigil with Silas. With all she had lost in this war, he understood why she would seek to hide from this latest blow, but he did not want her to prove the doctor's words. He knew an old woman at home who had lost her husband and all five sons at the Battle of Culloden. She had survived to grow old, cared for by others with a kind of superstitious kindness, as if she were a holy fool, but she had not said a word nor taken any part in the life of the community since the day she had learned of the deaths of her men. He did not intend that Addie share the same fate.

He could sense her in the shadows, just beyond his reach, and he wanted her back. He did not try to fool himself that it was for her brother's sake; he wanted her for himself. With that admission, the last barrier fell away.

"It is Iain. I am right beside you. Hear me. I did not lie to you. There is every reason to believe Darius is unharmed and will return soon. It will break his heart if he finds you like this." He paused, gathering his courage, feeling more apprehensive than ever he had on a field of battle. And then he confessed, "It is breaking my heart now." He kissed her very gently on the forehead.

Her breathing was even, her skin not as icy cold as it had been. He held her hand and spoke to her occasionally, but mostly he waited for her. He felt oddly at peace. Whether she had heard him or not, he had set his course now, and none of the obstacles in the way were as formidable as his need for her.

He looked up once during the night to see that Angus had come into the room and was watching him. He knew Angus had noticed and not approved of his growing interest in Addie, but he saw not condemnation, rather resignation and even a hint of approval.

Angus, too, had fallen under Addie's spell, and he didn't waste the breath to ask his colonel if he wanted someone to take over the night watch for him. He replenished the candles and added more wood to the fire against the chill of the November night, and then he left them alone.

Addie clung to the safety of the refuge she had found, trying to escape the voice that summoned her to come out. Something horrible waited for her, but the voice still pulled. She opened her eyes and saw everything at once—a new day's sun flooding into the room, the light gilding Colonel Traverne's face and catching in the sapphire of his eyes, a familiar face utterly changed. His emotions were no longer hidden. He was regarding her with such steady tenderness, she felt more warmth from him than from the sun. And he did not try to hide himself when he realized she was alert.

"Welcome back," he said.

She realized he was stroking her hand, just making small circles on her skin, and yet, the sensation was enough to hold her entire body in thrall. And then guilt washed through her in an icy wave as she remembered what she had done, where Darius was, if he were still alive. But when she tried to pull her hand away, to pull herself away, Colonel Traverne would not allow it.

Patiently he repeated his assurances that Darius would be all right, and he said, "You are not alone. I am with you." He was infinitely relieved to see awareness return to her and anxious to alleviate the raw pain he saw in her eyes. He spoke without reserve. "I know it is not rational or convenient. You are so recent a widow, you and I are political enemies, and none of it makes any difference." He lifted her hand to his mouth and kissed it. "Were there time, I would give it to you, but war speeds the clock, and despite all the trouble and my haste, I mean to court you. Pray do not reject my suit out of hand."

For a moment, she was caught again in his spell. She saw herself through his eyes, saw herself as a desirable woman, and she saw him, his goodness, intelligence, and honor. For a moment, she imagined leaning into his strength and letting him carry the weight of all the loss and death, but her loyalty and her treachery isolated her from his comfort as surely as a fortress of stone.

"Am I deluded? Are the feelings all my own?" he asked.

His calm tone did not cloak his vulnerability from her; nor could she lie.

"No, I cannot deny that you have become important to me. I liked you from the time I met you in Boston, though I was certain you were working for the Crown." He stiffened at that, and she nodded. "You see, nothing is simple about this. And I do not know how I feel. Silas will be part of me always, but I know that he is dead. And I know I am alive." She twisted her hands together, searching for words to explain something she barely understood herself. "But I don't feel alive! I feel as if I am just outside of myself, trying to put the pieces back together so that I can recognize myself again. I don't know who this woman is, and what I do know about her, I do not like." She stopped. She could not say that fear and guilt were the emotions she felt most clearly now.

"I like her well enough for both of us."

"Colonel…"

"Please, my name is Iain."

As soon as he said it, she could hear also what he had said to her while she drifted in the darkness, could feel the gentle touch of his kiss on her forehead. But his giving of his Gaelic name for her to use was even more intimate. It was more than an invitation to the familiarity of using first names; for Iain was his name in the world most precious to him, a world apart from English rule.

She could not resist the gift.

"Iain."

As soon as she said it, she knew she would never be able to distance herself with his military title again, even if she called him Colonel Traverne. This was different from discovering his name because one of his men had said it; this was the willful transference of the man he knew himself to be into her keeping. Whether she was prepared for it or not, a special bond existed between them.

"Ariadne, Addie," he caressed her names with his voice, but there was a gleam of mischief in his eyes at this acknowledgment that she also had two names.

They were discreet with visitors, but it took too much effort to maintain a formal mien before the household. It would have done little good anyway, for Angus, Duncan, and the servants were too aware of the shifting currents between the couple.

Iain didn't press his attentions on her, but now there was undisguised warmth in his eyes when he looked at her, and she felt so reassured by his mere presence, she began to seek his company, ignoring the voice inside her that warned she was forsaking good sense in order to have a champion to fight her demons.

She forced herself to continue to go to Valencourt's, but it was difficult to ignore the new tension in Robert Moore. He clearly considered her a risk now, though she continued to feed him every bit of information she gleaned at Darius's house, continued to betray Iain as she had betrayed her brother. And it did not improve her temper or Moore's when news reached the city that the French–American attempt against the British at Savannah had been a failure, not the success earlier bemoaned by the enemy. From the British perspective, this was further and much celebrated confirmation that the French–American alliance was useless. The French fleet was still rumored to be in American waters, but since no recent sightings of the ships had been made, apprehension about a naval confrontation was fading, and there was new speculation about what the British fleet would do now that it could ply the waters without interference.

Sometimes Addie found herself having internal arguments with Silas, trying to assure him that the French alliance could still save them, protesting against his skepticism, that even if the military actions had not worked, the money and supplies coming from France were vital. But Silas was dead, beyond her reach, and her doubts about the alliance had grown.

Winter would come soon. If the enemy wanted to mount an attack, it would most likely be in the South where winter and spring were the best seasons for war.

As much as she worried about her family in Virginia, the approach of the cold to New York was more immediate. Because she could do nothing for them, she tried to blind herself to the poverty of the host of refugees who lived on the edge of disaster. It was hard enough for them to find enough food and to stay alive under canvas and sticks in warm weather; the cold was sure to kill many. And it would be far, far worse for the American prisoners of war and for the starving men on parole wandering the city. She reminded herself constantly that the sooner the war ended, the more of these men would survive; thus anything she could do to hasten the finish was justified.

It was a justification fragile in daylight, impossible to sustain when the nightmares came. Sleep was her field of battle. She dreamed in excruciating detail. A grave was open in seeping earth, and there were bodies laid side by side in it, without coffins or winding sheets to shield them. Sometimes there were four—Sarah, Quentin, James Fitzjohn, and Silas—laid out in the order of their deaths. But then the grave would yawn wider, and Justin, Ad, the Castleton cousins, and Darius and Iain, too, would be there, corpses like the rest. Nearby wolves and feral pigs consumed the flesh and bones from other burials and waited for her to leave so they could feast there as well. The pigs' eyes were black; the wolves' eyes were golden, like hers. The bones were white, but the hues of flesh differed depending on the state of corruption from just a shade too pale for life to a dull greenish bronze, as if the substance were being transmuted into metal. She stared transfixed at the grave until the wolves howled and freed her to start awake to the sound of her cries. Then she would count the minutes until safety came with the sunrise.

The lack of sleep made each day more of an effort, each night more terrifying, and darkened the shadows beneath her eyes. And though Iain did not know the cause of her misery, he shared the burden of it, and was so worried about her, his own sleep was broken. But, again, he waited for her to come to him.

Finally her courage broke when she was awakened once again by her choking screams. This time it was worse than before because the stench of death engulfed her, pervasive and familiar. For an agonized instant, her heart pounded with the belief that all had been discovered and she was entombed not in the earthen grave, but deep in the belly of a prison hulk, with the dead and dying all around her, with the tidal waters sucking at the hull and at the shallow graves on the shore.

Reality crept back piece by piece, in the glow of embers in the fireplace, in the tangle of the bed linens, in the silence of the spacious chamber. She got out of bed shaking as if she were an old, old woman. And when she could steady her hands enough, she lighted candles against the gloom. She stripped off her sweat-dampened night-rail and bathed herself head to toe. Just lifting the pitcher to pour water into the basin took enormous effort, but the icy water felt good against her hot skin. She drew deep breaths, making herself smell the true scents of the room—lavender and rose, a hint of wood smoke, the tang of the oils and waxes used on wood.

Her heart slowed, her breathing quieted. She donned a fresh nightgown, one of Harriet's, soft and fine. She brushed her snarled hair until it was a long, smooth curtain. She thought of Tullia performing this task for her when she was a child, telling her stories, reassuring her with her voice and her touch, making it bearable that Lily, her blood mother, was gone forever. She longed for Tullia to be here with her, reassuring her once again, keeping the nightmares at bay. But Tullia was far away, in another life where she could at last give her love to a baby that was flesh of her flesh.

Addie had backed the demons into the murky corners; if she could endure until the dawn, she would be safe for the space of a day.

Her courage failed. She could not fight alone any longer and, suddenly, she was frantic to get to Iain, afraid only that he would not be in his chamber.

He was lying awake, but he thought he had slipped into sleep and was dreaming when the door to his room opened and he heard Addie speak his name, a soft plea as she approached the bed.

She was a ghostly apparition in the dim firelight, but when he opened his arms, she came into them, nestling against him, and he held her, rubbing her back, saying, "You are safe now; you can sleep," offering understanding and shelter, not demand.

The hard planes of his body, the sheer size and maleness of him were not strange to her; it was as if she had been held like this by him countless times before. The tension that had knotted her muscles ever since she had heard of Darius's capture drained away, leaving her feeling boneless, weightless, at peace. She closed her eyes and slept without dreaming.

Iain carried her back to her chamber just before dawn. As he laid her down in her bed, she awakened.

"The household will be stirring soon," he said by way of explanation.

But there was no alarm or confusion in her tawny eyes. She murmured her thanks and drifted back to sleep. He stroked her hair and the soft skin of her cheek and left with the image of her mouth curved in a smile.

He had not made physical love with her, and yet, he felt as if they had been lovers forever. It was an extraordinary sensation, as if his body and mind shared memories of her that had no measure in time. He had always considered himself a rational man, unlike many of his men who saw signs and portents everywhere and lived as much in an invisible world as in the visible. Now it seemed he had more of the Gael in him than he had known. Or perhaps for him, all the magic rested in Addie.

Addie spent part of the day at Valencourt's as usual and noted Robert Moore's obvious relief at the renewed ease in her manner. She could well imagine what his reaction would be did he know the cause.

This was time stolen out of the war. Whatever Iain believed, there was no future for them. In the maze her life had become in New York, she was sure of one thing—Iain should not trust her at all, while she could trust him with her life. He had vanquished the demons in her mind and had given her perfect rest. For those gifts, her body was a small exchange she would offer gladly.

When she went to him that night, he was waiting for her, still willing to provide nothing more than shelter if that were her choice. It was she who moved against him in demand, her mouth warm against his neck, tracing his face, finding his lips, feasting there gently, while her hands played over the muscles of his chest.

"You do not have to…" he began, not sure he could maintain his control, even less sure of why she was doing this. He wanted to believe her affection was a match for his, but some last vestige of sanity denied it.

"I have come to you. Do you deny me now?" Her whisper shivered against his mouth, and he surrendered. Her motives no longer mattered. Only a fool would refuse what he so desired.

He touched her with reverence, learning the curves and hollows of her body with patience, seducing her away from the past, from sorrow and loss, celebrating her beauty and his love in his native language.

She did not know the individual words, and yet, she understood his heart in the Gaelic. The sound coaxed an answer from her as much as his hands, his mouth, and the coiled strength of his body.

She had come to him for protection, willing to please but not expecting or wanting pleasure for herself. But even when she tried to control it, her traitorous body responded like a cat being stroked, moving sinuously against Iain, opening, inviting him in.

She had not made love for more than a year, but her body remembered, flaring to life from a small circle of energy that grew and swirled outward from her center until even her skin was burning.

"Now, come to me now!" she gasped, wrapping her legs around him and biting at his shoulder in the frenzy of her need. There was a brief stab of pain, as if her body had regained a semblance of virginity in the long solitude, and then Iain was part of her, and they moved in unison, knowing the dance perfectly.

When it was over, Addie waited for guilt to overtake her, but instead, she felt intensely alive. She and Iain were not untried youths; they were adults who had known love and were fortunate to have found it again. It could not last, but while it did, she would hold him dear and be grateful that such joy could exist in these dark times.

She sensed his question before he asked it. "We are alone. The ghosts cannot reach us here." It was the truth. Not for a second had she lost the knowledge that it was Iain, not Silas, who was making love to her. The scent and shape of him, the taste of his skin and the texture of his hair, his voice, everything about him was unique to him and different from Silas. She took his right hand and traced the calluses. Even these were different, caused by years of sword practice, the marks of a professional soldier. She kissed the patterns of war.

"I know who you are, Iain Traverne. You are a fine, honorable man, and a splendid lover." She laced her fingers with his to soften the blow of her next words. "You have my heart for now, but I make you no promises. We are still enemies. Someday I will leave, and you will not follow."

He was content and sleepy in the lingering haze of their shared passion, but he did not miss her deliberate use of "you will not," underscoring that it would be by his volition that he would stay with the British Army, and by her choice that she would go back to the Americans. It occurred to him that despite all he knew about her, he had not really believed her loyalty was as demanding or as valuable as his. Accepting now that it was he felt off balance, as if they had traded roles, for while there was no way to count how often men had claimed higher duty as a reason for separation or abandonment, it was disconcerting to have this woman he had come to love doing it. But for all of her resolve, he believed that given enough time, he could bind her to his heart.

He did not say any of this aloud. He tightened his fingers over hers. "One day, one night at a time; that is all anyone ever has. It will have to suffice for us, too."

She relaxed against him. It was futile for her to think she could be responsible for him when he alone was keeping her sane.

Iain reversed the chaos of her life. The days still held danger, the hazard of betraying herself as a spy, but the nights became a refuge. At night she was a woman well loved. During the day, she thought of

Darius, of Ad and Justin, and of Silas. But at night only she and Iain existed, complete with each other.

Iain was at her side when Clinton's aide, John André, now a brevet major and even more securely the favorite than before, came to the house to bring news of Darius. André was delighted to be the bearer of good tidings.

"Mistress Bradwell, your brother and Colonel Simcoe are both reported to be in good health, and plans for their exchange go apace. We hope to have them back with us before the new year. Sir Henry has been most concerned for their welfare."

"I appreciate his efforts. I have been so worried about Darius, and I long to see him again," Addie said, while inside another voice railed that Silas should have been as well treated. She acknowledged to herself for the first time that as long as Darius was not being harmed, it would be better were he to remain a prisoner, and Simcoe, too, so that they could no longer raid the populace.

Suddenly she felt as if André's dark eyes were seeing into her skull, and she gave him a brilliant smile, as if dazzled by his presence. Beyond his courtly manners, this young man was gaining influence by his sharp wits, and she did not want to be the subject of his interest for any length of time. Though he had made no comment, she was sure that within moments of seeing her and Iain together he had known they were lovers, and that troubled her. André being here was a mark of Clinton's favor for both Iain and Darius, and she did not want Iain to lose that for loving her.

Every compromise had its price, and now she knew the cost of hers. She was responsible for Iain, after all, and neither loyal enough to her political beliefs or hard-hearted enough to allow his ruin. She went through the motions of playing the good hostess, offering Major André refreshment and chatting about inconsequential things, while irreconcilable thoughts skittered around in her mind until her head felt as if it were being crushed in a vise. By the time André left, she was nearly blind from the pain pounding in her temples.

"I must retire. It is not your fault nor Major André's. It is a matter of the moon," she told Iain bluntly, and that much was true. Since she had come to New York, her woman's courses had been sporadic, but the heavy ache in her body had been warning her since the morning that the cycle was beginning again. She dreaded facing the dark alone, but she had nothing to offer him.

Iain seemed to agree, but late that night, he appeared beside her bed where she lay sleepless and miserable. When she started to protest, he said, "Hush, love. I am no juvenile to be afraid of this, and you are no jade who must perform every night." As he spoke, he lay down with her and began to rub the tight sinews in her neck and back and the taut drum of her stomach, not disturbing her fetal curl, easing her aching muscles until she was so relaxed she floated into sleep and did not stir again until full morning, long after Iain had left her.

She awakened to the knowledge that Iain's care of her had been more intimate and seductive than their coupling. The comparison occurred to her before she could stop it. Far from shunning her for her body's changes, Silas had been too careful of her, as if she were engaged in a female ritual so mysterious, no man could hope to understand it. And for her part, she had counted herself fortunate that it was rare for her to feel ill with it. But Iain had proven that a man could adjust to the cycle and offer practical comfort instead of awe. Maybe that happened often. Iain was an urbane man, while Silas had been nearly as innocent as she when they married, and they had lived their entire married life in war. She had no way to know what might have been had they grown older together in less trying times.

One forbidden thought gave way to the next—were it not for the war, Iain would be a good man with whom to grow older. But were it not for the war, Silas would still be alive and Iain probably never would have come to Boston on the Crown's business. She wrenched her mind out of the useless round, but there was no denying the deepening bond between her and Iain. And the household staff and Iain's men showed their approval by leaving the couple alone as much as possible and by deferring to both of them, as if they were master and mistress of the house.

Addie and Iain watched the first snow together, the few inches being enough to hide the filth of the city for a little while, enough to signal the end of the fighting season in that part of the country. On the last night of November, Addie felt very wifely when she saw Iain off to the celebratory supper given by Sir Henry for Scottish officers in honor of St. Andrew's feast day. Addie thought Iain looked the splendid Highland laird, but he spoiled the effect by pulling a dour face and complaining that he'd rather spend the evening with her than with fellow officers who would undoubtedly use St. Andrew as an excuse to drink too much. However, they both knew this was yet another mark of General Clinton's favor and not to be disdained.

The food and drink were plentiful and of high quality, and there were toasts and songs and enough talk of Scotland to make Iain feel as if he had been transported home. He enjoyed himself more than he had anticipated, yet all the while he felt the pull to be back with Addie, not wanting her to face the night alone. He was surprised at how difficult it was to keep his secret from the few officers who had become good friends. He wanted to tell them about Addie's virtues, intelligence, and beauty, wanted to tell them how lucky he was to have found her, Rebel passion and all. For the first time he understood men who babbled about their loves at every opportunity. It had not been this way with Jeane. Their union had been as logical as it was loving; it had not had this edge of danger and wonder.

He left the party as soon as he could, and he hastened home to Addie, hardly aware of Angus and Duncan guarding his back. When he came to her, his skin was still cold from the frosty night, and he tasted of sweet wine, but he was sober, and his voice was steady.

"You will like Scotland, and my family will love you nearly as much as I do. I want you for my wife. We can be—"

She put her fingers against his mouth unable to bear the pain and longing his words evoked in her. "Please, no more! You honor me, and I will not forget, but this is all we can have. We are safe only here. Outside of this house, we are enemies."

He had meant to say, "We can be married here or there," but now he could not. She was trembling as if she rather than he had been out in the cold.

What she would not allow him to say with his voice, he spoke with his body, wooing and reassuring her, seeking to bind her to him so closely that Scotland would not seem a far place by the time she went there with him.

She answered him in kind, with her heart and her body, trying to touch all of him, take all of him all at once until there were no divisions between them. But she knew what he did not, that this was the beginning of farewell, not of a new life together.

He fell asleep with his head cradled on her breast. He had worn a wig to the banquet, and his unpowdered hair was free of its queue and twined like heavy silk around her fingers.

"My sweet man, so wise in all save your trust in me." She whispered so low, he could not have heard her had he been awake.

She was resolved that she must leave as soon as Darius was exchanged. The clerks at Valencourt's had come to rely more and more on her in Darius's absence, and the least she could do for him was to help keep his business in order.

As for her business, she wanted to be quit of it and never again endure such a harsh conflict of loyalties. She did not think her dubious talents as a spy would be missed by anyone.

She regarded her plans calmly except when she imagined the actual parting from Iain. The desolation of that image was warning of how painful the reality would be, and her only defense was to savor every moment she had with him.

Three days later, it seemed her time with him was going to be even less than she thought. The enemy had withdrawn its troops from Newport, Rhode Island, a few weeks before, as if to concentrate all power in the stronghold of New York. But instead of sinking into the lethargy of winter quarters, many regiments were suddenly astir with orders to prepare for embarkation at short notice. The number of troops involved was considerable, and included those of Sir Henry's second in command, General Lord Cornwallis, who had returned from England after his wife's death. Rumor had it that both generals would be participating in the upcoming action, a mark of how important it was.

Although it was no secret that troops would be leaving New York and the surrounding encampments soon, where they were going was a mystery. Some had it that the troops were to be ferried quickly across to New Jersey for an attack on Washington's army; some said they would go to the West Indies to engage the French; and others claimed the South was the destination, where at last the Loyalists would flock to the King's standard.

Addie did not believe that Iain knew where he and his men were to go. At least he made no mention of it, and she could think of no way to pose it as a seemingly innocent question when the commander in chief of the British forces so clearly wanted the information kept secret. Iain worried about leaving her before Darius returned, but in a way, he was already journeying away from her. The professional soldier was very much in evidence. Now the daylight hours belonged to his military duties as he oversaw every step of getting his men ready, and at night there was a barely harnessed excitement about him, a restlessness that followed him into sleep even when he should have been exhausted and content from lovemaking. It was all very, very familiar to Addie.

She had no intelligence to pass along to Robert Moore, for he was far better informed than she. "They are going south," he told her, "and there is little we can do about it. The French have sailed away, and I fear the redcoats will take what they want." She had never heard such despair in his voice.

"They have Savannah, but little else," she pointed out. "They have been rebuffed before. Why not this time?"

"Perhaps they will be." There was no conviction in his voice. He glanced around once more, and then he said very quickly, "I may have to leave. I believe my room has been searched and that I have been followed about the city. If I go, you will receive word if you, too, should leave, but your brother's standing with the enemy makes you safer than I."

He moved away from her, attending to his duties as if nothing untoward had happened, but now she understood his despair, and she felt as if she had been stripped naked and branded as a spy before all eyes. She stayed where she was until she could control her breathing and the wobble in her knees. Moore had trusted her not to betray them both at his news, and she could not fail him.

She stayed as long as she usually did, and she worked on the accounts, soothed by the orderly rows of figures she recorded, being very, very careful not to make any mistakes, and all the while, waves of panic raced through her.

Despite the press of duty, Angus, at Iain's direction, came to escort Addie home, and she was infinitely grateful for his solid presence. She was unable to stem the sensation of enemy eyes watching every step of her progress.

That night she was as restless as Iain, clinging to him, though she knew she should be learning to let him go. But the night was full of terror again, and it was too easy to picture British agents tracking her down.

Iain was moved rather than dismayed by her behavior, taking it as a sign that she loved him enough to dread their separation, as any good soldier's wife would. He did not want to cause her sorrow, but since it could not be helped, he hoped she would miss him enough so that when he returned, she would agree to marry him, despite all the obstacles. In the meantime, the best he could do was to hold her close in comfort and love.

Addie saw Robert Moore the next day, but on the day following, he was missing from the shop, and one of the other clerks told her that Moore had been summoned home to his family's Long Island farm due to the severe illness of his mother. Addie had reason to be thankful that Moore had warned her that he might have to flee, for she was able to accept the tale with a proper expression of sympathy.

"I do hope she recovers swiftly. It is so worrisome when a parent is ailing."

As far as she could ascertain, none of the other clerks had any suspicions about Mr. Moore or her, but that hardly settled her nerves since now she had to await orders from an agent unknown to her. Unless it was a false alarm and thus safe for Mr. Moore to return, her usefulness was likely over. She kept reassuring herself that it would not be worse than that, that she would not be arrested. Moore had gotten away, and so would she.

Snow and sleet began to fall, matching the gloom in her heart. It was warm enough inside, but she shivered, thinking of the American prisoners and being selfish enough not to want to become one of them. When James Rivington came into the shop, Addie regarded him as just another trial in a difficult day. He had continued to treat her politely, but he also continued to print libelous attacks on General Washington. He did not come to Valencourt's often, for he and Darius were usually business rivals, although friendly ones, but occasionally they shared projects, such as book publishing ventures, as he had once shared them with Marcus Valencourt.

Today he announced that his press was overtaxed at the moment and asked if Valencourt's could take on some of the work. Addie left that decision up to the printer and went back to her task of sorting through a precious order of new sheet music that had just arrived from England.

Suddenly Mr. Rivington was peering over her shoulder, saying, "Ah, your brother is a canny rascal! He's managed to obtain pieces I haven't yet seen."

She quelled her annoyance as he began riffling through pages she had already sorted.

"Do not reveal your surprise at what I tell you." Low and fast, the words hissed into her ear, and she froze as she realized how clever he was, for both of them had their backs to the room, their faces concealed. Her mind leaped from one wild thought to the next, the only sensible one being that somehow he had found out that she was a spy and that he planned to use the knowledge against her.

"All right, tell me then," she murmured because she had no choice.

He picked up another piece of music, humming a little, and saying in a normal tone, "This would be a country dance to warm everyone on a cold winter's eve." His voice dropped again as he rustled the paper, and he leaned very close to her. "Sissy Nightingale orders you to leave New York as soon as you can. Word will arrive today that your brother Adrian is very ill and needs you, just as Mistress Moore needed her son to come to her. Neither is true. Have Colonel Traverne arrange your passage. If he asks it, Sir Henry will not refuse. Your true friends await your return to them." His voice gained volume again, and he hummed more notes. "It would take someone highly skilled to play this part without error."

She heard it then, beyond the double entendre of his words—the excitement he was enjoying in playing the dangerous game. That at least seemed in character for this flamboyant man, though nothing else did. She could not have been more shocked had the floor slipped out from under Valencourt's and the sea rushed in than she was to learn that James Rivington, that most earnest Tory, was working for Tallmadge and Washington. But he had used the code, and she had received a command she must obey. She hardly heard his parting words, spoken loudly enough for all to hear.

"When Darius comes home, I look forward to calling on both of you."

She went on sorting the music. The weather that had seemed so dismal became a godsend, keeping all but the most determined customers away. And it brought Angus to escort her home earlier than usual. Mentally she corrected herself; it was Darius's home, not hers. She took her leave of the clerks as if this were an ordinary day, and she steeled herself against taking a long last look at Valencourt's, though she doubted she would be back.

Being warmly wrapped in Harriet's fur-lined cloak was another reminder of Darius's kindness, and a lump swelled in her throat at the idea of not seeing him again before she left. But she could not afford to show such emotion when she was not supposed to know she was to be summoned away.

She hadn't long to wait. Iain joined her at the house shortly after she arrived, and he was bearing the letter for her. "This came under a flag to headquarters for you. It was opened and read there." His control slipped. "Addie, I am so sorry!"

She feigned puzzlement as she began to read, but she did not have to pretend shock, for everything was catching up with her, causing her to shake. The pain in Iain's face was unbearable. The dispatch drifted to the floor as she hid her face in her hands.

He put his arms around her. "Your brother is young and strong. He recovered from a terrible wound; he can survive this, too. I've

spoken with Sir Henry and arrangements are being made. Unless the
weather prevents it, you will sail at dawn. A message has already been
sent ahead to your lines."

He did not plead his cause by so much as a word, accepting that
her twin's need and claim on her was greater than his. That intensified
her anguish at her deception a thousandfold, but there was nothing
she could do to alleviate it. It simply grew worse as, like hot coals, he
heaped one kindness upon another.

"When you gather your things together, include those garments
your brother has given you. I know he would want you to take them
with you and to make good use of them."

She choked on a sob. "You know me too well." The irony of the
words jabbed at her.

"Indeed, I do. You would leave the clothes behind, lest you be
greedy. But your brother and I would have you take them so that
we need not worry that you suffer from the cold. And perhaps you
will remember us kindly when you wear them." His arms tightened
around her, and then he let her go. "You have much to do, and I
must return to headquarters. But I will come back to you as soon
as I can."

She watched him straighten and resume the mien of Colonel
Traverne. She watched the crisp swing of his kilt and the sway of the
plaid draped from his shoulder, and in spite of the danger, she wished
for a reprieve, for the storm to grow until the port was closed, just
for a few days, just for a little longer with Iain. But then she faced the
burden of continuing the lie of Ad's illness, and it was good to see
that the storm was fading as the hours wore on.

With the help of one of the maids, she packed her clothing,
compromising by taking some, but not all, of the garments she had
selected from Harriet's wardrobe; after all, she was going back to army
life, not to live in another city.

The servant made the task more difficult by sniffing back tears
through the whole procedure and saying, "Oh, Mistress Bradwell,
you've been good for this 'ouse, you 'ave. Won't be the same with
you gone."

Addie felt no guilt for having deceived the British Army, but it was quite another thing to have fooled Darius's staff who, whatever their initial reservations, had come to treat her and Silas very kindly.

Iain was back in time to share a late supper with Addie, though neither of them was hungry. Both were aware that the storm continued to wane, but it was as if the tension ebbing from the elements was flowing into them. There was at once too much and nothing to say, so at first they concentrated on practical matters.

Iain reviewed her travel arrangements in detail; then he paused, drawing a deep breath before he went on.

"I cannot accompany you this time. We are still under orders to be ready for embarkation, and I can't leave my men when final orders may be given at any moment. But Angus will go with you."

"It is not necessary. He will be sorely vexed if he is left behind when you sail," she observed calmly, but she felt as if the last hours with Iain were being ripped physically from her like pieces of flesh.

"It *is* necessary," Iain corrected her. "And even if orders are given before he gets back, there will be time for him to rejoin us. You know how long it takes to load a fleet and get it underway. It's a damn tedious business!" He fought against the rise of his anger. He was usually patient with the mundane details of military life—it was foolish to be otherwise—but he did not feel patient now.

By unspoken agreement, they made no pretense of retiring separately this night, but went to his chamber together, avoiding the sight of her luggage. She was dwarfed by the shirt Iain lent her for a nightgown, and he played lady's maid, brushing her hair until it crackled with energy. When they were in bed, they touched each other with patient hands, tracing familiar patterns and textures as if to remember with a deeper sense what the eyes could see. They were so closely aligned in their hearts and minds, they simply lay together seeking neither passion nor sleep.

"You will send word if you are with child?" he asked.

He had raised the subject soon after they had become intimate, for he had pictured her ripe with his baby and had felt far more pleasure than distress because he had also imagined both of them under his protection. Though she had not shied away from saying the words, he had heard the whisper of regret; no matter how much easier it had been for her to be free of the complications of pregnancy during the war, it was still difficult for any woman to admit she could not conceive. Iain had accepted her judgment, for she sounded very certain and had been married for several years, and his concern had shifted to reassuring her that her confession did not diminish her in his eyes. But now, he was haunted by the idea that she might be wrong after all and would be left to bear his child without his support.

"I am not with child," she said with utter conviction, before adding very softly, "I do love you, Iain Traverne, and I would have loved your child had I been able to create one with you, but that changes nothing. When I leave here, we will be enemies again."

"The war will not last forever." He wanted to ask her once again to marry him, but he heard the finality in her voice.

"No matter when or how it ends, it will not change the decision I made when it began. This is my country, and I will never be ruled again by the King or Parliament. Your Scotland, for all the wild beauty you see in her, is subject to England."

She did not have to recite the names; he heard them in the dark— Quentin and Silas dead; Ad lamed and now in danger of death from fever; Marcus Valencourt far away across the sea; and God knew how many more losses to come. His love, for all its power, was frail against such sorrow and the resolution that had grown in her because of it.

In that instant, as he had surrendered to loving her, so he surrendered to the reality of their separate lives. They lay holding each other until the time ran out.

Addie was ready to go when light began to spread across a cleared sky and sparkle on the snow and ice left from the previous day. A cold current of air promised to fill the sails.

The household staff assembled to bid her farewell, and she thanked each in turn, wishing she had more to give them, not even able to offer her tears in response to those shed for her leaving. She was washed as clean as the winter sky, left cold and devoid of emotion.

Iain, Duncan, and Angus saw her to the wharf where the trim coastal schooner waited. Her belongings and the crew were aboard as the last grains of sand raced through the hourglass. With Angus beside her, she faced Duncan and Iain, and felt the eyes of the sailors and soldiers who, already busy at this early hour, watched the little diversion with interest.

She nodded at the two men. "Thank you, Duncan, and you, Colonel Traverne, for your kindness."

Duncan seemed frozen in place, but Iain bowed in return, as formal as she. And that was all. Even when the ship was underway, she did not look back.

It was a cold, miserable, but efficient passage. Angus was never beyond her call, but there was nothing save silence between them until the Jersey shore was in sight. She saw the bright-green coats of Harry Lee's legion and knew that Justin and her cousins awaited her. Her numbness eased enough for her to turn to Angus, but even then, she had only the barest words to give him.

"Thank you for everything. I wish you all Godspeed home to Scotland."

He struggled to find English words, his emotions were too strong. He murmured to her in Gaelic, and she did not need a translation to hear his affection and sadness.

Her eyes remained dry, but her last sight of Angus was of him standing straight, a big muscular man, face marked by tears he did not deign to wipe away.

Chapter 22

"If I were not so happy to see you safe, I would strangle you!" Justin snarled in Addie's ear as he embraced her, and he warned, "I know what you've done, but the rest of them don't. They believe in Ad's false fever."

For a startled moment, Addie thought he was referring to her affair with Iain, and then she realized he was speaking of the spying that had necessitated her quick departure from the city.

He hugged her more tightly before he let her go. "I am so sorry about Silas. He was as much a brother to me as Ad or Quentin."

For her, there was some satisfaction in Justin's conflicting emotions and even amusement that the need for secrecy prevented him from scolding her as vigorously as he wished. But at the same time she felt so disoriented, everything seemed to be at a distance. She supposed she was offering the proper responses to her cousins and to the other men she knew in the escort since none of them seemed to find anything amiss, but she had the odd sensation that someone else was performing in her place.

Justin had brought Nightingale for Addie to ride, and she was grateful for the isolation provided by being in the saddle. The winter landscape was bleak, ruffled by an icy wind. The men kept noise to a minimum, alert for bands of Cowboys and Skinners who might view their horses and the small wagon that held their supplies and Addie's belongings as reason to risk an attack.

There was not enough daylight to see them all the way to Morristown, so they stopped at an inn for the night. It was a mean place, but warmer and safer than outside. Addie slept curled up on the floor in the sleeping chamber, preferring that to sharing one of the filthy beds with strangers. Justin, Reeves, and Hart each took turns sleeping beside her when they were not standing guard around the inn.

It was no place to have a conversation, but even had their surroundings been more amenable, Justin doubted his sister would have been forthcoming. Addie seemed as changed as her standing, a self-possessed widow who bore little resemblance to the anxious, hopeful young woman who had sailed to New York seven months ago. He reminded himself he hadn't known her as well as he thought even then because he had had no idea she had gone to New York as a spy. Ad hadn't known either, but still, Justin trusted that Addie's reserve would falter when she was reunited with her twin.

By the time they reached Morristown, Addie was weary of hearing reassurances that Ad would surely recover. Her brothers, Matilda, Major Tallmadge, General Washington, and two of his aides, Tench and Hammy, were privy to the ploy to bring Addie back safely, but that left a great number of people, including Hart and Reeves, who cared about Ad and worried that his life was threatened. She still believed that the American cause was just and that spying was one of the weapons that had to be used, but she had not foreseen how the web of lies would spread, spinning more lies, entrapping more and more people.

When the army had encamped at Morristown in the winter of 1776–1777, General Washington had established his headquarters at Freeman's Tavern, but this time, Mistress Ford, a widow whose husband had died on militia duty two years before, had offered her house to the general, refusing any payment. She and her five children had retained only the dining room and a small chamber behind it for their use, thus giving Washington all possible space. Even so, conditions were cramped due to the size of the staff, particularly for the aides, whether they were working at green baize-covered tables crowded together downstairs or trying to sleep upstairs, many to a room. Log additions were being added to both ends of the house to improve the situation.

The ruse of Ad's illness would have caused more upset than it had were it not for Tench and Hammy's mock-brave insistence that they would not let any contagion force them to forsake the company of their friend.

Addie was taken to see Ad immediately on arriving at headquarters, for not even past the front door could the charade be dropped. It was depressing evidence that as she had watched and reported anything that might be of interest in the enemy garrison, so enemy eyes watched everything here. And if the reason for her return were revealed as fraudulent, then everyone who had had contact with her in New York would be suspect to the enemy, and everyone included not just Robert Moore, but the innocent clerks at Valencourt's, and also Darius and Iain, and all those who served them. She could hardly support the weight of her guile; she could not bear that others be crushed by it.

When Justin saw the look the twins exchanged before the first word was spoken between them, he turned to leave, but Addie said, "Don't go. I'd rather fight with both of you at once than wage two battles."

Ad had felt as if he were going insane by inches as he had waited, confined to the small room, unable to do any work lest his handwriting be recognized. Under other circumstances, he might have enjoyed the respite from duty, but his worry about his sister had prevented that. He had had plenty of time to work himself into a high temper, but at the sight of Addie, his anger was transformed into concern. He could not see behind her eyes; it was as if that final tie, the one that had remained even after her marriage, had been severed.

Her voice flat, as if the story were about a stranger, she told them of searching for Silas, including every grim detail of prison conditions. She told them how weak and ill Silas had been. She included all the information that had not been continued in the two brief letters she had sent from the city.

"I did not want to believe it, but there was never any chance that he would recover. At least he died peacefully. He just slipped away from me."

It was unnerving to both of the men that their eyes burned with tears while hers remained dry.

To cover his emotion, Justin swore, "Those murderous sons of bitches! They ought to be hanged, every one of them, for so abusing our men."

"Not every one. You have not been listening," she countered, still without heat. "Our brother Darius and Colonel Traverne did everything they could and risked much to help me find Silas. Colonel Traverne went aboard the *Good Hope* and brought him off. Darius sheltered us in his house and made Silas's last days as pleasant as they could be. Darius is much more tender of heart than we knew, perhaps because of his own loss." She had written to them of Darius being a widower in her first letter from New York, so they knew what she was referring to.

They stared at her, uneasy at her defense of the enemy and, more, at her naming Darius their brother, a truth they tried to avoid thinking about. And it was particularly uncomfortable for Justin to consider that Darius might miss Harriet as much as he himself missed Sarah.

Addie answered them before they could ask the question. "I have not changed my mind or my heart. I am as loyal now to the cause of liberty as I have been since the first. But my loyalty cannot blind me to the truth that there are good men and women on the enemy's side. Our father proved that long since." She looked from one to the other. "I am sorry you have learned that I was spying in New York, but you cannot have worried about me more than I have worried about you whenever you have gone into battle. I was not very good at it, but I fear I might have been the cause of Darius being taken prisoner. He is a dangerous soldier in the field with his men, and it is better for our soldiers and civilians that he be kept from action. I accept the logic of that, but my heart is not logical. It knows I betrayed him, and I will have to live with that. If you want to know anything more about the information I gathered and how it was used, you will have to ask the general."

She watched the play of emotions on her brothers' faces, their concern for her mixed with their instinctive revulsion for the clandestine work she had done, and she could imagine too well what their reaction would be if she confessed that she had been Colonel Traverne's lover.

"We do have news of Darius," Justin said. He was still trying to understand the changes in Addie and all that she had gone through in New York, but this news, at least, should give her some peace. "He was not wounded, and I expect he will be exchanged by the end of the month."

"Have you seen him?"

"No, he is not being held here." He did not have to add that neither he nor Ad had any wish to visit Darius.

"Of course, you saw him when you met in battle, while I had not seen him since before the war began. He looks so very like Papa, it was strange to behold him at first. But Darius is his own man." She stopped, not wanting to torment them further with such reflections.

But then Ad said, "Letters from Papa, Darius must have some. Did you read them?"

"He never offered them, and I never asked. I believe they must contain too much that would bring us pain. But Darius did tell me that Papa is well, and Mary and the children also. Papa is fortunate that he has such strong connections in England; that is not true for many Loyalists." She thought she was resigned to their father's continued refusal to communicate with them, but the old hurt flared briefly before it was extinguished by the overwhelming weariness dragging her spirit down. She wanted to curl into Iain's arms and sleep.

She dreaded her interview with General Washington, but he was gentle with her, beginning by expressing his grief over Silas's death and assuring her that Robert Moore was still safely away from the city where he would remain, so that if he had caught the enemy's interest, that interest could fade in his absence. But if the British began a purposeful search for him, they would find that due to his mother's ill health, the family had removed themselves from their farm to travel to a more favorable climate.

"If it is necessary, the Moores will have time and warning enough to do exactly that," the general said.

Though Addie could not tell him their destination, the general was most interested in the enemy's preparations to sail from New York, and Addie dutifully listed those regiments she believed were going on the expedition, although she was certain he already had a more complete report than hers. He was even more interested in less tangible things, in the temper of the soldiers and the populace.

"The garrison is well provisioned, and those civilians who are important friends of the Crown lack for little, but many others live in very poor conditions. Huge numbers of refugees have come to the city with no means to support themselves, and there is a great lack of adequate shelter, for little rebuilding has been done since the fires."

Addie saw how worn Washington appeared. His army had dwindled to just a few thousand and was just as threadbare as ever, and he didn't yet have the usual winter comfort of his wife's company. Addie hesitated to bedevil him further, but she felt obligated.

"Your Excellency, I know there is little you can do while the enemy is so obdurate on the subject of prisoner exchange, but I must tell you that every horrible tale you have heard about the enemy's foul treatment of prisoners is true. Our men are being starved, beaten, deprived of every necessity of life, even of air to breathe, but they do not join the enemy. Their hearts are firmly fixed on you, as I know yours is with them. I speak to you of them because they have no voices now."

For an instant, he looked like a haggard old man, drained of energy, but then his expression hardened, and energy returned with his outrage. "I hear their voices always," he said. "No excuse the enemy makes can sound louder in my ears."

Although she had long known him as a valued friend of her Virginia family, now he seemed much larger than that, as if his public presence demanded more and more of him. She felt very small in comparison and understood more clearly than before why his officers and men wanted so to please him.

"I am sorry, Your Excellency, that I was not more effective in New York."

He looked faintly surprised, and then he smiled at her. "Perhaps it was not what you expected, but Major Tallmadge and I were quite satisfied with your work. Intelligence about the enemy most often comes in small pieces that, if we are fortunate, can be fitted together into something larger."

She was tempted to ask if she had been the direct cause of Darius's capture, but she decided she did not want to know, and was relieved when the general did not speak of it. But she could not forbear asking one question.

"James Rivington warned me to leave the city and told me how it would be accomplished. He is a fervent Tory, and he has printed such lies about you, how came he to—?"

Washington held up a hand as if to deflect the question, but his eyes were mischievous, and he suddenly seemed much less formidable. "We do not have so many friends that we can reject those who have come late to our cause. I trust you will not speak of his... ah, conversion to others."

"Of course I will not."

"Now we must all rejoice that your brother's recovery is going to be so swift." The mischief was even more visible, and Addie had no doubt that it was he alone who had devised the plan to get her out of New York without arousing suspicion.

Having spent enough time at headquarters to blind any hostile watchers to the truth, Addie was free to go to her lodgings, where Matilda awaited her.

"I hope it is all right." Justin was belatedly anxious about the arrangements he and Ad had made for their sister to lodge once again with the Dolbys, as she had during her first stay at Morristown. Familiar surroundings had seemed a good idea, but Silas had been with her then.

"If I sought to avoid everything and everyone who reminds me of Silas, I would have to leave the country, and he would still be part of me," she told Justin. But what she could not say was that as strange as it had been to be surrounded by the enemy when she had first gone to New York, now it was equally odd to see Continental soldiers everywhere. And she could not tell him that her heart was uneasy because Iain had a place there now, too. Where she lodged was of little significance against such inner conflict.

Matilda greeted her without reserve, throwing her arms around her and exclaiming, "Oh, I've missed you so much! And I am so, so sorry about Silas! I wish I could have been with you."

Addie hugged her in return, clinging to her warmth and innocence, grateful for both, but feeling like an old woman in comparison to Matilda. She willed herself to patience, sure that with time, she would fit into this new version of her old life. But even when she saw General

Knox and he openly expressed his heartbreak over the loss of a friend and one of his best officers, she viewed his tears from that distance where she now resided.

In the ensuing days, Addie tried to adjust to the once well-known pattern of a winter encampment. Ad's quick recovery to health and recall to duty were credited to the return of his beloved twin, and Justin was often out on patrol, the cavalry being charged with making sure no British force approached Morristown and with raiding enemy outposts where they could. In the past, Addie would have longed for more of her brothers' company, but now she was relieved when she could escape their scrutiny.

Some aspects of the encampment were too grimly familiar to everyone. Shortages grew worse by the day, and the paper money issued by Congress was now sixty to one against sterling, making farmers and merchants unwilling to accept it as payment for anything from fodder for the horses and meat for the men, to such small items as sealing wax and ink powder, while everyone was frustrated with Congress's inability to unsnarl its affairs in order to provide clothes, shoes, and blankets for the troops.

On top of this, the weather began to prove itself a worse adversary than the British. A snowstorm kept Mistress Washington from keeping Christmas with the general, stranding her in Philadelphia. And with the dawn of the new year, one blizzard followed another so closely that too often when supplies could be obtained, they could not be transported through the huge snowdrifts. Even the salt water of tidal rivers began to freeze, and there was talk of crossing the ice, as soon as it was thick enough, to attack the British garrison, but all that came of it was an abortive attempt against the enemy on Staten Island. It was unlikely that the enemy would attack in turn since such a great part of their force had already sailed off. The most likely destination was thought to be Charles Town, particularly because the failure to take it previously still rankled the enemy.

Addie had missed seeing John Laurens, who had been briefly at Morristown before her arrival. He had been sent north to plead for more troops in anticipation of an attack on Charles Town. He had stopped to visit General Washington prior to going on to appear before Congress in Philadelphia, but there was no help to give him. Ad had had a visit with John, and as he explained to Addie, he did not blame John for his bitterness, for when he had presented his plan for Black enlistment to South Carolina's legislature, he had been met with not only refusal, but also with derision and horror for having the temerity to suggest arming slaves. It had made no difference that the plan had Congress's support nor that the need for troops was so great.

"Perhaps it would have changed nothing, after all. But the situation as it now stands could not be worse," Ad said. "A huge enemy force is sailing for the target, it will have support from the garrison in Savannah, and there is little to stop it."

Addie did not point out that no one was absolutely sure of that target. Charles Town made sense. General Clinton might not be the best soldier in the world, but he was not enough of a fool to miss this opportunity made so much more attractive by the failure of the French–American attempt to regain Savannah. –

Darius would be with General Clinton. He and Simcoe had been exchanged on the last day of December and, by all reliable reports, Valencourt's Rangers had sailed away before ice had made the waters around New York too dangerous for shipping. Simcoe and the Queen's Rangers were posted on Staten Island and had been among those who had chased off the Americans.

There was relief for Addie in the knowledge that she need not worry for the present that Justin and Darius would meet again in battle. But she felt a keener loneliness with both Darius and Iain far away. It was unreasonable, as she could not have seen them anyway had they still been in New York, but that made no difference.

The dangerous weather, the trying conditions at Morristown, and the prospect of another British victory in the South combined to make tempers short and spirits low. Though Addie knew it was selfish to view it so, the general malaise served to camouflage her misery.

A dullness of spirit and an inability to rejoin the life around her characterized the days for Addie, but the demon dreams returned at night to awaken her to life so immediate and painful, it took all of her energy not to scream the house down. Every prisoner's face that she had seen came back to her, gaunt with privation, marked by death. And she saw Captain Trumble and his men as no less damaged by their captive freedom. And Silas was always there; not Silas as she had known him when she married him, but Silas as her dying child, so helpless that he could do nothing for himself, pulled down with the others into the grave grown vast as the sea.

It was worse when she dreamed of Iain, for then the two of them existed together in a place untouched by war. All the textures she had learned came back to her as if her hands were touching them again—the male solidity of him; the sleek muscles; the light silk of the hair on his arms and legs and the whorls on his chest, and the precise line of it bisecting his belly down to the thick thatch surrounding his manhood; the sword calluses on his hand and the small scars that marked his body from a long history of training and battles; the strong bones of his face—every part of his body was belovedly familiar to her. She drew in the spice and musk of his scent, felt his possession, and wakened each time to find herself alone, the bed warm only where her body had curled around the dream.

She knew Matilda would have shared her room and bed had she asked for company, but she was afraid of crying out in her sleep and betraying too much. Matilda treated her with such patience, trying not to fuss, but so clearly worried about her that it was hard not to confide in her because she was the most likely to understand. Her loyalty to their country was unquestionable, but that did not preclude her from compassion.

The most active American campaign of the summer had been carried out by a large raiding party sent deep into Native American territory. The people had fled while their towns, acres of fields, and thousands of fruit trees had been laid waste in retaliation for Native American attacks on white settlements. Matilda understood the reasons of it— the enemy's use of their Native American allies to terrorize the frontier remained one of their most effective weapons, and she knew the horror of it in the death of her father. But her father's Native American companion had been killed, too, and Matilda had the memory of the many Native Americans she had met at McKinnon before the war.

"Their towns were as fine as ours, long established, with mature orchards and fields that gave them enough so that even in the winter, they did not starve," Matilda told Addie. "Now if the enemy does not feed them, they will starve, not just the warriors, but the women and children, the very young and the very old. But the enemy will feed them, of course, not well, but something, enough to bind them even closer to the Crown. Such a tidy circle." She looked off into the distance as if she could see the dark, wild woods of her childhood. "I used to think I could always go back and that Luke certainly would, and McKinnon would go on as before. But it is never going to be that way again; everything is poisoned by hate, the land, and the people." She drew a sharp breath and covered her mouth in dismay, as if to take back her words, and then she said, "Forgive me, I did not mean to—"

"To distress the poor widow? I may be half mad now, but I will be fully so if everyone continues to treat me like a delicate invalid! Silas died; I did not!" It was Addie's turn to be shocked by her own outburst.

After a moment's pause, Matilda gave her a rueful smile. "I know, I've been as awful as the rest, treating you too carefully. I promise, I won't do it anymore. It would drive me crazy, too."

Addie felt closer to her than she had to anyone since coming to Morristown, but she conceded, "The fault lies with me more than with anyone else. My time in New York changed me. I thought I could fit easily back into this life, but every day makes me feel less a part of it. And when the other wives look at me, they cannot help but consider that their husbands may be taken from them. Silas dead is much more threatening to them than Silas missing."

"It will get better," Matilda assured her, but Addie doubted it as the dreams grew more vivid, the days more difficult, and Iain was not there to save her.

Even Mistress Washington, who was, like the general, usually very skilled at revealing only what she chose, regarded Addie with such sorrow in her eyes, Addie could scarcely bear to be in her company. At least she was spared the sharp scrutiny of Lucy Knox, since Lucy was expecting another child in a couple of months and so had not joined Henry at Morristown. But among the other wives who had journeyed to the encampment was Kitty Greene. Kitty was expecting a child even sooner than Lucy, but was determined not to be separated any longer from her Nathanael. Kitty had left their three children safely at home, and the fourth, named for his father, was born during yet another blizzard at the end of January. Homemade gifts from the soldiers flooded the house where the Greenes were staying, and Kitty was moved to tears by this generosity.

Addie gave Kitty the infant's quilt made for her by Mistress Willis. Mistress Willis had intended it for Addie and Silas's child, a child who would never be, and Addie thought that something made with such love and care belonged with the living. She held little Nat, marveling at the warm reality of him, and she felt her breasts swell as if to feed him. But even in this most intimate sharing with Kitty, Addie did not feel close to her. For all her coquettish ways, Kitty had gambled her life and that of her unborn child to be with her husband, and surely she would not understand how Addie had, after burying Silas, taken one of the enemy to her bed.

However, Matilda had been right. The officers' wives were adjusting to Addie's presence, accepting her for her own sake, letting Silas slip away into the shadows. Now the fault of distance was wholly hers. Silas was in the shadows for her, too, and the enemy was in her heart. Try as she might, she could not regret a single minute she had spent with Iain; unquestionably that would be judged a sin beyond redemption by women who, with their husbands, continued to give up every security for the sake of the United States. Her penance was that Iain was as lost to her as Silas, and she must carry the secret alone.

In defiance of the relentless weather and continuing shortages of everything, the pace of social life quickened. There were many friends of the cause in the region, and even with the snowstorms, Morristown was a far more congenial place than Valley Forge had been. The officers and their ladies organized sleigh rides, musical evenings, and made plans to start subscription dances, the cost of the gatherings to be shared among the subscribers.

Matilda and Ad tried to persuade Addie to accompany them to various events, but most of the time she was able to beg off. Though the women seemed to be adjusting, Addie's identification as a recent widow made it difficult for the young officers to know how to treat her since their normal high-spirited gallantry and flirtatious behavior seemed inappropriate toward her. Sometimes she felt older than Mistress Washington, and sometimes she felt rebellious enough to want to forget every sorrow and to dance the night away. Instead, she contented herself with watching the life swirling around her as if it were a play, and her detached view afforded her some entertainment.

"Hammy is developing quite a tendresse for Betsey Schuyler, isn't he?" she asked Ad one day.

He reacted with total astonishment. "Hammy and 'the little saint'? Great heavens! I should think not! What an unlikely pairing. He's had his eye on Cornelia Lott…" He paused, thinking about it. "And he hasn't minded us teasing him about her, which means he probably hasn't fixed his interest there. But Betsey?" Ad rolled his eyes.

Betsey was one of Philip Schuyler's four daughters, and she and one of her sisters were visiting with friends nearby. While not the prettiest of the Schuyler girls, the petite brunette had such lively dark eyes and so engaging and kind a manner, she had earned the sobriquet "the little saint." Given that Hammy's taste had heretofore seemed to run to brief dalliances with rather bold young women, she seemed an improbable choice. But when Ad considered the matter a little further he began to see the sense of it.

"Hammy stayed with the Schuylers when he was ill with fever more than two years ago. He certainly met her then. And her father is very influential in the state of New York. It would be a very advantageous match for Hammy."

"Shame on you! Advantageous or not, he's growing very fond of her, so don't twit him about it."

A few days later, Ad reported back to his sister. "I concede you the honors for superior observation. But Hammy's secret isn't likely to remain so much longer. Last night he nearly lost his life for love. On his way back from calling on Betsey, he was challenged by a sentry." Ad started to laugh. "The man is so besotted, he forgot the password. If a soldier coming along behind him hadn't offered it for him, he might have been shot. Imagine it, Hammy, who always has his facts in a row, made stupid by a wee girl."

"I think you're being cruel," Addie scolded him with a smile. "After all, it's not as if you have been perfectly serene throughout your courtship of Matilda."

"I am still not perfectly serene about Matilda," he confessed happily.

Addie thought of how far he'd come and how much Matilda had to do with it. Though his limp had improved, it remained severe enough to make his gait ungainly, and yet he was so confident in Matilda's love, it did not seem to bother him that he could not walk as smoothly as other men and could not dance at all. In Matilda's eyes, there was no more graceful human being.

Suddenly, Addie's light-hearted mood drained away, and she wanted to urge her brother to marry Matilda now because there was no way to know how much time they would have. But she kept her smile in place and said nothing. She was reminder enough of loss, and as long as Ad was one of Washington's most valued aides, his personal life must be subordinate to his duty.

Ad felt the change in her but did not question it. She had always been so steady; now her moods shifted so quickly, he could not discern a pattern. Day by day he was learning to accept this new twin who kept so many secrets, fearful that if he crowded her too closely she would flee from him entirely.

Addie had less patience with her changing moods. She had moved from feeling too little to feeling too much. Every day she expected the whirling emotions at her center to calm, but rather than that they grew more unstable so that both laughter and tears took her too strongly and at inopportune times. And while she felt well enough, given her broken sleep, she began to be aware of physical symptoms of her mental disquiet. Sometimes her body felt so full of energy, she could hardly sit still and would venture out even when the weather was foul. But just as often, the need to sleep would pounce on her so rapidly, she could hardly keep her eyes open, even if it was in the middle of a conversation or a meal. She wished the same impulse would overcome her restless dreams at night. Oddest of all, she began to crave foods that had been bountiful on her father's table before the war—Tullia's newly baked bread spread with freshly churned butter, the ripe fruits of summer, and the more exotic, particularly sweet-tart pineapple from the West Indies. She craved chunks of it encrusted with salt; she who had never eaten it that way when it was available; she who had never cared much about food; she who was pregnant.

She rejected the idea as soon as it entered her mind, but all of the puzzle pieces continued to fall into place, so obvious in their totality, she wondered how, even believing she was barren, she could have ignored them for so many weeks. She was carrying Iain's child.

She felt as if she had tumbled off Nightingale. She grew dizzy before she realized she was holding her breath and made herself find the normal rhythm again. Even the beat of her heart was alien, as if it might stop if she did not concentrate on keeping it going. She gave thanks that she was alone in her room with no one to observe her strange behavior.

And then it struck her that she was not alone. Very carefully she touched the slight curve of her belly. She was three months along but so thin, no one could see her condition. Her breasts had been tender for some time, but she had assumed that that was because her monthly flow had gotten off schedule again and her body was confused. She touched her breasts. Her body was not confused. It knew exactly what it was doing, changing itself to nurture the child within.

Her body recognized no political loyalties. In all those days and nights with Silas, no child had been conceived, but in the short weeks with Iain, her body had accepted a new life.

It was not guilt or despair, but sorrow, that came to her, more sorrow than she had felt on the day when Silas had been buried, and she heard her voice before she realized she was speaking aloud.

"Silas, I loved you for so long, when I was no more than a child I loved you. When I became a woman, I loved you. This should have been your child, and we should have had long, long years together, but you are truly gone from me now. Forgive me. This child was conceived with love on both sides, and I will do anything to carry it, bear it, and raise it as well as I am able."

She waited in such a strange state, willing to feel Silas's presence, but there was nothing, no stir of air nor brush upon her soul, only the empty room, so empty that the heavy silence of it pressed against her eardrums, and she welcomed the rising whine of the wind outside.

She touched her belly again, and she thought of life arising out of all the loss and death she'd seen, and it seemed not a disaster, but a miracle of survival. She longed for the quickening time to come, when she would feel the baby move, proving the existence of its life.

She needed the company and knowledge of women who had borne children, and the officers' wives would not do. If she remained among them, the details of her pregnancy would be before them, sure to cause speculation about paternity, for had Silas fathered the child, her pregnancy would be much further along.

She had finally written to Tullia about Silas's death, and she knew that Tullia and Prince would take her in, but it would be awkward for them to have a white woman staying with them. Nor would she consider asking Tullia to leave her family to come to her.

Addie understood what Matilda meant about feeling she could not return to McKinnon. Addie felt the same way about Boston. The house was still rented, and it didn't seem like home anymore in any case, with none of the family even in the town. Mary's farm was no answer either, for it had never been home to Addie, and she scarcely knew the tenants. And then she thought of Castleton, of being there with her aunts and Sissy, of going back to the place where her mother had been born. She felt as if a circle had been closed with the thought, and she did not doubt the welcome she would receive there.

She gathered her courage, and she spoke to Ad and Matilda together because she wanted her brother to have Matilda's support and because she wanted it, too.

"I cannot remain with the army any longer. I am with child, and I am going to Castleton to await the birth," she told them, making no effort to soften the blow.

Matilda gave a small gasp of shock, but Ad was immobile and silent, staring at her through narrowed eyes for a torturously long moment.

"It cannot be Silas's child." The gold of his eyes bored into hers. "It is your Scotsman's child, isn't it? Did Colonel Traverne force you?" The sneer in his voice made it clear he knew the answer already, and she could feel the fury emanating from him.

"It is his child. He did not force me. I went to him after Silas died. Iain is an honorable man. He would marry me if I would consent. He will never know of this child, but it was conceived in love, on both sides, and I rejoice in it."

She was completely serene, and Ad felt as if she were a stranger, which sharpened his rage with the fear of losing her entirely. "And what do you plan to tell your bastard of its paternity?" he snarled.

"If I am out of their view for a while, people will not keep such careful count of my life or my child's. I will give it Silas's name, and most will believe, or pretend to believe, that it is his child."

"Then you betray him twice."

"I did not betray him at all. I could not, for he died. He *died*, Ad. It is not just a word, it is the reality of preparing his body and seeing him buried. He is not coming back, not to me, not to you, not to anyone." The words had great impact because her voice remained even. "I am not asking for your approval, nor do I expect it. But you have a right to know why I am going to Castleton. You are a part of me."

He opened his mouth to say he wanted no part of the woman she had become, but Matilda's fingers dug into his arms like talons, and she spoke before he could.

"Addie, I think your decision to go to Castleton is a good one. You need to be where you can rest and eat properly. Unless Ad or I have a change of heart, someday I will be aunt to your child, and I want my niece or nephew to be born strong and healthy."

Ad could not have been more startled had a shell exploded in their midst. Matilda had always been careful about interfering between him and his siblings, and gentle on the few occasions when she had done so. But in her brief words, she had not only sided with Addie, she had also issued a warning that how he treated his sister and her child would directly affect his relationship with her. That Matilda would risk so much for Addie's sake impressed Ad as nothing else could have done. And abruptly, he realized that she had pulled him back from the abyss just in time. However he felt about Silas or Colonel Traverne—he winced inwardly at the soft way his sister had said "Iain"—or the child, Addie did not share his confusion. She was prepared to do anything, even alienate her twin, to ensure the safety of her child. She had entered a circumstance he could not fathom. Even if he were to have children with Matilda, he would still be denied the experience of feeling a new life growing inside his body. His anger dissipated.

"I can't understand everything you've done or why, but I love you, Addie, and I'll do whatever I can to help you get to Castleton."

He was as good as his word, sending a message to their uncle and making arrangements for Addie to travel to Philadelphia, though he left it to her whether or not she would tell Uncle Hartley about the baby. None of this was difficult because everyone assumed that Addie had found it too trying to be with the army so soon after her husband's death. The hardest thing for Ad was going to be telling Justin when he rode back into the encampment, but he would do it because it would ease Addie's burden.

Addie requested an additional favor, that he speak to the Chepmans for her. "I have seen them, but they pretend not to see me and scurry away. I know they feel more guilty than ever now, but I want them to know that Silas never regretted saving Tim."

"I'll talk to them," Ad promised, not voicing his doubt that anything could ever ease the Chepmans' guilt when the very existence of their son was a reminder of another man's sacrifice.

The Washingtons were as understanding as everyone else.

Martha confided, "My dear, I wish the general and I could go home to Virginia with you." She gazed into the distance as if she could see them both at Mount Vernon, though it had been nearly five years since the general had been there. "Someday," she murmured softly.

And though Addie saw Washington separately, his words were an echo of his wife's. "I regret that we will lose your company, but I envy you your destination," he said. "I would give much to see a Virginia spring after this dread winter."

Now that she was leaving the encampment, Addie wished she could feel as numb as when she had arrived. Only her driving need to get to Virginia made it possible to say farewell with dignity: farewell to the Washingtons, to Tench, Hammy, and the other aides, to General Knox and the Greenes, to Luke McKinnon, to so many people she had come to know and admire over the war years. When she had gone to New York in search of Silas, she had believed she would return to the army with or without him, but this was different. Though her friends could not know it, it was unlikely that she would travel with the army or see many of these people again.

"I hope we will be able to summon you back with less drastic measures than infecting Ad with another mysterious complaint," Tench teased her gently.

"Wherever I am, I will be confident that he has your wise counsel." Addie's grief lessened a little with amusement as she saw this seemingly imperturbable man could still blush at a compliment.

But nothing could ease taking her leave of Matilda. Addie had shared some of Harriet's clothes with her when she first arrived at Morristown, and she insisted Matilda accept more now.

"I want to take little baggage with me, though I will keep the cloak for warmth on the journey."

"Addie, I will soon be so indebted to you, I will never be able to repay you," Matilda wailed in protest.

"Indebted to me, oh, indeed not! It is quite the opposite. You risked a great deal to keep Ad and me from losing each other."

"That can't happen. It is as you said, you and Ad are part of each other, and I love both of you." Matilda's eyes filled with tears. "Are you sure you do not wish me to come with you?"

"I would like nothing better, but I need you to keep taking care of Ad and Luke. And I need you to send me all the news so that I won't feel as if I am in complete exile."

In the end, Matilda accepted the clothes because Addie gave her no option, and likewise the wagon and horses, except for Nightingale, were left in her charge, too. With the sorry state of the roads, Addie knew she would be safer and more comfortable on the mare than jolting along in the wagon.

Ad had planned to be part of her escort to Philadelphia, but Addie persuaded him not to on the grounds that his duties were too urgent and that perfectly reliable traffic was going back and forth with correspondence between Congress and the Army. In fact, she wanted to spare him because too long in the saddle still pained his lame leg. As a final argument, she pled sentiment.

"I would rather say goodbye here than draw it out," she told him.

Since he felt the same way, he agreed.

The night before she left, they shared a supper together with Matilda and Luke, but both McKinnons found reasons to leave the twins alone before the hour grew too late.

"Even if the enemy takes Charles Town, I doubt the war will reach Virginia. But if it does, I trust you will attempt nothing heroic and will stay out of its path," Ad cautioned his sister.

"You needn't worry. I have discovered already that I am not the stuff of which heroines are made."

Ad thought of all she had done and of what she was doing now, going to such lengths to protect the life of the child she carried. He shook his head. "Oh, Addie, I can scarcely give you good advice when you are such a poor judge of yourself."

"Good advice from the same brother who lent me his clothing for our adventures?"

It seemed perfectly fitting to let all their present concerns disappear as they recalled scenes from their childhood. Their knowledge of the losses they had suffered since then only served to sweeten the memories, and they laughed together, sharing their fondness for the bold, happy children they had been.

As he prepared to return to his quarters, Ad said, "I know it cannot be exactly the same in these times, but I hope my niece or nephew will grow up as well acquainted with joy as we were. When the child has arrived, I will tell our friends with discretion."

His claiming of her child as kin was, as he meant it to be, a benediction to Addie's heart.

In the morning, he and Matilda saw Addie on her way.

"Care well for each other," Addie bade them, holding her tears back.

Long after Morristown had disappeared in the snowy landscape, the image of Ad and Matilda standing together remained bright and clear in her mind.

*

To be continued…

Made in the USA
Monee, IL
26 November 2024

71319641R00240